Judy Nunn's career has been long and multi-faceted. After combining her international acting career with scriptwriting for television and radio, Judy decided in the '90s to turn her hand to prose.

Her first three novels, *The Glitter Game*, *Centre Stage* and *Araluen*, set respectively in the worlds of television, theatre and film, became instant bestsellers, and the rest is history, quite literally in fact. She has since developed a love of writing Australian historically based fiction and her fame as a novelist has spread rapidly throughout Europe, where she has been published in English, German, French, Dutch, Czech and Spanish.

Her subsequent bestsellers, *Kal*, *Beneath the Southern Cross*, *Territory*, *Pacific*, *Heritage*, *Floodtide*, *Maralinga*, *Tiger Men*, *Elianne*, *Spirits of the Ghan*, *Sanctuary* and *Khaki Town* have confirmed Judy's position as one of Australia's leading fiction writers. She has now sold over one million books in Australia alone.

In 2015 Judy was made a Member of the Order of Australia for her 'significant service to the performing arts as a scriptwriter and actor of stage and screen, and to literature as an author'.

Visit Judy at judynunn.com.au or on
 facebook.com/JudyNunnAuthor

A BRIEF WORD ABOUT JUDY'S THEATRE BACKGROUND

It's a little-known fact that Judy first trod the boards professionally at the age of twelve, playing Polly Hoppit in *Emil and the Detectives* at The Playhouse in her home town of Perth.

After that there was no turning back. Theatre was in her blood and remains there until this very day. At the age of nineteen she travelled to Sydney where she worked onstage for three years, concluding with the J. C. Williamson production of Neil Simon's hit play *The Odd Couple*, which toured Australia's capital cities for nine months, after which she took off for London, as ambitious young actors did in those days.

Judy worked for over five years in the UK, occasionally on TV and film, but predominantly as a leading actor in various repertory companies, on major tours, and also the odd stint in the West End.

Upon returning to Australia in the mid-seventies the theatre continued to claim her, and she performed leading roles for every major state theatre in the country, including Perth's National Theatre, the Queensland Theatre Company, the Melbourne Theatre Company, and Sydney's Old Tote Theatre Company where she played the title role in their final production, *The Lady from Maxim's*, at the Sydney Opera House in 1978.

These days most audiences would recall Judy from her many long-running television roles, but theatre was always, and still is, her first love as a performer. She says that to now write of those days 'treading the boards' is a labour of love; that it feels like 'coming home'.

JUDY NUNN

Showtime!

WILLIAM HEINEMANN

WILLIAM HEINEMANN

UK I USA I Canada I Ireland I Australia
India I New Zealand I South Africa I China

William Heinemann is part of the Penguin Random House group of companies
whose addresses can be found at global.penguinrandomhouse.com

Penguin
Random House
Australia

First published by William Heinemann in 2021

Cover design by Lisa Brewster, The Brewster Project
Illustration of theatre masks by McGill Design Group
Author photograph © David Hahn/bauersyndication.com.au
Internal design and typesetting by Midland Typesetters, Australia

Printed and bound in Australia by Griffin Press, part of Ovato, an accredited
ISO AS/NZS 14001 Environmental Management Systems printer

 A catalogue record for this
book is available from the
NATIONAL
LIBRARY National Library of Australia
OF AUSTRALIA

ISBN 978 1 76104 253 9

penguin.com.au

To the memory of John Gregg

'All the world's a stage,
And all the men and women merely players;
They have their exits and their entrances,
And one man in his time plays many parts . . .'

As You Like It, William Shakespeare

William (Will) Worthing (b.1858) m. Mabel Baker (b.1860)

Arthur (Artie) (b.1881)

Alfred (Alfie) (b.1881)

Prudence (Pru) (b.1883)
m. Tom Buxton

David (b.1912)

Alice (b.1885)
m. Raymond Sparks

Maxwell (Max) Worthing (b.1860) m. Gertie Smeed (b.1866)

Edward (Ted) (b.1884)

Sarah (b.1886)
m. Harry Redmond

Max (b.1917)

Elizabeth (Izzie) (b.1887)
m. Ambrose Watson

Albert (Bertie) (b.1895)

Emma (b.1901)

Michael (Carlo) Carlovsky (b.1850)   m. Winifred Small (b.1865)

Rosie Marks (b.1843)

Michael (Mick) (b.1879)

Anne (b.1890)
m. Christopher Mackie

Marten (Marty) (b.1899)

Marten (Rube) Reubens (b.1853)

BITS AND PIECES OF THEATRICAL TERMINOLOGY

'The wings.' These are the offstage areas either side of the stage.

'Prompt' and 'OP'. 'Prompt' refers to the wings on the left side of the stage (from the actors' perspective, facing out to the auditorium) and 'OP' ('Opposite Prompt') is the wing space on the right. The stage manager who runs the show always operates from the prompt corner, and is given full licence to yell out an actor's lines should he or she 'dry' (hence the term 'prompt').

'Dry'. To forget one's lines. Actors generally prefer to help one another out rather than risk the humiliation of a call from the prompt corner. And they do so most efficiently as a rule. It's not unknown for an actor to adlib in Shakespearean iambic pentameter. Very clever. The audience usually has no idea.

'Upstage', 'downstage' and 'centre stage'. Upstage is to the rear of the stage from the audience's perspective, downstage is to the front, and centre stage, not unsurprisingly, is where most actors favour whenever possible.

'Upstaging' is the practice of an actor deliberately placing himself upstage, therefore forcing a fellow actor downstage to turn his back to the audience – not a nice thing to do, in fact considered quite bitchy. 'Upstaging' doesn't have to refer to one's specific position onstage either. As a general term it can also mean to 'pull focus', in some way or another. A good example might be an actor who uses 'props' unnecessarily or who develops some physical mannerism that deliberately draws attention to himself. This practice has been employed by many actors over the years and does not endear them to their fellow thespians.

'Props', or 'properties'. These are any objects an actor uses onstage, be it a pen produced from the pocket of a costume, or a revolver taken from the drawer of a desk onstage. Prop tables are set up by ASMs (assistant stage managers) in the wings, both prompt side and OP, where actors collect their personal props before making their entrance, and onstage props are preset prior to each act. Many an ASM has copped it right royally for a prop not being where it should be, which can indeed make for awkward moments during a performance, particularly if the gun isn't there and the actor has to point a finger and go 'bang'. Mind you, most sensible actors check their props before curtain up. It's the intelligent thing to do.

'The flies'. Aptly named because this is the area high above the stage and out of sight of the audience from where all forms of effects and even massive objects are 'flown' in (think the chandelier in The Phantom of the Opera, the cart in Les Misérables, the helicopter in Miss Saigon, etc.). The flies were most important in the early days of theatre when, via a system of hemp ropes and pulleys and weights, backdrops, scrims and cycs were flown in to great effect.

'Backdrop'. Usually, as the word implies, a simple painted backcloth at the rear of the stage.

'Scrim'. Made of a woven mesh fabric, a scrim can be dropped to any part of the stage, its use being extremely versatile. Lit from the front it can appear opaque, depicting the scene painted onto it. Lit from the back it becomes transparent, depicting the scene behind. A simple but magical device.

'Cyclorama'. Commonly referred to in the theatre as a 'cyc'. Made of translucent material, it is positioned at the rear of the stage, stretched very tightly, usually curved at the sides and, with special lighting, gives the impression of vast space.

'Bump-in' and 'bump-out'. These are terms used on tour. When a show is being set up at a new theatre the company is 'bumping in', and when they're dismantling their set and their rigs, and packing away their costumes and props for the move on to the next theatre, they're 'bumping out'. A laborious practice, particularly if it's a tour of one-night stands.

'Follow spots'. As the term denotes, these are spotlights that focus upon a specific performer, or performers in the case of a duet.

'Stealing the limelight'. Lime being a major chemical used for lighting in the early days, 'stealing the limelight' referred specifically to an actor hogging another's spot.

'The half'. Now this is an interesting one. 'The half' is understood by most who are not in the trade to be the half-hour call before curtain up, i.e. the time when actors report for work. But in actuality this is not so. The half is not a half-hour at all, but thirty-five minutes. If the curtain goes up at, say, 8 pm, all actors are required to turn up at 7.25. This is presumably because it ensures the actors will be in the theatre half an hour ahead of the 'five-minute call', which is the all-important 'last standby'. 'The half' is therefore bizarre, but then so many things in the theatre are.

A NOTE TO READERS

Showtime! contains occasional passages and references that readers may find offensive, perhaps even shocking, particularly relating to minstrelsy and 'blackface'. I have made no attempt to omit or soften this, as minstrelsy was a highly popular form of entertainment worldwide during the period in which the book is set, particularly the earlier section. To apply today's views would not be true to the era, either historically or dramatically.

CURTAIN UP

TROUBLE AT MILL
1882

They all knew how the fire started. It was the clogs. Just one girl. A novice, probably first day on the job, who didn't know any better or simply wasn't thinking. She was only twelve years old as it turned out, but hadn't she wondered why the other women and girls left their clogs outside the factory doors? Hadn't anyone told her? Obviously not. But then all the workers entered those hideous cotton mills mindlessly, robots resigned to the endless drudgery of the day ahead, to the deafening clash of monster metal looms, to shuttles crashing back and forth and cogs gnashing like the teeth of giants. Who would notice that one small girl wasn't barefoot like the rest of them?

The mills were ghastly places, and Comberton Cotton Mill, built on the bank of the River Croal in the centre of Bolton, Lancashire, was no better or worse than the rest of them. Employing principally women and their children, it consisted of a massive single room ninety-five yards long and forty-four yards wide with a ceiling over fifty feet high. Thirty feet from the floor was a series of gantries, metal beams stretching across the entire space, and at regular intervals along each gantry were cast-iron wheels with leather belts that led to the looms below. The looms were driven by shafting from an adjacent engine and boiler house that employed a steam turbine-driven generator, and as the workers operated their machines – all 150 of them – the relentless action turned the air into a soup-like fug, muggy and stifling. Tiny wisps of cotton, invisible to the naked eye, choked the air, threatening also to choke the women if they forgot to breathe through clenched teeth.

The heat was not the only reason the workers left their clogs outside – although it was true they preferred working barefoot – it was because of the danger the clogs might present. Those clogs that had 'calkers', anyway. Commonly referred to as 'horseshoes', the iron calkers that were nailed beneath the wooden sole of some styles of clogs could spark off a fire if struck against the metal edge of a loom. Fire, always a threat in the cotton mills, was not an uncommon occurrence at the best of times; why add to the danger by wearing horseshoe clogs?

The young girl was wearing just such clogs. She was working a loom on the eastern side of the mill.

It was astonishing how quickly that one little spark from that one little clog became a firestorm.

For the first several moments the effect was magical. The tiny wisps of cotton, previously invisible, were now fairies, dancing, prancing in mid-air, a virtual wonderland shimmering in an unreal light. Then minutes later, the eastern side of the mill was ablaze, a tinderbox erupting, combusting, jumping from one machine to the next, destined to engulf the entire factory.

The workers had not paused to wonder at the sparkling world that had momentarily surrounded them. In a cotton mill, the merest suspicion of fire signalled the awful nightmare each of them suffered, the nightmare of becoming a human torch. They bunched up their skirts and ran between the machines screaming, all heading for the doors; those further down the line, particularly those on the eastern side, pushing, shoving, desperate to get to the front. Including the girl with the horseshoe clogs. But in the panic that ensued, some of them didn't make it in time. In fact, many of them didn't make it in time. As they spewed out into the cool afternoon air, quite a number were on fire.

Once outside, sanity prevailed – among those who had emerged unscathed anyway, particularly the older ones. They smothered the flames threatening to devour their sisters; they fetched water from the river in the many buckets that always sat beside the factory doors for that very purpose; they calmed the younger workers, some of whom were children, understandably terror-stricken and hysterical. The older factory workers were tough. These were women accustomed to hardship and the daily fight for survival.

'Mill's on fire! Mill's on fire!' Several ran down the street, yelling out the news, raising the alarm.

But it was unnecessary. Clouds of smoke billowing above the township was announcing to the whole of Bolton that Comberton Mill was in flames and already, several blocks away, firefighters were preparing the horse-drawn pump for action. They would not be able to extinguish the blaze, but hopefully they might prevent the fire spreading to adjacent buildings.

In the meantime, help came from another quarter. First on the scene were the two Worthing brothers, who worked at the nearby foundry. Twenty-four-year-old William and twenty-two-year-old Maxwell, young, strong and fit, arrived within only minutes, other foundry workers following along behind.

'Is everyone out?' Will yelled above the chaos as he and Max joined the team of women who had formed a bucket chain, which although doing little to douse the fire was proving useful for those poor souls who lay still smouldering on the ground.

'No,' the woman beside him yelled back, passing him a full bucket, 'our Gertie's still inside! She's done for, poor sod. Up on the work platform, no way she can get down.'

Forty-five-year-old Agnes Smeed turned away to accept the next full bucket in the chain. A lean woman, but as strong as a man, indeed stronger than many, she'd resigned herself to the loss of her youngest daughter. How many times had she told Gertie not to go up on the platform during her ten-minute break? 'It's dangerous, love,' she'd said, 'you could fall, or worse still, if a fire broke out you'd get stranded up there.' Those had been her very words, and now look what had happened. But Gertie was a wilful girl, just like sixteen-year-old girls were. She enjoyed sitting up there, eating her cheese and pickle sandwich, looking through the window at the outside world, or gazing down at the giddying spectacle of the mill floor thirty feet below. 'I like heights, Mam,' was all she'd say, not rude, but cheeky, the way Gertie always was. 'I like bein' up high.'

Well, she's paying for it now, isn't she, Agnes thought, heaving the next bucket to the young man who'd just arrived. *Nothing to do but keep working*, she told herself, *try not to think about what's going on in there, my little girl burning to death.*

'Right up among the gantries, she is, our Gertie,' Agnes said, 'not a hope.' And she turned away once again to accept the next bucket.

Max and Will exchanged looks, both aware of what the other was thinking. More foundry workers had arrived by now, eager to help with the chain and, handing over their buckets, the brothers raced to the western doors of the mill where the fire was less ferocious than it was on the eastern side.

They took off their jackets and, draping them over their heads, peered inside.

Through the fire and the smoke they could just make out the girl. She was up on the work platform that offered access to the gantries. But she was on the eastern side of the factory, which was fully ablaze, the narrow steel stairs that zig-zagged their way down beside the wall offering her no escape. Here on the western side, however, the steel stairs to the gantries, barely ten yards from where the brothers stood, were approachable despite the ever-encroaching flames.

'You can do it, can't you?' Will yelled above the noise of the fire.

'Course I can,' Max replied. Then he shouted across to the girl, 'Oi, you up there, Gertie, can you hear me?'

'I can.' The young voice came back loud and clear, although Gertie wasn't sure to whom she was yelling. Through the flames and smoke she couldn't see the men far below on the opposite side of the factory floor.

'Stay where you are! I'm coming to get you.'

'I'm not goin' anywhere.' Gertie was brave. Or rather, she was pretending to be. In truth she was terrified beyond belief, but just the sound of a human voice had lent her the strength to reply.

Will and Max ducked back outside.

'Buckets!' Will yelled to a number of the foundry workers. 'Bring buckets, we need water in here!'

As the men arrived with their buckets, Max dropped his jacket on the ground and took several deep breaths, filling his lungs, drinking in all the oxygen he could. He would need to keep his breathing shallow up there in the gantries, where the smoke would be thick.

Then he was back inside the mill, racing for the stairs, Will and the others following him, throwing buckets of water at the flames that licked his boots as he ran.

'Form a chain,' Will ordered the men, 'keep the water coming. These service stairs have to be kept clear so he can bring her down.'

One of the foundry workers, a close mate of the Worthing brothers who knew the double lives they led, was aware of what was about to happen, but the others were in a state of mystification. They could see the blurry shape of the girl over there on the other side of the mill, way up high among the flames. Bring her down? How?

Max took the narrow stairs nimbly three at a time, not touching the railings, which would be blisteringly hot, and when he got to the landing he paused, assessing the task that lay ahead, taking in through the pall the vague shapes of obstacles that lay in his path, the cast-iron wheels at regular intervals along the gantries. He slowed his breathing to a minimum, exercising only the very upper part of his lungs, avoiding the use of his diaphragm, and even his intercostal muscles. Up here the smoke was dangerous.

Then, holding his arms out either side at shoulder height, he stepped from the platform onto one of the gantries.

The metal beam beneath his feet was barely visible, which didn't at all bother him. One never looked down anyway, one always relied upon one's sense of touch, although one's sense of touch was difficult through a pair of boots and thick socks. On the highwire he favoured barefoot, but he'd be minus several layers of skin if he tried that now, wouldn't he? The thought for some reason vaguely amused him. This solid, steel beam was a damn sight easier than highwire. Under normal circumstances he could probably have run across the thing rather than the leisurely stroll he was taking. But he went slowly, with infinite care; this was a rehearsal for the trip back with the girl, which would be far more complicated. What if she became hysterical and tried to fight him? He mustn't think about that now.

He felt for the wheels with the toe of his boot, again not looking down, but relying upon touch, counting the number of steps between each wheel, measuring its height as he stepped over it. The distance and height were uniform. *That's good*, he thought, *that's good, makes things easier.*

Beneath him, the fire raged. The heat was intense and the smoke threatened to suffocate, but Max's focus did not waver. His bare hands felt as if they were burning so he balled his fingers into fists. Step after step after step, then over a wheel, then step after step after step and another wheel. It was a slow and methodical exercise, every movement carried out with the utmost precision.

And then he was there.

'What took you so long?' she asked as he stepped onto the platform.

Her face grubby with soot and grime where she'd rubbed at her eyes, she looked at him, feisty and daring, but he could tell she was petrified. He admired her pluck. She was standing on a pad of folded material to protect her bare feet – he guessed it was her petticoat – and she'd knotted her skirt together at the front to help prevent it catching sparks. *Practical too*, he thought. *That's good.* Then she started coughing. No, that wasn't good, that wouldn't do at all.

'Here.' He took his handkerchief from his shirt pocket and, folding it in half diagonally, tied it around her face like a bandit's mask. 'Breathe through your nose,' he instructed, 'and try to keep your breathing very shallow. Right here,' he said, laying the flat of his hand on her breastbone, 'right here, up high in your lungs. Go on, try it, no deep breaths, just try and pant; you know, the way a dog pants, little short breaths.'

She obeyed. The coughing stopped and he could feel the palm of his hand gently move to the light rhythm of her breathing. *Good*, he thought, *she takes instruction well. Good that she's slender too, just a slip of a thing really.*

'Ever walked the highwire?' he asked.

She shook her head.

'Well, you're about to.' He picked her up in his arms. Light as a feather. She was no heavier than little Jamie and he'd carried Jamie standing on his shoulders in last season's tour. But it was all about weight distribution; they had to get the balance right. He'd intended slinging her over his shoulders, but he'd have to hold her there, losing the use of his arms, and the imbalance would require quite a deal of compensation. Then another idea struck him. She seemed so bold, so brave, and yet also obedient, an excellent combination for a highwire performer. *Yes, it might work*, he thought. It was worth a try anyway.

'Stretch your arms and your legs out,' he instructed. She did so. 'Now stiffen all your muscles, tighten your body. Try and make yourself rigid, like a plank.' He felt her stiffen in his arms, but not enough. 'No, you're sagging in the middle,' he said, adjusting his grip on her, feeling the balance between the weight of her head and arms on the one side and her legs on the other. 'Point your toes as hard as you can.'

'Why?' she asked.

'Because it makes you turn your muscles on, that's why.' He gave an encouraging smile, urging her to obey, they were running out of time. 'Besides, it looks good.'

Gertie pointed her toes as hard as she could, feeling her calves and thighs harden. *He was right*, she thought. She balled her hands into fierce fists and felt the whole of her outstretched arms tighten. She hardened her stomach and her buttocks, rigid now, every muscle in her body as taut as could be.

'Good girl,' he said, 'good girl.' *Yes, she's got the message*, he thought. 'Now you stay like that, Gertie, you stay tight like that and don't you move, you hear me? You're my balancing pole and we're about to walk the highwire.'

He stepped from the platform onto the gantry.

The return trip started out easily enough. The girl was perfectly balanced in his arms and the routine was the same as it had been before. Step, step, step, then over a wheel, then step, step, step and another wheel. The familiarity was so comforting he was able to switch off from the inferno below, and the black smoke that all but engulfed them, and focus simply upon the repetition.

The major worry, Max knew, was whether the girl would be able to keep in her rigid state for the time required. She was no acrobat, her muscles were not accustomed to such tension, and if she were to cave in, as he suspected she might, they could be in trouble.

But she didn't. At least not until they were well over halfway across. Several times he felt her body quivering with the strain, but she didn't cave in at all; if anything she tightened even harder. *She's probably cramping by now*, he thought, *she might well be in quite a deal of pain. The girl's a real trouper all right.*

Down below, the men on the bucket chain continued to douse the service stairs. As they worked they kept looking up at the gantry, breathlessly following the couple's progress, expecting any moment that the two might fall into the hellhole that awaited them.

Will was at the head of the chain. He was dangerously exposed to the fire, which had intensified, but the bucket chain was proving effective, the flames around the stairs being kept sufficiently at bay.

He too looked up, but unlike the others he did not expect to see his brother fall. Not Max. Nonetheless, Will was surprised by the method his brother had chosen to employ. *He's using the girl as a balancing pole*, he thought. *How inventive, and how very like Max. Always loves a challenge, always trying out a new act. And it's working, what's more.*

Then, as they were nearing the finish, he saw his brother falter. *Something's wrong*, he thought, and for the first time he felt a jab of concern.

Up on the gantry, Max halted. The smoke had taken its effect and the girl was on the verge of coughing. Her lungs demanding air, any moment her mouth would instinctively open to suck in all her body needed. Her stomach muscles would spasm, she'd convulse and their balance would be lost.

'Don't give in, Gertie,' he urged. 'Don't breathe. Don't breathe at all. Hang on. We're nearly there.'

Without daring to breathe himself, Max continued his journey. He could see the platform now, only three iron circles ahead and only three steps between each. Could the girl hold her breath that long?

She could. And as he stepped onto the platform a great cheer went up from below.

'You can relax now, Gertie,' he said.

The girl sagged in his arms. She took a deep breath and was overcome with a bout of coughing. Then a moan, more like a growl, emanated from somewhere deep in her throat, her whole body knotted with pain.

He slung her over one shoulder, grasping her legs, feeling her bare calf muscles rock hard beneath his hand.

'I know, I know,' he said, 'we'll look after the cramp when we get outside. Just hang on for now, girl, hang on.' And he was zig-zagging his way down the steel staircase, arriving at the bottom to be doused by buckets of water as he made his way to the door.

Once outside, he carried her well away from the mill to the grassy riverbank where most of the women were gathered.

'Massage her legs,' he instructed, laying Gertie on the ground, 'and her arms and shoulders. Go deep, she's cramped up badly.'

The women did as they were bidden, strong hands digging in hard, Gertie moaning in pain.

Agnes Smeed, having left the bucket chain to arrive at her daughter's side, joined in, stretching Gertie's tightened limbs to their limit, the strongest and toughest of all the women.

'Well, that'll teach you, won't it, girl,' she said as she lent her full weight onto Gertie's outstretched leg, pushing it over the girl's torso.

'Ow, Mam,' Gertie squealed.

'You're going to cop it from your pa when he hears about this.' She pushed even harder, bony fingers digging into hardened muscles, and Gertie squealed again. 'Wouldn't be surprised if he gives you a right walloping, I can tell you that here and now.'

Agnes Smeed was distracting herself as she worked on her daughter. They said you weren't supposed to have favourites, didn't they? But of course you did. And Gertie was hers. Of the three she'd lost as little 'uns, and the three others she had, now full grown, Gertie had always been the one. The special one. As Agnes pummelled and pushed, she hoped people couldn't see the tears of sheer relief that cascaded down her cheeks. And if they did, she'd say it was just sweat, sweat from the fire and the exertion, that's all.

'Very impressive,' Will said, 'very impressive indeed.'

Will and Max were standing respectfully to one side, allowing the women space for their ministrations. The amount of bare leg on display would be considered unseemly by most and not for men's eyes. Not that they hadn't seen far more female flesh than this in the past themselves.

'An even better show than I'd expected actually,' he added. 'You were lucky with the girl, of course.'

'Yes,' Max agreed, 'very lucky with the girl, she's a natural.'

'Where is he?'

A young voice rang out loud and clear; Gertie certainly had a voice that carried. She was sitting up looking about, her skirt now demurely pulled down over her legs.

'Where is he?' she demanded. 'Where's my hero?'

'Go on,' Will nudged his brother, 'that's you.'

Max crossed to the girl and knelt beside her.

Silence reigned as they stared at each other for a moment or two, Agnes Smeed and the other women watching on.

'Thank you for saving me,' she said, 'that was real heroic, that was.'

He shrugged. 'All in a day's work.'

They shared a smile.

'You're a natural, Gertie,' he said. 'You should be in show business.'

ACT I

1

AN OFFER IS MADE

Max Worthing was my father and Gertie Smeed was my mother. They were married a year after the 'Great Comberton Mill Fire', as it became known. I don't know what was so 'Great' about that particular fire. Many a cotton mill had been razed to the ground, only to rise once again from the ashes, or so I'm told. But Comberton Mill was never resurrected; it just remained an empty burnt-out shell. Perhaps that's why they called the fire 'Great' – only a guess, mind, you never can tell about things like that, can you?

Anyway, Pa's heroic rescue of Ma, who was only sixteen at the time, became the stuff of legend. It was labelled 'a miracle'. Uncle Will came up with the term and made sure it was bandied about – he was the true entrepreneur in the family – and there were plenty of witnesses to back him up, so he couldn't be accused of show business hype. The story was headline news in the papers all over England, and Uncle Will even had a special picture taken in a proper photographer's studio, to use as artwork for a poster and handouts and billboards and things.

The photograph was black and white, of course, but he had it beautifully touched up and made into full-colour prints on paper. 'The Miraculous Max Worthing,' it said at the top, 'and his assistant The Daring Delores' – like many entrepreneurs Uncle Will favoured alliteration, said it gave things a special 'ring'. The picture was clever, awfully well rigged; I saw a copy of it myself years later in one of the scrapbooks that Uncle

Will maintained so religiously throughout his life. It showed Pa walking the highwire carrying Ma in her spangles, limbs outstretched, all smiles and pointy toes, as a human balancing pole. Beneath them was a bed of fire, which was fake, just red and orange paper with concealed lights, but very effective, reminding the punters of 'the miracle rescue' that had actually happened, and everyone flocked to see the 'real, live hero'. They couldn't use fire in the act itself, much as they wanted to, because the theatres wouldn't allow fire onstage, but they did incorporate dangerous elements – beds of spikes and knives that would have skewered them if they'd come a cropper, because naturally they worked without a safety net – the bigger the risk, the more thrilling the act. They tried a bed of snakes a few times too, Pa once told me, but the snakes wouldn't stay put; they kept escaping and scaring the punters.

Anyway, I'm getting ahead of myself – all this was further down the track when Ma had joined the show and they'd changed her name to Delores. Uncle Will said Gertie was no name for the theatre, and you'd have to agree with that, wouldn't you? I mean, really!

Uncle Will and Pa were born performers – 'naturals' they called themselves. 'You can always tell a natural,' they'd say. Oh dear God, if I had a quid for every time I've heard that!

Pa was the athletic one – a true acrobat right from the start, even when he was little, without a single lesson I might add. At least that was Uncle Will's famous boast. 'Your pa could walk as easily on his hands as he could on his feet right from the age of four,' he'd say. And of himself he maintained, 'They tell me as a wee thing I sang before I spoke, that the very first words I uttered were in song.' Mind you, you had to take a lot of what Uncle Will said with a grain of salt. He was a real showman, never one for letting the truth get in the way of things.

Uncle Will didn't do any of the physical stuff like Pa. Highwire and juggling and acrobatics didn't interest him in the least; he saw himself more as an actor and singer. And oh my goodness, yes, he did have the most marvellous voice, not to mention a truly incredible range. He billed himself as 'a Heavenly Tenor with the voice of an angel'. It was a very good sales pitch, but if the truth be known he was really a baritone. As I said, truth was immaterial to Uncle Will and he stuck to being a Heavenly Tenor throughout his life, simply because tenors were more popular with the punters.

Uncle Will was thirteen years old and Pa was eleven when they ran away to join a circus. It was Uncle Will's idea. He'd finished his schooling, he could read and write, and he was about to be sent off to work in a factory. Well, bother that, he thought. He'd probably have preferred to join a touring variety show where he could get to sing – as a boy he had the prettiest soprano voice – 'a natural', like I said. But there were no variety shows coming to town around that time so it had to be Hayley's Circus that was passing through. And of course there was no way his little brother was going to be left behind; Max and Will were a team.

From what I've gathered, I don't think their parents missed them all that much. They were the oldest of eight, a lot of mouths to feed, and they sent money home on a regular basis, so they were pulling their weight.

The circus quickly accepted Pa. A slip of a boy who could climb to the top of the pyramid and do a one-armed hand-stand? He was a godsend apparently. The youngest son of The Great Grazzinis Family Acrobatic Troupe had become a hefty fifteen-year-old and was causing huge problems with the pyramid.

Uncle Will presented a bit of a problem himself though. The circus wasn't quite sure what to do with him – they couldn't fit him into an act and he wasn't yet strong enough to work as a rigger or general labourer. Then he sang for them. Well, that did it. They built a special pedestal, dressed it all dreamy and cloud-like, and stood him on it in the middle of the ring where he performed 'Greensleeves' during the balletic sequence.

It was like he'd died and gone to heaven, this beautiful boy soprano with the face of a cherub and the voice of an angel, surrounded by girls in gossamer all twirling about him. You have to admit, it does conjure up a very pretty picture.

The brothers stayed with the circus for a whole four years, during which time Pa really honed his talents – acrobatics, juggling, trapeze, you name it, anything athletic – but highwire was his true forte.

Things proved a bit tricky when Uncle Will's voice broke, which happened virtually overnight when he'd just turned sixteen. He'd already shot up three whole inches and grown facial hair, all of which they'd taken pains to disguise, and then suddenly he was no longer a soprano. Being as talented as he was, he did manage the transition to tenor with surprising ease, but somehow 'Greensleeves' and the gossamer girls didn't work quite as well without a cherubic boy soprano.

The problem was soon solved by his stage presence though. Uncle Will could command an audience like no other, and with a voice that now matched his theatrical aplomb, he became the perfect ringmaster. By the time he was seventeen, he was running the whole circus, I'm told, or at least giving the appearance he was, because that's what a true ringmaster does, you see. A true ringmaster isn't really the boss – in fact, bosses make notoriously bad ringmasters. A true ringmaster is a showman who can sell each act with his sheer 'charisma' – and that's a word one does not apply lightly, believe me! Of course, the fact Uncle Will was very good-looking was an added bonus – tall, dark-haired and moustachioed, with eyes that burned. But then all the Worthings were good-looking. Some fair-haired and blue-eyed like Pa and me, some dark and dramatic like Uncle Will, dependent upon which side of the family you took after. Every generation of Worthings has been blessed. The boys have all been handsome and we girls have all been pretty, and that's not a boast, I assure you, just a fact of nature.

Uncle Will and Pa would have stayed with the circus even longer, but Hayley's went broke. I don't know why – this was all so long ago, way before my time – but I don't think Uncle Will was broken-hearted because, by then, he really did want to break into vaudeville and explore his talents as a singer and actor.

It wasn't as easy as he might have wished though. The Worthing brothers weren't well known on the vaudeville circuit and despite their respective talents it was difficult to stay employed. They got jobs here and there, sometimes together and sometimes apart, working different tours, which wasn't ideal because they didn't like being split up, but you have to go where show business beckons, and that's a fact.

Uncle Will met his wife, Mabel Baker, on a tour of *The Murder in the Red Barn*, a very popular melodrama in which he played the villain. When it came to melodrama he always preferred playing villains, maintaining a villain's lines were so much meatier than a hero's – a viewpoint with which I entirely concur. For my own part I always preferred a 'bad' woman to the role of a saintly one. But I digress.

Aunt Mabel was not an actress. Rather, she was employed by the management on a full-time basis as a costume designer, set dresser, and all round 'ideas' person. For a girl of only twenty she was immensely creative and oh so talented. Having learnt the basics of her trade very early in life, starting out as a seamstress in a factory workshop at the age of twelve, she'd come a very long way since then. While they were on tour she apparently referred to herself as a 'dogsbody' – a backstage worker, props master and jack of all trades – which is what Uncle Will thought she was when he met her and fell in love. Little did he know how invaluable she would prove in the many years to follow!

Theirs was a whirlwind courtship, and when the tour finished and Mabel left the company to marry her beau the theatre management was livid, but there was nothing they could do. Will and Mabel were inseparable and a year after their wedding she gave birth to twin boys, Arthur and Alfred, who instantly became known as Artie and Alfie. The arrival of the twins was a joyous occasion and cause for much celebration, but a change in circumstances that also called for a regular income. No more 'roughing it' between engagements. Mabel was quite happy to accompany her husband on tour, always bringing along her babies and offering her own specialist services to the management. But in between times, there was rent to pay for a roof over their heads, which inevitably led Uncle Will back to the foundry in Bolton. And more often than not, particularly during the general lay-off season, Max, too, would sign up for work there.

So how very fortuitous that they just happened to be there at the time of the Great Comberton Mill Fire, eh? Fortuitous indeed for me, and also for my brothers and my sisters, or we'd never have been born. Our mother Gertie (now professionally Delores) would have been reduced to ashes, and that's a fact.

As I said, Pa's heroism was headline news and Uncle Will incorporated it into the act they sold to the tour managements. Max Worthing was a hero the world wanted to see, and there was no going back to the foundry after that. No more mill work for Gertie either. She was only too keen to get away from factory life. Well, I ask you, who wouldn't be? Besides, she was a 'natural'.

Their greatest triumphs lay ahead of them though, down at the bottom of the world in Australia, where I was born in 1901. It all started with Harry Rickards' offer . . .

'We're looking at a goldmine, me old mates,' Harry raved in his customary exuberant manner, 'a veritable goldmine, and I mean that in the most literal sense, I can assure you. The punters down there, they throw nuggets onstage, you get showered in the stuff. At least you do in places like Ballarat and Bendigo. Blimey, those towns have become cities since the gold rush first hit back in the fifties.'

Being now early 1888, Harry wasn't quite sure if nugget-tossing was still a regular practice in the goldfield towns of Victoria, but he wasn't lying about the wealth to be found in Australia.

'The whole country's open slather for the likes of us performers,' he went on, 'particularly Melbourne. "Marvellous Melbourne" they're calling the place, and quite rightly so, I can tell you. Why, Melbourne's one of the world's fastest-growing and most cosmopolitan cities of the modern era. We're on the brink of a new century, me old mates, and they're just crying out for the likes of us down there.'

Upon Harry's repetition of 'the likes of us', Will cast a quick and meaningful glance in his brother's direction, but Max didn't notice. Max's boyishly handsome face was fixated, his piercing blue eyes focused firmly on Harry. His arm was around Gertie, who was cuddling baby Elizabeth, known as Izzie, while her other two little ones crawled around on the floor. Both he and Gertie seemed riveted by the glowing picture Harry was painting. Which was hardly surprising, Will supposed; Harry Rickards was very good at painting glowing pictures, a born showman prone to exaggeration, not unlike himself. *Takes one to know one*, Will thought wryly.

A further quick and meaningful glance to Mabel wasn't returned either, although Mabel didn't appear particularly entranced by Harry's sales pitch. They were, all of them, sitting around the old wooden table where the family regularly gathered to dine, and Mabel didn't even seem to be listening. Instead, she was gazing through the grimy front windows of their little cottage to the gloomy day outside, where her seven-year-old twins were playing in the muddy street with their younger sisters. The recent snow had turned to sludge, and she was probably hoping Artie and Alfie wouldn't get the girls' frocks all mucky. They could be so boisterous, particularly Artie.

Will rather wished his wife wasn't distracted and that she'd look his way. Mabel would know exactly what he was thinking about Harry and the tour the man was selling, and even if she disagreed with his own views, as she quite often did, she would know why he had doubts.

It wasn't that Will disliked Harry Rickards. Nor did he disrespect the man, far from it. They'd worked together on many an occasion and he knew Harry to be a fine comic performer. Indeed, Harry's cockney act as the pearly king, complete with stage suit and hat covered in shiny buttons, belting out in his booming baritone the musical hits of the day, regularly brought the house down. Harry Rickards was a talented *lion comique*, and a regular headliner on music hall bills.

But somehow, Will felt the combined talents of the Worthings were just that little bit superior to the rough and tumble burlesque favoured by Harry. He certainly didn't consider himself in any way *socially* superior; to the contrary, knowing a little of Harry's background as he did, he'd be the first to admit to his own inferior upbringing. Harry Rickards had been born in the East End of London, it was true, but he came from a staid, middle-class family while the Worthings – brothers and wives alike – came from factory stock, distinctly working class. As far as Will was concerned this was nothing to be ashamed of, but nor was it a life he wished to pursue. Will Worthing, who would turn thirty years of age in just two months' time, was fiercely ambitious. He wanted more for his family. He wanted more for Max's family, and for the families of their children. If, as an entertainer, Harry chose to cast himself lower on the social ladder, then it was his prerogative to do so, but the Worthings were travelling in a different direction. The Worthings were moving up in the world. Upon Will's insistence, they even spoke better than Harry with his constant use of cockney expressions and rhyming slang. Although it was true Gertie did lapse now and then, giving away her Lancashire working-class origins; they had to keep an eye on that.

'You listen to yer old mate 'Arry,' Harry continued, concentrating on Max, aware that the younger brother was hooked, while the older one was studying him astutely. Harry was aware also that Will was the one he'd ultimately need to convince. 'A top-class 'ighwire act like yours, why, you'd slay 'em in Australia . . .'

Why does he feel the need to drop his Hs? Will wondered.

'You and Delores working the way you do' – Harry gave Gertie a wink intended as a compliment, deliberately using her stage name when he knew full well she was always Gertie in private – 'without a net and all. Cor, what a duo you are! You could maybe try the snakes again like you did in Colchester, what do you say? That'd knock 'em dead. And there's plenty of snakes down there, I can tell you, poisonous ones too.

'And as for you, Will . . .' Harry finally turned his attention to the older brother. This would take a bit of work. 'With a tenor like yours, me old mate, the world's your oyster.'

He grinned engagingly. A stocky man with a broad, square face and eyes that sparkled with humour, Harry could be disarming at times, even downright beguiling, and he knew it. Just as he knew, or rather realised at that very moment, that this might not be one of those times. He needed a little more invention, he quickly decided. The grin disappeared, and so, to a surprising extent, did the accent.

'Given we'd be performing before a more *cosmopolitan* audience,' he said, choosing his emphases with care, 'I'd like to incorporate a broader range of acts in the show, Will, which means the *versatility* of you Worthings would be *invaluable*. We'd have a melodrama on the programme, of course; you as the villain, Max as the hero and Gertie as the heroine. Then in the variety section, along with the death-defying highwire double act and your Heavenly Tenor, I'd like to include a selection of your wonderful recitations, Shakespearean sonnets, perhaps.' Harry knew only too well how Will loved performing his recitations, particularly Shakespeare, and particularly the sonnets. 'And naturally,' he concluded with a triumphant ring and a flamboyant gesture in Gertie's direction, 'the bewitching . . . the enchanting . . . the Divine . . .' Pause for effect, both arms now showily extended. 'Dance of Delores.'

Will was neither disarmed nor beguiled, but he couldn't resist a smile nonetheless, simply in recognition of Harry's downright cheek. *You don't spin a ridiculous sales pitch like that to a born salesman*, he thought. *Takes one to know one, Harry, me old mate.*

The man really was incorrigible. But one couldn't help liking Harry Rickards. And what's more, Will recognised the fact that Harry was quite right. The versatility of the Worthings did make them invaluable. Above all, the versatility of Gertie.

Little Gertie Smeed – now Dolores Worthing and billed either as the Divine, the Daring, the Death-defying, the Delectable, or any number of other adjectives dependent upon which choice of alliteration most fitted the bill – had proved more than a 'natural'. Gertie had proved a show business phenomenon. Pretty as a picture with a cheeky smile and fair curly hair that caught the stage lights to perfection, there seemed nothing she couldn't do. Thanks to her husband's tuition she was by now a highly accomplished acrobat, and thanks to Will's training she could sing and perform more than adequately in both comedy and drama. But above all, and with no tuition whatsoever, she could dance. The Divine Dance of Delores, an act the Worthing brothers were still working on, incorporating a magic lantern, special lighting effects and Mabel's glorious costumes, was already proving a show-stopper. And it was all because of Gertie's God-given talent.

Gertie loved to dance. She always had, even as a little girl. She favoured an interpretive form of dance with a choreography all her own, inspired by the beauty of nature. The first rays of dawn, she would explain, creeping up over the horizon, then the ball of the sun rising majestically into a clear, clear sky. Or the flow of a river, serene to start with, then becoming rapids, running swiftly over jagged rocks, destined to crash in a mighty waterfall. Or it might be the wind in the trees, palms perhaps, swaying gently, then gathering to cyclonic proportions, ferocious and destructive.

The others were amazed. God only knew where Gertie's imagery came from. Postcards perhaps? When had Gertie Smeed seen a sun rise majestically? She'd never even seen a clear sky. She'd lived the whole of her life in the foggy north of England, where the sun rarely penetrated the smog that belched from the factories. And what did she know of rapids and waterfalls and palm trees and cyclones?

'Imagination,' she'd said airily when she'd first displayed to them her talents, 'that's what it is. Don't *all* performers got imagination?' And so amazed was Will at the time he hadn't even bothered to correct her grammar.

Over the past several years, Gertie's instinctive talent had grown exponentially and now her solo act, with the strength of an acrobat and the grace of a dancer, was solid proof that another true star shone in the Worthing firmament.

Harry's right on the money, Will thought. *The Worthings are practically a show on their own. And when the children are older, that's just what we* will *be.*

'So what're your thoughts then, c'mon, spit it out, are you up for adventure or not?' Encouraged by Will's smile, although not altogether gathering the reason behind it, Harry was once again addressing both brothers and their wives. And once again the accent was back in full force. 'Are you goin' to sit around 'ere in a miserable English winter where the business of show is all but brown bread, or are you goin' to come with me and my team of merry performers to the sunny climes of Australia, where the crowds are already queuein' and the streets are paved with gold?'

Max had been successfully beguiled already, but for him one added word clinched the deal. Adventure. Max was always up for adventure, and he knew Gertie was too.

'We'd be up for it, wouldn't we, Gert?' he said, but he didn't direct the remark to his wife, nor even to Harry. It was Will he was looking at. Will made the decisions these days. The Worthings were a team and Will was the boss.

But someone got in before Will could answer.

'Travel expenses and decent accommodation would have to be provided for all of us,' Mabel said, redirecting her eyes from the window to Harry, her pleasant, normally placid face now determined and even a touch stern. Harry had hit the right note with Mabel too, but it wasn't the 'adventure' aspect that held appeal for her. It was the 'sunny climes' that had drawn her attention from the sight of her children playing in the sludge of the street outside, where the air was damp and foggy. 'Seven littlies in all, mind,' she went on, 'none of these costs to come out of our wages.' Mabel, for all her artistic and creative talents, possessed a very practical side.

'Of course,' Harry agreed magnanimously, 'and anyways, when all's said and done, the twins are part of the show, aren't they? They're performers in their own right.'

It was true, the twins were being trained in acrobatics and had been for some time. Max would throw them in back somersaults or carry them on his shoulders as he walked the highwire, just simple tricks so far.

'I've had another thought for the twins though,' Harry continued. 'How about a magic act? The old disappearing routine. Put a kid inside the box, lock the door. *Abracadabra* ... open the door, box empty. *Drumroll and spotlight* ... kid revealed way up the back of the theatre among the punters. 'Ow about that, eh?' He shook his head as if lost in admiration at his own invention, but actually amazed that the Worthings hadn't come up with the patently obvious. 'Ah, identical twins, pure gold for a magic act.'

Will wondered himself why the idea hadn't occurred. It was probably because the twins weren't identical.

They're not, are they, he thought, looking through the window to where Artie and Alfie were chucking mud pies at the fence, spattering the girls as they did so, which naturally added to the fun. *They're not identical at all, in fact they're quite different. They wouldn't be to the punters though, would they? Not if we did their hair the same way and dressed them identically. Why didn't I think of that?* He felt caught out, even a tiny bit stupid, which was the strangest sensation for a man like Will Worthing.

'That's not a bad idea, Harry,' he said begrudgingly.

'So you're in!' Harry beamed. 'That's excellent!'

'No, no, I didn't say we were in,' Will interjected. 'I didn't say that at all.' He looked around at the others, who were waiting expectantly. 'We'll think about it, Harry, and let you know tomorrow.'

Harry rose instantly from the table, strode two steps and took his signature cloth cap from the peg near the door. He knew he'd won, that the rest of the family were hot to trot.

'I'll call back in the morning then, shall I?'

Mabel crossed to the door in order to show him out, which she considered only courteous, and the others stood politely, even Will, who felt himself a little railroaded.

'Fine, Harry,' he said affably enough, 'tomorrow morning it is. We'll discuss things then.'

They all said their 'ta-rahs' and Harry was gone.

The family settled down to discuss the matter, and as they did Will had the distinct impression he was on the losing side.

'Harry's worked the international circuit before, Will,' Max said. 'Not just Australia, he's been to America too, and he even toured his own company in South Africa a couple of years back.'

'Yes, yes, I know all that,' Will replied testily.

'So now he wants to tour a company in Australia,' Max continued undeterred. 'You have to admit, he's got the experience.' The brothers rarely disagreed, and as a rule Max was quite happy for Will to make the decisions, but adventure was beckoning.

'Harry's known to pay a decent wage,' Mabel said, mildly but determined to add her two-penneth, 'and if he foots all the added expenses as he said he would . . .' She left the rest hanging; she'd had her say.

Gertie didn't utter a word, but the big baby-blue eyes that glistened with excitement spoke multitudes. Will knew he was done for.

'Who else will be among Harry's "merry band of per-formers", I wonder,' he growled. 'I can promise you one thing. If I discover he's included any belchers or farters, we're not going and that's that.'

It was true, in previous tours they'd travelled with per-formers who'd belched and farted to popular melodies. Gertie had found their acts colourful and great fun, but Will hadn't. 'We're above that,' he'd said icily.

'Right,' Max agreed, 'no belchers and no farters.' He turned to his wife, unable to wipe the eager smile from his face. 'We're off to Australia, Gertie,' he said.

2

A JOURNEY IS EMBARKED UPON

A month later to the day, the Worthing entourage – brothers, wives and seven children – joined several other members of the Harry Rickards' Specialty Company, including Harry himself, his wife Kate, also a talented performer, and their own three children aboard the SS *Oroya*, shortly to depart the Tilbury docks bound for Australia.

Among the group was musician Frank Barcom, who regularly accompanied the Worthings' performances on piano accordion, and who had become more or less 'one of the family'. A seasoned performer of forty or so, with a Falstaffian appearance and a fondness for the drink, it seemed there was nothing Frank couldn't play, or for that matter, compose. He could create the most evocative melodies for Gertie's interpretive dances, he could accompany any classic aria or Gilbert and Sullivan piece Will chose to perform, and he knew every popular song of the era. The only trouble with Frank was keeping him sober, which didn't present an insurmountable problem in any event as he performed rather well when drunk. It was just getting him back to the digs after the show, which meant he very often slept things off backstage.

There was also a comedy duo called Lionel and Malcolm, an amiable pair of Americans in their mid-thirties, with whom both Harry and the Worthing brothers had previously worked. Lionel was tall and lanky, and Malcolm was short and stocky, and they had, slung over their shoulders as always, a banjo and ukulele respectively. One never knew when the two were going to burst into song.

And there was another double act unknown to the brothers, a pair of pretty young sisters with a North Country twang and the unlikely names of Lotte and Lieke. They professed to be Dutch, looked barely twenty, and evidently performed a song and dance turn of some description.

Will was relieved to discover there was neither a belcher nor a farter among the performers in the troupe. Harry had assured him he'd booked no such act, but Will hadn't altogether trusted him. He still didn't. And even as the steamer, having proceeded quietly down the Thames, now ventured into the open sea, he continued to bemoan the fact.

'Heaven alone knows what's in store for us,' he muttered to Mabel as he scowled at the rapidly receding coastline. 'Harry will line up other acts when we arrive and there's bound to be something in appalling taste.'

Mabel laughed. A pleasant but somewhat average-looking young woman – average, that is, among the many beauties that abounded in show business – Mabel Worthing had the most glorious laugh, infectious and genuine. It was her laugh that Will had first fallen in love with; her laugh and everything it represented. For Mabel, who could conjure up images of magical proportion out of no more than tinsel and frippery, was the most unpretentious, down-to-earth creature Will had ever met. She was the perfect foil for him.

'Oh, just listen to yourself, Will,' she said, 'you sound like the most awful snob.'

'Do I?' He was taken aback, shocked that she might even think such a thing. 'I'm not,' he protested. 'I'm not a snob at all, I'm —'

'Of course you are, silly, you're a talent snob of the first water as you very well know. Now stop spoiling the moment and just look at that.' She turned away from him to gaze once more at the coastline. The whole family was gathered at the ship's railings, along with hordes of other passengers drinking in the last sight of their homeland.

'England,' Mabel breathed admiringly. 'She looks very different from here, doesn't she? Majestic somehow.'

'It's the sea does that,' Gertie said, her eyes focused more upon the ocean than upon the distant land as she cuddled baby Izzie to her. Gertie was dreaming of a dance that would reflect the ocean in all its moods. 'I'm going to do a dance of the sea,' she said. 'All calm like this to start with, seagulls wheeling overhead.' She looked up at the gulls, swaying as she did, already feeling the patterns of their flight. 'Then I'll have the gathering of a storm' – she looked back at the waves – 'a mighty storm, all dark and threatening-like.'

'Yes.' Mabel instantly grasped the image as she always did. 'We'll have a layered costume,' she said. 'Chiffon. Peaceful blue on the surface, rippling gently as you move. Then, when the dance becomes a frenzy, the underneath layers will be a much darker blue, with white tips like angry waves. And we'll have a wind machine operating at stage level in order to keep the dark layers elevated . . .'

'Oh Mabel,' Gertie was enraptured, 'that be sheer heaven.'

'That *would* be sheer heaven.' Will corrected her automatically, but the women's exchange had delighted him. He did so adore creatively gifted people. And if that made him a snob, then so be it. 'Get back here, you two,' he said, hauling the twins down from the railings, which they had scaled with ease to perch precariously on top.

The SS *Oroya* carried five hundred passengers in three saloon sections plus steerage. The extended Worthing family had been allocated third-class cabins, which didn't bother them in the least. Harry was footing the bill after all, which was most generous – performers often paid if not their own way, then certainly those of their family. And besides, Harry and his own family were travelling as second-class passengers, they hadn't put themselves up there with the snobby first-class set. The Harry Rickards' Specialty Company remained an egalitarian affair.

The mood among the troupe was certainly amicable, indeed so much so that it rather placed them apart from the other second- and third-class saloon passengers, who found them decidedly odd. As they wandered around the ship's decks, rehearsing their lines, strumming their instruments, demonstrating the odd dance step here and there, or simply in animated discussion, people tended to give them a wide berth, and the ominous mutter of 'theatricals' would follow them as they passed.

'They'll get used to us,' Will assured the others as if it mattered, which it didn't in the least.

'They'll have to, won't they?' Max agreed with a lazy grin. 'They'll cop us full on in a couple of weeks.'

'And after they've copped us,' Gertie said, 'I bet we'll be the most popular folk on board. That's the way things go in the business of show,' she added impishly, and the others laughed.

Harry had gained permission from the captain for his company to give a performance aboard ship. Buckets were to be passed around at the end of the show, and the earnings would add to the coffers certainly, but there were other considerations of far greater importance, not the least being that performers simply loved to perform. This would keep his troupe happy. Besides, it was an excellent opportunity for the company to rehearse and get to know each other, both professionally and personally. They wouldn't present the show that was intended for Melbourne, of course; the sets, costumes and general equipment were not to hand anyway, some having been stowed in the ship's hold, others to be acquired upon arrival. Rather they would present *extracts* from the show, highlighting the performers' talents. Which was why they were currently rehearsing as they wandered the ship's decks.

There would be a full two weeks before the intended performance, which was scheduled for an evening shortly after their arrival at Port Said in Egypt. During the slow and sluggish trip through the Suez Canal there would be no particular weather issues with which to contend, and the intervening period would allow them time, it was decided, to discover their 'sea legs', as sections of the journey were bound to get rough.

Artie and Alfie were in their element aboard the *Oroya*, Artie as always leading the way. Both boys were adventurous, but Artie was the undisputed leader and Alfie his willing accomplice, which resulted in the most harmonious of sibling relations. Within only days there wasn't an area of the vessel they hadn't explored from steerage to first class, where they'd crept in unnoticed and roamed the posh lounges for a full hour before they'd finally been tossed out and ordered never to return. This didn't deter them from the foredeck promenade reserved for the first-class passengers though. Here they'd saunter along with a nonchalant air as if they were the children of well-to-do parents. Having inherited the family talent for acting, it was no hardship, and being attractive seven-year-old twins, perceived by many to be 'identical', they received a most favourable reaction.

'Oh, how adorable!' Women lounging in wicker chairs drinking tea would call them over and shower them with biscuits and sweets.

'Why thank you, miss,' they'd say in their best rounded vowels, or to an older woman, as if addressing royalty,

'That's very kind of you, ma'am.' They'd hoard these treasures in their pockets to share with their younger sisters, Prudence and Alice, and also their cousins, Edward and Sarah. Baby Izzie was too little; they didn't bother with her.

The equipment and general paraphernalia aboard ship was a further source of fascination for the twins, and also for young Prudence, who at five was a tomboy and easily led astray by her brothers. They were soon joined by Edward, who although only four was determined to be 'one of the boys'. With Pru and Ted on side, the Rickards children, too, soon joined in the fun and, the example having been by now firmly set, the ranks quickly swelled with other youngsters, including the ragamuffin kids from steerage. Between the lot of them they drove the crew mad, playing tag or hide and seek, dodging about among the masts and the funnels and the giant ropes and pulleys and spars. The *Oroya* was a veritable playground . . .

Until the weather struck.

The first storm hit in the Bay of Biscay, and it hit with a vengeance, the ship pitching and rolling, most passengers forced to remain below decks confined to their cabins or, those poor souls travelling steerage, cooped up in the gloomy hold. Only the hardiest of travellers ventured outside.

Mal de mer was rife. Places at dinner tables were conspicuously empty, and stewards ran hither and thither with buckets of carbolic and sea water to scrub away the involuntary messes that appeared all over the ship, in corridors and cabins, and also on deck when a desperate passenger hadn't made it to the railings in time.

The majority were sick for several days, including the members of the Harry Rickards' Specialty Company, with the one strange exception of Harry himself. Harry appeared immune to seasickness. Strolling casually about, his gait seemingly unaffected by the ship's rocking and rolling, he'd whistle a tune and raise his hat to the poor overworked stewards as they went about their unpleasant tasks. No doubt the many sea voyages undertaken in his past had toughened Harry Rickards' constitution.

But eventually, as the weather cleared, even the weakest of passengers had by then discovered their sea legs, no doubt to the relief of the stewards, who could now dispense with their buckets.

'Oh lovey, just look at that, will you. Have you ever *seen* such a sight? Did you ever *dream* that you would?' Gertie was leaning over the railing in a state of ecstasy.

'That's the Rock of Gibraltar, Gert,' Max said.

'I know,' she replied in wondrous admiration, not taking her eyes from the sight, 'they told us half an hour ago at breakfast, remember.'

Max did. But he'd also looked at the map hanging on the wall of the third-class saloon. 'We're entering the Strait of Gibraltar,' he said knowingly. 'That's Spain over there.' They were standing on the vessel's port side and he gestured at the steep cliffs that rose from the sea. 'If we go over the other side of the ship,' he went on, 'we'll be able to see Morocco.'

'Ooh really.' Gertie was hugely impressed, although she still didn't take her eyes from the Rock. 'How'd you know all that then?'

'Just things I've read.' He gave a casual shrug. He'd show her the map when they went back inside.

'Clever you.' Gertie would leave Morocco for later, she decided; the Rock had her full attention for now.

Both Gertie and Max had weathered the storm better than most, perhaps due to their physical fitness, who could tell, but after feeling queasy for a day and a night their bodies had soon adapted to the ship's motion.

Indeed, on the second day of the storm Gertie had insisted upon experiencing its full force up on deck. Max had accompanied her. Although still feeling a little unsettled himself, he wouldn't have her venture out there on her own.

He'd hung on to a spar in the wind-whipped rain and watched while, clinging to the railing, she'd dipped and swayed and pitched and rolled as if she were one with the ship. But she was staring out at the dark, dark ocean and he'd known it wasn't the ship's movement she was emulating, it was the storm. The storm and the anger of the sea. He'd been right.

'You'd best go below, miss,' a voice had said, and a young deckhand had appeared out of the unnatural gloom of the afternoon.

'I can't,' she'd said, turning to him, saturated, hair plastered to her face, eyes glowing with excitement. 'I can't go below. I'm living my dance.'

The young man had been about to insist, but Max had stepped from the shadows.

'It's all right,' he'd said, 'she's my wife, I'll look after her.'

The deckhand, little more than a youth, had eyed them up and down dubiously. 'Orright, suit yourself then.' And with a shrug he'd disappeared.

'Come on, Gert,' Max had insisted, grabbing her arm. 'You've lived your dance, love, we're going back inside.'

But when they'd returned, thoroughly drenched, to the poky little cabin where the youngsters were creating chaos, he had to admit he no longer felt in the least bit unsettled. He felt marvellous.

'Oh Max, lovey,' Gertie had said breathlessly, picking up Izzie who was squealing for attention, 'wasn't that wonderful?'

Water dripping all over her, Izzie squealed even louder.

'Oi, Ted,' Max had said, 'come and look after your little sister while your ma gets changed.'

Gertie, irrepressible as always, continued to relish every moment of the voyage to Australia. And after Max had shown her the map hanging on the wall of the third-class saloon, she followed their route assiduously.

'That's Mount Etna,' she told Mabel with pride several days later as they gazed at the towering volcano passing them by, deep lava flow fissures carved in its sides. It looked like a giant sentry allowing them safe passage; at least it did to Gertie. 'And see that really pretty town there ...' With two-year-old Sarah clinging to her skirts and baby Izzie cradled over her left hip, Gertie pointed with her right hand. 'That's Messina.'

Having left Naples just the previous day, the *Oroya* was now travelling slowly through the narrow strip of water that separated Sicily from the mainland of Italy, and the women were standing on the starboard side of the vessel.

'Good heavens above, Gertie,' Mabel said, astonished, 'how do you know all that?'

'Oh, I read it in a book somewhere,' Gertie replied airily. Then she gave the cheekiest grin. Everyone knew reading was not Gertie's strongest suit. Learning the lines of a script was as far as her talent with words went, and even then Max usually dictated her lines to her. Gertie had never read a book in her life. 'You haven't seen the map, have you, Mabel?' she said eagerly. And scooping little Sarah up, she slung the child over her right hip and led the way. 'Come on, I'll show you.'

Three days later, the ship steamed into the harbour at Port Said. The troupe must now start seriously preparing for their performance, which was planned to take place in two days' time during their cruise down the Suez Canal.

Mabel had already been applying herself diligently to the impromptu supply of costume and props that might enhance the show, the majority of the company's equipment being housed in trunks in the ship's hold. With regard to costumes, for the most part she'd simply added pieces of dressing to the basics the family carried with them.

Max, Gertie, and now also the twins, who had been incorporated into the highwire and acrobatic act, always travelled with leotards for training. The tight-fitting, supportive garments, in use for some time by professional acrobats, had recently been named after the great French gymnast Jules Léotard, who had previously referred to them as 'maillots'. Max, a great admirer of the man, found it only right they be known as 'leotards'. 'A worthy tribute,' he'd said, sounding very much like his brother Will. Max was not normally given to gravitas.

In any event, the leotards were easily transformed by the talents of Mabel, whose bulging bag of treasures never left her side, simply because, as she was wont to say, 'You never know when bits and bobs might come in handy.'

Hundreds of individual spangles, designed to catch the light, had been laboriously stitched to each black leotard, and bright fringing added to each sleeve. All four performers would wear colourful kerchiefs tied around their throats, presenting a dashing sight, perfectly befitting an acrobatic team.

The costume for Gertie's dance sequence had been transformed with equal ease. The one evening frock she'd packed for a special occasion that might take place aboard ship was a simply styled but very attractive satin dress of golden hue. Mabel had designed it herself and made it specially for the trip as a present for her sister-in-law. She'd replaced the large bustle currently in vogue with a smaller version in order to accentuate Gertie's lithe figure and, fashionably sleeveless and low-necked as the design was, the overall effect had proved most fetching. The two women had now decided between them that Gertie would perform a version of her 'sun dance', the glimmering texture of the fabric and the colour of the dress being deemed most appropriate.

The decision made, a tiara miraculously appeared, constructed from the bits and bobs of Mabel's bag. Made up of pieces of wire upon which were threaded glittering crystal beads and woven into a perfect shape, it would catch the light beautifully. As would the choker necklace, no more than glitter stitched onto a black velvet band, which looked for all the world like diamonds. Mabel then produced a long piece of lemon-coloured chiffon to act as a scarf, which could be used to simulate the rays of the sun as Gertie twirled her magic. And thus a costume had been born.

'It'll have to do,' she said critically as Gertie paraded before her.

'It's perfect,' Gertie exclaimed, 'you're a wiz, Mabel.'

Mabel's wizardry was not necessary in a number of cases, however, as many artistes did not relinquish their trademark costumes to the general cargo hold, perhaps for fear of losing their very identity.

Harry Rickards himself always travelled with his *lion comique* outfit of man-about-town 'swell', which included top hat, jacket, smart trousers, cravat and cane.

And as for Lionel and Malcolm, well, they were never without their tattered suits, their battered trilbies, their crisp white gloves and, above all, their makeup kits. Lionel and Malcolm were tramp comedians who performed under their own names. At least, it was presumed these were their own names; no one could be sure. Both onstage and off, they were simply known as Lionel and Malcolm. A highly successful duo comic act accompanied by banjo and ukulele and performed in 'blackface', their personas travelled with them wherever they went.

The likeable American pair had been performing in England for close on a decade now. They'd arrived from the United States with a minstrel show in the late seventies, and when the tour had finished, they'd simply opted to stay. 'Blackface entertainment' was tremendously popular throughout the whole of Britain, and they'd decided they could make much more money as a duo than they could as two members of a large minstrel troupe. And they'd been right.

So there was no need for Mabel to be inventive on their behalf, which might, even for her, have presented some problem, as she had no cork with which to mix blackface makeup in her bag of treasures.

A similar situation presented itself with young Lotte and Lieke, whose routine had turned out to be a clog dance, interspersed with popular songs. The girls always travelled together with their clogs, along with their peasant bonnets and their colourful Dutch skirts, a design more for young girls than young women as the hems stopped mid-calf. This was, of course, in order to show off their clever footwork.

Excellent, Mabel thought, *no help required there.*

From the outset of the journey, both Mabel and Gertie had wondered why the sisters had gone to such pains to pose as Dutch when they were so clearly from the English Midlands.

'Manchester, I'd say,' Mabel had remarked.

Gertie had agreed. 'And they're mill girls what's more, I'd stake my life on it. But "Lotte" and "Lieke"? Why are they pretending to be Dutch?'

Then they'd discovered that the sisters' act was a clog dance.

'I suppose they think the punters associate clogs more with Holland than with England,' Mabel had suggested pragmatically.

Supposition, however, was not good enough for Gertie, whose curiosity simply had to be satisfied. So she'd asked them straight out.

'Why do you call yourselves Lotte and Lieke?'

Despite the directness of the question, the sisters, who were a benign and pleasant pair, had taken no offence.

'Because that's our names,' said Lotte, who'd just turned twenty.

'But they're *Dutch* names, aren't they?'

'That's right. Our surname's Van der Laan.'

'Oh.' Gertie was momentarily stumped. 'You don't sound Dutch.'

Eighteen-year-old Lieke had taken over then. 'Our grandfather was Dutch,' she'd explained. 'We've never met him and we've never been to Holland – our mam hasn't either – but Pa wanted us to have Dutch names.'

'Oh,' Gertie said again, 'I see.'

She didn't really see at all, and it had become no clearer after questioning them further, but she'd reported the news back to Mabel.

'They're *part* Dutch,' she said.

'*Really?*' Mabel was amazed.

'Yes,' Gertie said thoughtfully. 'I think you're right though. I think they're using the Dutch link to sell the act. Funny that, isn't it? The punters all know we have English clog dancers.' Gertie found it most odd. 'Anyway,' she went on, 'I was right too, they're factory girls. Or were. They got into show business to run away from the mills.' Gertie certainly understood that part.

'Australia's a long way to run to,' Mabel commented drily.

'They heard about the gold rush and they're hoping to find husbands there.'

'Ah. That explains it then.'

The one performer among the family group who required no thought at all on Mabel's part with regard to costume was her own husband, Will.

Will Worthing loved everything there was to love about fine clothes. The finer the fashion, the finer the thread, the finer the cut, the better. And given his wife was a master designer and talented seamstress, he was not left wanting. They had to cheat on one element, it was true. Their budget did not allow for the finest of fabric, but the fashion and the cut were so superior one would never know. Particularly onstage. From double-breasted waistcoats and cutaway morning jackets to frock coats and capes, the everyday clothes Will wore were perfect for the theatre. Whether he be performing his recitations or giving voice to operatic arias in his Heavenly Tenor, or even playing a well-dressed villain, he presented a handsome and commanding figure.

There was little call for frock coats or capes, however, as the *Oroya* slowly steamed down the Suez Canal. For the past week the weather had become progressively hot and humid. Even the nights. In fact, so oppressive had the nights become that many second- and third-class passengers now chose to sleep out on the deck rather than in the stiflingly confined quarters of their small cabins. Women and children to port, men to starboard, the deck at least allowed them the slight breeze afforded by the motion of the ship.

The weather had been the principal consideration in choosing when the performance should take place, but the temperature had not. Conditions were calm and seasickness no longer an issue certainly, but perhaps someone should have thought to warn them about the heat. The captain and crew were doubtless so acclimatised to the tropics they no longer experienced discomfort, but . . .

No matter. As was the motto among the troupe, 'the show must go on'.

And so it did. They played to a full house of second- and third-class passengers, all crowded into the second-class saloon where a rostrum had been set up as a stage, and where the early arrivals gained seats at the front and the others gathered to stand up the back.

Lionel and Malcolm had prepared themselves in the late afternoon with the help of the twins, who'd agreed to meet them out on deck. The Americans had arrived fully costumed but for their gloves and hats, with hand towels tucked into their open collars. They'd each sat in a deck-chair and simultaneously opened their respective makeup kits. Even offstage they were a polished double act.

Artie and Alfie took the hand mirrors passed to them. Artie was to assist Lionel; and Alfie, Malcolm. The twins adored the Americans.

'This here's why we're doing our makeup outside,' Lionel explained, holding up a jar as he unscrewed the lid.

'Yeah,' Malcolm said, doing the same with his own jar, 'get a whiff of it and you'll understand all right.'

Artie and Alfie didn't need to put their noses to the jars that were offered them.

'Erk,' Artie said, both boys screwing up their noses at the stench, 'what *is* that stuff?'

'It's burnt cork,' Lionel said, waving his jar about in an effort to disperse the fumes. 'You burn a whole lot of corks to an ember, crumble them up and mix them with mutton fat.'

'It's the heat that's making it stink,' Malcolm said, also waving his jar about, the odour causing several passing passengers to glare accusingly at the group. 'This stuff freezes just about solid in England, but the tropics ain't so friendly.'

'Those folk are wondering which one of us farted,' Lionel remarked, loud enough for the passing passengers to quickly move on.

The twins laughed.

'All right, boys, hold them steady now.'

Grasping their respective mirrors by the handle, Artie and Alfie set them at the correct angle and watched closely as Lionel and Malcolm plunged their fingers into the jars and the procedure began.

When the Americans had blackened their faces and necks, they wiped their fingers on the towels tucked into their collars, screwed the lids back on the jars and tucked the offending mixture away. Then they carefully applied white pencil to the inside of their lower lids, accentuating the whites of their eyes, and from their kits they lifted out the sticks of bright red greasepaint with which to form the large classic mouth of blackface. During their minstrelsy days their accentuated mouths had always been white, but for their comic duo Lionel and Malcolm favoured red. And finally, the process was complete. They would leave the towels in place until the last minute when they could do up their collars with the minimum risk of soiling them, and they would add the white gloves, alleviating the necessity of hand makeup.

'Now all we have to do is try not to sweat too much,' Lionel said.

In order to do so, they stayed out on deck, skipping dinner and soaking up the breeze that came off the water. It was best anyway, they'd decided, that the punters shouldn't see them in makeup before the show.

'O, for a Muse of fire, that would ascend
  The brightest heaven of invention!
  A kingdom for a stage, princes to act,
  And monarchs to behold the swelling scene!'

With no introduction whatsoever, apart from Frank's short series of fearsome stabs on his piano accordion in order to shut up the punters, who indeed fell obediently silent, Will strode onstage and leapt directly into the Prologue of Shakespeare's *Henry V*. The opening Chorus speech was not only one of his favourites, but invariably applicable to the venue in which he was appearing, most tending to be of the 'humble' variety.

'But pardon, gentles all,
  The flat unraised spirits that have dared
  On this unworthy scaffold to bring forth

So great an object. Can this cockpit hold
The vasty fields of France? Or may we cram
Within this wooden O the very casques
That did affright the air at Agincourt?'

In both voice and stature he was nothing short of magnificent, and the crowded room was rendered silent. Even
the fluttering of fans, and of makeshift pieces of paper
serving as fans, ceased, as people sat or stood utterly
motionless. Such was the power of Will Worthing.

'Admit me, Chorus to this history;
Who, prologue-like, your humble patience pray
Gently to hear, kindly to judge, our play.'

It was the perfect way to open the show and as Will
offered a deep bow, the applause was deafening.

He cut it off quickly though. Pace was essential, no rest
between acts.

'And now,' he announced, 'I give you England's greatest
Lion Comique . . .' This accompanied by a grand gesture.
'The one . . .' Another grand gesture. 'The only . . .' And
another. 'Harry Rickards!'

He stood aside. Frank struck up a lively rendition of
'Captain Jinks of the Horse Marines' and Harry leapt onto
the stage, his booming baritone bouncing off the walls as
he strutted his stuff with all his customary aplomb.

Led by its two master performers, the show was off to
a wonderful start and things didn't let up from that
moment on.

Even the introductions to the acts were a star turn on
their own. As the tiny stage allowed no room to accommodate the customary easel and giant cards that accompanied
the announcement of each performance, and as there was
neither easel nor cards to hand anyway, Mabel's inventive-
ness had once again come to the fore. She always carried
a supply of cartridge paper in her huge bag of treasures
for just such occasions, and she'd drawn up the name of

each act in a beautiful cursive script accompanied by a suitably decorative motif. Little five-year-old Pru and her cousin, four-year-old Ted, had been delegated the task of introducing the performers and, standing together centre stage, they unfurled between them the paper bearing the title of each act. They took turns making the actual announcement, which the audience found most endearing, but things became extremely competitive between the two.

'Those loveable rogues . . . Lionel and Malcolm!' Ted bellowed at the top of his voice, and on came the laid-back tramps with their banjo and ukulele.

'The Sun Dance of The Divine Dolores,' Pru announced loud and clear, her voice pitched perfectly, and on twirled Gertie, tiara sparkling, chiffon swirling.

Another song from Harry followed, giving Gertie time to change. Then . . .

'The Wonderful Worthings' Family Acrobatic Troupe!' Ted once again, the announcement now louder than seemed humanly possible for a four-year-old. Both he and Pru had been thoroughly coached, show business being their destiny from the moment they were born.

Max and Gertie's act with the twins was a simple acrobatic performance. The conditions were hardly conducive to highwire so they stuck to somersaults, backflips and a family pyramid as the grande finale. Gertie climbed Max's body from bended knee to shoulders, where he lifted her above his head on his hands. He would have stood at this point, but if he had, the height of the ceiling would not have allowed room for the pyramid so he remained on one knee. The twins then climbed the two of them to stand either side of Gertie's shoulders, her arms outstretched, and the boys topped it all off with a one-armed handstand, legs spread wide, almost to the splits in order to avoid the ceiling. The tableau was perfect. The entire performance, accompanied by the verve of Frank's piano accordion and the speed at which the team worked, went down extremely well.

'And now . . .' Pru called in a voice designed to reach the utmost limits of any theatre. 'Lotte and Lieke from Amsterdam!'

The furled paper announcing the act, which she and Ted had revealed between them, was charmingly decorated with drawings of tulips. And on came the twins, clogs prettily and busily pitter-pattering away.

'They're no more from Amsterdam than you and me,' Gertie whispered to Mabel as they peered from behind the door at the side that led to the second-class kitchen, or rather 'galley' as they'd discovered it was known aboard ship.

'Shush, don't be unkind.'

'That's not a Dutch dance. That's pure Lancashire.'

'They're rather good, actually.' Mabel, always direct, always no-nonsense, was never saccharine, but nor was she ever unkind.

The girls *were* quite adept, Gertie had to admit. Their performance had all the accompanying sound of a standard clog dance, the heel-to-toe rhythm, and the shoe-to-shoe tap, but she couldn't help wondering whether the clogs they were wearing were of the 'horseshoe' style, which would certainly add to the effect. However, much as she studied each lift of the foot, from where she was positioned the angle was awkward, and she couldn't make out the metal studs.

By now the packed saloon was blisteringly hot, people although immersed in the show desperately fanning their faces, and Lotte and Lieke from Amsterdam, despite their talent, were proving a weak link. Even the popular songs they sang in pretty harmony were not enough to distract from the discomfort and the audience was growing restless.

But help was at hand.

'And now . . . the Great William Worthing!' Ted roared. 'The Heavenly Tenor himself!'

As Frank struck up an introduction on the piano accordion and Will Worthing strode onstage, the applause was instantaneous.

Standing to one side, accepting the ovation as his due, little Ted cast a triumphant glance at Pru, convinced he'd won the competition.

All was well again. Will Worthing's rendition of 'Ave Maria' brought the house down; who cared about the heat!

The show was an overwhelming success, as was proved by the donations that landed in the buckets handed around by the children, particularly those buckets proffered by Pru and Ted, who were still competing.

Gertie's words, furthermore, proved eminently prophetic. In the days that followed, the 'theatricals' were the most popular folk on board, so much so that the first-class passengers demanded a show of their own.

The troupe happily obliged, but not before they'd performed another show, this time in the afternoon and on deck, for the passengers travelling steerage. At the closure of this performance, there were no buckets passed around. Everyone was content to work for the pure joy of performing, and for the pure joy their show afforded their audience.

Surprisingly enough, the results of the bucket collection that followed the performance in the first-class saloon was roughly the same as the sum collected after the second- and third-class performance; around four pounds in all.

'That's how rich folks get rich, I suppose,' Gertie remarked with an acid tone. 'Rich folks hang on to their money.'

Early the following morning, the *Oroya* arrived in Aden Harbour in the Middle East and, after refuelling and taking on fresh supplies, she set off across the Arabian Sea bound for Ceylon and the docks of Colombo south of Asia.

It was in Colombo that the Harry Rickards' Specialty Company had their first taste of mangoes, and the children, Artie and Alfie in particular, couldn't get enough of them. For the next several days the twins walked around the ship's decks with faces stained vivid orange.

'Can you get these in Australia?' Artie asked, sucking away at a dry mango stone long devoid of flesh.

'Only in the northern parts,' Harry explained; being well-travelled, he was the only one among them au fait with mangoes. 'They're a tropical fruit, you see.'

Upon leaving Colombo, the ship embarked upon the next major leg of its journey, the crossing of the vast Indian Ocean, bound for Australia. They would not stop in the western port of Fremantle, but continue around Cape Leeuwin, their initial port of call being Adelaide, before then continuing on to Melbourne and Sydney. But the first sight of land would be the southern coast of Western Australia.

The days dragged by interminably with barely a ship in sight, the odd glimpse of a distant freighter enough to drag passengers out on deck simply to view something other than the endless blue of the ocean. In the meantime, the principal distraction during the day was shoals of flying fish, and during the night, the clarity of a sky and stars never seen before.

'Just look at that, will you, Mabel,' Gertie whispered in awe, baby Izzie fast asleep clasped to her chest, as she lay gazing up at the jewelled sky. The weather was hotter than ever and most nights they were sleeping out on the deck now. 'That's a sky you don't get back home.'

'It's beautiful all right,' Mabel agreed, cuddling little Alice, also fast asleep, beside her. 'I don't think I've ever seen anything quite so beautiful.'

'Even you couldn't design something like that, could you?' Gertie said; not facetiously, she was being quite serious.

Mabel didn't say a word. She just kept looking up at the sky.

Their nights of sleeping on deck were numbered, however, as the weather once again hit with a vengeance.

Fierce tropical storms came from out of nowhere, lashing the boat, flooding the decks, smashing things about in cabins and saloons. And then as quickly as they'd arrived they were gone, leaving everything cleanly washed, innocent rainbows in the sky, a bright sun shining down, as if they'd never visited. Until they came back for a return performance, freshly invigorated and as violent as ever.

Most of the passengers were again suffering seasickness, praying desperately the trip would come to an end, and even those not overcome with *mal de mer* were starting to long for the feel of solid earth beneath their feet.

Then . . .

'Land! I see land!'

Whether Will Worthing was the first aboard the *Oroya* to see the coast of Western Australia that day is debatable, but he was certainly the loudest.

'Land ahead!'

Perhaps others on deck had been wondering whether, through the heat haze, they could make out the coastline. 'Is that land?' they might have been muttering to one another, but it was Will Worthing who made the announcement. Will Worthing's stentorian tones, which could reach the gods of any theatre clear as a bell, rang out about the ship for all to hear.

They had arrived.

3

A NEW LIFE BECKONS

The tour of *Rickards' New Comedy and Specialty Company*, as it became known after the show had been fully rehearsed and mounted, was quite a spectacular affair, featuring musicians, soubrettes and minstrels, a mix of vaudeville and variety aimed to please. It proved successful enough. Perhaps not quite the 'goldmine' Harry had promised, but certainly enough to whet the collective appetites of the Worthing family. They played Adelaide, Sydney and Melbourne, along with any number of big regional towns, and the following year Harry took the tour to New Zealand. By which time, Uncle Will and Aunt Mabel, Pa and Ma, and most definitely all the children, were well and truly won by the Antipodean lifestyle. They liked New Zealand, very pretty they agreed, but they simply adored Australia. Melbourne in particular. 'Marvellous Melbourne' Harry had promised, and he'd been quite right.

The heyday of the gold rush might have been over, but you'd never have known it in Melbourne. At least that's what Ma always said. Oh my, how she'd rave on about those early days. 'The rosy days,' she called them.

'Oh, the excitement, lovey,' she'd say, 'the heady excitement of it all. Melbourne was one of the great cities of the world back then, right up there with London and Paris and New York. She was a harlot and a grand lady all in one; mucky back lanes seething with muggers, and pimps touting the wares of poor working girls; broad boulevards with elegant ladies and gents strutting about in their finery, and honey-coloured stone buildings that glowed gold in the gas lamps. There was electricity too, you know, just not in the streetlamps – that didn't happen until five or six years later – but all the big theatres had electric lights, and oh my, what a sight! A wall of electric lights all the way up Bourke Street . . .'

The mention of theatre always brought Ma to the point of ecstasy; there'd be no stopping her after that.

'Oh, those theatres, lovey, my goodness, those theatres! Melbourne was a cauldron of entertainment, a bubbling cauldron, I tell you. Why, it seemed you could walk around any corner and into a theatre, be it of the big, flashy kind or a downstairs gas-lit hole in the wall, and catch any sort of show you wanted . . .'

No wonder the Worthings decided to stay put, eh? With a rave like that you'd be surprised if they didn't, wouldn't you? So when Harry returned to England, that's just what they did. They stayed put and found jobs with other theatre managements. They missed their old mate Frank Barcom, who'd been virtually one of the family for years, but not being of the same adventurous spirit, Frank pined for England and went home with Harry and the others.

Harry himself was going to come back though. He was going to tie up his affairs in the Old Country and return to Australia where he'd set up his own theatre circuit, that's what he said. And being Harry Rickards, no one doubted he'd do just that.

In the meantime, there was no shortage of work for the Worthings; big shows, small shows and shows that were in between. Variety, music hall, vaudeville . . . Classical, comic opera, panto . . . The Worthings could slot themselves in anywhere and everywhere, it seemed. The pay wasn't grand, mind, but they managed to scrape by without having to seek employment outside their sphere, which is something few performers can boast.

Uncle Will, Pa and Ma toured a number of times with J. C. Bain's and Harry Clay's vaudeville and minstrel shows, and when they did Aunt Mabel would stay in Melbourne with the littlies, who by now were mostly school age. The family had determined the children were all to be educated in the three Rs until they were at least twelve, perhaps even fifteen. And the best part was, they got all this learning for nothing! Given the Worthings' 'pecuniary instability' – a favourite term of Uncle Will's – it had been presumed the kids would have to go to one of the ragged schools that catered for the offspring of paupers, private school fees being out of the question. But no, that wasn't the case at all. Thanks to the government's *Public Instruction Act* there was 'free, secular and compulsory schooling' (that's what Aunt Mabel said they called it) available for all children from the ages of six to fifteen. The state schools didn't cost a penny! Isn't that marvellous? Aunt Mabel said the only added expense was the shoe leather she wore out walking the tribe back and forth each day. She herself, of course, never stopped working. Fresh costumes and props kept appearing from nowhere.

Shortly after they returned from one of the tours, Uncle Will was offered a wonderful run in *The Pirates of Penzance*, a J. C. Williamson production at the Princess Theatre in Melbourne. Uncle Will adored Gilbert and Sullivan's comic operas, and so it appeared did the great JCW himself, so the marriage was a happy one.

James Cassius Williamson's theatre company, the most successful in Australia, was commonly referred to as The Firm. And over the ensuing years, I'm happy to report, various and sundry members of the Worthing family were regularly employed by The Firm in both Melbourne and Sydney, along with many national tours.

Uncle Will was determined whenever possible not to split up the family, so during the run of *Pirates* they all stayed at their favoured digs in the middle of the city. This was the

Victoria Coffee Palace hotel, fondly referred to as 'The Vic'. Situated just behind the Town Hall in Little Collins Street, The Vic was a 'temperance hotel' and, although it looked rather fancy, was warm and cosy and didn't cost the earth. Then, as luck would have it, Ma and Pa landed work with a variety production at the Opera House in Bourke Street. Actually, their employment had nothing at all to do with luck but rather talent, as they were billed with two different acts altogether – The Wonderful Worthings' Daring Duo (a highwire act minus the twins who were at school), and The Dance of The Divine Dolores. The Worthings were certainly versatile, you have to say that much.

Not for one minute did the family regret their decision to stay in Australia. Ma even worked hard on improving her literacy skills, determined to write regularly to the mother she accepted she may never see again. 'Not that Mam'll be able to read my letters, mind,' she said, 'but Betty our oldest will, and that'll keep her happy.'

They still didn't regret their decision when the depression hit in the early nineties. And in 1893 when the banks closed shop – and I mean quite literally, the banks closed their front doors and locked people out, can you believe that! The whole country was crippled. Even then, Ma managed to laugh about it.

'No point us doing a run on the banks like everyone else, lovey,' she told me, 'we didn't have any money in the bank. Not a penny, not a farthing. Everything went on new costumes and props – got to keep the acts fresh – and what was left went on food and rent. What would we need with a bank?'

It was a hand-to-mouth existence throughout the depression years, but the Worthings managed to survive. There was always one or two of them working, earning enough to support the others, and as usual, Uncle Will had his clearly defined views on the matter.

'In times of hardship, the theatre always survives,' he'd proclaim. And this wasn't just referring to the economic depression of the nineties, I hasten to add. I've heard him come up with these views on numerous occasions over the years. 'People need entertainment during periods of great adversity,' he'd say. 'Believe me, they'll find that extra shilling for the escape the theatre offers.' Then he'd add with great pride, 'We must never underestimate the importance of our calling.'

I don't know if you've gathered yet, but Uncle Will could sound just a little pompous now and then. We all loved him for it though. When you're as charismatic as Uncle Will you can get away with a lot.

Funnily enough, it was during the depression years that Ma discovered the dance that would prove her greatest success of all. Well, she didn't discover it actually – Aunt Mabel did. And Aunt Mabel didn't really discover it – she stole it. But then, in those days, everyone stole acts from everyone. Nothing stayed original for long.

'Come with me,' Mabel said urgently, grabbing Gertie by the arm and hauling her to her feet.

'But I haven't finished my tea yet,' Gertie protested. It was lunchtime on a cold winter's day and, after lingering over the last of her fish paste sandwich, she was halfway through her second cup of tea at Parer's Crystal Café.

Parer's, at the top end of Bourke Street, was a favourite haunt of the Worthings. After sending the children off to school, or if it was during the holidays to picnic and play in Fitzroy Gardens, they would gather at Parer's for either a late breakfast or an early lunch. Standing four storeys high with ornate arched windows, sturdy stone balconies, and topped by an elaborate cupola, Parer's Crystal Café and Hotel was well beyond the family's means when it came to accommodation. For socialising, however, the ground floor café was not. Parer's Crystal Café, one of the most popular gathering places in Melbourne, was not the preserve of the wealthier clients, who booked into the hotel's upstairs rooms, but the fashionably favourite haunt of many from all walks of life. There was a distinct air of luxury about the place, with its ornamental fountain, elaborate floral arrangements and mirror-covered walls.

Will, Mabel, Max and Gertie would settle themselves on the crimson velveteen settees and, for a good hour or more, they'd eke out their second sixpenny pot of tea, which sat on the round marble table before them as they discussed new acts, new scripts, or new ideas in general.

The principal discussion these days was how to get around the problems presented by the depression. How they might reduce production costs – the creation of sets and backdrops and costumes – without adversely impacting the imagery. And most importantly, what form of show would entice audiences, in straitened times such as these, to part with their meagre funds? Comedy, it was decided. Music, dance, acts of a spectacular nature – everything the Worthings had at their fingertips – and above all, magical effects! In times of woe the people needed more than laughs; they needed magic!

'Smoke and mirrors,' Mabel would say. 'The best effects are so often the cheapest.'

'Tinsel and fairy dust,' Gertie would add.

The management of Parer's welcomed show business folk and no one ever asked them to move on. Parer's epitomised to the Worthings all the glamour of Melbourne. There was even a spacious billiards room out the back where men gathered to smoke and discuss weighty matters, or to tell jokes and simply exchange yarns.

'Forget about the tea,' Mabel insisted, 'you have to come and see something.' She looked about, as if suddenly noticing. 'Where are Will and Max?'

'They're out back in the billiards room. Some fella wanted to chat to them. About a show I think.' Gertie had been very much enjoying sitting on her own watching the fancy people who strutted about demanding to be noticed, and the stitched-up old maids who acted so proper, sipping tea with their pinkies extended; there was always such a lot to see at Parer's. Will and Max had finished their sandwiches anyway, and the man who wanted to talk to them had been craving a cigar. So had Will for that matter. As women were not welcome in the billiards room, Gertie hadn't minded in the least staying where she was. Besides, she couldn't stand the smell of cigars.

'Where did you get to, Mabel?' she asked. 'We wondered why you left The Vic in such a rush.'

'I wanted to check out something I'd heard,' Mabel replied, giving Gertie's arm another tug. 'Hurry up, we don't have much time. Put your coat on, it's freezing outside.'

'Time for what?' As she felt herself being dragged away, Gertie struggled into her coat and looked reluctantly at her teacup, although she knew by now the tea would be cold.

'You'll see.'

'Shouldn't I let the boys know I'm leaving?' There was the touch of a whine in Gertie's voice; Mabel was being decidedly bossy. 'And what about the kids? They're in the park.'

'Will and Max won't care in the least, and the kids will be fine, as you very well know. They're playing with the Baker tribe and Barb's bound to be there.' The young Baker children went to the same state school as the Worthings, and the families had become good friends. Given the alliteration factor, Will maintained that Bob and Barb Baker should have been in show business.

'Good grief,' Mabel went on, 'even if she's not there, Artie and Alfie are twelve years old – they can bring

the others back to The Vic. Now hurry up or we'll
miss the curtain, and you know how rude that is.' They
were outside the warm café and in the chill of Bourke
Street now.

'What curtain?' Gertie gave up and hastened her pace.

'A benefit matinee at the Royal. The Ada Delroy Company's performing.'

The nearby Theatre Royal was among the finest of
Melbourne's many magnificent theatres. After being burnt
down in 1872, it had been rebuilt even bigger and better
in order to meet the demand of the city's boom days, and
now over twenty years later could seat 4,000 people over
four tiers. A massive space with an opulent high-domed
ceiling and equally opulent balconies, it was designed to
overwhelm, and did so most successfully.

Mabel and Gertie arrived with only minutes to spare
and, stepping inside the lavish foyer, they found it all but
deserted; the audience was obviously already seated.

Gertie instinctively made for the box office, but Mabel
stopped her.

'It's all right, I bought the tickets half an hour ago,' she
said, delving in her handbag, 'follow me,' and she headed
for the doors that led directly to the dress circle.

'Oh my,' Gertie said with raised eyebrows, 'the classy
seats, are you sure we can afford this?'

'They're half the normal price,' Mabel assured her. 'The
management knows it'll only be a small house, they're
not even opening the two upper tiers. It's a benefit performance after all.'

'Who's the benefit for?'

'The homeless and destitute, I should think,' Mabel said,
not archly, but with a smile. 'There is a depression on,
you know.'

'Oh yes. Of course.' Gertie returned the smile, not
feeling at all rebuked. 'Silly me.'

'Mind you,' Mabel continued, 'the Ada Delroy Company's probably happy to use the performance as a final dress rehearsal – they're about to go on an overseas tour, India I'm told.' Again, the comment was made with no element of spite, just Mabel's inherent practicality. 'A very good idea,' she added. 'I'm sure if we had our own company we'd do the same. Everyone benefits that way, don't they?'

She handed the tickets to an usherette and they entered the impressive dress circle, Gertie following her down to the front row, where they began edging past those already seated.

Mabel had been right: for such a very large theatre, the house was small. *Can't be more than five hundred*, Gertie thought, eyes flickering around the auditorium. They slid into their seats.

'Oh my,' she said again, but this time in a whisper, 'front row, centre.' She always whispered when she was in a theatre auditorium. Didn't everyone?

'Yes.' Mabel's reply was also whispered. 'I wanted you to have the best possible view.'

They sat silently drinking in the magnificence of their surrounds. With theatre in their blood, there was no need to whisper further. Will Worthing always called such moments 'theatrical osmosis'.

The show, which was termed 'vaudeville' by the Ada Delroy Company, was a classic form of variety, with around ten diverse acts presented in rapid succession without announcement. 'Variety' – a superior form of the more vulgar British music hall designed for the lower classes – had proved popular in Australia, and lately entrepreneurs had adopted the term 'vaudeville', a style of multi-act theatre that had emanated from America. Variety and vaudeville had become synonymous with each other, and in both, anything and everything could be expected.

Ada Delroy's show was no exception.

Mabel and Gertie sat through a series of acts that progressed with such remarkable speed they seemed an assault on the senses; a strongman and his wife (who seemed equally strong); a large woman with at least a dozen cockatoos perched on her shoulders and outstretched arms (the birds obedient to her every command); a ventriloquist with an exceptionally rude doll (whose insolence appealed very much to the audience); and an acrobat-juggler who could tumble and somersault in between catching multi-coloured batons (*Max does it so much better*, Gertie thought, wondering why on earth Mabel had brought her here).

Then came the moment. The last act before the interval. There was no announcement, as there hadn't been for the previous performers, but given the musical introduction, this was clearly the highlight and the moment everyone had been waiting for. This was Miss Ada Delroy herself.

All of a sudden the theatre was plunged into darkness, the house lights were turned off and the stage was black, the audience momentarily blinded. Then, simultaneously, shafts of light appeared from all directions, spotlights trained centre stage, and there she was, a spectacular butterfly with gigantic gossamer wings, poised and about to take flight.

The music swelled, a glorious waltz, and as Ada Delroy danced, the spotlights following her every move, the diaphanous gown and the giant wings changing shape and colour, billowing about her to become clouds and waves and rivers, creating images that, particularly to an imaginative brain, were nothing short of spectacular.

Gertie leant forward, hands gripping the wooden railings of the dress circle, utterly transfixed.

Mabel was carefully studying every artifice employed to create the effect. She observed six 'follow spots' in all, two operated from the wings, two from the balcony boxes and two from either side of the dress circle. Necessary for a big theatre, she thought, but you'd only need two all-up in a small venue, maybe even one would do. Very effective to start with a total blackout too. The changes of colour she dismissed as easily achieved, just circles of different coloured gels rotating in front of the spotlights.

She turned her focus upon the costume. Pure silk, and white in order to successfully reflect the colours, but how *much* silk, she wondered. There had to be at least fifty yards to produce that amount of billowing. The main trick, of course, was the sticks. You couldn't see them beneath the fabric, but Ada Delroy was dancing with sticks in her hands, extending the length of her arms, creating those giant wings that could swirl the light fabric into every shape imaginable. *Perfect for our Gertie with her strength and flexibility*, Mabel thought, elated. The dance was everything she'd heard about, and more. An ideal vehicle for The Divine Dolores.

'It's called The Serpentine Dance,' she explained an hour or so later as she and Gertie walked down Bourke Street on their way back to The Vic, the collars of their coats pulled up around their necks to ward off the cold.

They could have left at the interval, but they'd stayed for the whole show, aware that Ada Delroy was to perform again; the last act on the bill, which had quite rightly received a standing ovation, an encore and several curtain calls, despite the small house.

During the interval, they'd remained in their seats, discussing in hushed tones the technicalities of the act, the use of the sticks, the amount of silk fabric, the lighting effects . . .

'You couldn't even *see* her through the costume,' Gertie had whispered, still lost in awe, 'she just *became* things . . .' A struggle for words to describe the indescribable. '*Spiritual* things, as if she was part of the universe . . .' Gertie had petered out at that point.

But Mabel, as always, had stuck to technicalities. 'She'd be wearing a body stocking, a flesh-coloured leotard – easily done. And every trick she's using will be perfect for your dances, Gertie,' she'd added with uncharacteristic excitement. As a rule it took quite a lot to get Mabel worked up, but the imagery had had its effect upon her too, stirring her creative juices.

'The Serpentine Dance,' Gertie now echoed as they turned the corner heading for Little Collins Street. 'You mean it's actually got a *name*?'

'That's right.'

'Then how can we steal it? I mean, Ada Delroy puts on an act like *that* and it's got a *real name*! Give us a break, Mabel,' Gertie scoffed, 'we can hardly steal it, can we?'

'Why not? *She* did.'

'Eh?' Gertie came to an abrupt halt, nearly causing a collision with two people walking behind them.

Mabel came to a halt also, and they stood to one side, making way for passers-by.

'Ada Delroy stole The Serpentine Dance from Loïe Fuller,' Mabel said a trifle smugly. 'Three years ago, to be precise, when she saw Loïe perform it in New York at the Madison Theater, Ada made it her own and she's been performing it ever since.'

'But it's so original.' Gertie couldn't help being just a little shocked. 'She'll cop it from Loïe Fuller, won't she?'

'Only if she goes to Paris.'

Gertie looked suitably mystified, as Mabel had intended she should.

'Loïe – who's really Marie Louise Fuller from Chicago – moved to Europe shortly after the Madison Theater run,' Mabel went on to explain, 'and she'll never come back. Why should she? She's currently the toast of Paris, performing at the Folies Bergère. I'd say there's not much chance of Ada getting sprung for nicking her act, so long as she steers clear of Europe.'

'How do you know all this?'

'Several of Ada's crew are staying at The Vic. They're really nice blokes.' Gertie's dubious reaction implied 'so much for loyalty', but Mabel was quick to come to the crew members' defence. 'No, no, Gert,' she assured her, 'it's common knowledge, honest it is. Everyone knows Ada pinched the dance. She doesn't broadcast the fact to the general public, of course, but it's no secret among show business folk.'

'Well, it still seems wrong to me,' Gertie said primly.

Mabel threw back her head and laughed her gorgeous laugh. 'Oh Gertie, love, you're a wonder, you really are. A true innocent.'

Gertie might have felt a little peeved had someone else made the comment, but when Mabel laughed that laugh of hers it was impossible to take offence.

'Why?' she asked.

'Do you know how many Serpentine Dances must be popping up all over the world right now? We won't be stealing anything that hasn't been stolen a dozen or more times, nothing's sacred in show business. Now come along' – she started once again walking briskly down the street – 'we have to tell the boys about our brand-new top-of-the-bill act.'

Gertie matching her pace, Mabel continued without drawing breath, 'All we have to do is make sure your Serpentine Dance is the best there is. And with your talent, Gertie Worthing, believe me that won't be hard.'

Will and Max were certainly intrigued by the news of a brand-new act, but as things turned out they had news of their own. The man who had been craving a cigar and a chat about business in the back billiards room of Parer's

Crystal Café had come up with a proposition of great interest to the Worthing brothers.

'The first half of the show minstrel style, the second half vaudeville, and we split the profits right down the middle, what do you say?'

Hubert Manders was an American showman who'd 'followed the gold dust trail to Australia in the seventies'; at least that's the way he put it. 'There's riches to be found in boom towns without having to break your back digging,' he'd enthused. 'I knew it at the time, and I was proved right – those miners were aching for entertainment, and my minstrels were just what they wanted.'

Now in his mid-sixties, but trim, dapper, neatly bearded and moustached and looking a decade younger, Hubert Manders still toured his minstrels, although the original troupe members had long since disappeared to be replaced on a regular basis by younger, fresher performers. There were plenty of minstrel players from whom to choose, and not all of them were white. Over the years many black entertainers had arrived from America following the work that beckoned. Talented performers; juba dancers, gospel singers, comedians and acrobats. But when it came to minstrelsy they too were required to wear the cartoonish 'blackface' makeup, just as they had back home. In minstrelsy it was essential everyone be as black as the white performers.

With vaudeville now the fashion of the day, however, the popularity of minstrelsy was on the wane, and although Manders' Mellow-tone Minstrels had a well-established reputation, Hubert had decided it would be wise to join forces for the next regional tour he intended to mount in the spring. Having heard excellent reports of the Worthing brothers, he'd attended several shows where the family's performances had been featured, and he'd been struck by the talent and versatility of their acts.

'*Manders' Mellow-tone Minstrels and Worthing Brothers' Variety Extravaganza*,' Hubert had grandly proclaimed, painting a sign in the air, 'that would be one fine mix, do you not agree?'

As usual, Will had been spokesman, but a quick glance to his brother had assured him Max was equally eager. Here was their big chance. There was just one problem.

'I do indeed agree ... However, I'm afraid we don't have sufficient funds available to co-produce a tour,' he'd said circumspectly. 'Not right at this moment anyway ...'

'Of course, of course,' Hubert interrupted, his tone most jovial; he'd known this would be the case and was quite prepared. 'I'll look after all production expenses. We'll take it out of the profits before we make the split at the end of the run. And I promise you I'll keep good, clean books, which you'll be free to check whenever you wish. Now, what do you say?'

What *was* there to say? The Worthings were in.

There was a lot to be done over the next two months before the tour's commencement in the spring, not least of which was the creation of their new top-of-the-bill act, The Serpentine Dance of The Divine Delores. They'd discussed the possibility of changing the name, Gertie insistent they should.

'I dance my own dances,' she'd protested, 'not someone else's.'

But Gertie was no match for Mabel.

'They *will* be your own dances, love,' Mabel had said reasonably, 'the name only refers to the *form* of the dance. The choreography and the theme will be all yours.'

'But I don't want —'

'The Serpentine Dance is becoming famous, Gertie,' Mabel had continued, still reasonably, but in that voice of hers which brooked no argument. 'Ada Delroy's getting rave reviews, there are already other imitators, and people are queuing up to see it. We simply let the audience know that yours is the best.'

When Mabel was adamant, no one else got a look-in. For one reason only. Mabel was always right.

She now set about with a vengeance creating the costume, painstakingly working with fifty yards of white silk, ensuring each seam was virtually invisible. Any new choreography would present no problem for Gertie, whose dances were already interpretive; she needed only to familiarise herself with the use of sticks. Mabel had decided the sticks should be canes, which would allow for a certain flexibility, and that they should be bent at the end to avoid damage to the fabric. This was no doubt the device favoured by both Loïe Fuller and Ada Delroy, she presumed, as it was eminently practical.

A further idea of Mabel's was the addition of the magic lantern, which they'd already been using to form an impressionistic background for Gertie's dances. Now, with the use of slides, they would project specific images onto the silk itself. Instead of merely changing colour, the costume would mirror the various themes of the dance, an effect that was to prove extraordinary.

Hubert Manders hired a rehearsal hall and work commenced in earnest.

The twins were taken out of school. They were about to turn thirteen anyway; it was high time they joined the business.

Artie and Alfie were thrilled to be part of the tour, just as they had been during the run of *Rickards' New Comedy and Specialty Company* all those years ago. These days it was only during the school holidays that they could perform with the family, and then only when the dates and venues conveniently matched. They'd continued to rehearse, honing their skills, their acrobatic and highwire by now well developed, but it was the magic act in which they proved most valuable.

Harry Rickards' idea of a disappearing act for the twins had been quickly embraced by Will Worthing. So much so he'd come up with a brand-new magician routine for Max, the disappearing act being the finale. The acquisition of conjuring tricks, including a 'magical top hat', had presented no problem, and Mabel had provided a dramatic high-collared, full-length black cape that swirled to perfection, along with a dress coat housing many a secret pocket from which any manner of items could be produced.

Not unsurprisingly, Max had proved a perfect magician. Performing totally in mime with his customary grace and precision, he'd established as always a warm and personal relationship with his audience. One of the twins acted as his assistant, further engaging the audience given his extreme youth, while the other remained standing by for the disappearing finale. They'd had the whole thing off pat before they'd embarked upon their journey to Australia, and had they wished to fetch up from the ship's hold the custom-made box with its fake backing, they could have performed it on board. But there would have been little point. The passengers all knew the boys were twins and, as the family agreed, 'You can't have the punters one step ahead.'

The situation had become quite different once they were performing in Australia. And as the years passed, the Worthings took great care to keep things that way. The twins were to remain a mystery.

'The ace up our sleeve,' Will would declare with a smile.

In everyday life, Artie and Alfie's dissimilarities were highlighted, which wasn't really difficult because they were indeed dissimilar; by now Artie was even a good inch or so taller than Alfie. They'd both inherited the dark hair of their father, but Artie wore his long and shaggy while

Alfie's was neat and clean cut, which rather matched their personalities. Their respective dress styles also matched who they were: Artie favouring casual clothing, sometimes overly so, and Alfie preferring smarter apparel, again their personal choices. The two were purported to be brothers with no mention of twins. No one was any the wiser. And most certainly no one, even for one minute, had any trouble telling them apart.

Except when they were called upon to perform the magic act.

Artie and Alfie loved the deception. In fact Artie and Alfie *revelled* in the deception, both onstage and even at times off. Artie never complained about having his hair cut neat and short to match Alfie's; Alfie never complained about the special shoes with lifts that added an inch or so to his height; and neither ever complained about being identically dressed. Offstage, when they were simply 'brothers' and not 'performers', they reverted to their distinctive personalities anyway, Artie wearing a sloppy cloth hat to cover his lookalike hair. But *on*stage, the deception went far beyond the magic act and the disappearing trick. They took turns during every show and in every act. Sometimes it would be Artie on Max's shoulders during the highwire routine and sometimes it would be Alfie . . . Sometimes it would be Alfie completing the pyramid in the family acrobatic sequence and sometimes it would be Artie . . . And who knew which boy would be performing as the magician's assistant, and which boy would be revealed at the finale?

The family was always aware of who was who, but the other members of the company were not. Offstage they all knew the young Worthing boys, and they would never divulge the secret of the disappearing trick, for this would be the ultimate show business betrayal. But onstage, the performers and musicians and crew had no idea which brother was which. Even bumping into them backstage, they couldn't tell the difference. And it wasn't just the boys' physical appearance. There was no giveaway trait, no evidence at all of the individual boys they knew.

To Artie and Alfie it became a delicious secret, melding together, creating between them a third person who was neither one nor the other, but a hybrid creature they could call upon at will. And every now and then, they did.

The family had commented upon the 'game' the boys played from time to time, and Will was all for encouraging it. Harry Rickards was right, 'identical' twins were pure gold for a magic act.

Rehearsals ground on relentlessly night and day as they worked on new acts, six in all, incorporating the added effects Mabel came up with; the mirror ball, the smoke machine, the sound effects, the magic lantern, all put to reinvented and highly effective use. They were co-producers now; a whole half of the bill would feature the Worthings. The thought pleased Will no end: *I always said we were a show on our own.*

Then, it seemed before they knew it, rehearsals were over and they were all set to go.

But Gertie nearly put a spoke in the works at the very last minute.

'I got something to tell you,' she loudly announced.

It was Saturday and the whole family, including the children, had gathered at Parer's Crystal Café for a farewell lunch, the kids at one table scoffing down ice cream, their parents at another with sandwiches and the ubiquitous pot of tea.

The tour was due to depart on Monday and this time they could not afford to leave Mabel in Melbourne with the youngsters; as stage manager, she literally ran the whole show. But what to do with the younger children?

They didn't want to take them out of the state school, which was 'compulsory'; what if they weren't accepted back in? Fortunately all had been solved by Bob and Barb Baker. The five younger Worthing children, now ranging in age from eleven to six, were to bunk down with the Baker tribe at the ramshackle house they rented in Prahran, a boys' and girls' dormitory assigned to all. The Bakers, who were certainly not well off, welcomed the extra income on offer, and the kids welcomed the prospect of bunking down in swags. A happy arrangement all round.

Gertie carefully placed her teacup back on its saucer. 'I'm pregnant,' she said.

A deathly silence followed. Then simultaneously . . .

'What!' from Will.

'Are you sure?' from Mabel.

Gertie chose to answer Mabel. 'Pretty much,' she said. She'd been aware of the possibility for several weeks, having missed her second time of the month. She'd been wondering whether she should keep it a secret, but she'd decided that wouldn't be fair. 'And I've always got it right in the past, haven't I, lovey?' she added with a glance to Max.

'Yep,' Max agreed. He wasn't particularly fussed. They'd discussed the matter the previous night.

'But this is a five-month tour.' Mabel again, deeply concerned.

'I know.' Gertie grinned broadly. 'I'll be well and truly showing at the end of it, won't I just!'

'Hardly a laughing matter,' Will said huffily.

'I'm not laughing, Will,' she assured him, 'honest I'm not. I've performed in the past when I've been "well and truly", and I don't get that big, not even at the end. Besides, you'll never see me belly in all that silk.'

'*My* belly.' The correction was instinctive; there was no way he could prevent himself.

Gertie *did* laugh then. 'Well, *my* belly won't look as good in spangly tights, so you might have to drop me from the acrobatic routine in a couple of months.'

'One of the twins and me can cover that though,' Max said.

'One of the twins and *I*.'

'Yep,' Max smiled lazily, 'us too.'

'Are you sure, Gertie?' Mabel asked.

''Course I'm sure. I'm as tough as old boot leather, you know that.'

Mabel nodded. Yes, Gertie was a trouper, they *all* knew that.

Two days later, the members of *Manders' Mellow-tone Minstrels* and *Worthing Brothers' Variety Extravaganza* paraded down Bourke Street in a series of horse-drawn omnibuses and carriages bound for the towns of the Victorian goldfields.

The Worthing brothers were on the path to becoming entrepreneurs.

4

FIRST STEPS

The following weeks became something of a blur, as was always the case on tour. The Worthings were well accustomed to the exhausting process of life on the road; they knew it by rote and could have quoted it verbatim . . .

Travel all day, arrive in town, drop off costume skips and stage equipment at theatre, book into digs arranged by advance man, gobble down whatever supper the pub or boarding house might choose to dish up, and collapse into bed.

Up early following morning, walk to theatre and bump-in; hang backcloths, set up scenery, rig lights, arrange costumes, props and dressing rooms. After bump-in, walk back to digs, a bite of lunch, and smarten up for a bit of a promotional wander around town. Punters like nothing more than a chat with show folk, and the pallier the chat the bigger the walk-up ticket sales that night.

Arrive at theatre early in order to check local firemen have set out buckets of sand and water in case there's a problem with stage lights – the quicklime used in lamps highly flammable, fire posing a constant threat – then prep for performance. Makeup, hair, costume, and it's on with the show.

Curtain up at half past seven, down at half past ten, perhaps later if it's been a corker of a show with encores, then bump-out. Ensure lights are cleaned and made safe – again fire precautions – pack away costumes, scenery and equipment for collection in the morning; walk back to digs, light supper and to bed.

Up early next morning ready for buses and coaches, which have been housed overnight at Cobb & Co's livery stables, and repeat whole experience all over again. And again. And again. In smaller towns anyway. Then, oh, the luxury of bigger towns, where the run might be for several nights, a whole week even, the Royal Princess Theatre in Bendigo and the like. A run like that's as good as a holiday.

The work was hard and relentless, but the Worthings thrived, for this was their home. The theatre was where they belonged and they thrilled to its call, the oohs and ahs from the audience music to their ears, the applause and the encores their rightly earned reward. Whether the house was large or small, they never walked through a performance, never took a show for granted. 'If you don't love your work,' Will would say, 'then you're not any good.'

They all loved their work, and they were all very good. Now more than ever, for this was *The Worthing Brothers' Variety Extravaganza*. This was *their* show. Or half of it was.

The eight members of *Manders' Mellow-tone Minstrels* were a mixed bag of varying ages and sizes, all white, and all male. Hubert Manders had in the past travelled with a larger troupe, often including one or two black players, and even at times a female performer. Now, given the fact he only needed to fill half the showbill, he had cut down on numbers to create a neat, tight show in the old form that had stood him in good stead throughout his early days. His players performed typical minstrel songs and dances and presented comic sketches featuring the popular stock characters audiences had come to know over the years. There was the 'happy-go-lucky plantation slave', the 'primping dandy', the 'loveable mammy' and her counterpart the 'old darky', along with the 'black soldier' and the 'provocative mulatto wench'. Between them they sang and danced and exchanged repartee. Two musicians, also in blackface, accompanied the players, one on banjo and one on fiddle, and there was the constant rattle of a tambourine.

The Worthing family found the minstrel performers easy to get along with, a friendly bunch, with the possible exception of Geoffrey and Clive, who played the 'loveable mammy' and the 'old darky' respectively. Geoffrey and Clive, both American and in their late fifties, were a somewhat disgruntled pair. They'd been treading the same minstrel boards for over thirty years and had become jaded in the process. They were talented, there was no doubt about that, bouncing off each other with perfect comic timing, the harmony of their duets a delight, but an element of spontaneity was missing.

'They're tired,' Mabel astutely observed, 'and it shows. What's more, their attitude's affecting the other members of the troupe. The whole show's a bit lacklustre if you ask me.'

Will took the opportunity to drive home his argument yet again. 'They don't love their work,' he said, 'that's the problem.'

Mabel and Will both had a point. Whether or not the troupe was directly influenced by Geoffrey and Clive was debatable, but the members of *Manders' Mellow-tone Minstrels* had been performing together for quite some time, and the show had become a little stale. Which was precisely why Hubert Manders had decided to bring the Worthing brothers into the equation. Perhaps minstrelsy itself was becoming stale, Hubert had thought; perhaps it would be best to team up with someone else, share the entertainment load half-and-half.

It had been a wise choice on Hubert's part. The first half of the show was received well enough; audiences very much enjoyed minstrels. But the second half of the show was another matter altogether. The second half of the show was an out-and-out winner!

> '*All the world's a stage,*
> *And all the men and women merely players;*
> *They have their exits and their entrances,*
> *And one man in his time plays many parts,*
> *His acts being seven ages . . .*'

Will opened the second half of the show with another of his favourite Shakespearean speeches, this time from *As You Like It*. He hadn't chosen the opening Chorus from *Henry V*, pertinent though it was, for the simple reason he'd performed it on previous tours of the Victorian goldfield towns. But Jaques's speech, he decided, was eminently suitable, being so deliciously theatrical.

> '*And then the lover,*
> *Sighing like furnace, with a woeful ballad*
> *Made to his mistress' eyebrow . . .*'

The audiences loved it! Will Worthing and William Shakespeare were a perfect marriage, and by the time Will got to the end of the speech he all but brought the house down.

> '*Last scene of all,*
> *That ends this strange eventful history,*
> *Is second childishness and mere oblivion,*
> *Sans teeth, sans eyes, sans taste, sans everything.*'

He played it for all he was worth and they howled with laughter, stamping their feet and calling for more. The perfect way to open a show.

Will Worthing, of course, did not *give* them more, but left them wanting. Any encores belonged to the *end* of the show.

In fact, the audience was given barely enough time to recover their senses as a drumroll interrupted the applause and the family acrobatic team bounded onto the stage. Max, Gertie and Artie – or perhaps it was Alfie – at their spangly best.

They were followed by Will's Heavenly Tenor, accompanied by piano, bass, violin and flute. Of the four musicians Will had employed, two were conveniently versatile, being equally skilled in percussion instruments, which was particularly handy for the magical act.

The mere sight of Will Worthing aroused in the audience a fervour of enthusiasm, and a similar reaction ensued when Max returned with Alfie (or Artie?) to perform the highwire. The punters had clearly embraced the Worthings.

Following the highwire was another Heavenly Tenor, allowing time for a wardrobe change, and then came Max the Magical Marvel and his talented young assistant.

The punters' immediate recognition of the acrobatic and highwire duo did not in the least curb their enjoyment. If anything the familiarity enhanced their pleasure. Max Worthing had already charmed them as a gymnast, and as a magician he would go on to win their hearts.

The act was visually dazzling, Mabel having employed the use of a mirror ball and also a smoke machine, which every now and then gave forth a brief burst, catching the coloured lights most effectively. But it was Max's performance that mesmerised.

Max took to the stage in utter silence, swirling his black cape, juggling his top hat, which seemed to disappear and reappear in the sparkling lights, his movement lithe and graceful, as much dance as mime. At the completion of each sleight-of-hand trick his young assistant would react in a similar vein. Accompanied by a musical sting, the lad would offer a pirouette and a triumphant gesture to highlight the feat. The twins had been well coached by their uncle.

As always, Max Worthing had his audience entranced, playing to every corner of the house, be it large or small. Indeed, so entranced were they by his charm they didn't seem to notice that the act in itself was really nothing new – just smoke and mirrors when all was said and done. Which made the finale so truly spectacular . . .

A low drumroll as the young assistant steps into the box. A further drumroll as the door is closed and the box, on castors, is wheeled in a circle to display to the audience its solidity and the fact there is no trapdoor beneath it. Dramatic increase of drumroll as magician himself circles the box, black cape swirling, then prepares to open door. He does so. Door opens, clash of cymbals, box is empty.

Applause from audience. But . . .

Further drumroll as magician holds both arms high, gesturing to the rear of the theatre. All heads turn. Further dramatic drumroll, clash of cymbals and there, revealed in the sudden glare of the spotlights, high up where everyone can see, is the young assistant.

Gasps of amazement. The house goes wild. Even those sceptics, who wonder whether the box may have had a fake back, whether the boy may have slipped out under cover of the magician's swirling cloak to hide behind the black tabs at the rear of the stage, are flummoxed. They have no answer. There was simply no time for the boy to have got from the stage to the back of the theatre. This was a true illusion, the sort wrought by only the most accomplished of magicians.

The disappearing act was a winner every time. In fact, it was difficult to think how one could *best* such an act. But the Worthings could.

People rarely recognised Gertie as the woman who had performed in the acrobatic routine. But it wouldn't have mattered if they had. The Serpentine Dance of The Divine Dolores quickly developed a life all its own, the effect transcending the very dancer herself.

The stage went to black. The whole theatre went to black, even the house lights normally set to a low level throughout the performance. The total blackout always unsettled the audience, most of whom wondered whether something was wrong. Then the faint strains of a waltz could be heard and on came the limelight follow spots, three in all, each hand-operated and each focusing a beautiful silvery beam upon, it would seem, a spill of something white on the stage. The waltz grew a little in volume, and slowly the white turned to muted shades of pink and apricot as a form came to life. A woman's form to start with, but growing exponentially, fed by the music that swelled. Taller and taller the form grew, changing shape and colour, the softly muted shades becoming shafts of vivid gold as the sun spread its rays and embraced the day.

Having painted the sunrise, the dance then went on to paint the day itself, changing colours and shapes in astonishing mutations.

The bright beams of the follow spots illuminated every movement and mood of the dance, as Gertie swooped and whirled and rose to hover majestically, then dived again to flutter in a frenzy of anger or agony, who could tell, only to rise once more and float in a billowing wave of serenity. Those watching saw whatever images they chose, the selection endless and open to all forms of interpretation. They would talk about it afterwards. Some saw eagles, some rivers and rapids, some angry seas, some rolling clouds, and some saw all of these things. But everyone was in agreement about the end of the dance. Here the imagery left no one in doubt about its intention.

Mabel had wisely decided against the use of slides. She would not project specific images from the magic lantern as she'd originally intended. 'I was wrong,' she'd said, 'the dance must speak for itself. We'll just use the gel, colour changes only, let the audience see what they want to see.' But when Gertie had come up with her idea for the end of the dance, Mabel had had an instant rethink.

'You remember those nights out on the deck of the *Oroya*, Mabel,' Gertie had said. 'That sky, those stars . . .' The deep sigh that followed might have appeared overly theatrical to some, but not to those who knew her. Gertie was transported; she was there on that ship, gazing at that sky, reliving that moment. 'You told me I was looking at the Milky Way, remember? Well, that's how I want to end the dance. I want to become the Milky Way.'

Of course, Mabel had thought. 'And so you shall, Gertie,' she'd said, 'and so you shall.'

The Serpentine Dance of The Divine Delores appeared to finish in a reverse of its opening, the vivid gold of the sun becoming muted shades of pink and apricot. Here was the sunset, fading away with the music; both the day and the dance were over.

The previously billowing image was now drained of colour. White and with barely a ripple, it remained poised, and the audience was on the verge of applause. But the dance was not over at all. Before their very eyes, the white turned into the blackest of night skies, clear and cloudless and dotted with diamonds. The waltz was now replaced by a simple flute, and as Gertie danced, gliding about the stage with effortless grace, constellations appeared, stars, planets, a crescent moon . . . The audience was floating in the Milky Way.

The silence was breathless, no sound but the flute, the theatre held spellbound. Then finally Gertie stopped dancing. Her arms spread wide, the universe froze. The flute stopped. Blackout.

Gertie's dance was the perfect grande finale, and she always obliged with the encore the audience demanded. But she never repeated the Milky Way. They'd agreed, or rather Mabel had dictated, the magic lantern and the imagery it provided was to be used sparingly.

'Just for that last-minute frisson,' she'd said, 'when the punters think they've seen it all. Good to have something up your sleeve. Send them away talking.'

As the weeks passed, the goldfields towns melded into one another, grand though so many were with their broad main streets and their fine stone buildings; Ballarat, Bendigo, Daylesford, Maryborough ... But not for one minute did the Worthings become complacent, each member of the team using the tour in his or her own way to improve a performance or create something new.

Max, always the perfectionist, was forever rehearsing his magic act, introducing fresh tricks, embellishing old ones. And he drove the twins mercilessly in the acrobatic and highwire sequences; whichever of the boys was performing they had to be equally skilled. Besides, they were thirteen now and stronger and fitter since they'd been on the road; time they learnt more difficult routines. He never pushed Gertie though. Gertie was pregnant and beginning to show. They'd soon have to leave her out of the acrobatic team, all the more reason to work the twins harder.

As for Gertie and Mabel, they never let up. There was always a new idea ...

'I'm going to do a bird dance,' Gertie announced.

Mabel said nothing. A 'bird dance' as such didn't sound particularly new, but one could never be sure what was going to spring forth from Gertie's fertile imagination.

'An *Australian* bird dance,' Gertie went on, 'because I think it's possible to dance *sounds*, don't you?'

Mabel didn't really think so at all, but she gave a 'why not' shrug.

'I want to dance the sounds of galahs and cockatoos and kookaburras.'

'Ah yes.' Mabel could see where this was coming from now. She and Gertie had had a conversation some time back about the murderous calls of Australian birds as

compared to the melodious songs of their English counterparts. The subject of their chat had obviously remained
festering in Gertie's brain and now demanded some form
of visual expression. 'Perhaps we could throw in a magpie
for a touch of melody?' she suggested, more in jest than
anything.

'Mmm.' Gertie sounded unsure. 'It's actually the raucous
ones I want to dance. They're so . . . you know, so . . .' As
usual she ran out of words.

Mabel had a sudden image of Gertie as a kookaburra,
high on a branch, head thrown back, cackling its crazy
laughter. Then as a cockatoo showing off, hurling itself
about in the sky with its bizarre, look-at-me screech. *That
could actually work*, she thought. *Not for The Serpentine
Dance, but perhaps as a separate piece . . . A feathery
costume that would shimmer as she flies, colour changes,
a magic lantern background of trees . . .*

'We'll do it without music,' she said briskly, 'we'll use
sound effects instead. Will and Max can practise their
bird calls; the audience will swear they're hearing the real
thing.' There were times, she told herself, when one simply
had to be literal. 'A cacophony of cockies and kookaburras,' she announced, thinking how Will would just love
the alliteration, 'and we'll throw in the warble of a magpie
for good measure.' *Yes*, she thought, *that'll definitely
work. Something different, make the punters sit up.*

But of them all, it was Will who was using this time on
the road to his greatest advantage, for Will was focusing
upon every facet of the tour's production. He had come to
realise that, for all his knowledge of the theatre, he'd been
inattentive to many aspects of production that, as a hired
performer, he'd taken for granted, or perhaps considered
merely boring.

Hubert Manders' lengthy experience as a producer
together with his entrepreneurial expertise were proving

invaluable to Will Worthing, who was noting down every detail of every lesson learnt. The theatre bookings, which were to be confirmed well up-front, the hire of advance men to arrange accommodation and plaster bill-posters about town, the transportation, the box office and ticket sales, the feting of the press, the pre-tour publicity, and of course the all-important local newspaper reviews.

Both Will and Max had long been aware of the need for publicity and the significance of reviews. Over the years, they'd printed their own handouts and even staged their own publicity stunts ensuring they'd make the newspapers. And the reviews of every show in which they'd appeared had been eagerly awaited, personally cut out by Will and pasted into a scrapbook, along with every other piece printed about them, as proof positive of their triumphs.

But Hubert Manders went a step further. As an entrepreneur Hubert Manders went many, many steps further.

'Just look at the *size* of it,' Will had said to Max when they'd arrived in Ballarat. 'They'd need a sixty-foot ladder to get that up there.'

They were standing on a corner in Lydiard Street looking at the bill-poster that covered one whole storey of a wall.

'Hubert told me he made it that big so it'd get in the papers, and it did,' Will said. 'Then people complained about it and that got in the papers too. He told me he made the first complaint himself – under a false name, of course – just to get the whole thing started.'

'Smart,' Max agreed, 'very smart.'

'He does that sort of thing all the time,' Will said, 'and have you noticed how he fetes the press?' The question being rhetorical, he didn't wait for an answer. 'After the bump-in, while we're all "doing-the-rounds" about town, he gets in touch with the local journalist who's going to be reviewing the show and invites him out for a drink. Quite a number of drinks,' he added wryly. 'Then he spins yarns, butters the chap up no end, and . . .' Will shook his head in grudging admiration. 'Our Hubert's a clever operator, I'll give him that much.'

Max smiled knowingly; he could all but hear the clock-like ticking of his brother's brain. 'Not as clever as you'll be, Will,' he said, 'not as clever as you'll be by half. I'd put money on that.' Max meant every word.

They'd been on the road for well over a month when it happened. They were playing the Theatre Royal in Castle-maine, a typical goldfields town with a broad central street and an imposing stone clock tower that stood out as the landmark it was intended to be. The locals were justifiably proud, not only of their post office and clock tower, but also of their theatre. So important to the townspeople was the theatre that when it had been gutted by fire in 1887, leaving nothing standing but the original stone walls, it had been resurrected, rebuilt and refurbished to an even grander state within just one year. Now, five years later, the Theatre Royal was proving as popular as ever.

Manders' Mellow-tone Minstrels and Worthing Brothers' Variety Extravaganza had been booked in to the Royal for a five-night run from Tuesday to Saturday and the houses had been excellent throughout the whole week. This, their last night's performance on Saturday, was totally sold out.

The minstrels were well received, performing to an appreciative audience, but as usual it was the second half of the show that brought the house down. The punters went wild for Will, both his recitation and his Heavenly Tenor; they couldn't get enough of him. They loved the acrobatic team and the highwire duo too, and by the time Max the Magical Marvel appeared they were right in the mood; they couldn't get enough of Max either. The magic act's final disappearing routine was an absolute triumph, producing rousing cheers and even a standing ovation from some; they could have finished the show there and then. But the grande finale was yet to come. And Gertie didn't disappoint.

Given the raucous show of approval Max had received while taking his bows, it was astonishing how quickly the audience calmed down, and how completely silent they soon became. There was the total blackout's usual rustle of confusion, then as the limelight spots came up on the crumpled form, and as the form grew to become the sun, there were the customary gasps of astonishment. But after that, nothing. Nothing but the strains of the waltz. All else was silence. It was as if the audience was holding its collective breath. Which it undoubtedly was.

Finally the end of the dance, the moment when Gertie froze and the universe froze with her. Then blackout. The curtains closed, the house lights were brought up to their normal performance level and the audience erupted.

Following the dance, Gertie would retire to the prompt side of the wings, where she'd wait while the audience went wild. Then the curtains would reopen, the stage lights would come on and she'd make a grand entrance, taking her bows bravura-style to the stamp of feet and the cries of 'encore'. If the house was small and they'd decided between them there was to be no encore, the other members of the company would join her onstage and they'd take their final curtain calls together. If there was to be an encore, as was invariably the case, she'd return to the wings, a blackout would ensue – of stage lights only this time – and the spotlights would reappear, two focused centre stage, the other following her on from the prompt side as she made her entrance.

After her encore, Gertie would remain onstage to take her bows, never 'milking the moment' as many performers would be wont to do, particularly given the tumultuous applause afforded her. She would take two bows only, then she would signal with a nod either side to the wings, the follow spots would disappear, the stage lights would come up and, to a rousing refrain from the musicians backstage, the other members of the company would join her for the final curtain call.

Such was the order of things with *The Worthing Brothers' Variety Extravaganza*. A neat and tidy finish, bearing the stamp of Mabel's efficiency and Will's 'leave 'em wanting more' policy, it was the way they concluded every show.

But not this time. Not this final Saturday night performance at the Theatre Royal in Hargraves Street, Castlemaine.

Of the three follow spots, two were operated from the 'opposite prompt' side, or OP as it was known, and one from the prompt side. This was the same side from which Mabel ran the entire show, taking personal control of the magic lantern, which she would entrust to no one, while cueing the backstage crew, lighting, musicians and sound effects.

'Stage lights down,' she now said.

The stage lights faded, signalling to the audience that The Divine Delores was about to perform her encore. The applause died away in anticipation.

Gertie stood poised, waiting.

'Stand by, Trev,' Mabel said to the stagehand operating the spotlight machine.

She walked briskly upstage to the black tabs at the rear, behind which the musicians were housed.

'Go music,' she instructed, and strode back to her position in the prompt side corner.

Not a sound from the audience now as the gentle strains of the waltz could be heard.

'Go limelight.'

Trev turned on his machine. From his position near the wall beside the ropes and pulleys that operated the

backcloths, he focused the follow spot directly upon
Gertie as she prepared to make her entrance. The two OP
operators quickly took their cue from him and focused the
intense beams of their own limelight spots centre stage.

'You're on, Gertie.'

Gertie raised her arms, lifting the silk high with the
sticks so it billowed, a cloud of white. She was about to
glide onstage when behind her the spotlight hissed and
crackled, the heated chemicals at war with each other as
was known to happen on occasion. Then suddenly, from
out of the machine sputtered an angry cascade of sparks,
a fountain of fireworks aimed directly at Gertie.

From that moment on, everything happened with unpre-
dictably blinding speed . . .

The silk, loose and flowing as it was, instantly ignited, the
flames taking hold in barely a second. Gertie dropped
the sticks, intent upon beating them out with her hands. But
it was too late. Already she'd become a torch of fire.

Mabel raced for the nearest water bucket. Trev the
stagehand, panic-stricken, dropped the machine. Flames
licked at the dusty floor and as he instinctively dived to
retrieve it, he collided heavily with Mabel. The bucket
slipped from her hands, falling to the ground on its side,
the water spilling uselessly.

From the opposite side of the stage, Max could see it all.
After his magic act he'd remained in the wings to watch
Gertie dance. He always did. He loved watching Gertie
dance. Now he was watching Gertie go up in flames.

He strode across the stage, long black cloak held wide,
caught in the glare of the OP spotlights that were still
focused centre stage. And, bizarrely, the waltz played on.

Upon reaching the prompt side he enveloped Gertie in
the cloak, and hugging her firmly to him dropped to his
knees, taking her to the floor, rolling with her, smothering
the very last of the flames.

'It's all right, Gert,' he whispered urgently, 'it's all right, love, it's all right, you're safe.'

She was whimpering, and he knew the horrors this held for her; he was witness to those nightmares she had.

'You're safe now, Gert,' he whispered, covering her face with kisses, speaking as he might to a child. 'You're safe now, love, you're safe, no more fire.'

She stopped whimpering and he helped her to her feet, looking her up and down to see how badly she might be burnt, but she appeared surprisingly unharmed. The full wrist-to-ankle body stocking she wore beneath the silk had protected her.

'You're lucky, love,' he said. 'Thank God for leotards, eh?' He gathered her to him, his arm around her, encasing her in the cloak, aware of the shivering throughout her entire body; the terror had not left her.

Mabel could hear the audience becoming restless. The waltz played on, but there was no encore. The punters were puzzled. This wouldn't do at all. They needed to close the show.

'Are we up for a company curtain call?' she asked Max. But it was Gertie who answered.

'Of course we are.'

Mabel turned to poor Trev who was by now close to a blithering idiot, convinced he'd nearly killed the star.

'Get Will and one of the boys from the dressing room for curtain call,' she barked, 'quick as you can.'

'Yes, yes . . .' He dashed off, still muttering 'I'm sorry, I'm so sorry,' as if it was his fault, which it really was not. All forms of stage lighting were notorious; many a theatre had burnt down because of them.

'Stage lights up,' Mabel said, while at the same time signalling with a wave of her arm to the two spotlight operators OP.

The stage lights came up and the follow spots disappeared.

'You're on,' she said.

'But the costume,' Gertie weakly protested. 'What about . . .'

'We'll worry about the costume later,' Mabel said. 'Take her on, Max.'

As Max shepherded Gertie onstage, still protectively cocooned in his cloak, Mabel dashed up to the black tabs, stuck her head through the side and barked a command.

'Cut the waltz,' she said to the musicians who were still gamely playing on. No one had cued them otherwise. They'd heard the crash of the lamp, but accidents did happen so they'd carried on regardless, and they would continue to do so until ordered to stop.

'Curtain call,' Mabel ordered, 'and make it big.'

The audience was bemused by the change in music, the waltz now becoming a rousing refrain that more befitted a circus parade. They were bemused, too, by the sight that greeted them, which seemed at odds with such a musical choice. Bemused certainly, but entertained nonetheless.

Only minutes previously as they'd been awaiting an encore, they'd seen the magician, caught in the spotlights, stride boldly across the stage, cloak held wide either side of his body like the wings of a great, black bird. Now here he was, back again, with the glorious dancer, The Divine Dolores no less. But she was so *small*. The huge presence that had engulfed the stage and transported them with her imagery was now nestled in one wing of the magician's cloak, and she was *tiny*! The revelation of this amazing fact was surely part of the show.

Max undid the cloak, fastening it around Gertie's shoulders, where it sagged to the floor. He stepped aside, spread his arms wide and, after a grand gesture that embraced the whole house, turned to acknowledge The Divine Dolores.

Gertie dropped humbly to the deepest curtsy, all but disappearing within the cloak, and the audience forgave the lack of encore in an instant. Most even forgot they'd been waiting for an encore. How could this diminutive woman, so dainty, so pretty, have had such an assault upon their senses?

The applause was deafening.

Then on strode Will Worthing, The Heavenly Tenor himself, and with him the magician's young assistant.

Will and Alfie (for it was Alfie this time – he and Artie always tossed a penny for the curtain call) also made a grand show of acknowledging the house before bowing to The Divine Dolores. After which Gertie rose to her feet and blew kisses far and wide to the audience, making sure they landed in every area of the house.

Then, as the rousing musical refrain – which now seemed more than fitting – continued, the members of the company took their curtain call to an audience that cheered, yelled bravos and rose to its feet. The Worthing family's final performance at the Theatre Royal, Castlemaine, had been an unmitigated triumph.

There was the bump-out to contend with that night, but Mabel wouldn't allow Gertie to lend a hand. Or Max for that matter.

'Take her back to the pub and look after her, Max,' she said. 'I can tell she's rattled something terrible, which is hardly surprising when you think about it.'

'Yes,' Max agreed, 'she has nightmares.'

'I know.' Mabel smiled at his apparent surprise. 'We all know, love.' Travelling as a family, often housed close together in cheap digs, did he think they hadn't heard the occasional screams in the middle of the night? 'Take her back to the pub. We'll see you there later.'

Gertie's principal concern had appeared to be the costume. 'Oh Mabel, I'm so sorry,' she'd said shakily as Mabel had helped her change. 'I'm so awfully sorry, your beautiful costume.' She looked forlornly at the damaged silk, at least half of which was burnt, as if for some strange reason it had all been her fault. 'What on earth will we do?'

'We'll mend it, Gertie, that's what we'll do. I'm carrying plenty of spare silk, and tomorrow's Sunday, I have all day. Stupid of me not to be travelling with a spare in the first place.'

Gertie looked as if she might cry, and Mabel knew that when someone was distraught mollycoddling them was not the right answer.

'You're lucky the costume was silk, not cotton.'

'Oh?' Puzzled, but a definite flicker of interest.

'Cotton's far more flammable.' Picking up the costume, Mabel examined the damage. 'The silk ignited so quickly because it was loose and hit directly by the sparks. But see here?' She ran her fingers down an edge that appeared very evenly burnt. 'The fabric was starting to seal itself. The flames were actually dying down. Cotton wouldn't have done that. Max would never have been able to smother the fire so easily if you'd been wearing cotton.'

'Oh.'

'So . . .' Mabel gave an efficient, typically Mabel nod. 'Weren't you lucky?'

'Yes. Very lucky.'

Max, too, tried to play down the episode, aware that Gertie was fighting off the reawakening of her terror as best she could.

'We're going to have to stop making a habit of this, Gert,' he said, as they wandered arm in arm back to the pub in Mostyn Street. They were staying at the Albion, one of the grand goldfields pubs built at the height of the boom, always a popular choice for travelling players.

'Stop making a habit of what?' she asked.

'Well, I can't be on hand to rescue you every time you decide to set yourself on fire now, can I?'

She smiled, loving him for the joke. 'My hero,' she said.

'Always will be, love.' He patted her hand. 'Funny, isn't it, this thing you've got about fire? Cotton mills and theatres, the two biggest fire traps in the whole darn world. You sure can pick 'em, Gert.'

'Yep, funny that.'

It wasn't funny later, though, when Gertie awoke in the dead of night racked with pain.

'What is it, love, what is it?' Beside her, Max was instantly awake and filled with alarm. She was squirming in agony, clutching her belly.

He jumped up and pulled back the bedclothes.

'Oh dear God. Oh no. Oh dear God, no.'

There was blood all over the sheet. To his horror-struck eyes, the bed appeared drenched with it. Panic engulfed him. What was he to do?

Gertie knew. 'Get Mabel,' she said through clenched teeth, 'it's the baby.'

Max raced along the hotel corridor to his brother's room where he bashed on the door with all his might, yelling for Mabel at the top of his voice.

The door opened in only seconds to reveal Mabel and Will side by side, both in their nightwear, both understandably startled.

'It's Gertie,' Max panted, 'the baby . . .'

Mabel immediately took control. 'Get water,' she said, 'buckets and bowls, whatever you can round up. And towels, get as many towels as you can lay your hands on. And get some clean sheets too if you can find them.'

Then, in her nightdress, without even fetching a gown, she was off down the corridor to Gertie's room.

It was some time before the actual miscarriage took place, the lead-up lasting throughout the rest of the night, the foetus, sac and placenta being finally expelled in the early hours of the morning.

Mabel had dismissed the men following their arrival with water and towels and fresh sheets, as instructed. Men served no purpose at times like these; they were not accustomed to the sight of so much blood. She thought of sending Will and Max for a doctor, but the process was happening so quickly she didn't see much point. So she remained with Gertie, nursing her, comforting her, replacing the towels that were by now capturing the large, liver-like clots of blood, praying that the baby would appear with one of these clots. The sooner the better, and the safer it would be. Mabel had had two miscarriages herself in the past; she knew what to expect.

'It was a boy, love,' she said as Gertie lay back, wan, exhausted and as pale as the fresh sheets Mabel had just placed on the bed.

'Oh.' Gertie's sigh of regret was heartbreaking. 'I wanted a boy.'

Mabel looked across at the bowl where she'd placed the baby, still in its sac, tiny but fully formed, every little limb, every finger and toe flawlessly fashioned. *So beautiful,* she thought, *but such a sad, sad thing to see.*

'Not this time around, I'm afraid,' she said. 'Maybe next time, eh?'

'Yes. Next time.'

'Hold the towel there, love,' Mabel instructed, placing Gertie's hand on the folded towel positioned between her legs. 'You'll keep bleeding for a while yet.' She stood. 'I'll let the boys know you're all right, and I'll send them off to find some food – we need to get your strength back.'

Gertie automatically obeyed instruction, holding the towel in place, but she didn't seem to have heard Mabel.

'I wanted a little brother for Ted,' she said. 'Max did too.' Her voice was weak, but she was clearly determined to have her say. 'We wanted two boys and two girls, just like you and Will got. That's a nice number, don't you think?'

The food could wait for a moment, Mabel decided. She sat on the bed and held a damp face cloth to Gertie's forehead.

'Yes, love, four's a very nice number,' she agreed.

'I always been strong,' Gertie went on. She seemed puzzled, concerned, and a touch of the old Lancashire twang had returned to her voice. 'I always been much stronger than I look, you know?'

'Oh yes, love, I know that all right, we all do. You're a constant surprise, believe me.'

'So why did I lose the baby? What did I do wrong?'

'It wasn't you, Gertie. It was the fire. Terror could cause a miscarriage, wouldn't you say? And you were terrified, love, you know you were. I truly think that could do it, don't you?'

'Yes,' Gertie agreed thoughtfully, 'you're probably right.' A steely light of determination crept into her eyes. 'It won't happen again, though, I can tell you that much,' she said. 'I'm going to get pregnant as soon as I can, and I'm going to have a boy. Max and me are going to have a brother for Ted.'

'Good on you, love.' Mabel stood; time for food. She pulled the bed linen up over Gertie's legs, covering the towel, which was already bloodied. 'I'll send Max in and I'll come back with some breakfast.'

'Oh goodie . . .' The pale little face lit up. 'I'm that hungry.'

You're strong all right, Gertie, Mabel thought, *you're strong and you're tough. Which is just as well because you've got today and tonight to get over this – Monday you're back on the road.*

'Don't you go away now,' she said with a smile. 'Max'll be here in a couple of minutes.'

'I'm not going anywhere.' Gertie returned the smile. 'I'm waiting right here for my hero.'

Mabel draped a hand towel over the bowl, picked it up and carried it away with her. They really didn't need to see their tiny, perfectly formed son.

5

INTRODUCING CARLO AND RUBE

Ma soldiered on incredibly after the miscarriage she suffered in late 1893. My heavens but she was a trouper, just like Aunt Mabel always said. They left her out of the acrobatic routine for the rest of the tour, but she performed The Serpentine Dance of The Divine Delores the very next night, and every night after that (bar Sundays) for the next three months or more.

Digressing briefly, you'll be pleased to hear, I'm sure, that she gave birth to a son barely two years later – my brother, Albert – which meant by then she had the four children she'd planned. There was Ted, Sarah, Izzie and now baby Bertie, two boys and two girls, just the way she wanted. She hadn't counted on me. I came along in 1901, a right surprise that messed things up well and truly I'm sure.

But back to the tour, or rather its outcome. That tour of '93 was the start of it all. According to Uncle Will anyway. And I must say, also, according to the scrapbooks he kept so meticulously. Oh my goodness, those scrapbooks! They were like a mania to Uncle Will throughout the whole of his life, bordering on a religion to which he was so devoted, and I'm not exaggerating, I swear. There was a purpose to them, mind. They were not only proof of the Worthings' triumphs, they were an invaluable source of reference and publicity. He'd haul them out at the drop of a hat to anyone he needed to impress – fellow entrepreneurs, potential co-producers, theatre managers . . . And of course the press!

Uncle Will quickly adopted Hubert Manders' tricks. Working as a double act, they'd fete the local critic in every town they played. Over drinks, while Hubert launched into his customary spiel, Uncle Will would pull out the scrapbook and show off the Worthing reportage as solid evidence of their fame. The rave reviews, the heroically posed pictures, the gossipy tattle of their derring-do from the past; they were the brightest stars in the whole of the vast theatrical firmament, or that's the way they appeared, because that's the way Uncle Will sold them. All of which pleased Hubert Manders no end, for he well knew that the Worthings were a far greater attraction than his minstrels.

Now, I ask you in all honesty, if you're a critic on a country newspaper, would you give bad press to a show after seeing and hearing a sales pitch like that? Particularly when you've been treated to many an ale by your friendly hosts? You wouldn't dare really, would you?

But you want to know something? My opinion, for what it's worth? I don't think it was the buttering up of the press that did it at all. Or the glowing reviews for that matter. I think it was purely a case of the good old grapevine. The punters were passing the word around – *The Worthing Brothers' Variety Extravaganza* was a show that just had to be seen. Oh, I tell you, there's no better publicity than word of mouth. Never has been, never will be.

They finished the tour with a week's booking in Sydney. The Royal Standard Theatre in Castlereagh Street, a smaller venue, not one of the big city theatres, but specialising in vaudeville and very popular, with a ready-made audience always hot to trot. Well, there wasn't a spare seat to be had for the whole run. Sydney just loved the Worthings. And the act that got them all talking? Yes, you've guessed it: The Serpentine Dance of The Divine Delores. Ma was the toast of the town.

That dance really set her up, you know. Even made headlines some years later; it's all there in Uncle Will's scrapbooks. The critics started getting fancy, you see, analysing The Serpentine

Dance as some unique style called 'symbolism' and saying it was all tied up with 'The Art Nouveau Movement'. Ma wouldn't have known what any of that meant. She told me as much, said she didn't know what on earth they were talking about. But these were the terms the snooty set was applying to Loïe Fuller in France – trust the French to come up with something like that, eh? – so Ma was tarred with the same brush whether she liked it or not.

Apparently Loïe Fuller got so fed up with imitators she tried to patent her Serpentine Dance, but the American Copyright Office wouldn't have a bar of it. I can tell you here and now, it wouldn't have made any difference to Ma if they had. Apart from the use of sticks and all that silk, she'd been doing the same sort of dance since she was sixteen years old. Younger! Since before she was married – before she was even a Worthing! Gertie Smeed had invented the art of free dance long before the Loïe Fullers and Isadora Duncans of this world strutted their stuff.

The tour had been a runaway success for the Worthings, proving their viability as entrepreneurs, and during the eighteen-hour train trip back to Melbourne, Uncle Will and Pa made plans for the future. Strongly influenced, I might add, by Aunt Mabel's considerable input.

It was agreed they'd have to work in a partnership until they'd built up the necessary funds to employ other acts and set out on their own, but although Hubert Manders was keen to mount another joint tour, they were reluctant to ally themselves with him. At least not quite so soon.

Aunt Mabel was firmly of the opinion that they shouldn't become known as one half of a show that had grown stale. 'Keep Hubert on side in case we need him,' she apparently said, 'but for now we must seek out someone newer and more innovative.' Aunt Mabel could be ruthless at times.

So who do you think that someone 'newer' and 'more innovative' turned out to be? None other than Harry Rickards.

True to his word, Harry had returned to Australia intent upon setting up a theatrical empire of his own – and in the middle of an economic depression, would you believe! He bought the Garrick Theatre in Sydney, tarted it up no end, renamed it The Tivoli and opened to a fanfare of publicity in 1893. A bold move, but he pulled it off. Oh, Harry was a clever entrepreneur all right. He went on to become lessee to any number of theatres in capital cities around the country, and so the Tivoli circuit was born. The original 'Tiv' in Castlereagh Street, Sydney, remained his flagship theatre, though, and he had every right to be proud of it.

Anyway, in those early days, Harry needed the Worthings as much as the Worthings needed Harry, so over the next several years they partnered up for quite a number of shows, in Melbourne and in Sydney and out on the road.

But to Uncle Will it all seemed a bit of 'a walk down memory lane', so to speak, like they were repeating themselves, not really moving on the way he'd have liked. I suppose that's because Harry was very much sticking to the old format that had served him well, a mix of music hall, burlesque and minstrels. Uncle Will wanted more classy stuff, more drama – particularly Shakespeare – which by now I suppose doesn't come as much of a surprise to you.

The idea, they decided, was to find full-time partners who were not set in their ways, but open to new ideas. 'Partners we can mould to fit our own purpose,' were Aunt Mabel's exact words, I believe. 'Perhaps even partners with a ready-made show that we could take over.' Like I said, Aunt Mabel could be ruthless.

The others agreed as always, particularly Uncle Will, who was only too aware that his wife was the smartest of them all. Besides, he was very keen to move on. It wasn't too far off the end of the century by then, and 1900 seemed to Uncle Will an excellent time for the Worthings to set their sights on becoming masters of their own destiny. He asked Aunt Mabel which particular show she might have in mind, as she quite clearly had a plan.

'What about *Carlo and Rube's Big Show Bonanza?*' Aunt Mabel said, no doubt offering up the suggestion in all apparent innocence before sitting back and waiting for the bomb to explode. At least, that's the way I see things happening.

Carlo and Rube! Now there's a couple of names to conjure with. My goodness, what a pair!

Michael Carlovsky and Marten Reubens were inseparable and had been since early childhood. This was probably because, as just two among the many thousands of pauper urchins who roamed London's slums, their earliest existences had been equally wretched, equally deprived.

Michael, or Carlo as he was known, was the elder by three years. He'd been born in 1850 around St Giles High Street, an area at the top of Shaftesbury Avenue known as 'The Rookeries', because it was here people huddled together like roosting rooks, even sleeping on rooftops when there wasn't a room to be had, which was quite often the case. The dingy rooms the fortunate among them were lucky enough to share were referred to as 'sties'; their places of amusement, usually for the purpose of fighting or gambling, were 'dens'; and their children were known by many a name perceived as only fitting by most. They were 'guttersnipes' because they lived around the filthy drains like the brown-feathered wading birds called snipes; they were 'mudlarks' because they scavenged in the low-tide mud of the Thames in the hope of finding something they might sell; and they were 'street Arabs' because they roamed the lanes of old London Town in wandering groups, wild and unsupervised.

Carlo was the youngest of three siblings, his two sisters quite a deal older. His father deserted the family, and when his mother died both girls just up and disappeared, leaving him alone. The older girl was twelve by then and quite possibly already working the streets, but in any event she and her ten-year-old sister, in their fight for survival, did not relish the prospect of being responsible for a little brother. A month or so later, Carlo was caught stealing, adjudged an orphan and placed in St Jude's Orphanage and Home for Wayward Boys. He was six years old.

Marten, or Rube as he became known, arrived at the orphanage just two years later. An only child, his mother too had died, but he hadn't been left on his own to fend for himself. The landlord of the tenement building, wanting the room immediately vacated, had taken the child directly to the police station and dumped him. Rube was placed in St Jude's Orphanage by order of the courts in 1858. He was five years old.

Young Rube was unable to cope with the violence that existed among the child inmates of the orphanage. He was not the street-smart, tough, savvy boy that Carlo was and he suffered some terribly bullying. Until one day Carlo came to his rescue.

'What's your name?' Carlo asked, hauling the ginger-haired boy to his feet. He'd chased off the two who had been bashing him.

'Marten,' the boy said, wiping his bloodied nose on the sleeve of his grubby shirt, 'Marten Reubens.'

'You're going to have to learn how to fight, Rube,' Carlo said. 'I'll teach you if you like.'

Marten Reubens had been Rube from that day on. And from that day on Carlo had been Rube's hero, despite the fact Rube was actually the far brighter of the two.

Being the quick learner he was, and with his confidence now boosted by the only friend he'd known in his very short life, Rube rapidly absorbed all Carlo taught him about fist-fighting, and between them they became a formidable pair. So formidable, in fact, that by the time they were ten and thirteen years of age respectively, tutor and pupil were all but untouchable. Others at the orphanage knew better than to challenge them.

Just two years later, Carlo and Rube decided they'd outgrown St Jude's, insufferable as it was, and that they could do far better on their own. So they ran away and joined a travelling boxing troupe. They stayed with the troupe, working through the seasonal months when the boxing tent did big business, for a whole four years.

The troupe was run by an innovative but disreputable Irishman called Paddy O'Donnell, who knew the value of tough cockney kids who could fight like the devil; street kids willing to work for little more than their keep and the love of doing battle. To Paddy, Carlo and Rube were money in the bank. No matter they were fifteen and twelve, they were more than a match for boys far older. At times he'd even pit them against adults. They were his prize pair.

Paddy was right to value the boys as he did. Carlo and Rube quickly became favourites among the men who flocked to the Irishman's boxing tent to cheer on the fighters and lay hopeful bets on the winners. The troupe travelled a well-worn path through the industrial Midlands and north of England, setting up their tent in fairs and showgrounds and even the occasional circus. Here they performed to mill workers and miners who were starved for entertainment and loved nothing more than egging on one of their own to challenge a 'pro'. At first, any encouragement to fight Paddy's 'boys' was directed towards the younger workers, of which there were many, but the regulars soon gathered this did not result in anything approximating fair odds so they started calling for older and tougher opponents. Then, when Paddy obligingly agreed to such a seeming mismatch, they'd more often than not lay bets on the boys. Here was good sport, even if on the odd occasion they found themselves backing a loser. The boys' popularity soared.

Surprisingly enough, Carlo tended to lose more often than Rube. Not because he was the lesser fighter; indeed given his added years he was the stronger of the two and, like Rube, he was quick and light on his feet. 'My boys are as agile as monkeys,' was Paddy's proud boast. But Carlo just loved playing to the crowd. He'd pump the audience up before the fight, strutting showily about the roped-off, makeshift boxing ring like a handsome young peacock. Then when the bell rang, he'd charge boldly from his corner, a David to the Goliath who was challenging him. Performance was everything to Carlo. So much so that occasionally he'd lose focus and his opponent would land a lucky punch.

Rube never lost focus. Rube fought with his brain, or so he said, and it certainly appeared that way. He'd start out slowly, dodging and weaving, reading his opponent's tactics before making a move, adding up the weight factor, the footwork, the favoured style of jab and punch. Then when he finally came in for the attack, his opponent by now tiring, he always seemed several steps ahead, as if he knew exactly what was going to happen next, which he invariably did.

There was no competition between the boys themselves. Carlo didn't mind in the least losing the odd match; to the contrary he rather enjoyed the experience. The crowd was so much on his side that most would boo the winner anyway. And as Paddy O'Donnell held up the challenger's hand announcing the man's victory, Carlo would accept his defeat in true heroic fashion. He'd clap his opponent on the back and circle the ring acknowledging the crowd with gratitude, showing what a truly good sport he was.

He was never incapacitated to the point where he couldn't enjoy his defeat; Paddy would never have allowed that to happen.

Paddy had special rules and signals for his 'boys'. It was true he had special signals for his other six fighters too, but the hard-and-fast rules applied most particularly to Carlo and Rube. Under no circumstances were they to take too much punishment. If an opponent appeared a potential danger, which was unusual, they were to put on a show for the crowd certainly, but they were to throw the fight before risking any serious damage. And if Carlo, through his inattentiveness, were to cop a lucky punch that decked him, then he was to stay down and concede defeat.

The rules were simple, the signals readable, and the boys obeyed them to the letter, for which Paddy was thankful. His boys were too valuable to lose, especially Carlo whose looks were a huge added bonus.

'I'm not riskin' a busted nose or a cauliflower ear with that one,' he'd say to his drinking mates, 'the lad's a bleedin' Adonis. They adore him, men and women alike.'

There was no doubt Carlo was handsome, and in a flashy daredevil way that well suited his chosen profession. Tall, with a fine head of glossy brown hair, a moustache to match, and a raffish grin that he used unashamedly to his advantage, men respected the way he teased and tantalised his fearsome opponents, and women found him fatally attractive. By the time he was sixteen he'd bedded any number of easy conquests, from wide-eyed young virgins to worn-out wives of forty. There was ample opportunity among the female workers in the mill towns to the north.

Carlo couldn't understand Rube's lack of interest in sex. Sure Rube was only thirteen, but that was old enough, wasn't it? Carlo had had his first girl at the age of twelve, around the same time he'd started shaving.

'You should take your head out of those books, Rube,' he'd say, 'have a look around at the girls instead, you don't know what you're missing.'

But Rube would only shrug and return to his book. At every town they visited Rube's first port of call was the local bookshop, which he would seek out with fanatical zeal. Books were Rube's passion. He read voraciously, devouring everything in sight, hungry for knowledge and revelling in the beauty of the written word.

Carlo put his friend's lack of interest in girls down to the simple fact that, being baby-faced and still devoid of facial hair, Rube was probably a late developer. He must stop teasing, he told himself; the day would come. And of course Rube was brainy, which probably had something to do with it. Carlo was willing to admit that between the two of them Rube was the brains.

By the time Rube was fifteen, however, still baby-faced but now nuggetty of build and sprouting a sparse, gingery moustache that matched his hair, Carlo was driven once again to tease him about girls.

'Didn't you even *see* her?' he nagged, a comically incredulous raise of his eyebrows. 'Didn't you notice the way she *looked* at you?'

'Of course I *saw* her,' Rube replied with a touch of exasperation, 'and of course I'm aware she *looked* at me. We were *talking* for goodness' sake, where *else* was she going to look?'

'But she was *set* on you, Rube,' Carlo insisted, 'she was set on *you*, do you understand? *You* not *me* . . .' *Well, naturally she wasn't set on me*, he thought, *I was already taken, wasn't I?* 'You could've had her, mate, but you just didn't notice.'

It was a Sunday and they were in Chester, a beautiful town, one they knew well. The previous day's boxing shows at the annual Spring Fair had been a roaring success – Paddy's tent always drew good crowds in Chester – and on this their Sunday afternoon off, Carlo and Rube had decided to visit the markets.

Chester's marketplace, like every market throughout the whole of Cheshire, was a wondrous place, particularly on a bright and cloudless, azure-blue spring day. Stalls abounded with every form of fresh produce direct from the farmers: fruit, vegetables, flowers; milk, cream, cheese; poultry, meats, sausages; and from one stall the tantalising aroma of fresh baked bread, scones and biscuits.

There'd been quite a crowd gathered about the stall that sold ale out of barrels and freshly made Melton pork pies, and before long Carlo had engaged two girls in conversation. Or rather they were women, factory workers in their early twenties. Carlo had concentrated on the attractive one with long fair hair, buying her an ale and edging her aside, a glance to Rube signalling him to do likewise with the other, a plainer girl with mousy hair but a pretty smile.

Rube had read the signal correctly, buying the girl an ale and chatting quite animatedly, the girl responding in kind. They'd appeared most interested in each other, which had delighted Carlo.

An hour later, however, upon bidding farewell to the girls, Carlo had been left totally bewildered.

'See you tonight then,' he'd said to his fair-haired girl.

'You surely will,' came the reply with a saucy promise.

'Bye,' Rube had said.

'Bye,' from the mousy-haired girl, who'd appeared even more bewildered than Carlo.

'What's *wrong* with you?' Carlo had demanded as he watched the girls walk off. 'Are you *mad?*' He turned to Rube, incredulous. 'Didn't you even *see* her?' And he'd launched into his tirade. He'd arranged to meet the fair-haired girl at a tavern that evening – 'for a drink', as they'd agreed, but they both knew the tavern had rooms upstairs.

He'd presumed Rube had been working along much the same lines. 'Didn't you notice the way she *looked* at you?'

But as Carlo had continued to berate him, and even as Rube had responded, his mind was elsewhere.

'Actually,' he said thoughtfully when Carlo, aware he was making no inroads, had finally given up, 'I had a very interesting conversation with that girl.'

'Oh,' the response was dry, 'how exciting.'

His cynicism was lost on Rube. 'She comes from a big family, oldest of eight kids, youngest just turned six . . .'

Carlo didn't say a word, but his expression spoke multitudes.

'Their father deserted them four years ago . . .'

Oh, poor things, Carlo's expression said, *do you seriously think I fucking care!*

'He left his wife and kids and took off for Australia, to Melbourne and the goldfields in Victoria, she told me —'

'So what!' Carlo couldn't remain silent any longer. 'So a bloke runs out on his family, what's new about that? Happens to the best of us. What do I care if he leaves his kids penniless? What do I care if —'

'Ah, but you see, he didn't.'

Rube's interruption confused Carlo. 'Eh?' he queried.

'He sent a whole stash of money home to his wife.'

Carlo remained mystified, but intrigued, aware that Rube was actually hinting at something. 'What do you mean?'

'I mean he got rich, that's what I mean. There's a gold rush happening down there in Australia, Carlo. I've read about it in the newspapers. People are flocking to Melbourne from all over the world. They have been for some years, so the papers say. And now this girl tells me her dad goes there four years ago and sends home a stash of money? Don't you see what I'm getting at? That's where we should be going, mate. That's where the money is.'

It hadn't taken long to convince Carlo. Rube after all was 'the brains'. True, he might be a bit thick when it came to women, but he was invariably right about everything else.

Carlo was not misguided in considering Rube 'the brains', but his view was not just by way of comparison, for he himself was certainly not backward. Gifted with the natural cunning of a true survivor, Michael Carlovsky was quick-witted and canny. But he did not have the enquiring mind of young Marten Reubens. Few did, particularly among those born into a life of squalor and deprivation.

From a very early age Rube had always loved to learn. As a child, he would gather gems of knowledge like a nesting bowerbird, but unlike the bowerbird with no drive to impress. He simply liked to collect interesting facts and, as he grew older, to store away for reflection beautifully written passages of prose and verses of poetry. He blessed the insufferable St Jude's Orphanage and Home for Wayward Boys for offering him a basic education. Who knows? Without St Jude's he might never have learnt to read and write. Although deep in his psyche Rube had the feeling he would somehow have taught himself. He couldn't imagine a life without books.

Following that day in the Chester marketplace, Carlo and Rube started saving every penny they could. Carlo even managed to blackmail Paddy O'Donnell into doubling their pay. 'If you don't, we're off,' he threatened. And Paddy believed him. They made good money boxing from then on, particularly when they rigged a match and got someone to lay bets for them. In the off-season they signed up for factory work; neither was lazy, not when they had such an enticing objective. By now both were consumed with gold fever.

It took them exactly one year. They left England in the spring of 1869 aboard the barque *Queen of the Seas*.

Carlo was nineteen and Rube sixteen, and they were bound for Melbourne, Australia.

Upon their arrival, they found themselves destined for disappointment. Or so it appeared.

'You're too late, mate,' they were told by a fellow Cockney in the streets of Melbourne when they'd simply asked for directions to an outlet where they might buy a tent and panning equipment. 'There's no more gold. No more alluvial stuff anyway. The rush is over, all the fields are worked out.'

The man had then gone on to bemoan the day he'd set off from London to find gold at 'the arse end of the earth'.

'Because that's what it is down here, my friends,' he'd said, 'the arse end of the bleedin' earth. Four whole years I spent camped out there near Ballarat and what have I got to show for it? Nuthin'. Not one fuckin' farthing. You're better off heading home, boys, cut your losses while you can.'

The man's words had made sense to Rube; the peak of the gold rush had been some time back. He cursed his own naiveté; they'd obviously left their run too late.

But Carlo refused to be deterred. Carlo's lust for adventure still ran hot.

'One bloke's opinion, Rube,' he urged. 'Just one bloke, that's all, there's got to be other stories out there.'

And there were. One story in particular, which they heard only days later in a backstreet tavern when they'd been asking around.

'Oh, there's gold out there all right,' the man said, 'of course there's gold.' They were sitting at a table whose grimy window looked out onto a gloomy laneway, the tavern dim and gas-lit even though it was mid-afternoon. The man's name was Douglas. He was a Scot, around forty or so, and they'd bought him a drink when they'd discovered he had a story to tell.

'Have you not heard of the "Welcome Stranger" nugget?' he asked.

Carlo and Rube shook their heads, but exchanged a quick glance of suspicion – was the man spinning them a yarn? Best he wasn't, for his own sake; they didn't like being taken for fools.

'Discovered earlier this very year,' Douglas went on, 'in February it was. The biggest alluvial gold nugget ever to be found in the whole, wide world.'

'Whereabouts?' Carlo asked.

'A place called Moliagul, about thirty miles west of Bendigo.'

'*Alluvial* gold, you say?' Rube's tone was mistrustful. 'I thought there was no alluvial gold left?'

'Well, obviously there is, laddie,' Douglas said, unaware of how much Rube detested being called 'laddie'. 'The "Welcome Stranger" nugget was found in Black Gully, just one inch below the surface, and that's about as alluvial as you can get now, wouldn't you say?'

The Scot probably didn't intend to sound patronising, but Rube, still baby-faced and often taken to be even younger than his now seventeen years, bristled.

'And you'll never guess in a million years what its total weight was . . .' Douglas polished off the last of his ale in the dramatic pause that followed as the two waited expectantly. 'A whole 2,332 ounces,' he said, thumping his empty mug down on the table. 'The "Welcome Stranger" weighed over ten stone, can you believe it? That's more than my wife weighs, and she's no sylph, I can promise you.'

'Who discovered . . . the nugget?' Rube asked. He couldn't bring himself to say the "Welcome Stranger", it sounded too absurd. *We're being had*, he thought.

'Two Cornish miners, John Deason and Richard Oates. They've become quite famous, which is no surprise considering.'

The Scotsman hadn't registered Rube's underlying animosity, but Carlo had.

'Let me get you another ale,' he said, signalling the girl who was doing the rounds of the tables. He cast a dagger-like look to Rube that said *watch it*, and leant forward eagerly. 'Tell us more.'

The girl was beside them in a second; she'd had her eye on Carlo from the moment he'd walked in.

'So what'll it be?' she asked suggestively, the breasts in her low-cut blouse offering a promise. She worked after hours when the tavern closed, but she'd do this one for nothing, God he was handsome.

'Same again.' Carlo gestured at the three mugs of ale, even though he and Rube hadn't finished theirs. He'd noticed the breasts, but they were of no interest to him.

'I met a chap who has a piece of the "Welcome Stranger",' Douglas proudly announced as the girl left, disappointed that she'd made no impression. 'He was a friend of Deason's. He showed it to me, what's more, a solid piece of the nugget itself.'

Oh, so the bloke just gave away pieces of his whopping-great, world-breaking nugget, did he? Rube thought, but he said nothing.

'Go on.' Carlo was spellbound.

The Scot was happy to oblige, pleased he had a captive audience and that another drink was on the way.

'When Deason and Oates *finally* got the giant thing out of the ground,' he said, 'and bear in mind they had to use a *crowbar* to do it – they broke a pick handle in the attempt to lever it up – they loaded it into a dray, carted it off and gave it a good clean. But when they got it to the bank several days later, it was way too big to be weighed on the scales so they had to call in a blacksmith, who cut it into smaller pieces.'

'So how do they know that the whole thing weighed in at . . . whatever it was, I've forgotten.' Mindful of Carlo's warning glare, Rube tried to sound pleasant, but didn't quite succeed.

'As I said, 2,332 ounces, laddie. Or thereabouts,' Douglas added hastily, not wanting to find himself caught out. 'It varies a wee bit either way, according to which reports you read.' He liked to be specific as a rule – it sounded more impressive – but the lad seemed to doubt him. 'They arrived at the net weight of the nugget by weighing in the whole lot, you see, including the gold that was contained in the crushed quartz that had been prised off it, and also the pieces that broke away when it was cut up.'

The drinks arrived.

Carlo and Rube drained what was left in their mugs and the girl cleared the table with a regretful glance at Carlo, who didn't notice.

'Deason gave away the pieces that broke off the nugget to friends of his,' Douglas said after taking a swig of his fresh ale, 'and I met this chap who had one of them. In a tavern much like this,' he added, looking around the dingy ale house. 'And that's how I come to know the full story of the "Welcome Stranger",' he concluded with an air of triumph. He'd dined out on the story many times.

'How much did Deason and his partner get for it?' Carlo asked.

'Close to ten thousand pounds,' Douglas said, 'which they split between the two of them. Money like that . . .' He shook his head enviously. 'Oh my, you'd live like a king, wouldn't you?'

Carlo didn't need to hear any more. Carlo was fired up and raring to go. He wanted to set off the very next day.

'Black Gully, at a place called Moliagul about thirty miles west of Bendigo,' he said, having memorised every detail.

Rube was more circumspect.

'We'll have to check out the bloke's story,' he said.

They did, only to find the Scotsman's every word was true. The 'Welcome Stranger' nugget was the biggest ever discovered, just an inch or so below the surface, and earlier that very year.

They bought a horse and dray and headed for Bendigo.

'We'll give it three months,' Rube warned, 'no more.'

The three months never eventuated.

'A fool's errand,' Rube said early one wintry evening six weeks later as they hunched over their campfire, frozen fingers nursing tin mugs of tea. 'Always was.'

Carlo, who was equally disheartened, took the remark as a personal criticism. 'So what do you think we should have done then?' he demanded belligerently. 'Go on, you tell me. Should we have given up without even trying? We travel halfway around the world and —'

'I'm not blaming you, mate.' Rube's response was mollifying; Carlo always became over-defensive when he thought he might be in the wrong. 'None of this is your fault, it's the law of averages, that's all.'

Slightly mystified and suitably distracted, Carlo waited for the clarification he knew was forthcoming.

Rube gazed about the surrounding countryside that had once no doubt been attractive, but cleared of vegetation and in this wintry weather was now a boggy expanse of well-trodden mud. Theirs was the only campsite visible at the moment, but the landscape testified to the presence of others before them.

'Too many people have been and gone,' he said, 'and there'll be more who'll follow and never give up. They'll delude themselves daily in the hope of finding gold. But they won't. Even if there's gold still here, which there might well be, not everyone can get lucky. Law of averages, you see what I mean?'

'Are you saying we should quit already?' Carlo was surprised; they hadn't done their three months yet, and Rube was never a quitter.

'Hunting for gold? Yep.' A decisive nod. 'But getting rich? Nope.' Rube's smile as always was engaging, and on this occasion also just a touch enigmatic. 'There's money to be made from all these people.'

'What you got in mind, Rube? C'mon, spit it out.' *Enigmatic* was lost on Carlo. 'What are we going to do?'

'We're going to do what we do best, Carlo. We're going to fight.'

Rube had had his alternative plan in mind from the day they'd first arrived in Bendigo, where they'd bought their supplies before heading off to make camp at Black Gully. As their horse and dray had plodded through the outskirts of town, he'd seen the boxing show, which was set up in the fairground, tough men standing in a line, a showman extolling their talents. They'd both seen it. Carlo had even made some flippant remark about their 'previous lives following them', but Rube had thought, *So they have touring boxing shows here, how interesting. And that tent's much bigger than Paddy's was.* He'd also observed the excellent crowd the tent show had attracted. *Well, there's always that,* he'd thought, and he'd made a mental note of the name on the banner above the platform where the boxers were standing. *Barney O'Banyon's Boxing Bonanza. Another bleeding Irishman,* he'd thought.

Having now made their decision, it took them no time at all to find the troupe, which was currently performing at the Maryborough Showgrounds; Barney O'Banyon's tent show was well known in the area. And becoming one of Barney's boxers turned out to be an even easier exercise.

'I'll take you on if you can prove yourself,' Barney said, eyeing Carlo up and down. The kid's looks would be a big draw and he appeared fit; if he could fight he might well be a real winner. But the other? 'Not you, boy,' he said with a shake of his head, 'you're too young.'

'Put me up against any one of your fighters,' Rube dared him, eyeing the half-dozen or so men who stood on the platform. 'What about that bloke there?' He pointed at the biggest and toughest, a thuggish-looking Pole close to six feet tall known as Killer Kaminski.

'Don't be daft,' the Irishman said scathingly, 'he'd pulverise you in seconds, and what sort of show would that offer me speccies?' The spectators who attended Barney O'Banyon's fights were always affectionately referred to as 'speccies'. 'Besides, they'd have me guts for garters if I allowed such a match.' Barney had to admit though, he respected the kid's nerve. 'All right, you can take on young Dodger. Best of three rounds.'

Nineteen-year-old Dodger was so named because he was the speediest and most agile of Barney's stable. Nobody could land a punch on the boy as he danced about the ring, unerringly finding his own mark while remaining untouched.

'Don't take him out too soon,' Barney whispered instructions to Dodger. 'Give the speccies a fight, make it two rounds.'

But Dodger didn't make the end of round one. He'd met a worthy dance partner in Rube and couldn't land a punch of his own. Then when Rube, having assessed the pattern of play, honed in for the attack, young Dodger was taken completely by surprise. One punch did the trick, even with the padded mittens provided. Rube had intended it would; he was out to prove himself.

Funnily enough, Rube went on to become really good friends with Dodger, who hailed from Wagga Wagga in New South Wales. The son of a sheep shearer, his real name was Ben, but Barney, who liked all his fighters to have labels, had come up with 'The Dodger'.

'So he named you after the Artful Dodger,' Rube said approvingly. 'That's really good, that is.'

'Who's the Artful Dodger?'

'He's a character in a novel by Charles Dickens,' Rube explained. 'A novel called *Oliver Twist*.'

Dodger, who wasn't sure about this, checked it out with Barney.

'Of course,' Barney said without the slightest hesitation, which very much impressed Dodger, who hadn't known that Barney read books.

Carlo and Rube were happy touring with *Barney O'Banyon's Boxing Bonanza*. The members of the troupe were amicable enough, any aggression having been satisfyingly expressed in the ring, the speccies arrived in healthy numbers wherever they went, and the takings were excellent.

After a year on the road, and having discovered that boxing tent shows proliferated far more in their newly adopted country than they did back in England, the two decided to start up a troupe of their own.

'Why work for another man's profit?' Rube wisely commented. He'd been congratulating himself for some time now. After all, he'd been right, hadn't he? There was money to be made from the hordes who'd arrived during the gold rush and stayed on in the area, either as merchants, tradesmen, farmers or the like. Wherever this number of people were settled, any form of entertainment was bound to prove a winner.

Once again, they started saving their earnings, and fed by such an incentive they didn't find the task difficult. *Carlo and Rube's Boxing Bonanza* sounded altogether too good to resist. To Carlo anyway. Rube wasn't so sure.

'I think Barney might get a bit mad if we nick "Bonanza", don't you?' he mildly suggested.

'Why?' Carlo countered with more than a touch of belligerence; his heart was set on the title and he had no intention of budging. 'Barney doesn't *own* the word, does he?' For someone really clever, Carlo thought, that seemed a dumb argument. 'He can't stop us!'

Rube backed off. He'd let the matter go for now; they'd cross that particular bridge when they came to it.

But something happened before they came to that particular bridge. In 1875 they met the girls. And superficial though the meeting at first appeared, the girls were to change the course of their lives.

6

THE FURTHER ADVENTURES OF CARLO AND RUBE

'You're a wonderful showman,' Rosie said, offering her gloved hand to Carlo. 'A natural-born talent, I can tell, far and above the average, extraordinary in fact.' The words themselves might have sounded gushing, but their delivery was not. She was looking him directly in the eye and appeared to be just stating a fact. 'I admire those with a gift like yours.'

Returning the handshake, Carlo was flattered, but simultaneously dumbstruck. Her eyes were the deepest blue, or were they violet? Whatever the colour, they were intense, hypnotic; he couldn't break from her gaze.

'Thank you,' he said simply, which was uncharacteristic; in the presence of a beautiful woman – and she was certainly beautiful – his innate charm always sprang to the fore.

'You should be master of your own show,' she said, 'leading your own troupe instead of being just one of them.' She finally released his hand. 'I'm Rosie, by the way.'

'Hello, I'm Carlo.'

'Yes, I know.'

'Oh?' He was puzzled. How could she know? The label Barney had assigned him was 'Gentleman Johnny' because of the way he wooed the crowd.

'I enquired,' she said.

She may have released his hand, but she still held his gaze and the seductive smile she now proffered only devastated him further.

Beside her, the other girl, who was fair-haired like Rosie, a little shorter but also attractive, offered her gloved hand to Rube.

'I'm Gilda.'

'Hello, I'm Rube,' he said, his response echoing Carlo's.

'Yes, I know.' Again, how could she know? Given his baby face, which he kept clean-shaven these days, his gingery moustache never quite successful, Rube's label was 'The Kid'. But her smile was humorous rather than seductive as she added, 'I enquired.'

Rube liked her instantly.

It was unusual for women to attend one of Barney O'Banyon's boxing shows, particularly women like these; fashionably dressed, prettily bonneted, well-spoken – yet with just the faintest hint of a twang that a well-tuned ear might find suspect – and above all, young. As a rule, any women in attendance were of the rougher variety and certainly not young, more often than not the weathered wives of miners or farmers, as hardy as their husbands.

These two aren't as young as they first appeared though, Carlo thought, as his senses recovered from the initial onslaught of her personality. *Not right up close like this. They'd have to be around thirty, perhaps even older.* Not that he minded in the least. Twenty-five-year-old Carlo preferred older women. *They're bold as brass too*, he thought, *openly waiting for us outside the tent, not caring what people might think. That can mean only one thing, surely. They're making themselves available. Rosie is anyway.*

'We noticed you at the fight,' he said, smile debonair, charm now well and truly back in place, 'didn't we, Rube?'

'Yep, sure did,' Rube said with a wink to Gilda, sharing their recognition of the very obvious flirtation game being played between their respective friends. 'Difficult not to.'

The boxing troupe was at Wagga Wagga, or rather nearby, the circus's big top and accompanying sideshows having been set up that very morning in an open field just one mile out of town. This was the troupe's first day performing, but *Barney O'Banyon's Boxing Bonanza* had been booked to travel with the circus for a whole three months, as had most of the other sideshows. After their two-week run at Wagga Wagga, the entire entourage would pack up and move on in a vast convoy of animals and vehicles to other regional towns in New South Wales before travelling over the border into Victoria. The circus was one of comparative modesty, no elephants or big cats, at least 'not yet' as the owners were wont to say with the hint of a promise, but the brass band-led procession was always impressive. Girls in plumed headdresses rode bareback on prancing show ponies, garishly painted clowns performed their buffoonery in open oxen-drawn wagons, and gymnasts executed backflips and walked on their hands alongside the endless miscellany of vehicles as the parade passed through small country towns en route to the larger centres where they would perform. The circus convoy was more than a means of transportation; it was a prime advertising opportunity, as its owners knew only too well.

'So what are you girls doing at a *boxing* show?' Carlo queried, the risqué raise of an eyebrow signalling this was surely an outrageous action on their part.

'We wanted to check out the opposition,' Rosie replied smoothly. 'That's us over there.'

She pointed across the broad grassy path, which was still relatively green but destined to become a mothy, well-trampled avenue as the week progressed, to where the other row of stalls and sideshows were set up, some still being erected. A workman in dungarees was rigging a huge banner above the tent to which she pointed.

'THE FABULOUS FAIRWEATHER SISTERS, EXOTIC DANCERS AND CONTORTIONISTS EXTRAORDI-NAIRE,' the banner read in large letters. On either side was a colourfully painted picture of a veiled woman in a bizarre costume of supposedly 'Eastern' appearance, one dancing seductively, the other performing a backbend that defied belief, elbows resting by feet, head peering through legs. Beneath, in smaller letters, the banner promised '*An assault on the senses. Prepare to be transported to a world of feminine mystique.*'

'That's *you*!' Carlo gaped at the poster, then back at Rosie and her equally respectable companion. *Extraordinaire?* he wondered. *Feminine mystique?* He'd seen French postcards of the obscene variety that men regularly passed around and he was shocked. 'Are you two some sort of strip show then?' he blurted out, Rube beside him just as flabbergasted.

'Certainly not,' Rosie primly responded, 'we're dancers and contortionists just as the banner says.'

'We're not really sisters though,' Gilda chimed in, 'that part's a lie.'

'We mostly perform in vaudeville and burlesque,' Rosie went on, ignoring Gilda, 'sometimes on tour, sometimes in town, depending on the show. Backwater halls, big city theatres, you name it we've played it,' she said airily. 'We're very versatile. And as you can see,' she added with a flamboyant gesture at the banner, 'we can also play circus sideshows.'

Rosie considered the circus a decidedly downward step, but it was a step they'd taken in the past and would no doubt take again in the future, hence she'd acquired the tent and had the banner made up. One had to grab whatever one could get in the ever-fickle world of show business. But she and Gilda were survivors, and even a circus or fairground sideshow was an improvement on their previous life. At least here there were no middlemen to rob them of their earnings, like the pimps of yesteryear and Madame Simone at the 'gentlemen's club'.

Rosie Marks and Gilda Grant, both thirty-two, had met five years previously at the Beauchamp Gentlemen's Club, an elite brothel that catered for only the wealthiest of clients in the heart of Sydney. They'd been experienced working girls by then, having plied their trade in various establishments from the age of eighteen, but upon discovering they shared a common, and very saleable, commodity that served their trade well, and for which they'd become known, the bond between them had been instant.

'You're double-jointed too?' Rosie had asked in amazement when they'd been returned, along with the other girls, to the general quarters out back, where they would await the summons to attend whichever gentleman had made whichever one of them his choice. As the girls had been paraded before the clients in the plush bar and lounge of the Beauchamp, the madam had extolled the virtues of the club's latest recruit, namely the fact she could manipulate her body into extraordinary positions.

'Another of my ladies who is very *flexible*,' Madame Simone had said, her glassy smile taking in both Rosie and Gilda. 'An ability, gentlemen, that exquisitely enhances the sensual delights.'

Gilda had given Rosie a brisk nod. 'Born that way. See?' And she'd promptly sat on a hardback chair and wrapped her ankle around the back of her head.

Far from considering Gilda a threat, Rosie had embraced her as an ally, and they'd made a good team. Performing in the lounge for the men before whom they were paraded, they would dance seductively with each other and contort their bodies into unimaginable poses. They sometimes performed together in private too. There were always those clients who enjoyed a *ménage à trois*, and particularly a *ménage à trois* as bizarre as these two could provide. Rosie and Gilda, despite their age – and twenty-seven was old in their chosen profession – remained the most popular of the Beauchamp's ladies.

But, aware time would not prove their friend, and with thirty looming, they'd decided to give up the game and direct their considerable talents elsewhere. Why not show business? They'd learnt a great deal in the last several years, the madam having promoted them in the most exotic terms: 'the ultimate experience', 'an assault upon the senses', 'extraordinaire', 'a world of feminine mystique'. Madame Simone had a way with words.

Inspired by such terms, Rosie and Gilda had choreographed their dance and contortionist act accordingly. They would entwine their bodies with each other as they danced, twisting their limbs into positions of genuine contortionism, it was true. But the end result, rather than being grotesque, was suggestive and to many decidedly erotic, particularly costumed as they were in shimmering, transparent apparel beneath which they were scantily clothed. 'Exotic' was the image they had chosen, and in order to avoid any suspicion of vulgarity, they'd adopted the name 'Fairweather' and billed themselves as a 'sisters act'. Which to their mind was all very respectable.

'You must come and see our show tomorrow, Carlo,' Rosie said.

'You too, Rube,' Gilda added with something that seemed like a touch of mischief.

Carlo couldn't wait. And even Rube, to whom exotic female dancers didn't hold great appeal given he'd much prefer to settle down with a good book, had to admit he was intrigued.

The following day they quickly changed and ducked out in between fight sessions, both having polished off their opponents in double-quick time, much to Barney's annoyance.

'You could have milked it a bit more,' he grumbled.

But Carlo and Rube paid him no heed. They were outside in seconds, mingling with the crowd among the hurly-burly of the fairground, where the cries from men touting sideshows starring sword-swallowers, strong men, freaks and tattooed ladies vied for prominence and the smells from food stalls tantalised.

They queued up to buy tickets for The Fabulous Fairweather Sisters.

'Their man's an amateur,' Carlo said critically of the fellow in dungarees, who was selling tickets while intermittently touting the show through a speaking trumpet. It was the same dungaree-clad man who'd been rigging the banner the previous day. 'Just look at him, will you. All the panache of a cowherd.'

'Roll up, roll up, showing on the inside,' the man called in lacklustre fashion, 'The Fabulous Fairweather Sisters, exotic dancers and contortionists extrordinry . . . Roll up, roll up . . .' And then he'd repeat the same spiel as he doled out tickets and change from the cloth money bag tied at his waist.

Rube agreed. 'Where's the sales pitch?' he said. 'And whatever happened to *extraordinaire*?'

'You'd think they'd dress the bloke in something decent too, wouldn't you?'

The signs did not auger well, and they prepared themselves for disappointment.

But they were not disappointed.

From the moment they entered the tent along with the rest of the crowd – and as Carlo muttered to Rube it was not a bad turnout at all – the atmosphere became charged with promise.

A fiddle was playing, quietly, teasingly; an innocuous, balding little man of indeterminate age seated upon a stool in the corner of the tent. He was not positioned on the wooden platform where the girls would perform and was barely visible to most, but Rube's eyes sought him out. The sound was tantalising.

God he's good, he can really play the thing, Rube thought admiringly. There was something else too, lending itself to the atmosphere, calming the crowd, which would normally be jostling for prime position. *Incense,* he thought, *that's what it is. They're burning incense. Jasmine, I think. That's clever, the fiddle and the incense, perfect mix. Excellent way to arouse the senses.*

And this was only the start. There was a great deal more intended to arouse the senses.

The Fairweather Sisters received no introductory announcement. The music was introduction enough, changing tempo and volume, rendering the audience instantly silent. Then, from behind the curtains of the canvas dressing room at the rear of the tent, they appeared. Slender figures, their faces veiled, wearing snugly fitted headdresses that sparkled and costumes of 'Eastern' appearance, romantic, mysterious, and also alluring, the shape of their bodies clearly visible through the gossamer outer layer. The taller of the two wore red, the other orange, and as their bodies entwined, their arms slowly reaching upwards, curling around each other, they could have been a flickering flame.

As the act progressed, the women performed duets – exotic dances as promised – and solos; contortionist skills mingling with the dance, also as promised. Both performers displayed their talents well and the music varied suitably for each dance, some slow and sensuous, others more fiery. But it was the finale that left the audience breathless.

The final dance, a duet, started out slowly, sensually, the women making connection, but in a tentative way. The touch of hands. The duplication of steps as they gazed intently at one another. The feeling that each was fascinated by her own mirror image. Then steadily, relentlessly even, the music became more intense. Like a magnet, it seemed to draw the dancers together until, finally, they melded.

The audience's rapt attention remained focused solely upon the women, but Rube's eyes couldn't resist seeking out the little man on the fiddle. *Who is in control*, he wondered, *who's leading who? Are the dancers following the musician, or is the musician following the dancers?* But the little man wasn't even watching the women. He was just sitting on his stool in the corner playing his fiddle, by all appearances in a world of his own.

The dancers were on the floor now, writhing together on the wooden platform that served as a stage, then rising and entwining their bodies even more intricately to the point it was impossible to tell whose limbs were whose among the tangle of red and orange. They'd become a fire, and as the music grew more passionate the fire grew wilder and more frenzied, until finally the two froze, their bodies now one inextricably tangled entity, their hands fingers of flame clawing for the sky. And as they froze, the music became a single, long, ecstatically quivering chord.

The chord did not die away beautifully as might have been expected, instead being shrilly replaced by a sharp, exclamatory note that shook the audience from its collective spell and announced the end of the performance.

Upon the violin's jarring note, the women parted, turned coolly to their audience, and clasping each other's hand took their bows with great dignity then retired to their dressing room. The Fairweather Sisters' show was over.

'I tell you what,' Carlo said, while he and Rube waited outside the rear of the tent as they'd been instructed, 'that's one of the most erotic things I've ever seen. And I've seen a few erotic things in my time, I can promise you.'

'Yes,' Rube replied in all seriousness, 'they're very good. The musician's good too.'

Carlo made no comment; he'd given up on Rube.

Rosie and Gilda appeared barely ten minutes later, stepping out from the rear of the tent, where the specially designed door flap led directly from their dressing room. They'd learnt to avoid any audience members who might be lying in wait. The dungaree-clad man stepped out just behind them, having remained on guard beside the dressing room as the audience left, this too being deemed a necessary precaution.

'Thank you,' Rosie said as the man passed her the money bag he'd untied from his waist. 'Bartholomew, isn't it?' She tucked the cloth money bag into the beaded reticule that dangled from her wrist and pulled the draw-string tight, the weight of coin now requiring her to hold the reticule club-like, sagging at her side. It was a healthy sign that obviously pleased her.

'That's right, miss. Bart for short.'

'An excellent turnout for our first performance, Bart.' Her smile was friendly, but her eyes issued a warning. 'I counted the numbers, as I told you I would.' She would count the takings just as assiduously, the man would learn.

But Bart was no fool. 'Of course, Miss Fairweather.' He was an employee of the circus; he wasn't going to risk his job scrounging a few shillings from these two. 'I'll be back in an hour.' The sisters' performances were to be hourly. He nodded to both women.

'Thanks, Bart,' Gilda called after him as the man took his leave. 'So what did you think?' she asked brightly, turning to Carlo and Rube.

'You were wonderful,' Carlo replied, 'both of you. Wonderful.' He marvelled at the way they were absolutely unrecognisable as the dancers he'd just been watching. Of course their headdresses and veils had served well as disguises, but they were once again the two respectable women he'd met yesterday; it was remarkable. *And also damned erotic*, he thought, looking at Rosie and remembering the dance.

Rosie met his gaze boldly. 'Glad you liked us,' she said, knowing exactly what he was thinking.

'I don't think much of your man though.' Carlo was not in the least concerned she'd caught him out as she obviously had. Surely the object of the dance was to enflame men's desire.

'I know. He's just a workman, we pay the circus for his services. Unfortunately we lost our regular man who travels with us.' She wasn't about to admit their 'regular man' had been her lover of two years and that he'd recently left her for an eighteen-year-old soubrette with whom they'd performed in a burlesque show.

'Your musician's really good,' Rube said, still fascinated by the little man with the fiddle. 'Does *he* lead the dance, or do *you*? I couldn't work that out.'

The question was refreshing. Rosie and Gilda had never been asked about their musician. In fact, no one ever seemed to notice Vasily. Or, sadly, his music, which both women agreed was the most important component of the show. Without Vasily's violin there would be no force that drove them; they would simply be two women suggestively contorting their bodies.

'The musician leads the dance,' she said. It seemed the easiest answer and it was, after all, close to the truth. 'Vasily is our inspiration.'

'I should like to meet your Vasily . . .' Rube was aware of Carlo's incredulous expression that plainly said *why, what on earth for?* 'The man is talented and deserves to be congratulated,' he added firmly, for Carlo's benefit more than the women's.

'Yes, I agree he's talented,' Rosie said abruptly, 'but he will have disappeared somewhere, he never stays around after the show. He'll be back in an hour.'

'We'll tell him you liked his music though,' Gilda chimed in, once again brightly and with a smile. To Rube, she seemed by far the more amenable of the two. 'It will please him, I'm sure.'

'If he understands, that is,' Rosie said. 'He's Russian, can't speak much English, or at least pretends he can't – you never know with Vasily, he keeps to himself.' *We're wasting time*, Rosie was thinking, *we need to get to the point.* 'Shall we find something to eat?' she suggested, treating Carlo to one of her special smiles. He was the one she had her eye on.

'Excellent idea.' Carlo offered her his arm and she took it.

Gilda took the arm Rube proffered and the four wandered out into the main concourse of the fairground, looking for all the world like two respectable young couples who knew each other well. Perhaps even looking like lovers.

'So how did you meet Vasily?' Rube asked, as they strolled through the milling crowd towards the area where several food stalls were set up.

'We worked together in the same variety show several years back,' Gilda replied.

They had certainly worked together, but whether the term 'variety show' could be applied was debatable. Vasily had been employed at the Beauchamp Gentlemen's Club. Madame Simone had instantly recruited him upon discovering him playing for pennies from passers-by in George Street. Madame Simone knew talent when she saw it, just as she also knew the value of creating 'atmosphere', and from the outset this strange little man's music had been perfect.

For his keep and a very meagre stipend, Vasily had played his fiddle while the incense burned and the girls paraded, a heady mix of sensations, tantalising and inviting. Following Gilda's arrival, when Madame Simone's *very flexible* ladies had performed before the clients, his music had become even more evocative, which was rather uncanny as tucked away where he was, standing in the shadowy corner of the lounge, he never watched the two, seeming instead to sense their dance.

'When the variety show closed Vasily joined up with us full time,' Gilda went on to explain.

'You were lucky,' Rube said, 'he's quite a find.'

'Yes, he is,' she agreed. 'Are you having sausages and mustard or bread with cheese and pickles?' This time it was Gilda who seemed, although not brusque like Rosie, just a little evasive.

Not that it mattered; Rube wasn't interested in enquiring any further, aware all of a sudden that it was getting close to lunchtime and he was extremely hungry.

They'd arrived at the food stalls; there were three in all. One, run by a German couple, sold fat pork sausages cooked on an iron brazier and served with mustard; another offered thick slices of bread cut from the loaf, topped with chunks of cheese and freshly made pickles; while the third sold confectionery: crystallised fruits, liquorice and toffee, together with paste candy and boiled sweets of every description.

The men opted for sausages and mustard, the women for bread, cheese and pickles, all of which Carlo insisted upon buying, after which they wandered away from the busy fairground to find a space of their own. Many were doing likewise, families picnicking on rugs, others perching on tree stumps or logs. The field where the circus was set up had recently been enlarged, with freshly cleared areas providing many a perfect picnic spot.

Carlo and Rube found a log for the women, and once they were comfortably settled, hunkered themselves down on the grass and ate their sausages with gusto. Pork fat and mustard dribbled from the brown paper in which they'd been served – a messy exercise, but who cared? They were both hungry.

As he ate, Carlo watched Rosie, delighting in the way she attacked her own food. Not messily as he was, but with no pretension either, just a healthy animal-like appetite. He found her unbelievably attractive.

Rosie was fully aware of his eyes on her, not even furtively, but gazing in open admiration, which didn't in the least bother her. She wanted him to admire her; it was part of her plan. And once her hunger was assuaged, she put the remnants of her bread and cheese to one side and got to the point.

'I mentioned to you that we recently lost our regular man who travels with us,' she said, her fingers ferreting briefly inside the frilled sleeve of her dress to produce a lace-edged handkerchief. As she delicately dabbed at the corners of her mouth she directed her attention solely to Carlo, ignoring Rube and Gilda who might as well not have been there.

'Yes,' he replied, swallowing the last of his sausage and screwing up the brown paper, which he tossed aside, 'the man who touts your act is a circus employee, you said. Pity,' he added with a shake of his head, 'he's really terrible. No showmanship at all.'

'Yes, yes, we both know that,' Rosie said a little impatiently, 'but I'm afraid there's not much we can do about it. The trouble is, you see, we lack a protector. Bart is paid to set up and dismantle our tent and to tout and sell tickets, no more. The circus transports our tent for a fee, and we travel with our own horse and buggy. It is therefore advisable we have a protector.' For the first time since broaching the subject, she included Gilda with a brief glance, then as her eyes returned to Carlo, her expression softened. So did her voice, and the effect was most becoming. 'Two women openly travelling alone present a vulnerable target for unscrupulous men who might wish to take advantage ...' Her eyes did not leave his as she returned the handkerchief to the sleeve of her dress. 'As I'm sure you can imagine ...'

'I most certainly can.' Those eyes, that intense focus: he was once again mesmerised.

'We are all of us travelling with the circus, are we not? And for a whole three months.' She'd checked with the circus; the boxing troupe was committed to the three-month run. 'Perhaps ... Carlo ...' The hesitation before she uttered his name sounded like an open invitation to her bed, which in truth it was. 'We might find a way of travelling together. Perhaps ... "Gentleman Johnny",' she smiled, 'you might become our protector?'

'Gentleman Johnny,' she'd scoffed to Gilda just the previous day as they'd watched the boxers up on the platform, Barney O'Banyon touting the talents of each, 'he's no more a gentleman than I am a lady. But by God, he's a handsome devil, and if he can fight the way he's being touted he'll fit the bill perfectly.'

Rosie Marks did not miss the French lover who'd recently left her, but she very much missed the purpose he'd served. Both women did. Louis had been their manager, protector, showman and worker, all of which had made it worthwhile splitting their takings three ways. Three ways after paying Vasily his meagre pittance, that is.

'Yes,' she'd said later as they'd waited outside the boxing tent having watched the fight, 'our "Gentleman Johnny" will do very nicely. And we won't even have to pay him.' Rosie had recognised Carlo's type; she'd found him so very readable. His cockiness, his love of women, his sexual appetite. *He's mine for the taking*, she'd thought. 'An excellent showman too,' she'd said, 'better even than Louis. Pity he's performing in the boxing show. Perhaps we'll be able to lure him away with us at the end of the tour, what do you think?'

'Perhaps,' Gilda had replied. She would believe anything possible of Rosie when it came to men. Which was rather strange, she thought, because Rosie didn't particularly like men. Or sex, for that matter. To Rosie, both men and sex were simply a means to an end.

'They have their uses, Gilda, as we both well know,' she'd often said over the years, 'but men are truly odious creatures. Whenever possible, you and I are far better off without them.'

'It would be an honour to undertake the role of pro-tector during your travels,' Carlo said with the true gentlemanly flair he'd perfected over the years. 'An honour and a personal privilege, I can assure you.'

Rube wanted to laugh. Carlo had sounded so preten-tious, and Rosie's manipulation had been so obvious. But then that was Carlo, wasn't it? *Always thinks he holds the cards when he doesn't really.*

Gilda smiled benignly from one to the other. *There goes Rosie, she's done it again. He has no idea.*

But Carlo did have an idea. He wanted to be manipu-lated. Of course he did.

Rosie's face lit up, her glorious smile reflecting the depth of her gratitude.

'We're staying at the Australian Hotel,' she said. 'You must come into town tonight and we'll toast the deal with champagne.' Every good deed deserved a reward after all. 'Both of you,' she added with another glorious smile to Rube; the men were obviously close friends and Gilda could keep 'The Kid' happy; it was an excellent way to do business. 'This is cause for celebration.' She beamed from one to the other.

They *did* go into town that night, all four of them, in the women's horse and buggy, which was housed with the countless circus and sideshow vehicles of all descriptions, and the horses and oxen that drew them.

Given his suspicions, Rube hadn't wanted to accompany Carlo and the women. He'd said as much in private.

'I'll just be in the way, Carlo,' he'd said. 'I think Rosie has her eye on you.'

Carlo certainly hoped so. 'I think you should come as a matter of courtesy, Rube,' he'd suggested. 'Gilda would like you to, I'm sure.'

But Rube had continued to protest, saying he'd much prefer to stay back at camp. Like most of the workers and performers, they lived on site, camping in tents if the weather was inclement or sleeping under the stars, tucked into their swags beside the vehicles and equipment. Food was cooked over open fires or on iron braziers, and town was visited only when fresh supplies were needed or when men felt the craving to get drunk, which was quite often.

'Do it as a favour for *me*, mate,' Carlo had urged, secretly hoping that Gilda might seduce Rube. 'I'd really like you to come with us.'

So Rube had joined them. Rube always had trouble resisting Carlo.

Wagga Wagga, known to the locals as simply 'Wagga', was a well-established town and, among its substantial number of public houses, the Australian Hotel in Fitzmaurice Street was one of the most popular, boasting excellent stables at the rear and comfortable lodgings for weary travellers.

Upon their arrival, they left the horse and buggy in the competent care of the stablehand and made straight for the lounge where Rosie ordered champagne, which strangely enough was available. The Australian Hotel was known as a most convivial gathering place and prided itself on a broad selection of liquor, much of which was delivered by an 'importer' of questionable background. Rosie insisted upon the bottle being added to the expenses she and Gilda would incur during their two-week stay.

'Put it on our room bill,' she said grandly as if she drank champagne every day of the week, which during her years at the Beauchamp she invariably had.

'To new friendships,' she toasted when the bottle had arrived in its ice bucket, and Carlo had made a great show of pouring their glasses with an expertise that signalled he, too, was accustomed to drinking champagne every day of the week, which was testament to his skill as a performer.

'To new friendships,' they echoed and clinked glasses.

They drank, all four, Rube loathing the taste, which he found a very poor and bitter substitute for apple cider, Carlo feeling decidedly let down, he too never having tasted champagne, and the women being instantly transported to the gentlemen's club, despite the fact that this 'champagne' tasted distinctly inferior.

'And a further toast' – Rosie leant seductively close to Carlo, a teasing whisper – 'to our new protector. We're very grateful, aren't we, Gilda,' she said, but she wasn't looking at Gilda.

'Yes, we are,' Gilda replied, pleasantly but unnecessarily, Rosie and Carlo having eyes for no one but each other. Then she turned to Rube. 'We're very grateful ... both of us,' she said, with an intimacy that he found somehow jarring.

'I hope you won't think me ungrateful' – he rose from his chair; he simply had to get away, even just for a moment – 'and I really don't mean to be rude, but I'm afraid champagne is not to my taste. I'm going to get myself an ale, if you'll excuse me.' He gestured at Carlo's glass. 'Carlo?' he queried. Surely Carlo couldn't abide the stuff either.

'No, no, Rube, I'm fine thanks.' Carlo took a hefty sip of his champagne to prove how delicious it was.

Rube set off for the bar, feeling embarrassed and also annoyed. Mainly with himself. He'd suspected the outcome would be something like this. Why did he always give in to Carlo?

'How odd.' Rosie watched him go. She was surprised and, given her liaison with Carlo was such a foregone conclusion, felt free to speak quite openly. 'I thought we might see if the hotel had another room for the night.'

'Sadly, no.' Carlo observed his friend with regret, but resignation. 'He's never shown much interest in girls. Don't know what's wrong with him,' he added, turning back to Rosie with a winning smile. 'I've given up trying.' He'd recognised the invitation from Gilda and hoped she wasn't offended. 'Sorry, Gilda,' he said.

'I don't mind,' she replied, and she genuinely didn't. She'd much prefer to sit and talk. She liked Rube, and what's more she sensed he liked her.

Rube returned from the bar with his ale, and barely ten minutes later Carlo and Rosie left. Rosie was utterly brazen. 'Would you like to see our room?' she said, and rising to her feet she held out her hand. She didn't expect an answer and didn't get one. He simply took the hand on offer and they were gone.

'Tell me about yourself, Rube,' Gilda said, unfazed, pouring the dregs from the champagne bottle into her glass. 'You don't want that, do you,' she said, upending the contents of his own glass into hers. 'How did you and Carlo meet? What made you take up boxing? I'm most keen to hear your story.' Gilda was always keen to hear other people's stories, which she considered so much more interesting than her own.

So Rube told her of his background, of the orphanage and of Carlo and his introduction to boxing; he found Gilda very easy to talk to. And as Gilda listened, she began to suspect that she and Rube might have quite a bit in common.

The others returned within the hour, surprising Rube, who'd anticipated walking back to camp on his own, although he'd been wondering how to address the problem of leaving Gilda alone, which seemed rather rude. He'd had no cause for concern, however. Rosie had had other plans from the outset.

'Let's eat,' she said, 'I'm told they make an excellent stew here.' To Rosie the business part of the night was over; she'd transported her new protector to sexual heights as planned and she was ravenous.

They relished their meal, all four, dunking hunks of bread into steaming bowls of stewed mutton and gravy and vegetables, chatting away about the travels that lay in store as if they were already old friends. Rube noticed that Carlo seemed as much preoccupied with Rosie as with the stew, but he made no comment, the reason being glaringly obvious.

During the walk back to camp, too, he made no comment, hoping that Carlo wouldn't go on about sex the way he so often did when he'd made a conquest. Rube simply wasn't interested.

But Carlo didn't go on, because this time, unlike his customary sexual encounters, the conquest had not been his at all. It had been Rosie's.

Carlo had never had sex like that before. He'd never been so transported. She'd played his body like a musical instrument. In fact, just the way he liked to play a woman's body, tantalisingly, provocatively, employing every means possible to prolong the ecstasy. Rosie had been in total control throughout, and already Carlo was lost.

Their trysts became a regular routine throughout the circus's two-week run at Wagga, but Rosie never allowed him to stay the night, even when he begged her to let him book another room. 'Just for the two of us,' he'd say.

'A waste of money,' she'd reply dismissively.

Rube would occasionally join them on the trip into town, chatting in the lounge with Gilda, whose company he very much enjoyed, then tucking into the hotel's hearty stew when the others returned. The general talk over their meal was always relaxed and convivial, with no hint of the lustful passion that had been aroused in one of the nearby hotel rooms. During the walk back to camp, however, Rube would have to put up with Carlo's ravings, which far from being boasts of his sexual prowess as they had been in the past, had now become earnest professions of 'love', which Rube found a little worrying. It appeared very obvious to him that Carlo was being manipulated. *But so what*, he told himself, *no point in saying anything. He'll find out soon enough.*

Rube put the thought aside. Besides, he'd discovered something else to occupy his mind, something unbelievably exciting. Wagga Wagga had just opened its own free public library. To Rube, nothing could have been more thrilling; he hadn't even known such places existed. He joined up immediately and took out a copy of the collected plays of William Shakespeare, thus embarking upon a love affair of his own.

'Do you know how Wagga Wagga got its name?' Carlo asked.

He and Rosie were looking out over the pristine waters of the Murrumbidgee River, the surrounding vegetation lush and green, the Riverina landscape splendid in the spring. They'd just completed their respective late-morning shows, and after sharing a picnic lunch with Rube and Gilda as they often did, Carlo had suggested a walk down to the river. He'd joked that they needed to escape yet another reading of Rube's from his precious book of Shakespeare, but that was only an excuse. Carlo relished any possible opportunity to be alone with Rosie, to woo her as the true lover he'd become in less than two weeks. She was everything he wanted in a woman.

'Wagga Wagga?' she queried with an enigmatic smile; it was always impossible to know what Rosie was thinking. 'No idea whatsoever, do tell me.'

'It's a Wiradjuri word, "wagga",' Carlo said. 'They're the local Aboriginal people from around these parts,' he explained, 'and "wagga" means "crow" in their language.'

'Really?' She appeared fascinated.

'Yep, that's right. And there are lots of crows around here, so they double up on the word, you see – Wagga Wagga – that means "place of many crows", or "meeting-place of crows". I bet most people don't know that.'

'Well, *I* certainly didn't,' she said. 'How very interesting. Where did you learn all this?'

'Oh, I read it somewhere,' he replied airily. He hadn't. Carlo rarely read anything, books and even newspapers being strictly Rube's realm. He'd heard about it from Dodger. Dodger was so happy to be back in the town of his childhood that he'd gone on about Wagga to anyone who'd listen. Under normal circumstances, Carlo would have been his least appreciative audience, but circumstances were no longer normal. Carlo had been extremely attentive.

'I'm most impressed,' Rosie said.

They were the words he longed to hear. He so wanted to impress her.

She turned to him, her face raised invitingly, and when he kissed her she returned the kiss with such tender affection his love overwhelmed him. He was also very quickly aroused, but the moment his erection became obvious, she withdrew from the embrace. Still gently, caringly.

'No, no,' she said, 'not here, not now . . . We'll wait for tonight.'

Her kiss had been a reward. *He's mine*, she thought, *he's smitten and behaving like a lovesick fool.*

Rosie was pleased. Everything was going according to plan.

7

CARLO, ROSIE, RUBE AND GILDA

When the circus tour came to an end three months later, there was no pain of parting, nor was there any agony of decision-making. The die had been cast.

'You're such a wonderful showman, Carlo,' Rosie had said. 'A natural-born talent like yours belongs in the theatre!'

Looking on, both Rube and Gilda had wondered whether she recalled these were virtually the same words she'd said when the four of them had first met. They'd both wondered, too, why she considered it necessary to say them. Carlo would do anything she wished; he needed no flattery.

But this time Rosie was actually being genuine in her praise. If Carlo were to join forces with The Fairweather Sisters, he would serve a far greater purpose than that of mere protector. They would incorporate him in the act. With his skills as a showman, he could woo any audience he chose; Rosie sincerely admired a talent like that.

Given the spell she had cast over him, it was no great surprise Carlo was prepared to leave the boxing troupe and embrace a whole new world of show business. But it was somewhat of a surprise that Rube was quite happy to follow suit.

Carlo was of course delighted; he hadn't relished the prospect of a life without Rube. And he openly displayed his delight to Rosie when she voiced her misgivings, saying in that remote, cold manner of hers that they surely didn't need an extra team member.

'Oh, just you wait, love,' he'd eagerly replied. 'Rube'll be of real value, I can promise. Rube's clever. He'll be the brains, you'll see.'

Rosie had remained displeased and didn't even bother to hide the fact. Rube's decision had taken her totally by surprise. They didn't need 'The Kid'; he'd be intrusive. She'd naturally presumed they'd be leaving him behind.

Gilda hadn't been in the least surprised.

'Oh, you won't break that pair up,' she'd said, which further displeased Rosie.

A fact of which none was aware, even Carlo, was that Rube had no problem at all abandoning the boxing troupe. He didn't even particularly like fighting, he never had. There was no killer instinct in him, no desire to do harm to his opponent; he simply responded to the challenge on offer. He enjoyed the tactics a fight involved, he enjoyed testing himself, focusing upon his opponent, and the bigger the better, which he supposed meant he was at least competitive. He liked to win. The same way he liked to win a game of chess. A self-taught player, he invariably bested an opponent he met across a chessboard too. In fact, to Rube, life was rather like a chessboard, every game presenting fresh possibilities; a new move, a surprising twist up ahead, a different way of looking at things . . .

'I think we should incorporate Vasily in the act a whole lot more than we do,' Rube said. 'The man's a virtuoso.' Even as he spoke, a further idea occurred. 'We could title him on the bill, "The Fairweather Sisters, accompanied by Vasily the Violin Virtuoso". Dress him up showy and give him an opening solo. Very classy. You could double the length of the act all over again and ask for double the money.'

They were nearing the end of their four-month tour
with *Hayden Barron's Big Show Burlesque*, having played
to good houses at the Opera House in Melbourne before
going out on the road. The Fairweather Sisters act was
already nearly double its original length given Carlo's
role as Master of Ceremonies, in which he introduced
himself, told the audience of the sisters' exotic history, and
made regular appearances throughout their performance,
weaving stories of the mystical background that related to
each of their dances. All was jargon and all performed with
Carlo's customary verve and charm. Their fee had been
upped accordingly, and Rosie had learnt to listen to Rube.
It had been Rube, after all, who had written the material,
and he seemed so eerily capable of speaking with Carlo's
voice. Rosie recognised that 'The Kid' was indeed clever,
which made him of use, although it didn't mean she liked
him any the more. She found his presence more intrusive
than ever, aware that the power she held over Carlo and
Gilda did not apply to Rube.

They signed on for another tour with Hayden Barron's
company the following spring, this time in partnership with a minstrel production, and the new act they'd
rehearsed now headed the bill in the burlesque half of the
show. Vasily the Violin Virtuoso was highlighted with an
opening solo as planned. Dressed to the nines in a crimson,
brass-buttoned jacket and illuminated by a limelight spot,
the little Russian made no objection. He just stood there
and played, his mind somewhere else, as it always was
from the moment his bow drew its first note. When his solo
had received its rightful and healthy round of applause, he
would quietly retire to the wings from where he would
play unseen until he reappeared for the final curtain call.

And there was a further change to the act. At Rube's
suggestion Carlo now joined the sisters in a duet. He was
a natural dancer, moving with grace but also command,

and as he held his arms out from one to the other, drawing them to him, it appeared the two were vying for his favour. Then, during the finale he stood at the rear of the stage watching them, motionless, a remote and inaccessible figure, as if his mere presence were forcing the women's passion to feed upon each other. The mixture of power and voyeurism was extremely effective.

'It gives a sort of story to the act,' Rube had suggested to Rosie and Gilda. 'Carlo becomes something of a puppeteer. He could be a hero or a villain, up to the audience to decide . . .' Rube had started to get carried away at that point and had gone one step further. 'We could even change the name of the act,' he said. 'Instead of being The Fairweather Sisters you could be Rosie Krantz and Gilda Stern.'

There were blank looks all round.

'What the hell does *that* mean?' Carlo demanded.

'It's a play on words,' Rube explained, 'or rather names. We're making the act classier, so we give the audience something to think about.' More blank looks. 'You know,' he prompted, 'Rosencrantz and Guildenstern.'

'And who the hell are *they*?' Carlo once again, the women remaining silent.

'Who *were* they more like – they were Hamlet's mates. Hamlet was the dominating power in their lives. Now that could *really* add to the story . . .' Rube was suddenly carried away by the potential of such a breakthrough idea. 'At the end of the dance, you could actually *be* Hamlet, Carlo.'

'Hamlet who?'

'*Hamlet!* By William Shakespeare.' Rube looked from one to the other, finally taking in the blank expressions of all three. 'Don't you get it? The names! Rosie and Gilda . . .' His voice petered out; he knew he'd become overexcited. 'Never mind.'

By the end of the tour, Rube's ideas had become more grandiose and more far-reaching than ever. Young Marten Reubens had discovered in himself a relish for show business. And he was ambitious. Show business, to Rube, had become the ultimate chess game.

'We should form our own company,' he declared.

Rosie was dubious at first. It seemed to her that Rube was gaining far too much control; she was not accustomed to others taking over her life.

'It makes sense, love,' Carlo cajoled. 'Rube and I intended to start our own boxing troupe anyway, and we've saved a lot of dough between us. We'll put the money into burlesque instead.'

Given the boys were footing the expenses, Rosie quickly acquiesced, although she did wish he'd stop calling her 'love'. Yes, they shared a room when they were on tour, and yes, they were lovers, but that didn't mean he could treat her as if she were his *wife*. Rosie Marks was nobody's *wife*.

'*Carlo and Rube's Big Show Bonanza!*'

Carlo was the one who came up with the name.

Rube didn't find it particularly original himself, 'Big Show' having been nicked from Hayden Barron and 'Bonanza' having been nicked from Barney O'Banyon, but it had a certain ring to it so he didn't mind.

Rosie did. Rosie was piqued that The Fairweather Sisters didn't come in for a mention.

'It's just a producers' name, love,' Carlo assured her. 'You'll be heading the bill, I can promise you.'

Rosie had to be satisfied with that, which she supposed was only fair.

They had no trouble finding acts willing to sign up, many being performers they'd worked with before, some only recently. Friedrich and Sonya, a married couple who swallowed swords, came directly from *Hayden Barron's*

Big Show Burlesque, as did Bella with her team of trained dogs, and the Pinkingtons: mother, father and six young children who harmonised a cappella.

There were other acts with whom Rosie and Gilda had worked in the past: Goliath the strongman and his wife, Vesuvia; a ventriloquist called Ivan; Susannah, a young soubrette who warbled winningly; and Madame Katarina, a thickly accented European clairvoyant who insisted upon being as mysterious offstage as she was on.

Along with a small band of musicians numbering six in all, there were only two new acts that none of them knew, and both passed the test of audition. One was an Aboriginal snake handler called Jimmy, who wore a turban and billed himself as 'Abdul', and another was a mild-mannered gentleman called William Downes, proudly boasting 'two acts for the price of one'.

William, who billed himself as 'Blow Me Downes', was both a farter (although he preferred the term 'flatulist') and a belcher, and had proved hugely popular in the large outback towns of Victoria. William had extraordinary control of his sphincter muscles, bowel and intestinal wind and, splendidly attired in evening dress, would fart animal noises; mice and dogs and lions, squeaks and barks and growls of every description; birds too, the cackle of a kookaburra, the screech of a cockie, the mournful cry of a crow. But his true triumph was the finale, when he would fart 'The Blue Danube', during which people would rise to their feet and waltz in the aisles. A little later in the programme, when he made his return to the stage to perform his belching act, demonstrating again extraordinary control, this time of his stomach, lungs and oesophageal muscles, his finale would invite a standing ovation, as he wisely chose to belch 'God Save the Queen'.

Carlo and Rube's Big Show Bonanza now had its full complement of performers, and rehearsals commenced,

Carlo playing Master of Ceremonies throughout, Rube
plotting the sequence of the programme and generally
taking on the role of director, while also confirming theatre
bookings, designing posters and organising advance men.
This was the chess game Rube so enjoyed.

They rehearsed in Melbourne before taking to the
road. After a six-month tour, during which any kinks
in the show would be ironed out, they would return to
Melbourne, for a season once again at the Opera House
in Bourke Street, which specialised in burlesque and where
they were known.

The fact that Carlo and Rube considered Melbourne
their home base was another factor that irked Rosie, to
whom Sydney had always been home. But when she tried
to raise any form of objection she was quickly howled
down.

'Oh no,' Rube stated categorically, 'Melbourne's the
mecca when it comes to theatre, no doubt about that. We
have to base ourselves here.'

'He's right, love,' Carlo said.

Rosie wanted to kill them both. She also wanted to kill
Gilda.

'I don't care,' Gilda had said with a shrug when she'd
tried to get her on side. 'I don't mind where we live.'

What was happening, Rosie wondered, why was her
life getting so out of hand? Rube appeared to have total
control with Carlo's full approval and Gilda didn't care!
What's happened to my *say in things*, Rosie fumed.

The four of them planned to share rooms as couples
throughout the tour, just as they had during their previous
tours with Hayden Barron. It was cheaper that way, and
less complicated, everyone presuming they were married.
Rube and Gilda didn't mind; there were always two beds in
the room, and they'd become very good friends. Although
in the early days, there had been some awkwardness.

Particularly on one occasion when Rube had found Gilda's honest, forthright manner, which he'd come to so admire, extremely confronting.

It had happened a full month into their first tour with *Hayden Barron's Big Show Burlesque*, on a very cold night when she'd climbed into bed with him.

'Let's share a bit of body warmth, Rube,' she'd said. 'It's bloody freezing and there aren't any more blankets, I've looked in the cupboards.'

Gilda was making no sexual overture; she knew he wasn't interested. But she had felt his body tense at the mere nearness of her.

'Relax, sweetie,' she said, snuggling up to him, 'just relax.'

He remained frozen, unable to move.

Aware he found the situation uncomfortable, Gilda nonetheless refused to give up, rolling over on her side instead and placing her back to him. 'Cuddle up to me, Rube, come on now,' she urged. 'For God's sake, let's try and get warm.'

He did his best to obey. He, too, rolled on his side, facing the lacy neck of her nightgown and the tumble of fair hair that was vaguely visible in the light from the street gas lamp that shone through the chink in the cheap curtains of the hotel window. But he couldn't 'cuddle up'. Given the narrowness of the bed, their bodies were virtually touching anyway, but he simply couldn't bring himself to make any further contact with her.

'All right,' she said good-naturedly, 'better than nothing I suppose, we'll leave it at that. Now go to sleep.' He could hear the smile in her voice as she added, 'And don't worry, Rube, your secret's safe with me, it always has been.'

But sleep was impossible for Rube. He lay there in that threatening bed with that threatening body in its threatening proximity, every muscle in his body tense. He sensed through her breathing that she was drifting off, and when he was certain she was asleep, he very cautiously rolled onto his back, creating what little space he could between them, and stared up into the gloom, trying to pretend she wasn't there. But he couldn't pretend he hadn't heard her words.

'Your secret's safe with me, it always has been ...' And she'd said it with such humour, such candour, as if they shared some special confidence. What exactly did she mean? Was she intimating he was homosexual? Had she presumed this was why he was not sexually interested in women? But that wasn't so. Was it? He'd known for the whole of his life that he was not a lover of women, not physically, although many women he liked and admired, Gilda being one. But he'd also known for the whole of his life that he was different.

Gilda had unwittingly raised the spectre that had once bothered Rube. In the early days, when Carlo had constantly nagged and teased him about his lack of interest in women, he'd wondered whether it really was a matter for concern. Was there perhaps something unnatural about him? Could he perhaps be homosexual?

He'd even put it to the test once. A man had made advances towards him, strangely enough a boxer in Paddy O'Donnell's troupe, which at the time, and his being only sixteen, Rube had found further cause for worry. Had the man sensed something in him that he'd been so emboldened to reveal himself? The practice of homosexuality was a criminal act.

Rube had reluctantly agreed to a liaison with the man, who'd wanted to bugger him, but he hadn't allowed it. The man had not dared become aggressive, knowing only too well the baby-faced lad's skills with his fists, and the event had proved little more than a mutual masturbatory exercise, which had left Rube with no desire to repeat the experience simply for the sake of sexual gratification.

He'd felt wrong afterwards, even a little sordid. He'd deduced, therefore, that he must be asexual. He'd read that term somewhere. Neither women nor men interested him sexually. The sexual act itself held no interest for him, he'd further decided, unless perhaps love was involved. If there was love, he'd thought, then perhaps things might be different. Which, he'd determined, made him a romantic. Having come to that conclusion, Rube had been quite happy to remain asexual. And now Gilda had reawakened his uncertainty. If she was so sure there was a 'secret', then there must be something wrong with him. Rube felt distinctly unsettled.

The following morning, Gilda jumped out of bed, grabbing her small bag of toiletry items and struggling into her robe.

'Race you to the bathroom,' she said as she always did, the bathroom invariably being down the hall and invariably involving a queue if the pub was a busy one. It was an ongoing joke; Rube always let her go first, and she knew that more often than not, he used the chamber pot that sat beneath one of the beds.

When he didn't answer, she looked back at him, and realised in an instant that she'd made a mistake. He was sitting up on the bed, obviously self-conscious, and she could tell he was avoiding meeting her eyes.

Oh hell, she thought, *what did I say? What the hell did I say?* That's right, she remembered. 'Your secret's safe with me,' that's what she'd said, but she'd been joking, didn't he realise that?

Her bladder felt about to burst, but she could hold on, she decided, and she sat on her own bed, a safe distance between them, cursing the fact that she might have threatened their comfortable relationship. She and Rube were akin to brother and sister; the siblings, as they'd agreed, neither of them had ever had.

'Sorry, Rube,' she said, the comment sounding casual, but signalling her sincerity nonetheless. There was no point in lengthy discussion. 'I was making a joke, that's all.'

'Yes.' He looked at her and smiled. He felt no animosity. The fact that he questioned himself was hardly Gilda's fault, was it? 'Yes,' he said, 'I know you were.'

No, Gilda thought, *you don't really know, Rube. There's a whole lot you don't know. Oh my dear, dear friend, I know you better than you know yourself.*

She returned the smile with a wealth of affection. 'You're not alone, Rube. You and I are a whole lot more alike than you think,' she said, 'believe me, we are. And one day I might just tell you.'

Then she jumped to her feet. 'In the meantime, I'm busting. I'll leave you to the chamber pot. And no more bed cuddles from now on, I promise,' she called over her shoulder as she rushed from the room, praying the bathroom queue wouldn't be too long.

The subject, whatever it may have been as Rube sometimes wondered, was not alluded to again and they reverted to their comfortable 'sibling' relationship. The sharing of a room was never a problem, and their friendly 'goodnights' were often exchanged over the clearly audible sexual pounding of Carlo and Rosie from the room next door when the walls were thin, which, unlike the solid stone walls of the pubs, was quite common in the cheaper boarding houses.

Oh, how Rosie envied Gilda her celibate existence.

Like all first 'out of town' runs, particularly those of a newly formed theatrical company, the tour had its ups and downs in the early days.

Bella's team of trained dogs, miniature poodles all six, were highly intelligent but also highly neurotic, and they did not take kindly to Jimmy's snakes. The mere sight of the reptiles in their wire travelling cage was enough. Five of the poodles would back off whimpering to cower behind Bella's skirts, while the leader of the team, a male called Rolf, would front up to the cage barking incessantly, obviously considering the creatures a personal threat. Rolf's barking would in turn unsettle the snakes, and the whole situation threatened to become a terrible state of affairs. It appeared, under such circumstances, Bella had no control over her dogs.

But Jimmy fortunately did. Jimmy had a way with all animals. Which was just as well. He quickly befriended Rolf and, once he'd gained the dog's trust, introduced him to the largest of the snakes, a harmless green tree python called Clara. As Clara slithered all over Jimmy, the dog watched on, more fascinated than threatened. If the snake was no threat to his new 'boss', then surely the snake was no threat to him. And with the team leader no longer panicked, the other dogs fell immediately into line. For Jimmy, the situation was easily remedied.

Bella was grateful. Or rather she was thankful. But as Rolf kept seeking out his new best friend, she decided, deep down, that she didn't really like Jimmy. They were *her* dogs, weren't they?

There was a further unspoken clash of personalities, this time involving Susannah, who was twenty-two years old and exceedingly pretty, as most soubrettes were, given the flirtatious roles they were called upon to play or to sing. Susannah's songs were decidedly saucy, and her bouncy curls and even bouncier body served her well.

From the earliest days of rehearsal, it had been obvious Susannah found Carlo extremely attractive. Most women did, so this was not surprising, but as Carlo was married to Rosie, or at least appeared to be, most women tended to observe a certain distance. Susannah was not most women. Whenever she was in his presence, and she contrived to be

so as often as possible, Susannah's curls and body bounced
in an ever-livelier fashion. The way, too, that she 'sang'
her greetings and farewells in girlish falsetto was downright suggestive.

'Good morning, Carlo,' might well have been 'I'm all
yours, Carlo.' And 'Good night, Carlo,' sounded very like
'Come to my bed, Carlo.'

Needless to say, Rosie detested Susannah. For God's
sake, what *was* it about soubrettes!

Rosie never allowed her animosity to show, however – it
would have been beneath her dignity to do so, and besides
she knew she had no cause for concern. Carlo was aware
of Susannah's infatuation certainly, and he responded
in the flirtatious manner his nature demanded he must,
but it was obvious to all he had eyes only for Rosie. Her
dignity thus remained intact, but it didn't stop her despis-
ing Susannah, and before the show even hit the road, she
contrived to rid herself of the irksome girl.

'I'm wondering, Rube,' she said thoughtfully, 'whether
we might not be a little top-heavy on the musical side.'

They were nearing the end of the rehearsal period and,
as now was the time to make any last-minute refinements
to the production, she'd sought him out personally.

'Oh? In what way?' Rube was always willing to listen to
Rosie's ideas; she had a great knowledge of show business.

'Well,' she said, still pensive, still appearing to mull over
her thoughts, 'we open with a solo from Vasily, and we
feature him again during our dance . . .' She was ticking
off the events with her fingertips. 'We have musical accom-
paniment from the band throughout most of the acts,
and then there's also the Pinkington family's harmony.
I'm wondering whether we really need the vocal talents
of Susannah. Besides which,' she added decisively, giving
her argument the final clinching comment, 'I think the
soubrette act is rather weak.'

'Ah . . .' It was Rube's turn to mull over his thoughts. She'd taken him very much by surprise – he hadn't considered Susannah's act weak at all – but he mentally went through the programme, visualising each act in turn. And as he did, he recognised one element that would be missing if they rid themselves of the soubrette. 'No,' he said finally, 'I'm afraid I can't agree with you on this one, Rosie.'

'Why is that?'

Rube didn't hear the acid-like tone that had crept into her voice. Or if he did, he was so accustomed to its timbre, he didn't relate it to their current conversation.

'Susannah's very pretty and she's very young,' he said. 'We'd miss that element if she left. The show's a bit short on youth as it is.'

The comment did not go down at all well.

Of even greater significance to Rosie was her realisation that from a practical perspective Rube was quite right, which meant she was left with no possible rejoinder. To argue the case would be to give away her personal feelings, which she had determined would remain secret. But she was now further alienated from both Susannah and Rube. *That moll of a soubrette*, she seethed, *and that homosexual pervert!* How she detested them. And she was shortly to be out on the road in their company for a whole six months!

'You do not vorry for your man,' Madame Katarina the clairvoyant muttered in an aside to her barely a week later, on the very last day of rehearsal. 'He loff only you. For the girl, *pooph*,' a dismissive wave of her hand, 'he haff no interest. Never he vill.'

'I don't know what you're talking about,' Rosie said coldly.

Madame Katarina was another of whom Rosie was not particularly fond, but then with the exception of Gilda there were few who had ever held a place in her affections. She had no reason to actively dislike the woman, apart from the fact that she didn't understand her, and Rosie didn't like any*one* or any*thing* she didn't understand. Rosie was accustomed to reading and manipulating, to her own advantage, every person and every situation that confronted her.

In truth, Madame Katarina was a mystery to them all. A pleasant enough woman in her forties, dark-haired, hooded-eyed, no one knew how her clairvoyance proved so successful. Unlike most mystics, she employed no assistant to act as an 'accomplice' and when she called a volunteer up onstage, holding her hands out before them, feeling their 'aura' and hearing her 'inner voice', her revelations of their past were more often than not correct. To the point where, on occasion, the subject was even reduced to a state of hysteria. Where were her tricks? And a further mystery, no one knew where Madame Katarina came from. Despite her name, she was not Russian, and her abominable accent offered no clue. Even Vasily, who spoke several languages, couldn't hazard a guess as to her ancestry. She never spoke of her background and no one asked her directly – show business folk did not pry – but every now and then, for no apparent reason, she would offer a word of well-meaning advice. This was just such an occasion.

'He vill vish to marry you,' she went on, unperturbed by the coldness of her reception. Katarina had been visited just the previous night by her inner voice, and she believed that Rosie deserved to know the truth. 'He vill vant also for you to bear his child.'

Rosie was outraged. How dare Carlo talk about her behind her back. 'What's he been saying? Who's he been talking to? Who told you such a thing?' she demanded.

'He say no thing, he talk no one. Is my voice, it tell me.'

'I see.' Rosie refused to be mollified; the woman was a charlatan out to impress, and she would have none of it. 'Then I suggest you tell your voice to mind its own business.'

Katarina shrugged, still unperturbed. Some were believers, some were not; it mattered little to her. 'Very vell,' she said, infuriatingly unruffled, 'you vait, you vill see, time vill tell.'

Only days later, they were out on the road and the hard slog had begun. Town after town, show after show, playing small halls and huge theatres alike, adapting wherever they went as all tours must.

The reviews were praiseworthy: 'There is entertainment for one and all, young and old alike, in *Carlo and Rube's Big Show Bonanza*' ... 'An amusingly vivacious brand-new burlesque, deftly hosted throughout by the charismatic Mr Carlo himself . . .' Word passed along, audiences flocked and business was good. Carlo and Rube loved every minute of it. Their very own company, just fancy that. They'd discovered their true metier. They were slaves to no one.

'Better than dancing to someone else's tune,' Rube said, and Carlo agreed wholeheartedly. This was where he belonged. An orphan from the East End of London starring in his very own show! What more could a man want?

But as the tour progressed, Carlo discovered there *was* something else he wanted, something he had never before considered and that he now suddenly longed for. A wife, and a son to bear his name. Why not? Now was the time. He would shortly turn twenty-eight years of age, and already he had the woman he wished to be his wife.

He chose the last performance of the tour to make his declaration. They'd played to a packed house and during the company's final curtain calls, of which there'd been many, they'd received a standing ovation. Tomorrow they would embark upon the trek back to Melbourne to prepare for their season at the Opera House where, according to Rube, the advance bookings were excellent. The timing was perfect, Carlo decided.

As the curtain closed on their final company bow, he took her hand and turned to her.

'Let's get married, Rosie,' he said, and he dropped theatrically to one knee, oblivious to who might be watching. 'This is a formal proposal, my love,' he declared with his customary flair. 'Will you do me the honour of becoming my wife?'

'Oh, for God's sake, get up!' Rosie hissed.

The performers were dispersing to return to their dressing rooms, and she could see from the other side of the stage the 'I-told-you-so' look from Madame Katarina, who remained motionless, staring at them.

'I said get up,' she hissed again as Carlo, still on one knee, kissed her hand.

He obligingly jumped to his feet, his grin showing he was not in the least offended.

'We're as good as married anyway, love,' he said reasonably, 'we might as well make it legal.' *It'll be better for the child if we're legally married*, he thought, but he wouldn't mention his desire for a son. Not just yet. Rosie could turn surprisingly cantankerous if she thought someone was planning her life. She liked her independence, and he admired her for that.

'So what do you say?' He drew her close, his smile at its most devilishly winning. 'Shall we tie the knot when we get back to Melbourne?'

'We'll talk about it at the end of the season,' she said.

'An excellent idea.' Her reply was as good as a 'yes' to Carlo. He was content to wait.

He's become far too cloying, Rosie thought. She was heartily sick of him by now and had been for quite some time; she did so dislike sentimentality. She would leave him at the end of the season.

*

The Opera House opening was a splendid affair. Word had preceded them, Rube had wooed the press, and audiences and critics alike were not left wanting.

'A refreshing new show under a refreshing new banner,' the *Melbourne Advertiser* declared. 'We have no doubt this popular burlesque entertainment, which is of the highest calibre, will prove pleasing to audiences.' And after singling out a number of the various acts, most particularly The Fairweather Sisters, the critic went on to proclaim: 'Theatre producers beware, Messrs Rube and Carlo have joined your ranks and are destined to become a force to be reckoned with.'

Carlo and Rube raised their tumblers; fine imported Scotch whisky, what's more, not the local-made variety that came from Ballarat.

'This is just the beginning,' Rube said, and the two of them clinked glasses. They'd rented a house in Carlton for the Melbourne run, and were now in the kitchen sitting up late and gloating over the review that promised to be the making of them, Rosie and Gilda having retired for the night.

'To the beginning,' Carlo toasted, thinking of the many beginnings he now anticipated. Marriage to Rosie. A son to bear his name. Life simply could not be better, he told himself as he swigged back the fine Scotch, vaguely aware that he actually preferred ale.

But as things turned out, Rosie refused to marry him. Even under circumstances that appeared not only propitious but eminently practical, she refused to budge on the matter.

Towards the end of the season when, as planned, he revisited the subject of matrimony, she seemed not to hear him. She had news of her own, and whatever he had to say was of no interest to her.

'I'm pregnant,' she snarled.

Despite her obvious ill-temper, Carlo could not disguise his delight. 'But that's splendid news,' he said, gathering her in his arms and spinning her about the room. 'Oh Rosie, love, that's absolutely splendid news, and all the more reason to marry . . .'

'No, it's not,' she growled ominously, breaking free of him. 'It's not splendid news at all, and it's certainly no reason to marry.'

He ignored her mood, choosing instead to rejoice in the fact he was to become a father. Rosie had always been mercurial; difficult to fathom and even more difficult to please, she'd come around to marriage once she'd had the child.

Rosie had been furious to discover she was pregnant. How had she allowed this to happen? She'd always taken such care. She couldn't remember a time when she'd allowed a man to ejaculate inside her. Well, there was just that once, but she'd been very young and it had been a case of rape, impossible to avoid. The perpetrator had been her stepfather, but her mother hadn't believed her, which she supposed in one way or another had set her on her life's trajectory. And in becoming an expert at her chosen trade, she'd been most adept at eluding the greatest threat of all. She would bring a man to the very brink, then manipulate her body to avoid the final moment of ejaculation. It had always worked. But not this time apparently. This time, somehow, she'd been caught out. Carlo was to blame, and she loathed him for it.

She had, of course, discussed her predicament with Gilda, as she always did, Gilda being the only person in whom she ever confided.

'I'm going to have an abortion,' she declared.

'How far gone are you?'

'I don't know, I can't be sure, I haven't been keeping a close watch on my monthly times.' Rosie cursed herself;

she'd never been this complacent before. 'Two months at least, probably a little more.'

'Too late,' Gilda said briskly. 'Too late and too risky.'

'I won't opt for a back-street hatchet job by some old crone, if that's what you're worried about,' Rosie argued with a touch of desperation. 'I've heard there are doctors in East Melbourne who —'

'No, you won't, Rosie.' This was to be one of those rare times when Gilda took control, and she didn't mince her words. 'You won't have an abortion, it's far too dangerous. Doctors can botch things up too, you know. You could end up bleeding to death and your body found in some godforsaken back lane or floating in the Yarra. Doctors are ruthless,' she said, her voice harsh, condemnatory. 'Doctors aren't going to risk getting caught and going to gaol for the women they've mutilated.'

Rosie listened, aware that Gilda spoke from personal experience. Gilda herself had had an abortion that had nearly killed her, and at the hands of a doctor. She'd been sixteen years old, and upon discovery of her pregnancy her father had thrown her out onto the streets. Her lover had paid for the abortion, but when things had gone wrong he'd run off and left her.

'I nearly bled to death,' she'd told Rosie as they'd compared backgrounds all those years ago at the Beauchamp Gentlemen's Club, discovering that, along with the fact they were both double-jointed, they had so very much in common. 'He might have been a doctor,' Gilda had said scathingly, 'but he was a real butcher of a one, chopped me around good and proper. I'll never be able to have children.'

'Lucky you,' had been Rosie's caustic response, and they'd shared a hearty laugh, infertility being the ideal state of affairs for a working girl. Gilda hadn't admitted that she would rather have liked to have had a child.

'So what am I expected to do?' Rosie now demanded, more vulnerable than Gilda had ever seen her, but belligerent too, angered by her predicament.

'You'll tell Carlo, and you'll have the baby,' Gilda replied, decision made.

'I won't marry him,' Rosie countered, 'and I certainly won't stay with him.' Knowing she was cornered, she spat out the words with all the venom she could muster, and Rosie had plenty of venom to hand. 'He's destroyed my life, the bastard, he's ruined my body, he's —'

'We'll talk about all that after the child's born.' Gilda remained the one making the decisions, and they both knew it. 'You can't just run off and have a baby without any support. You need Carlo.'

The season at the Opera House was extended six weeks, by which time Rosie was definitely starting to show. She disguised the fact in her daily dress, and the costumes for The Fairweather Sisters act were adapted, a seamstress designing shifts to be worn beneath the gossamer so the shapes of the dancers' bodies were not visible. There was one person, however, who very clearly recognised Rosie's condition. And something else besides.

Madame Katarina signalled her knowledge not with an 'I-told-you-so' look this time, but rather with an expression of approval, as if the right decision had been made.

Rosie was unnerved. Did the woman know she had contemplated an abortion? Surely not.

But Katarina did. Her inner voice had been adamant. She'd known Rosie was pregnant before Rosie herself had, but she hadn't known whether Rosie would keep the child; her voice had been vague about that part.

For the rest of the season, Rosie refused to meet Madame Katarina's eyes. The woman was unsettling and her presence insufferable.

*

At the end of the run, when the company parted ways, Carlo, Rube, Rosie and Gilda bunkered down in the modest stone house in Carlton to await the birth of the child. There was a whole five months to go and Rosie loathed being cossetted. She also loathed being pregnant, seeing herself become more bloated and unsightly with each passing day. But the uglier she appeared in her own eyes the more beautiful she seemed to Carlo, who insisted she be waited upon hand and foot; nothing was to threaten the birth of his son.

Gilda took on the role of nursemaid, which further irritated Rosie, and Gilda prayed, as did Rube, that the child would be a boy. Carlo appeared unable to recognise the possibility of another gender.

While the others remained principally holed up in the house, Rube was out and about busily organising the next *Big Show Bonanza*. Given the fact they were steadily devouring their profits, they would need to partner up with another company this time, but there were funds enough for a half-share in production costs put aside in the tin trunk he kept under his bed. And besides, they now had a name. Following the success of their first production, other entrepreneurs were only too willing to join forces. Including their former employer, Hayden Barron, who, far from being offended by their use of his 'Big Show' slogan, considered it an asset they could put to good use.

'We give them two "Big Shows" for the price of one, Rube,' he eagerly suggested. 'What do you say? *Hayden Barron's Big Show Burlesque* in partnership with *Carlo and Rube's Big Show Bonanza*. Sounds darn good to me.'

It was certainly worthy of consideration, Rube thought, although they might reassess the billing.

Determined not to eat into the capital he'd stashed away, Rube sought employment utilising the other talent he had readily to hand. On Friday and Saturday nights he fought bare-fisted in a gambling den at the top of Lonsdale Street, Melbourne's red light district. Here men were pitted against each other like fighting cocks, others gathering around, laying bets and urging them on to the death.

Rube invariably won, but he often came home a little bloodied and with the telltale sign of bruised knuckles.

'What on earth happened to you?' Rosie would demand.

'Got into a fight,' he'd say.

Carlo, of course, guessed the truth and was grateful, but he said nothing, aware that Rube would prefer it that way.

In the meantime, Rosie saw her pregnancy through with gritted teeth, praying for the whole ghastly episode to be over.

And finally it was. The midwife, a highly experienced woman whom Carlo had lined up well in advance and to whom he paid a handsome fee as promised, delivered the child at the convenient time of five o'clock in the afternoon. The child was a boy.

Carlo was ecstatic, Gilda and Rube relieved, and Rosie thought, *Thank God that's done with*.

But as soon as she had recovered from the birth, and determined as she was it took her little time to do so, Rosie resolved to leave just as she'd planned. Barely two months later, she put her plan into action. The baby's arrival had aroused in her no maternal instinct; to the contrary she detested the infant. She did not want a child, she had never wanted a child, and she refused to be saddled with one. She was thirty-six years old and must utilise to her best advantage the relatively short time she had left.

Rosie's plans were clearly defined. Even at her age, admirers abounded, and she knew how to attract them. Gilda was the key. The two of them working together. The Fairweather Sisters' dance was a magnet to men, not only the hoi polloi but also the rich. She could literally feel the waves of lust as she and Gilda writhed together during

the final duet. And she could always pick the wealthy out
from the crowd, those in their well-cut suits of the finest
cloth, the same sort of men who frequented the Beauchamp Gentlemen's Club. Which one among them did not
fantasise about a *ménage à trois*? So? The right man for
the right price could *have* a *ménage à trois* if he wished.
And should the experience prove as breathtakingly erotic
as he'd hoped – and she and Gilda would ensure it was –
he could have a repeat performance whenever he wished.
Again, for the right price, of course. What man could resist
such an arrangement? Rosie's plan, in essence, was to find
a rich patron.

Gilda had no particular wish to leave. Happy with
her current life, she had no particular wish to pursue the
strategy Rosie intended either. She offered no resistance,
however, aware that Rosie had made up her mind and
that opposition would prove futile. She understood, too,
Rosie's need to disappear with no word of warning, no
form of goodbye. The parting from Carlo needed to be
brutal in its finality. That much was all too obvious.

But Gilda could not leave without farewelling Rube. She
pretended to Rosie it was all part of the plan.

'I can make sure Rube and Carlo are out of the house,'
she promised.

'How?'

'I'll tell Rube to come up with something, another
business appointment or whatever.'

'He'll want to know why, won't he?'

'Not if I choose not to tell him. Rube will do whatever
I ask.'

'Good.' Rosie shrugged. She didn't care one way or
another, so long as Carlo was out of the house.

Gilda waited until the night before their planned departure. She and Rosie had surreptitiously packed their bags
that afternoon while the men were gone, Carlo now

accompanying Rube on his many business meetings. Their cases were stashed under Gilda's bed, their coach tickets to Sydney booked and paid for, and a hackney carriage would pick them up at ten in the morning to take them to the Cobb & Co livery stables.

It was not particularly late, but the couples had retired for the night, Carlo and Rosie to the double bedroom with its little cot in the corner where the baby slept, Rube and Gilda to the other bedroom with its two single beds. The small cottage had only two bedrooms, so they shared as they had on tour.

'I have a favour to ask of you, Rube,' Gilda said.

They were already attired in their nightwear, she in her gown, he in his nightshirt, and Rube was surprised when she turned up the gas lamp in its wall bracket and perched on the edge of her bed.

'A favour?' he queried, sitting on his own bed. 'Of course, ask away.'

'I don't know if you have business to attend to in the morning, but if not, can you invent something and get Carlo out of the house?'

'Mind if I ask why?' Even as he made the query, Rube was sure he knew the answer.

'Rosie and I are leaving.'

'Yes.' He nodded, and Gilda could see he was not in the least surprised. 'I'll miss you,' he said.

'I'll miss you too,' she replied, 'very much.'

'Rosie won't be taking the baby, of course.' Rube was not asking a question; he knew the answer to this also.

Gilda didn't even reply, just the merest shake of her head.

'You don't *have* to go, Gilda,' he gently urged. 'I'd be happy to look after you. You don't have to go, really.'

'Oh yes I do, Rube,' she said, 'oh yes, I really do. Rosie's all I have, you see. Rosie's my whole world. Just as Carlo is yours.' She smiled. 'You remember a long time ago when I said you and I were a whole lot more alike than you think?'

'Yes.' He remembered quite clearly. He hadn't known what she meant then, and he didn't now.

She could tell that he didn't understand. Which was as it should be, she supposed. He had no idea. He probably never would. Her smile broadened fondly, and her tone was rather like that of a mother to a child. 'Well, take it from me, we are, my dear, we're more alike than you'll ever know.' *The only difference being the law does not perceive my love as illegal*, she thought. *Oh darling Rube, you'll love him until you die.*

'We'll be leaving at ten in the morning,' she said briskly, getting back to business before he had time to ponder further, 'so Carlo will need to be out of the house before then. But don't stay away too long because baby Michael will be left on his own.'

'Of course.'

She stood. 'I couldn't leave without saying goodbye to you, Rube, you've been such a fine friend to me.' She crossed the several steps to him and, bending down, took his face in her hands and kissed him on the lips, the gentle, chaste kiss of a sister. The goodbye was forever, both aware it was unlikely they would see each other again, and that even if their paths did cross, the relationship they'd shared was over. 'I couldn't leave also without saying I'm sorry,' she added in the most heartfelt fashion. 'I'm so very sorry.'

He wondered what she felt she should be so very sorry about – presumably leaving the child. Over these past two months, in her nursemaid capacity, her fondness for baby Michael had vastly exceeded that of the child's own mother.

'It's all right,' he assured her, 'we'll manage.'

'Bedtime,' she said, once again brisk, and crossing back to her bed, she reached up and turned off the gas lamp.

'But we saw Hayden only two days ago,' Carlo protested the following morning; he wanted to stay home and play with the baby. 'And we're not even sure if we're going to take up his offer.'

'He wants to see us again,' Rube said firmly. 'Our appointment is at ten.' Hayden Barron's office was exactly the right distance away, a good twenty-minute walk there and another twenty minutes back. Even if Hayden wasn't around, the timing would be perfect. It was just on half past nine.

They left ten minutes later.

Hayden was not there as it turned out. In fact, no one was there; the office was locked.

Rube insisted upon waiting for a good further ten minutes in case the man was running late, and when Hayden still didn't arrive, he shrugged good-naturedly.

'Probably my fault, I must have got the day wrong.'

Carlo grizzled all the way home, Rube attempting to placate him with comments upon the fine weather and what a pleasant morning it was for a stroll.

The baby was crying when they walked in the front door, and chaos instantly threatened.

Carlo raced into the bedroom, picked up the child and rocked it in his arms, his face livid at the sight of his son abandoned, crooning noises alternating with yells for Rosie.

Having followed close behind, Rube decided that brutality was the only option. Carlo was about to rage around the house, babe still in his arms, searching for the women.

'They're not here,' he barked.

'What?' Carlo halted abruptly.

'They've gone. They won't be coming back. Rosie's left you, Carlo.'

The moment seemed to freeze, the tone of his voice, the very weight of his words and their meaning irrevocable.

Carlo remained staring at Rube, both of them speechless, and as he did so he continued automatically to rock the whimpering baby cradled in his arms. Perhaps it was the motion, or perhaps the silence, or perhaps a mixture of the two, but the child stopped crying.

He looked down at the boy. So did Rube, and the moment was broken.

'We'll have to hire a nursemaid,' Rube said, grateful for some practical course of action he might take. 'I'll get onto that right now – we have money put aside.'

He dived from the room, thankful to get away if only for a minute or so and allow Carlo his privacy. In his own bedroom, he pulled the tin trunk out from under the bed and opened it. The money was gone.

So that's what Gilda had been 'so very sorry' about, he thought. Rosie would not have known the money was there. Gilda must have told her.

Rube couldn't bring himself to feel anger. Not towards Gilda. If anything, he felt pity rather than anger. Love was such a strong emotion, he thought. Poor Gilda. She'd do anything for Rosie.

He slowly walked back to the other bedroom where Carlo was sitting on the bed, his full focus on the baby whose tiny hand was wrapped fiercely around his little finger.

Rube sat beside him, watching the play between father and infant, finding the connection touching.

'The money's gone,' he said, but Carlo appeared not to hear him. 'We'll be all right, mate,' he continued with a heartiness he thought appropriate. 'Hayden Barron will put up the money for the co-production and we'll reimburse him out of the profits. We'll come back stronger than ever, you'll see.'

Still Carlo remained silent, his focus remaining on the baby, and they sat for a while longer. Then . . .

'She didn't love you, Carlo.' Rube felt compelled; he simply had to say it, he didn't know why.

Finally Carlo spoke. 'Yes, I think I knew that,' he said, 'I just didn't want to admit it.' An infinitesimal shrug. 'Pride probably.' He looked up, his eyes meeting Rube's at long last. 'I will marry, though, Rube,' he said. 'I have a son, and a son needs a mother.'

Rube was instantly heartened by the strength he saw in his friend's eyes. He grinned his baby-faced grin. 'Good. We'll find you a wife then. A mother for Michael.'

They'd come up with the name Michael between them, or rather it had been Rube's idea. Over the many years of their friendship they'd practically forgotten that Carlo's real name was Michael. It had seemed most appropriate.

They shared a smile. Rube was happy for Carlo. So very happy that Rosie hadn't destroyed him.

ACT II

8

AN UNEASY ALLIANCE
IS ENTERED INTO

Carlo and Rube had been around for years. Their *Big Show Bonanzas* were famous, but Uncle Will considered them decidedly 'old hat', despite the fact he'd never even been to one, which when you think about it isn't really fair. He pooh-poohed Aunt Mabel's suggestion of a possible partnership with Carlo and Rube, and very roundly, so I'm told. Called their shows 'burlesque of the lowest order', the sort with strip dances and dirty ditties and even 'farters' and 'belchers', both of whom he absolutely abhorred. Oh – digressing just a bit if you'll forgive me – Ma found farters and belchers ever so funny. Talented too, I might add.

'Truly, Em,' Ma would say to me when regaling her tales of yesteryear, as she so often did, 'you've no idea how much muscular control that would take. I mean, just think about it . . .' Then she'd burst into a fit of the giggles. 'And oh, lovey, talk about laugh!' When she'd calmed down, she'd give a sigh of regret. 'What a pity they don't have those sorts of acts these days, the world doesn't know what it's missing.'

Anyway, getting back to the matter at hand, Aunt Mabel was quite cross with Uncle Will for being so dismissive of *Carlo and Rube's Big Show Bonanzas* when he hadn't even seen one. She assured him there were no farters and belchers in their current show, which had recently opened in Melbourne to splendid reviews, and that he should darn well go and see for himself.

'They're massively popular,' she insisted. 'They've built up a huge following over the years, and if we joined forces with them we'd reach the broadest market we could possibly wish for.'

Much as Uncle Will always respected Aunt Mabel's opinion, it appeared he was going to dig his heels in nonetheless, and that's when Pa entered the fray. Max strongly disagreed with his brother, and this time he wasn't going to keep quiet about it. This time, what's more, he wasn't going to shy away from throwing Uncle Will's age-old dictum right back in his face.

'You've always maintained "it's the business of show where'er ye go", Will,' Pa firmly stated. 'That every audience should be served equally. "Give them what they're after and leave them wanting more," that's been your motto. And from what I hear, Carlo and Rube do exactly that, just as every good showman should.'

Apparently Uncle Will took offence at his theory of 'the business of show' being bandied about so disrespectfully. And never one to take kindly to criticism, he got huffy to the extreme.

'There is no need to play to the lowest common denominator, Max, in order to gain cheap applause,' he scorned haughtily, the way only Uncle Will could. 'Audiences need to be taught, otherwise they risk being left in the gutter. It's up to us to educate them!'

Well, that sort of hoity-toity response didn't go down at all well with the family, not according to Ma. And before anyone else could get a word in, it was she who piped up.

'There's no such thing as cheap applause. And what audience is going to applaud a snob anyway?'

That stopped Uncle Will dead in his tracks, and Pa and Aunt Mabel gave Ma her own round of applause. Ma really did have a way of summing things up at times.

Uncle Will was shocked by the inherent accusation in Ma's words, and also by the fact that it was Ma who'd said them.

I mean, little Gertie never criticised the great Will Worthing, and here she was all but calling him a snob. He didn't see himself as a snob, of course. A perfectionist, yes, but never a snob.

So you see it was Ma's intervention that put paid to the argument. (Oh dear me, she was proud of that!) Uncle Will was forced to go to Carlo and Rube's show just to prove he wasn't a snob. 'What a lark,' as Ma was wont to say.

This particular *Big Show Bonanza* of 1899 was currently performing at the Princess Theatre in Spring Street, which had just come under the sole management of George Musgrove, the previous 'Triumvirate' partnership of J. C. Williamson, Musgrove and Arthur Garner having dissolved earlier that same year. The Princess was destined to operate in a state of flux under a rapidly changing succession of lessees and owners over the next decade, which was possibly fortuitous for the likes of Carlo and Rube. At least that's what Uncle Will thought.

'That a magnificent theatre like the Princess is forced to stage such productions,' he lamented, 'when it should be home to grand opera and great drama . . . to Verdi, to Shakespeare . . .'

Uncle Will was still complaining the very night they went to the show, and in Ma's opinion still sounding like a snob. Didn't he remember he came from years of music hall and burlesque and variety? Didn't he realise there was a huge demand for such entertainment, indeed far greater demand than there was for opera and Shakespeare? Variety shows packed the grandest of Melbourne's theatres, didn't he know that?

When Ma expounded upon this topic – privately, of course, not in Uncle Will's hearing – Aunt Mabel stood up for her husband, and in the most motherly fashion.

'Oh Gertie,' she said, 'of course Will knows all that. He just so adores his Heavenly Tenor and his Shakespeare. Best we let him rant on, love.'

The whole family went to the show, every one of them, including all eight of the children, even little Bertie who was only four years old. The kids weren't going to miss out on a *Big Show Bonanza* – everyone knew what fun was in store.

Everyone except Uncle Will it seemed. But my goodness, was he about to change his tune! Oh dear – what a show! And that particular performance! Of all the performances the family could have chosen to attend, it had to be that one! My, oh my! The stuff of legend, I promise you. There was such a to-do about it in the press the next day that Uncle Will saved the clippings. They're in the scrapbooks, and they don't even relate to a Worthing production! Unbelievable! Uncle Will said at the time they belonged in the scrapbook as proof the family was present at an event that would make history in the theatrical world.

⌘

Will gazed about the auditorium of the magnificent Princess Theatre, one of the favourite theatres in which he'd performed; comic opera for the most part, *The Pirates of Penzance*, *The Mikado* ... Did this make him a snob? Of course not. Such performances required talent, that was all. One needed to know how to sing, how to project one's voice and one's presence. He simply preferred talent and professionalism to gimmickry and cheap tricks, which by no means made him a snob.

Will Worthing was offended by the inference he sensed from his family. It was totally undeserved.

They were seated in the front row of the dress circle, Mabel having insisted upon only the best, and for the whole twelve of them despite the cost.

'I want you to see the show from its best vantage point,' she'd stressed, 'so you can take in the quality of the staging and effects. Very important to gauge their expertise if we're to contemplate a partnership.'

Over my dead body, Will had thought.

The house lights started to fade as did the chatter that surrounded them. Every member of the Worthing family had been sitting quietly, even reverently, the children having inherited their elders' respect for the theatre, but those around them had been in the customary state of pre-show restlessness. Now, with darkness enveloping them, the audience fell silent, all focus upon the stage as the curtains parted.

From the orchestra pit, music swelled slowly. Romantic to start with, strings for the main part, and matching the swell of the music the stage lights gradually intensified to reveal a magical world. The painted backdrop was a colourful boulevard scene, al fresco cafés and diners and passers-by, very Parisian, and as the lights played upon the cloth, seeming to give it a motion all its own, the music grew accordingly, other instruments joining in, becoming busy and bustling. Before the audience's very eyes, the scene was coming to life.

The overall effect was extraordinary, the Princess Theatre being rightfully proud of its sophisticated, state-of-the-arts electrical stage lighting with its complex rig and adaptability.

Then, for no apparent reason, the stage lights went to black, leaving eyes momentarily fighting to adjust. The music however kept busily playing, and the audience was given little time to ponder upon whether there may have been a mishap as very quickly the backdrop became a blank screen, and all of a sudden they were looking at the real thing. A Parisian boulevard, diners at tables, people scurrying by. The colour was gone, the scene now black and white, but the audience was watching real, live action. There were gasps of wonderment followed by an immediate and spontaneous burst of applause.

Mabel and Will exchanged looks. While the eyes of others had been adjusting, they'd seen the exchange of backdrop and blank screen that had been operated from the flies, and they could now see quite clearly the position from where the bioscope projector was being operated, although others were currently too distracted to notice.

Mabel's look said 'clever', and the nod that accompanied it said 'excellent way to open the show'.

Will's look said 'effective, yes', and the shrug that accompanied it said 'gimmickry nonetheless'.

They returned their attention to the stage. They never spoke during a performance, not even in a whisper, considering it rude to the performers, but their looks invariably conveyed all they needed to say.

The Worthings had recently considered incorporating film in one of their own acts, having seen, at Harry Rickards' invitation, its first use by the magician Carl Hertz at The Tivoli only several years previously.

'It's bound to catch on,' Mabel had said. 'The audience went wild.'

But Will had been sceptical. 'Gimmickry,' he'd said, 'just fancy gimmickry.'

Even Harry himself had been dismissive, calling film a passing novelty. 'Who wants to see a flat picture when they can see the real thing?' he'd said.

Mabel hadn't been so sure at the time, and now, watching Carlo and Rube's use of the bioscope, she was having further thoughts.

The film, which lasted barely a minute, flickered to a halt, the blank screen disappeared, and when the stage lights once more came up the Parisian backdrop had been magically replaced with another, again flown in from high above by the hardworking stagehands. This one, gaudy and eye-catching, screamed its message loud and clear – 'CARLO AND RUBE'S BIG SHOW BONANZA' – and in smaller letters just below: 'Featuring Stars of the Southern Cross'.

Will found the sign's blatancy crass to the extreme. No style and no subtlety, just as he'd expected.

Then, a fanfare from the orchestra pit, and in the fierce glare of a follow spot, Carlo himself entered from the prompt side and strode to centre stage, holding his hand up in order to stem the immediate round of applause, while also graciously acknowledging the show of appreciation.

Top-hatted and smartly attired in black tailcoated evening dress, he welcomed the audience and introduced himself as 'Carlo, your host for the evening.' Then he doffed his top hat to the house and threw it into the wings, where it was no doubt deftly caught by a stagehand – he preferred to work bare-headed, hats tending to shadow the face – and went on to rave about the thrilling experience in store for those 'lucky enough to be here tonight'.

'A bonanza of extravaganza,' he enthused, 'a goldmine of entertainment, pure nuggets of the finest talent, featuring our own homegrown stars of the Southern Cross . . .' And he proceeded to list, with equal enthusiasm and in the most florid of terms, the various acts that were to follow.

Will watched in stunned amazement. This was surely the worst tack a Master of Ceremonies could take. The audience was already here; there was no call for a sales pitch. All that was needed was a quick showy intro to each act and then let the performance speak for itself. But even as he watched, Will very quickly realised he was wrong. Carlo was not just an MC. Carlo was anything but 'just an MC'. Carlo was an act in himself.

Will studied the man as he wooed the audience. There was no doubt he was talented, and a natural talent at that. *Always the best*, Will thought, *you can't beat natural talent*. The voice could possibly do with a little more depth, but it reached every corner of the theatre, nothing wrong with his vocal projection. And the man's looks, too – that was a big added bonus.

Carlo's looks surprised Will Worthing. The two had never actually met in person, which was not altogether surprising, Will distancing himself as he did from forms of theatre he'd ceased to find interesting. He'd seen pictures of the man in the newspapers though, and also on posters and leaflets, portrait shots mainly, taken for publicity purposes. A handsome man certainly, but he'd presumed the photographs were touched up; studios could do anything these days. Carlo was, however, even more handsome in the flesh, or so it appeared. Of course there was the stage lighting and the makeup, Will reminded himself, which would account also for the fact the man looked so much younger than one might have expected. He'd assumed Carlo was far older, having been in the business all the years he had, but the man's youthful figure and the vigour of his performance, how did he do it? The magic of the theatre naturally, there was always that, but ... *Good God*, Will thought, *he has to be over sixty*.

Carlo was actually forty-nine, just eight years older than Will himself. Will didn't know that, but he was soon to find out.

Following Carlo's opening performance, which thoroughly captivated the audience, the show progressed quickly and efficiently. Carlo ensured that it did, his introduction to each act brisk but colourful: a witty opening remark for a comedy routine ... a dramatic punchline for something spectacular ... a pertinent comment upon the strong or heroic ... Every act was given its due, not just with empty patter, but its own unique observation.

Good scripting, Will noted, wondering whether Carlo had written the material himself. If so, he thought with begrudging admiration, he'd have to add 'clever' to 'talented'; the man was actually rather impressive.

The overall show was slick, Will had to admit, although there seemed an over-abundance of comedy, much of it unnecessarily ribald and not to his taste. The audience loved it, however, his own children at times all but rolling in the aisle. And as for Gertie! Well, Gertie always adored gutter humour. He cast a sidelong glance at Max. Max too was enjoying much of the comedy, he could tell. No accounting for taste, he supposed.

There were animal acts too, which Will chose to ignore: three chimpanzees in costume behaving like humans, two of them smoking cigars, drinking ale and flirting with the other one dressed as a saucy girl; a bespangled young woman performing a contortionist routine on top of a llama that wandered dolefully around the stage; surely such acts belonged in a circus. But Carlo himself remained riveting throughout.

Then came the magician act, obviously the show's highlight.

'And now our *pièce de résistance* . . .' Carlo, alone in his follow spot, announced from centre stage. 'The Great Galdini, magician and illusionist extraordinaire, ably assisted by his wife, The Beautiful Cassandra.'

Being the *pièce de résistance*, the act obviously demanded no further introduction, and with a flourish Carlo retired to the wings.

As the magician pair bounded on accompanied by apposite music and lighting, the stage underwent a metamorphosis. Black tabs were flown in as a backdrop and a false proscenium arch appeared from nowhere, glittering panels on either side and an equally glittering overhead archway creating a stage within a stage, a magical world of its own.

The effect worked visually, but Will and Mabel exchanged yet another of their knowing glances. There would be a technical reason for such a reduction of performance space, and being a magician act it was no doubt the need for masking, probably during the illusionist's grande finale routine. Will and Mabel had seen it all before.

Once again Will closely studied the performance; magicians were naturally of great interest to him. Galdini's mime and sleight of hand were both excellent and the act polished, but to Will's mind the man wasn't as good as Max. He didn't have Max's personal connection with the audience, nor was he as graceful. But then few were. And any illusion he might choose to present could not possibly best that of the twins.

Artie and Alfie, now eighteen years old, still played the game they'd shared for the past decade, taking turns in who was to be the magician's assistant and who was to be the finale's reveal. No one outside the production knew there were Worthing twins, and those insiders privy to the fact never knew who was performing in which capacity on the night. The boys continued to enjoy the deception.

The Great Galdini's performance was coming to its conclusion and, as Will and Mabel had predicted in their one glance, the grande finale was to be an illusion of vast proportion. So vast, in fact, that it warranted the return of the show's master, Carlo himself, this being a unique experience demanding introduction.

'And now, ladies and gentlemen,' he proclaimed, a drumroll having heralded both his appearance and the import of his announcement, 'the *denouement* for which you have all been waiting . . .'

Will could sense a breathless anticipation; the audience obviously *was* aware of something about to happen, something that had been reported in the newspapers, or some word that had got around. Having only recently returned from tour, he was unacquainted with the latest local news. An excellent reaction, he thought, wondering what was about to ensue.

'The disappearing tiger!' Carlo declared. 'Everything you have read and heard of The Great Galdini's mastery is about to unfold before you, right here on this very stage . . . Behold!'

Another drumroll as he gestured to the OP side. All three of them gestured in unison – Carlo, The Great Galdini and The Beautiful Cassandra – while from the wings two stage-hands pushed out a trolley upon which sat a large cage.

'The tiger!' Carlo bellowed, dramatically and perhaps a little unnecessarily as a wave of gasps rippled through the audience like wind on water.

Inside the cage was indeed a tiger, prowling restlessly, unsettled by the lights and the drumroll and the general commotion.

The stagehands set the cage in its central position, quickly locked the trolley's wheels and disappeared. Clad in black as they were and with only a short distance to travel given the false proscenium arch, they'd been virtu-ally invisible to the audience. And they would be totally invisible during the magical effects when they would enter from upstage to wheel the cage behind the black tabs, while an identical second cage was flown in from the flies. A very simple trick, but most effective.

'The tiger,' Carlo continued seamlessly, 'which, through the mastery of The Great Galdini, will disappear before your very eyes . . . Thence to be returned' – dramatic pause for effect – 'as a *kitten*!' He bashed the front of the cage with his hand, a signal for the animal to growl and slap back with its giant paw, either due to its training or its irri-tation no one was sure, least of all Carlo. Or for that matter the Galdinis, who had bought the beast from a circus that was going bust; they didn't know its background.

The big cat obeyed, baring its teeth with a snarl, whacking its paw against the bars, and another ripple of gasps, very audible this time, ran through the audience.

'A *tiger* turned into a *kitten* . . .' Carlo emphatically enthused, pacing downstage, arms outstretched, embracing the whole of the house from the front row of the stalls to the back row of the gods. 'A feat never before witnessed on any stage in the world . . .'

The music was about to strike up, and Carlo, with a final word and a flourish, was about to leave the stage to the Galdinis and their mime and the impressive display of special effects. But that was as far as he got. There was not a sound from the orchestra pit, and the gasps had become far more than a ripple. Both the musicians and the audience were alarmed, and with just cause. Behind him, the gate of the cage had slowly swung open. And the tiger stood there, facing directly out front, surveying the freedom that beckoned.

The Galdinis, posed either side of the cage as they were, exchanged looks of horror. One of them would have to slam the gate shut, but which one? Neither could move; husband and wife were simultaneously rooted to the spot.

Then the decision was made for them. The tiger stepped out from the cage, negotiating the one-foot drop from the trolley with threatening elegance.

The Beautiful Cassandra gave a terrified scream and headed for the wings OP while The Great Galdini raced for the prompt side, equally terrified but cursing his wife. He'd never wanted to do this trick in the first place, but she'd insisted exotic animals were the latest thing. And the bigger the better. Cassie could be so dumb!

Carlo turned to see what all the ruckus was about. He froze. The tiger was standing centre stage, its eyes following the direction from whence the screams were still audible. The screams stopped. Someone had shut Cassie up.

The tiger turned its attention to the next distraction. Which was Carlo. It took a step towards him, then paused, yellow eyes unblinkingly fixed upon this creature of interest.

Those in the front row of the stalls were starting to panic; people were getting up out of their seats prepared to flee. Then . . .

'No, don't go,' Carlo said, the voice of calm, but also the voice of compelling authority. 'There's no cause for panic, I assure you. It's all part of the act.'

And they believed him. They sat back down in their seats.

The musicians in the orchestra pit knew better. Being the professionals they were, however, they did not disrupt the performance, choosing instead to quickly and silently steal away.

Carlo was left to put on a show. He faced the tiger.

'Here, kitty,' he said. 'Here, kitty, kitty,' and incredible as it was, there were laughs from the house, nervous laughs perhaps, but laughs nonetheless.

So far so good, he thought, adrenaline coursing through his veins; he had them under control. He took off his tailcoat. Standing there in his slender, well-cut trousers, his silk vest, shirtsleeves and bow tie, he cut a fine figure, and holding the tailcoat out in front of him like a cape, he adopted a matador pose.

'*Toro*,' he said, '*toro . . . toro . . .*' He'd heard that word somewhere; perhaps Rube had told him. Bullfighters used it, and he thought it meant 'bull', which would make sense. He didn't dare jiggle the tailcoat, as a matador might his cape, for fear of agitating the beast, but this was showtime – he had to make things entertaining.

The tiger, totally focused upon Carlo and perhaps intrigued by the coat, started to pad very slowly towards him, intent upon investigating. Carlo, equally slowly, backed away.

'*Toro*, kitty, *toro*,' he said. The mention of 'kitty' didn't raise a laugh this time, the audience holding its collective breath, not daring to break the moment.

As if in slow motion, man and beast circled the stage, Carlo cautiously backing, the tiger following. Or was it stalking? Was it at any moment about to pounce?

At one point, Carlo, in his determination to entertain, gave the coat a small jiggle and the tiger swiped a huge paw at it. A shared gasp from the audience. A very taut moment. No, he decided, he wouldn't try that again. But the tiger did seem intrigued by the coat, Carlo realised, his mind racing. What lines would Rube come up with for a situation like this? Rube would write something witty, wouldn't he? Carlo wasn't very good with patter himself; Rube wrote all the material.

'Tigers and kittens are very closely related,' he said, keeping his voice calm in order not to excite the beast, but making sure at the same time it reached well out into the auditorium. The acoustics at the Princess Theatre were excellent, as he knew. 'They're all just the same, really,' he went on. 'It's only a matter of size, wouldn't you agree? Here, kitty,' he called once again, the coat still held at arm's length, 'here, kitty, kitty.' No laugh, but he hadn't expected there would be.

The circle was nearly completed now. They were back to the cage; beside him was the open gate. Did he dare? He backed a step or two further. The tiger was beside the open gate now. Yes, he decided, he did.

Carlo jiggled the coat, more vigorously this time, and as the tiger once again swiped at it, he quickly pulled his arms into his chest, the animal's paw missing him by inches. Then, in one swift action, he hurled the coat into the cage and stood facing the tiger, wondering which option would find favour. *What's it to be*, he thought. *The coat or me?*

But as fate decreed, the tiger automatically followed the source of its interest. The coat. Its circus trainer had used a cape, which the animal had always found irritating. With a snarl, it leapt into the cage.

Carlo slammed the gate closed, giving the bars a brief rattle to ensure the catch had firmly locked, then whirled about to face the audience.

'Olé,' he said, which was another bullfighting term he'd heard somewhere, 'good kitty.' Adopting full showman pose, he again triumphantly embraced the house. 'The tiger did not exactly disappear, I grant you,' he announced, 'but as you can see, it did become a kitten.' *Beat that*, he thought. And he took his bows to thunderous applause, while behind him the tiger, now slumped on its belly, ripped into the tailcoat, tearing it to shreds.

Along with the rest of the audience, Will Worthing couldn't quite believe what his eyes had just seen. But unlike many, he knew the whole episode had been a ghastly mistake and that anything could have happened. The sheer gall of the man! *You have to respect guts like that*, he thought.

Backstage, the adrenaline having instantly deserted him, Carlo was throwing up into a fire bucket.

The meeting was arranged for a week later at Parer's Crystal Café, which remained the Worthings' favourite gathering place. Will had booked a table, but Carlo and Rube were already waiting when he and Max arrived with Mabel and Gertie.

Carlo made the introductions. 'Michael Carlovsky and Marten Reubens,' he said as they both rose to their feet, 'otherwise known to the world as Carlo and Rube,' he added with a flashy grin.

'William and Maxwell Worthing,' Will replied stiffly, accepting the hand on offer.

'Otherwise known to the world as Will and Max,' his brother interjected, giving one of his easygoing smiles as they shook hands all round. Why did Will have to be so pompous? Sure the man was being a bit showy, but so what? No call for antagonism. 'And this is Will's wife Mabel, and my wife Gertie.'

Mabel and Gertie extended their hands, shaking as firmly as the men had, which was always their way upon introduction.

'Ah yes,' Carlo said, 'The Divine Dolores. An honour.'

He bent to kiss Gertie's hand, and as his lips lingered just that little too long, Max felt his own prickle of antagonism. *Don't you try things on with my Gert*, he thought protectively.

But Gertie wasn't taken in by the performance. 'If we're going to work together, Gertie'll do,' she said, and Max wanted to laugh.

'Of course, Gertie it is then,' Carlo replied graciously. 'Please do take a seat, ladies.'

He gestured to the crimson velveteen sofa – the men would take the hardback chairs – and they all settled themselves comfortably.

Carlo hadn't actually been 'trying things on' with Gertie; she wasn't his type. Pretty enough, but too small; he liked fuller-bodied, majestic women. His nature simply dictated he flirt with a pretty woman. It was what they liked after all, wasn't it? And a pretty woman deserved admiration.

So the brothers have seen fit to bring their wives, he thought a little critically – this was a business meeting after all. The Divine Dolores, yes, that was understandable, but the plain woman, Will Worthing's wife? What was she doing here? *Strange that such an arresting-looking man should have such an ordinary wife.*

'I should have brought my wife along too,' he said, smiling winningly at the women. 'Winifred would have so loved meeting you, but she recently gave birth and is at home with the baby.'

Why should you have brought your wife? Mabel wondered. *This isn't a social gathering, we're here to talk business.* But she returned the smile pleasantly enough.

'Oh, how lovely,' Gertie's face lit up, 'you have a new baby. Your wife must be very happy.'

'Yes, she is.' The smile she gifted him was so genuine Carlo found himself captivated. *She really is extraordinarily pretty*, he thought. 'We're all very happy.'

He exchanged a look with Rube. Happy? Ecstatic would be more apt. Winifred had given birth just one month ago to a son whom he'd named Martin. After Rube, of course. With twenty-year-old Michael grown to manhood and little Anne, his half-sister, having just turned nine, Winifred's production of a second child had proved the greatest triumph of all. Carlo could not have been more proud. He now boasted two sons.

'We've been recreated, Rube,' he'd said as they'd toasted the baby's arrival. 'Michael and Martin.' He'd raised his glass. 'To the two of them. Mick and Marty. Brothers, just like you and me.'

'To Mick and Marty,' Rube had echoed. He was as proud of the boy as the child's father himself. Baby Marty was a joy to them both.

'You certainly picked the right night to see the show,' Carlo said. He'd been delighted to hear the Worthing brothers had witnessed his triumph with the tiger. 'I shan't be repeating that performance in a hurry, I can promise you.'

'You handled it brilliantly,' Max said.

'Well . . .' Carlo returned a nonchalant shrug. 'What else could one do?'

'He vomited afterwards.' Rube's comment, made good-humouredly with no malice, was deliberate nonetheless; he thought Carlo was laying it on a bit thick. These men were skilled performers, they knew the score.

Carlo darted him a glance, annoyed. He wanted to retain the hero image, particularly in front of Will Worthing, who he suspected didn't altogether approve of him, although why was beyond his comprehension.

But upon this matter, Will was surprisingly understanding. 'I'd be amazed if you hadn't had some sort of violent reaction,' he said, 'given the assault upon your nerves such an incident would have. Adrenaline is an amazing thing, is it not?'

'Indeed it is,' Carlo replied, thankfully.

'In my opinion,' Will went on, voicing yet another of his many theories (which were invariably pre-empted with 'in my opinion'), 'an occasional attack of the nerves is good for a performer – keeps him on his toes, avoids the risk of complacency. And of course the moment he's before an audience it disappears. The same with minor afflictions, don't you find? A bout of hay fever or hiccoughs disappears onstage, only to reappear the moment one returns to the wings.'

Carlo nodded knowingly, although he'd never experienced such episodes himself. He'd never experienced any form of nerves, either. Not until he'd been confronted by a tiger anyway.

'Same if you're pregnant,' Gertie added. 'You vomit before you go on and you vomit when you come off, but you never vomit onstage.'

When are we going to get around to talking business? Mabel wondered.

Then Rube saved the day.

'Shall we order some tea and sandwiches and get down to business?' he suggested.

Thank you, Mabel thought. She already had a feeling that she rather liked Rube. There was nothing remarkable about his looks; a stocky little man, mid- to late forties, with gingery grey hair that was thinning, he didn't carry

his age as well as his friend, Carlo, but in the strangely
baby-like face there was a gentleness and an intelligence
that she found intriguing.

They ordered mixed sandwiches, ham and chicken, with
a special round of fish paste for Gertie. The Worthings
could afford ham and chicken these days, even imported
pâté if they wished, but due to either habit, nostalgia, or
perhaps pure preference, Gertie had retained her taste for
fish paste.

They didn't leap straight into a business discussion –
the small talk continuing as they ate – but the conversation
was productive nonetheless, every word pertaining to show
business, and everyone aware they were being assessed.

'Your Serpentine Dance is an absolute masterpiece,'
Carlo said to Gertie, 'a highlight to top the bill in any
variety show.' Both he and Rube had seen past productions
of the Worthing brothers and they very much admired the
family's talent as performers.

Gertie nodded her thanks, accepting the compliment
as graciously as she could with a mouth full of fish paste
sandwich.

'We loved the magician act too, Max,' Carlo continued,
'you're so much better than our Great Galdini. Rube and
I would both have to admit that, wouldn't we, Rube?'

'Absolutely,' Rube agreed, reaching for another ham
sandwich.

They all shared a smile, and Carlo went on, determined
to hold forth with one purpose in mind. He wanted to
know ... *What does the plain woman do? Surely she
should be home minding children. Why is she here?*

'And as for your Heavenly Tenor, Will ...' He shook his
head and, hands raised heavenwards, gestured theatrically
as if words could not suffice. 'Sublime, simply sublime ...'

'Thank you.' Will's response was dignified, although
a touch brusque. He doubted this peacock of a man was

qualified to pass an opinion on the art of performance. Carlo was not a true creature of the theatre, despite his many years in the business. After all, what was his particular talent as a performer? *He neither sings nor acts nor has a specific skill*, Will thought. *He's a show-off, that's all. A masterful one, and a talent, yes, but a shallow talent.* Will had come to a definite conclusion with regard to Carlo, and he very much doubted he could work with the man.

Having so far commented upon the talents of three Worthing family members, Carlo turned his attention to the fourth.

'I'm sorry to say, Mabel, I don't quite recall seeing your performance . . .' he said tentatively, but he didn't get any further.

'That's because there isn't one,' Mabel interjected, 'I don't perform. I do other things.'

'Oh.' *She's blunt as well as plain*, Carlo thought. 'Like what, may I ask?'

'I work backstage.' Mabel gave a shrug. 'I make costumes . . .'

A seamstress, yes, she looks like a seamstress.

'Mabel runs the show,' Max said. 'She's the Worthings' mastermind.'

Will felt a stab of annoyance. He found Max's comment unnecessary; it didn't at all suit his image. Carlo would have presumed that he, as the family patriarch, ran the show.

'Ah,' Carlo said, 'a woman at the helm, how very interesting.' It wasn't. He sensed Will's annoyance, which was blatantly obvious, and didn't for one minute believe Max. There must have been some falling out between them, he thought, for Max Worthing to needle his brother so. 'May I say then, Mabel, you do a remarkable job. The Worthing brothers' productions are splendid. If I were to make just one minor suggestion though,' he added humbly, 'and I hope my presumption in doing so doesn't offend, the programme you offer could perhaps do with just a dash more humour.'

The remark, although directed to Mabel, was intended for Will, and it was very much intended to annoy the man further.

Carlo was fully aware he'd been not only assessed but found wanting by Will Worthing, and he didn't care in the least. He'd done his best to be agreeable, but the man had passed judgement on him. Will Worthing was a pompous prig who needed to be brought down a peg.

'Audiences do so crave amusement, I've found,' he said, again to Mabel and very pleasantly, but just patronisingly enough to really irk Will Worthing.

'I'm sure you're quite right, Carlo,' Mabel replied, 'I'll bear that in mind.' She smiled to herself. *Well, well, it's happening already*, she thought, *the clash of egos. There's too much charisma in this room.*

'I must say, Will, I have very much enjoyed your Shake-speare.' It was Rube who intervened, inwardly cursing Carlo as he did. *Stop provoking the man!*

Rube too had recognised the clash of personalities and hoped it would not interfere with the intended business of the day; he was very keen to form a partnership with the Worthings.

'Oh, really? Which particular one did you see?' Will acknowledged and allowed the all-too-obvious change of subject, which was no doubt wise, but his tone remained icy. He would not be won over by hollow flattery – what would these tricksters know of Shakespeare?

'Several,' Rube replied. 'Two from *Henry V* – the Agincourt speech and the Prologue address from Act One, both of which I might add are particular favourites of mine – and I also adored your rendition of Jaques' "Seven Ages of Man" ... So terribly *funny*,' he added, with a meaningful glance to Carlo.

'Ah.' Will was not only mollified, he was distracted; things had suddenly become interesting. 'Yes, it's a wonderful piece to perform. For an actor who can handle comedy, that is. In my opinion' – and off he went again, another pet theory – 'comedy is far more difficult than drama or tragedy. Any actor with the requisite vocal skills can handle drama, but comedy requires so much more delicacy. The emphases infinitesimal, but of such importance, and the timing of course crucial. The nuances of comedy —'

'Perhaps we should get down to business?' Mabel gently suggested, once again thankful to Rube for the distraction that had proved so effective.

'Yes, yes, of course, my dear, you're quite right.' Will was not in the least offended; Mabel often stopped him mid-stream. He was even accustomed to the odd reprimand. 'You're pontificating, Will,' she'd say bluntly, and she was always right. He did tend to allow his passion to take over. How could he not? The subject of theatre was so devilishly fascinating.

'We're most interested in the slant your *Big Show Bonanza* is taking in promoting homegrown talent,' he said, initially addressing Rube, then including Carlo also, his annoyance momentarily forgotten. 'In fact, the slogan you've adopted – "Featuring Stars of the Southern Cross" – we find quite inspiring.'

Will appeared to be using the royal 'we' with reference to himself, but he didn't actually intend to take the credit, the idea having initially been Mabel's, as most of the Worthings' innovative ideas were. 'We discussed its implications at some length, didn't we,' he said, turning to Mabel and Max. As the patriarch he'd commenced proceedings, which was as it should be, and it was now only right they both have their say.

With a barely perceptible nod, Mabel indicated Max should take the floor first. She sensed Carlo was not accustomed to a woman leading the troops.

'Yes,' Max said, putting down his teacup and opening the discussion in all earnestness. 'We firmly believe, as you obviously do, that we should forge a new path for Australian performers. The major entrepreneurs appear to think no show will survive without an overseas star heading the bill, that even the majority of support acts should be imported. As I'm sure you're aware, they pay talent scouts in America and England to report on the international variety circuit, they make regular trips themselves —'

'Harry Rickards is always going overseas,' Gertie piped up, eager to have her say. 'He has an imported headliner in every one of his Tivoli shows. I've heard they're planning to bring out W. C. Fields, at least that's what my friend Mary-May told me.'

'Who's W. C. Fields?' Carlo asked, mystified. Unlike Rube, he didn't read the entertainment columns of the newspapers.

'He's a comic juggler,' Gertie said, only too happy to inform, 'hugely popular on the American circuit. He does a tramp act with a trick pool table and billiard balls that brings down the house, Mary-May says ...' Mary-May was an American vaudevillian who'd recently become Gertie's best friend – Gertie made friends with everyone. 'Oh, you should hear her go on, he's ever so funny, Mary-May says —'

'The Firm too has a similar policy.' Another gentle interruption from Mabel; Gertie also occasionally needing a little reining in. 'JCW himself strongly believes in the importation of stars. He brought Sarah Bernhardt out in '91, and it was such a huge success he hasn't stopped since.'

'And the Fullers as well,' Max added. 'Ben Fuller makes regular trips to America and England and also to Europe, particularly Paris, in search of "fresh novelties", as he calls them.'

Will took over at that juncture, aware they'd made their point and that it was time for him to sum up the case.

'We believe, as you clearly do,' he declared dramatically to Carlo and Rube, 'that we can create our own Australian stars and that, furthermore, we can attract the audiences to embrace them. "Featuring Stars of the Southern Cross" could become an anthem to this country. An anthem of which we could all be rightly proud!'

There was no doubt about it, Rube thought, and so begrudgingly did Carlo: Will Worthing in full actor-manager mode was downright impressive.

But I only came up with the slogan to save money, Rube thought. *Imported stars double the budget; locals come at half the price.*

Rube's mind was working overtime. He'd been intrigued by the theatrical legitimacy of the Worthings and the opportunities a partnership with them might offer. Another turn in the chess game of life, he'd thought. Fresh ideas . . . new moves . . . But this? This was something altogether different. This was a brand-new chess game.

'It's a grand idea, Will,' he said, 'and one with which we concur wholeheartedly, don't we, Carlo?'

'Oh yes,' Carlo replied, 'yes, we most certainly do.' Carlo wasn't sure why Rube was so eager to join forces with the Worthings, but he always agreed with Rube when it came to business. Rube was the brains.

They settled down then to discuss the various intricacies of their forthcoming partnership, the choice of acts they would incorporate in their production – hopefully, as they agreed, just the first production of many – the out-of-town tour dates, the major city theatres they would line up . . . But Rube's mind was elsewhere. Rube was dwelling upon the broader spectrum that now presented itself.

'Why don't we look at a partnership not just as producers, but lessees?' he suggested during a brief lull in the
conversation. 'And on an ongoing basis? We could lease
our own theatres, say one in Melbourne, one in Sydney, let
them out to other producers, when we don't have a show
of our own, but over time build up audiences that come
to recognise here is where they get to see their very own
favourites, their homegrown stars.'

A pause ensued. This was a much bigger plan. Mabel,
not unexpectedly, was the first to grasp it.

'Brilliant, Rube,' she said, 'brilliant.' She knew she'd
liked him from the moment they'd first met. Now she
knew why.

How come I didn't think of that? Will wondered.

Rube's so damn smart, Carlo thought admiringly.

'It seems we have a plan,' Max announced.

They ordered champagne to celebrate the beginning of
a true partnership.

Carlo grinned impishly as they raised their glasses. 'We
shall have some humour in our shows though, shan't we,
Will?' he suggested.

Will didn't deign to answer.

Gertie muttered in an aside to Mabel, 'I reckon there'll
be some feathers ruffled along the way.'

To which Mabel returned a nod that plainly said, *oh
yes, there will indeed.* 'What a lark, eh,' Gertie said.

Little could either of them have imagined . . .

9

NEW FRIENDSHIPS ARE FORGED

As the dawn of a new century loomed ever nearer, the talk on all Australians' lips was the inevitability of Federation. The people had been called upon to vote and already two referendums had been held, the majority of citizens proving very much in favour of a Federal Parliament. There were stumbling blocks along the way, however. In the 1898 referendum, New South Wales had not received the 80,000 necessary votes to pass the bill. As a result, the following year when the second referendum was put to the people, Edmund Barton himself, leader of the NSW Federalists, personally drove his gig and horses throughout the entire state and also Queensland calling upon citizens to vote 'yes'. The campaign was intense, newspapers and pamphlets planting the seeds of Federation in every remote corner of the country. By the time Referendum Day arrived on 28 June, it seemed every Australian was aware of the part they could play in this all too significant historical event. And they won! But there was a further stumbling block: Western Australia. The WA Premier, Sir John Forrest, maintained that the farmers and country businessmen of his state did not want Federation. As it turned out, however, the miners did, and they rebelled! A petition signed by almost 30,000 citizens from the goldfields was sent to Queen Victoria requesting separation from Western Australia. What was to be done? Was the country to become a Federation of only five colonies instead of six?

Most Australians agreed it was just a matter of time before WA would give in. Surely, they would have to . . .

'Of course they'll give in,' Rube said, steering the general chat to politics, although he could tell Carlo and Will weren't remotely interested. Rube himself followed political affairs very closely, he always had, reading every newspaper and every published report he could get his hands on. 'A representative from each Australian state – that is except WA, of course,' he added drily, 'is sailing to London to meet with the Colonial Secretary. Between Joseph Chamberlain and the five of them, they'll twist Western Australia's arm, you just wait and see.'

Max nodded; he too had been following events closely. But it was Gertie who jumped in with a passion.

'And the sooner they do the better,' she said firmly. Gertie, who in the past had shown little interest in politics, was surprisingly committed to the Federalist movement. For one reason and one reason only. 'The sooner they bring in Federation, the sooner they'll give women the vote and the sooner we'll be able to fight for our rights.' Gertie was all for the suffragettes' cause.

'It's downright disgraceful,' she'd said time and again, 'that even in show business women are paid less than men. Why, the number of times my Serpentine Dance has topped the bill, and some bloke with a tatty, second-rate ventriloquist act gets paid more!' Gertie was truly outraged. 'That shouldn't happen, not in our game. You should get paid for the value of your act, not for whatever bleeding sex you was born.' So outraged that she would lapse into her old working-class vernacular.

'What do you reckon, Mabel?' she now said, calling upon support from a fellow suffragette. 'When Federation gives us the vote, you'll be able to deal with theatre managers yourself instead of having to hand everything over to Will.'

Mabel gave a cursory nod that might have passed as agreement, although she doubted any theatre manager would welcome doing business with a woman. But she rather wished Gertie would shut up. Always protective of Will, she was aware such a comment could have appeared belittling. Mabel was such a strange combination of motherliness and cold hard practicality.

In this instance, though, she had no need for concern; Will hadn't even heard the remark. Nor had Carlo. Both were far too distracted, with other things on their mind as they discussed the forthcoming tour. In past meetings, the title, the dates and the venues had all been amicably agreed upon:

The Worthing Brothers in partnership with
Carlo and Rube present:
THE MUSICAL VARIETY EXTRAVAGANZA OF 1900
Proudly Featuring Stars of the Southern Cross . . .

The show was to go on the road for three months in order to iron out any kinks, before travelling by train to Sydney for a grand gala opening at the Criterion Theatre on the corner of Pitt and Park streets. 'The Cri', as it was affectionately known, was a favourite venue of Will Worthing's. Built in Italianate Neo-Renaissance style, with an interior of Georgian design, it seated close to a thousand, but had an 'intimate feel' and was 'classy', or so Will maintained, and few could disagree. Upon its opening in 1886 the *Sydney Morning Herald* had deemed the Criterion 'a great advance on Sydney theatres', remarking that it made the audiences feel 'far nearer London than usual'. High praise indeed.

A further tour was to follow the opening at The Cri. The company would travel by steamer to Adelaide, and then on to Tasmania where they would perform at the Theatre Royal in Hobart, before finally returning to Melbourne for a triumphant closing season at the Princess Theatre.

As was to be expected, however, they were encountering some friction in the final drawing up of the programme, and the selection of the several new acts and performers they would need to employ.

'We'll have to incorporate a strong musical theme if we're to successfully carry off a variety show at the Criterion,' Will said, having ignored any opening chat about the current political situation, which was of no interest to him.

They were seated again at Parer's Crystal Café, which they'd adopted as their headquarters, all six of them, the women on the crimson settee as usual.

'The Cri's known to specialise in musical presentations,' he went on, 'comic opera and the like, so audiences will arrive with certain expectations.'

Will had been keen from the very outset to construct the programme along the lines of his personal preference. He'd been against the inclusion of minstrelsy, which hadn't bothered the others, but he'd met with some opposition when he'd vetoed the employment of exotic animal acts.

'But exotic animals are hugely popular,' Carlo had argued, 'particularly the chimpanzees. And they're *funny*, what's more!' A deliberate dig.

'They're trouble,' Will said dismissively. 'I prefer to find comedy from the *human* quarter, if you don't mind.'

Carlo actually *didn't* mind. He didn't mind in the least; he'd found working with animals annoying himself, particularly recalling his run-in with a tiger. But he couldn't stand Will Worthing's superior tone.

'Oh, so we get our laughs from your *Shakespeare* then, do we?' he queried with a haughty sneer of his own.

'Quite possibly, yes,' Will countered, the two men squaring off across the paper-littered coffee table like a pair of combative fighting cocks. 'Shakespeare wrote a great many comedies with a great many laughs . . .'

'Which I'm sure a great many people find greatly amusing . . .'

'Yes, they do! *Intelligent* people most certainly do!'

'What about Irving Sayles?' Gertie's voice broke in before the spat could go any further.

They turned to look at her, where she sat with her little dish of fish paste sandwiches delicately poised in one hand, staring back at them wide-eyed and innocent.

'Irving's one of the funniest men in show business,' she said, 'and he sings and dances like a dream. You'll get your comedy and your music all together in the one act, Will. Irving Sayles is your man.'

'Irving Sayles is a Negro,' Carlo said.

'So?' Gertie more wide-eyed and innocent than ever.

'So what about the "Stars of the Southern Cross"?' Carlo's voice had lost its edge; he would never be sharp with Gertie – he liked Gertie – but he was confused. 'An American Negro hardly fits the bill, does he?'

'Of course he does,' Gertie replied airily. 'We wouldn't be bringing him into the country, would we? He's already here. Irving's been in Australia for ages, he came out the same year we did in '88. We did a tour with him in the early nineties, remember?' She looked around the table, but before anyone could answer, sailed blithely on. 'He got married right here in Melbourne just two years ago, to an Englishwoman what's more. And he's never going back to America, he told me so himself. He's one of us all right.'

'I think Irving Sayles is an excellent idea,' Max said. 'He's a first-rate performer on all levels.'

'Good to have a mix in the show too,' Rube agreed. 'The word is "variety" after all. And Gertie's spot on, we wouldn't be bringing him in from overseas. He wouldn't be an import.'

'When you come to think of it,' a laconic comment from Mabel, 'who *isn't* an import? Who *hasn't* come from overseas?'

There being no rejoinder, the remark halted them all momentarily. But Carlo was baffled by more than the remark, he was baffled by the woman herself. What was it about Mabel? He still couldn't work her out. *She doesn't play games*, he thought. He'd originally presumed this was because she was plain and didn't have the natural gift other women possessed. But he'd quickly realised this was not the case. *She's more like a man*, he'd thought. But he'd come to recognise this too was not the case. Mabel Worthing remained something Carlo couldn't quite grasp.

'So we're in agreement about Irving,' she went on briskly. 'That is, of course, if we can get him – we'll have to pry him away from Harry and The Tiv.' Irving was a great favourite of Harry Rickards.

Irving Sayles, born in Quincy, Illinois, had come to Australia as a very young man, little more than a youth, with the Hicks-Sawyer Minstrels. His solo song-and-dance 'Father of a Little Black Coon', which had featured in the show, had become an instant hit, earning nightly encores, and two years later, when the minstrel group had broken up, he'd stayed on in Melbourne, performing both solo and double acts to great acclaim.

Yes, they decided, the agreement was unanimous: they were most certainly in favour of Irving, whose combined talents as acrobat, comedian, dancer and singer they very much admired. 'An all-rounder,' as Will Worthing was wont to remark of such performers, 'and all-rounders are worth their weight in gold.'

'And what's more,' Gertie added, determined to have the final say, 'Irving's the loveliest man in the whole, wide world.'

Gertie well remembered the time she'd confronted Irving Sayles with a question that had puzzled her since her arrival in Australia. She'd worked with minstrel groups a number of times back home in the Old Country, but the players had always been white. Here in Australia, where minstrelsy had proved so very popular, she'd discovered there were many black American performers working alongside their white counterparts, which she'd further discovered was often the case in America.

'Can you answer something for me, Irving?' she'd said. It was the interval during an afternoon matinee, and they'd been sitting on the back steps of a theatre called the Royal or the Palace or the Grand or Her Majesty's in some large outback town. It had been a long tour and she couldn't recall the particular outback town, or the particular theatre, all of which seemed to be named after theatres she'd known back home.

'I can try,' he'd replied, looking out at the dusty dirt road.

'Why do Negro minstrel performers have to wear "blackface" when they're already black?' she'd asked in all innocence.

He'd smiled his gentle smile, which in real life was so at odds with his exuberant onstage personality. He was actually several years younger than she was, but he seemed so much wiser. So much more worldly. At least, he did to Gertie.

'I suppose because a lot of us just ain't black *enough*, Gertie.' And when the answer hadn't appeared to satisfy her, he'd gone on a little further. 'I think the requirement in a minstrel act is one of uniformity, you know? We all gotta be real shoe-shine black, with big white lips and big cartoon eyes . . .' He rolled his eyeballs in comical fashion.

'That's what people find funny. And when we put on all those airs and graces . . .' He jumped to his feet and struck up the pose of a minstrel 'dandy', then broke into a Juba flatfoot dance, body undulating in perfect rhythm, feet gliding effortlessly across the red-dust ground, hands slapping and patting his arms, chest and cheeks. 'Well now, they find this downright funny too.'

'But isn't that insulting to you black people?'

'Mmm, maybe.' He nodded thoughtfully then sat back down on the steps and smiled again, a cheeky smile this time. 'But not if you look at things the way I do. You see, the dandy is really imitating his white plantation boss, making the boss look like a fool, so who would you say is laughing at who?' When she'd looked a little blank, he'd summed it up for her. 'Minstrels are something of a contradiction, Gertie. White folk pretending to be black folk who are pretending to be white folk sort of comes around full circle, don't you think? The white audience don't know it, but they're really laughing at themselves. That's the way I choose to see things anyway.'

Gertie adored Irving. In fact, she'd be quite prepared to admit, even to Max, that she was just a tiny bit in love with Irving Sayles.

Despite some minor conflict, which was invariably due to an ego clash between Will and Carlo, there was much they were all agreed upon. It was a foregone conclusion that Carlo would MC *The Musical Variety Extravaganza of 1900*. Even Will, and perhaps especially Will, was prepared to admit, albeit begrudgingly, that Carlo was the best Master of Ceremonies in the business. Or at least the best he'd witnessed, and he'd witnessed many. He'd been relieved to discover, nonetheless, that all of Carlo's scripts, down to the very last word, were written by Rube. *Just as I suspected*, he thought, *a talented showman, but not necessarily clever.*

Several of the Worthings' most popular acts were to be retained, although the material for each would be brand new.

Gertie and Mabel had already devised fresh themes, costumes, visual effects and choreography for The Serpentine Dance, which was always in demand with people queuing down the street. Mabel had decided that, in keeping with the inspirational slogan 'Stars of the Southern Cross', the opening dance should feature a didgeridoo and clapsticks, with a projected background of desert, spinifex and mulga trees, Gertie to be in ochre-red silk, the colour of the very land itself.

'I'll wager most audiences have never even *heard* a didgeridoo and clapsticks, let alone seen them in action,' she said. She and Gertie hadn't seen or heard them either until recently, when they'd encountered a black man and his son busking outside the main railway station in Flinders Street. The sight and sound had fascinated them both. 'Of course we'll have to find a couple of Aborigines willing to come on tour,' she said thoughtfully.

Mabel wondered if the man from the railway station might be interested; he'd been most helpful when she'd given him money and enquired about the instrument. But he'd probably be gone by now; the horrified passers-by had avoided him as if he were something contagious. *Poor man*, she thought, *why would they do that? People are so frightened of things they don't understand. Different altogether from show business folk. We just thrive on mystery.*

'Oh well,' she continued briskly, moving to the next item on the agenda, 'I'm sure we'll manage somehow. I'll ask around.'

It had been decided Max would perform a solo juggling and highwire act, accompanied throughout by the ten-piece band they intended to employ. This was another of Mabel's suggestions.

'I see the performance as being dance-like,' she'd declared, 'almost balletic. One-on-one with an audience, Max is a genius,' she'd explained for the benefit of Carlo and Rube, 'everyone thinks he's performing just for them. We'll orchestrate every look, every wink and every flick of a finger. This is why we need the best piano player we can get, one who'll lead the band and work with Max as a team . . .'

That was when Will had jumped in. 'Georgie,' he'd said, with a ring of triumph.

'Georgie, that's right.' She wouldn't tell him she'd already been in touch with Georgie Washington, the black American pianist who coincidentally bore the name of the first US president; she'd let Will think this was his idea. 'I'll line Georgie up, let's hope he's available.' She already knew that he was.

The biggest change in the Worthings' routine, however, was to be the magic act, which had been restructured altogether. Max, Artie and Alfie had been working on the new act for some time now, but it was yet to be performed before an audience. *The Musical Variety Extravaganza of 1900* would see the debut of The Wonderful Worthing, Master Illusionist, an act to rival that of any magician the world over. But The Wonderful Worthing would not be Max.

Max had passed the baton to his eighteen-year-old nephews. Artie and/or Alfie were no longer to be an assistant to the magician, they were to be the magician himself. The idea had been Max's.

'It goes without saying that a pretty young woman, tantalisingly dressed, is a far more effective distraction to the audience than a young male assistant,' he'd said. 'Furthermore, we'll bring the house down with the final illusion if it's the magician himself who's transported, rather than the magician's assistant.'

Max had thought through his plan with care, and his enthusiasm was contagious as he'd gone on to explain. 'We can vary the finale's reveal with each performance too, so the audience doesn't know where or how the magician is going to reappear. He could be hanging upside down from the rafters, for all they know. The boys are accomplished acrobats, they can manage all sorts of stunts, and a reveal like that's bound to get in the newspapers and set everyone talking. The punters will probably come to the show time and again, just to see where the magician turns up next.'

Mabel had instantly embraced the idea and in typical fashion had taken things one step further.

'I think we should drop "magician" from the title altogether,' she'd said. '"Illusionist" is more fitting and much, much more stylish.'

Max wholeheartedly agreed. And so was born The Wonderful Worthing, Master Illusionist. Artie or Alfie – for who would know which one was which when they adopted their onstage persona – was destined for stardom. It was further decided their younger sister Prudence, shortly to turn seventeen, would share the billing as a distractingly pretty assistant. All three were very excited.

But Mabel's instruction to her sons, issued in private, was strict and held a distinct warning.

'You boys work hard,' she ordered. 'With your Uncle Max out of the act, we risk losing a top-of-the-bill performance. We don't want anything second-rate. You make sure you don't let me down now!'

They didn't dare. And the endless rehearsals became competitive, albeit in a friendly way. The brothers were still very close, but neither was prepared to be outshone by the other. They would share, as they had for the past decade, the task of who would perform onstage and who would be the reveal, and no one, not even their fellow performers, would be able to tell the difference. Artie and

Alfie, so unalike in real life, always brothers, never twins, still revelled in their deception and the hybrid third person they'd created between them, the person who was neither Artie nor Alfie.

Will's Heavenly Tenor was naturally to be employed to its fullest advantage throughout the show, and they decided upon a series of male and female Gilbert and Sullivan duets. This, of course, necessitated the employment of a soprano, so they held auditions. It wasn't long before they hit upon the perfect choice.

Maeve Gallagher was twenty-six years old, a fiery, statuesque redhead from Ireland. And she simply oozed sex appeal.

'Things are seldom what they seem,
Skim milk masquerades as cream.'

Carlo leant against the door frame at the back of the hall watching the girl rehearse with Will. They were performing 'Things Are Seldom What They Seem' from *HMS Pinafore*, a very bawdy duet, and even in these early days of rehearsal, Maeve was giving it her all as 'Buttercup', rubbing her backside against Will's groin, bending over and wriggling her hips provocatively as she looked out front and sang to an imaginary audience. *God, the man must surely have an erection*, Carlo thought.

Then the girl's eyes met his. She'd been aware he was watching. But Carlo didn't look away. Nor did Maeve . . .

'Highlows pass as patent leathers;
Jackdaws strut in peacock's feathers.'

Instead, she winked as she sang, and gave another wriggle of her backside. Carlo returned the wink. He couldn't wait to be out on the road with Maeve Gallagher.

Several other auditions were held too; a supporting baritone for the G&S bracket – Carlo didn't bother going to that audition – a team of skirt dancers to titillate the masses with a show of legs (he certainly attended that one), and a young actress to play opposite Will in the balcony scene from *Romeo and Juliet*.

Rube and Will had thoroughly outvoted Carlo in the Shakespearean choice.

'Didn't you intend to perform a *comedy* piece?' Carlo had asked cuttingly.

'We're doing comedy throughout with the G&S segments,' Will had replied with equal edge. 'Rube and I have decided upon the balcony scene.'

'*Romeo and Juliet* has always been my favourite,' Rube said with fervour.

'Mine too,' Will agreed wholeheartedly. 'In my opinion, or rather in my *personal* opinion,' he added, uncharacteristically backing down just a little, 'of course others may well differ, *Romeo and Juliet* contains the Bard's most poetic passages.'

'And also the greatest romance of them all,' Rube said.

'Indeed.'

The one true bond in the entrepreneurial partnership remained Will and Rube's mutual love of Shakespeare.

Carlo gave up.

Surprisingly enough, they did not find the Juliet they wanted among those who auditioned. For the simple reason that no one quite matched up to Gertie.

Gertie had performed Juliet to Will's Romeo in the past when the budget had been tight and they'd relied solely on family, but they'd long since decided not to double up her appearances, allowing full focus on The Divine Dolores. Now, after several auditions, they were forced to rethink that decision. Under stage lighting, Gertie, although thirty-four, looked as young and ethereal as ever, her natural innocence seeming somehow to glow. Her voice was lighter than those of most actresses who specialised in Shakespearean roles, it was true, but that only enhanced the reality of her performance. Gertie was the perfect Juliet.

The same could not quite be said of Will's Romeo. As far as appearances were concerned anyway. Will Worthing was still an impressive-looking man, his carriage proud, the flecks of grey in his fine head of hair always blackened, but at forty-two his body wore the thickening of middle age. It was plainly evident he was no youth. This did not bother Will in the least, and had anyone dared mention the fact, which no one ever did, he would have scoffed at them.

'Do you seriously believe a *youth* could play Romeo?' he would have scathingly replied. 'One needs a *voice* to perform the finest poetry in the English language.' His was the common view among actors – and producers and directors and theatre managers for that matter – most Romeos were in their forties, and all of robust, full-bodied voice. Will personally felt much the same about actresses, and if the truth be known, he would have preferred to be playing opposite a weightier voice than Gertie's. But when the others, Mabel in particular, had so approved the choice, he'd said nothing. He loved Gertie dearly and would never hurt her feelings. There were times when Will Worthing's softer side came to the fore. Although not often displayed, it was always there underneath, as Mabel well knew.

During the rehearsal period, the families became acquainted with each other, although Carlo and Rube rather lost sight of who was who in the numbers of Worthing children.

'This is Ted and Sarah and Izzie and Bertie,' Gertie said, having lined her children up in their order of ages; Ted, soon to turn sixteen, being the oldest, and Bertie, not yet five, the youngest.

'And this is our Alice,' Mabel said, indicating fifteen-year-old Alice, who offered the firmest of handshakes to both men. 'You know our other three, of course.'

'Of course,' Rube said with a smile to the twins. 'The Wonderful Worthings . . .' They didn't look remotely alike;

one would hardly even guess they were brothers. Watching them rehearse Rube had wondered how the act could possibly work, but he put his trust in Mabel, who assured him it would.

'And The Beautiful Pandora,' Carlo added, beaming at Pru. It had been decided to give Pru a stage name; 'Prudence' was not appropriately tantalising.

Rather than disrupt rehearsals, they'd devoted a Sunday for family introductions over a lunch to be held at the Worthings' house in Cremorne.

'With all our tribe, much easier if you come to our place,' Gertie had insisted.

Both Worthing families shared the rambling old house down by the river Will and Max had bought several years previously. In its early days it had belonged to a farming estate, but the once affluent residential area of Cremorne had become increasingly industrialised as tanneries and soap-making factories had set up along the banks of the Yarra, culminating in the Richmond Power Station in 1891. The Worthings' house was no longer the grand residence it had once been, but it was big and served their purpose.

'A stepping stone, Max,' Will had announced, 'a mere stepping stone. We'll both have homes in Toorak one day.' Toorak was the wealthiest suburb in Melbourne, which made it quite possibly the wealthiest suburb in the whole of the country. Toorak was the symbol of success upon which Will had set his heart. 'And that day is not far off, I swear,' he'd vowed.

As promised, Carlo had brought along his family too: wife Winifred; older son Michael, a strapping twenty-year-old; nine-year-old Anne; and newborn baby Martin, who was fast asleep in his perambulator.

'Mick, Anne and Marty,' he proudly announced after introducing the diminutive Winifred.

The Worthings were rather taken aback by Winifred. She wasn't at all the sort of wife they'd envisaged for Carlo. In fact, Will's reaction was not dissimilar to that of Carlo's upon first meeting Mabel. *How odd that such a handsome man should have such an ordinary wife*, he thought.

Winifred Carlovsky was a bony little woman; not ugly – on close inspection not even plain, with a pleasant face and pretty hair tucked up inside her very conventional bonnet – but she was the sort of woman who did not attract notice. Which was possibly one of the reasons Carlo had married her.

Winifred Small had been nineteen years old when Carlo had employed her as a live-in housekeeper and nanny for five-year-old Michael. He'd always joked about her name. 'Small, how very apt,' he'd said upon their first meeting.

True to her name, Winifred was certainly small of stature, but she was hardy, and had quickly proved an excellent housekeeper, nanny, and of far greater impor-tance, a caring mother figure for young Mick. Carlo had found her a welcome change from the succession of nannies he'd hired over the years, some of whom had fallen in love with him, thereby becoming intrusive upon his life, others with whom he'd had a casual affair, thereafter neglecting their duties; all proving in one way or another disastrous. Winifred was different.

After four years of devoted loyalty, Carlo had decided it would be to everyone's advantage if he was to marry Winifred. She would gain a husband, little Mick would gain a mother, and as she was young and healthy, he might hopefully father another son. Besides, he liked her.

Winifred had accepted the proposal, but not in an overly effusive fashion, instead agreeing on a practical level that it would serve everyone's purpose. She admitted, and quite truthfully, that she was grateful to embrace him as a husband and provider, but she did not admit to the deeper truth that she loved him. This fact she would keep always to herself, in the knowledge that a man like Carlo would never conform to the restraints of marriage, nor would he stay with a woman who demanded he should. Winifred was not only hardy, she was intelligent, and eminently sensible.

They had married in 1888 when she was twenty-three years old and he thirty-eight, and in the decade that had followed Winifred had suffered the roué nature of her husband, aware of his infidelities, but thankful Carlo did at least practise discretion on the home front.

It was true, Carlo's many dalliances took place out on the road or when he was performing interstate. This was not altogether in consideration of Winifred's feelings, but rather in deference to his family and his standing as a father. Carlo took parenthood seriously.

The day was crisp and clear, and they dined at the huge family table set up on the back verandah that looked out over the Yarra. The younger children were sent off to play on the grassy slope leading down to the riverbanks, Gertie and Mabel having made up a picnic lunch for them so they wouldn't bother the adults.

'You go on and look after them, Ted,' Gertie said. 'We don't want to have to fish anyone out of the Yarra, do we?'

'You too, Alice,' Mabel ordered. 'There's chicken and salad sandwiches in the hamper for you two as well, and some apples and plenty of cake. Off you go now, you're in charge.'

Ted and Alice accepted their roles with reluctance but resignation for this was currently their lot in life. Both were profoundly envious of Artie, Alfie and Pru, and longed to take up their place as performers. But they were in their final year of schooling and knew it wouldn't be long now. Every Worthing child was to complete his or her education until the age of sixteen: those were the rules.

They dined on platters of oysters to start with, Max having made a quick trip over the Princes Bridge to purchase them freshly shucked from one of the many oyster bars that dotted the inner-city streets.

'A poor man's feast, fit for a king,' Gertie proclaimed to the table after unashamedly sucking an oyster straight from its shell. 'Remember when we first got here we was stony broke, and all we could afford was a glass of ale and a punnet of oysters? Threepence a dozen they was back then.' She ignored the warning glance Will darted at her as she picked up another oyster. 'Well, they're still a poor man's feast,' she went on, 'and they're still fit for a king.'

Max nodded agreement and grinned at his wife. He loved the way his Gert was always just Gert, no pretensions about her. Grabbing an oyster he followed suit, aware it would irritate Will but not caring in the least. Max never allowed his brother to ruffle him.

To avoid the sight of Gertie slurping down a second oyster and his brother about to do the same, Will turned his attention to Mick Carlovsky, who was seated beside him. He found the young man most intriguing. As devilishly handsome as his father, but in a very different way, fair haired and blue-eyed, Will couldn't help wondering about the mother. She too must have been quite a looker. He'd heard Carlo's first wife had died many years ago, although he hadn't heard how, childbirth possibly.

'So you're not interested in becoming a performer, Mick?' he asked. *Pity*, he thought, *with looks like yours, you'd have the matinee matrons swooning in the aisles.*

'No, not in the least,' Mick replied. 'As a matter of fact I'm not really interested in any aspect of show business.'

'Oh.' Will's surprise held an element of shock. The lad's response had not been in any way rude and no insult had been intended, but it was such a brutally honest admission he was taken aback. He was also confused.

'But I was under the impression . . .' he said after a moment's pause while he gathered his thoughts, 'that for the past four years you'd been a valuable employee of your father's company.'

'Oh yes, that's true.' Mick reached out to the nearest platter, gathered a number of oysters and put them on his plate. 'Since I graduated from school I've worked with Uncle Rube on many aspects of the business, front-of-house, box office, accounting, keeping the books, all that sort of thing,' he said, adding a squeeze of lemon juice. 'But it's not where my real interest lies. I'll never belong in show business.'

'Ah, I see.' Will didn't see at all, but he watched, fascinated, as Mick raised an oyster shell to his lips, tossed back his head and sucked the contents into his mouth with a panache that appeared truly stylish. By now, everyone had taken up Gertie's lead. 'It's the only way,' she'd said and they'd all begun obediently slurping.

'Gertie's quite right, isn't she?' Mick turned to Will with a smile as unassuming and winning as any Will Worthing had seen in his life. 'A poor man's feast, fit for a king.'

Will couldn't help himself; he was utterly disarmed. Unlike the father, the lad appeared totally unaware of the impact his looks and personality had on others.

'So tell me, Mick,' he asked, 'where exactly *does* your interest lie?'

'I'm going to join the army.'

'Oh.' Another frisson of surprise bordering on shock. 'And how does your father feel about that?' *Carlo surely won't allow such a thing*, Will thought.

'He wasn't too happy at first,' Mick admitted with a grin, then he noticed Will's empty plate. 'Aren't you having any oysters?'

'No, no.' Will fluttered a hand of indifference; the whole table was now slurping back oysters, and he wasn't a particular fan of the things anyway. 'But you go ahead, please do.'

Mick downed his second oyster with an elegance that equalled the first and continued, 'Uncle Rube talked Pa around though.'

'Really? How?'

'Uncle Rube talked us both around actually. You see, I wanted to join the Victorian Mounted Rifles. A couple of friends from my old school days joined up just this year, and it seemed no time at all before they were off to South Africa to fight the Boers.' Oysters now forgotten, Mick eagerly warmed to his theme. 'I can't tell you how much I wanted to be with them,' he said. 'I'd have given *anything* to go to war, really I would. A life that serves a real *purpose*, you know? A life outside show business.'

Again, the lad meant no disrespect, but Will had trouble maintaining a civil demeanour given such a dismissal of his noble profession.

'But Uncle Rube got me seeing things in a completely different way.'

'And what particular way was that?' Just a touch of coldness in the tone now, which fortunately Mick failed to detect.

'Uncle Rube said no purpose would be served in going off to another country to get killed in a war that really has nothing to do with us.'

'I quite agree.' *Clever Rube*, Will thought.

'I'm going to wait until the government forms its own Australian army,' Mick declared, 'and then I'll be able to embark upon a career in the military. A career that will lead to a *lifetime* of purpose.' His face glowed with a happiness verging on beatific.

'And your father doesn't mind you foregoing show business for a military career?'

'No, Pa doesn't care in the least.'

Which was possibly the greatest shock of all to Will Worthing. *Carlo doesn't care?!* But the answer quickly struck home. *Of course he wouldn't care, he's not a creature of the theatre. Carlo's the amateur I always took him to be.*

In truth, the situation had been neither as simple as Mick had painted nor as Will now assumed. Carlo had very much wanted his son to remain in the family business. He'd been immensely proud of Mick's education, the boy having graduated with excellent marks from the ultra-exclusive Melbourne Academy, and he'd been proud too of the invaluable part his son had played in the running of the company business. It had come as a terrible blow to discover the lad wanted to sign up and go to war in South Africa.

'I can't and won't allow that, Mick,' he'd said firmly. 'You'd probably get yourself killed, and for what? It's just adventure you're after, like any young man.'

'No, Pa, it's not,' Mick had protested. 'I want to join the Victorian Mounted Rifles, I want to serve a purpose . . .'

The boy was clearly determined and Carlo had been lost for an answer.

As always in times of crisis, he'd turned to Rube. And as always in times of crisis, Rube had come up with a solution.

'Bide your time, Mick,' he'd advised. 'You're only twenty years old, and if you go about things the right way, you could serve a far greater military purpose than getting yourself killed in a war that has nothing to do with your own country.'

Mick had listened attentively as Rube had gone on. He loved his father dearly, but Uncle Rube was, and always had been, the greatest influence in his life.

'I have it on good authority,' Rube had said, 'that after Federation, which as we all know will happen any day now, the various state militias – *including* the Victorian Mounted Rifles –' he'd added meaningfully, 'will be united under the new Australian flag and become a real army. Why not wait until then and be part of a great new adventure? A noble cause that will serve you a lifetime.'

Uncle Rube's advice had made sense to Mick. But it was Carlo who had been truly grateful for the further advice Rube had offered in private.

'The new army will not be authorised to engage in war anywhere but on Australian soil, Carlo,' Rube had said. 'I've made enquiries and been told the army is to be solely a national defence force. Furthermore, the military will not be called upon to sort out domestic situations as the state militias once were. Civil unrest like riots and protests are to be left in the hands of the various state police. All of which means Mick will have an honourable career serving in the defence of his country just as he wishes. But unlike the fate that may await his friends in South Africa, his life will not be under threat.'

And that was all that ultimately mattered to Carlo: the preservation of his son's life.

'Who cares about show business,' he'd said as he'd given the lad his blessing and wished him well, 'a career in the army will be a fine life for you, Mick.'

Gertie and Mabel were now clearing away the oyster platters preparatory to setting out the light meal that was to follow.

'Eat up,' Gertie commanded, and Mick hastily downed the three oysters left on his plate.

'So all I have to do now is wait for Federation,' he said to Will, grinning as he wiped his fingers with his napkin. 'And it can't come quick enough for me, I can tell you.'

The commotion occurred barely fifteen minutes later. Everyone was about to tuck into their food, with the exception of Winifred, who had disappeared to feed a restless baby Marty his bottle. Artie and Alfie had set fresh plates on the table, Max had poured glasses of ale for those who wanted them, Pru was buttering bread rolls for all, and platters of cold meats and salads were being passed around, when suddenly young Ted appeared on the verandah. He'd come up the back steps that led down to the grass, dragging along beside him by the scruff of his neck his younger brother, Bertie. Both were dishevelled, soaking wet and covered in mud, and fifteen-year-old Ted was very, very angry.

'He did it on purpose,' he loudly declared, releasing the hold he had on the collar of Bertie's sodden shirt.

'Did not,' Bertie declared equally loudly, standing his ground.

'You just wanted attention, you little brat! You were out to cause trouble, like always!

'Was not,' Bertie fired back, 'I slipped.'

'You could have drowned.'

'I can swim.'

'Not in a current like that you can't!'

'All right, that's enough, you two.' Gertie broke up the spat. She'd instinctively risen from the table at the sight of her sons in such a mess, but when she'd ascertained there was no real harm done she'd sat back down. 'You're dripping all over the place. Now go and get cleaned up, the pair of you.'

The two stood scowling at each other for a moment, Ted simmering, Bertie defiant. Then . . .

'You do that again, Bertie,' Ted said, quietly this time although a definite warning, 'and I just might not come in after you.'

But the little boy wasn't prepared to accede defeat altogether. 'I *can* swim,' he muttered rebelliously, and he walked off with all the dignity a four-year-old could muster.

The stunt *had* been deliberate. Bertie had dared himself to jump in the river. He was nearly five and he wasn't scared of the water or being in over his depth. He'd decided to test himself. But deep down inside, he'd known Ted was watching out for him and that if something went wrong Ted would come to his rescue. Ted was Bertie's hero.

Young Ted was about to leave, but Gertie stopped him.

'Ay Ted,' she called, and when he turned back to her she wrinkled her nose in that funny way she did when she was conveying a special message to one of her children. 'Thanks, lovey, you done good.'

Ted nodded, both aware no more need be said. Gertie had recognised the source of his anger, how truly scared he'd been by Bertie's stunt. Ted adored his baby brother.

'He's a cheeky little bugger, our Bertie,' Gertie announced to the table as she speared herself a lump of chicken breast. 'More trouble than he's worth sometimes.'

And the lunch continued most successfully.

The company worked hard over the ensuing months, and then it seemed, with lightning speed, the 31st of December was upon them. After a riotous New Year's Eve that saw in the birth of a brand-new century, *The Musical Variety Extravaganza of 1900* was about to hit the road.

10

A ROCKY ROAD IS TRAVELLED

As was the purpose with all out-of-town tryouts and any tour of a brand-new show, flaws were revealed during the early run of performances. In the case of *The Musical Variety Extravaganza of 1900*, however, the principal problem, which manifested itself glaringly in the very first performance, came from a most unexpected quarter.

'But, soft! What light through yonder window breaks?
It is the east, and Juliet is the sun!'

They were opening the second half of the show with the balcony scene, and the titters started from the very moment Will stepped out onstage. He looked handsome, imposing in his tights and tunic, and his voice was as always magnificent. What could possibly be wrong? He projected a little louder with a vocal power that demanded silence.

'Arise, fair sun, and kill the envious moon,
Who is already sick and pale with grief,
That thou, her maid, art far more fair than she.'

But the titters continued; they grew, even, spreading through the audience like a virus.

Gazing up at Gertie, where she stood serenely beautiful on the vine-covered balcony, Will struck a stance of heroic proportion, defying those who dared laugh at the greatest romantic speech written in the English language.

'Be not her maid, since she is envious:

Her vestal livery is but sick and green
And none but fools do wear it; cast it off.'

Still the titters continued to grow, and the bolder he performed the louder they became. He forged on regardless,
at one point ignoring the balcony and looking directly out
front, commanding respect.

'See, how she leans her cheek upon her hand.
O, that I were a glove upon that hand,
That I might touch that cheek!'

The titters were no longer titters. They'd become laughs
now. The audience was *laughing* at him!

'Ay me.'

Up on the balcony, Juliet spoke.

He whirled about, gesturing to his love high above.

'She speaks:
O, speak again, bright angel!'

More laughs, bigger and louder. Will was mortified.
What was going on? But he was angry too. How *dare* they!

Some performers might have taken the punters to task,
demanding they shut up, in which case there was always
the risk they would hurl things at the stage. But Will was
not such a performer and this was not burlesque, nor was it
music hall – this was the poetry of William Shakespeare.
He remained in character, prepared to continue bravely
soldiering on, but all of a sudden something unheard of
occurred. He dried. So shaken was he that for one brief
moment the words he knew and loved so well totally
escaped him. How could this happen? Will Worthing
had never been known to dry. Never! And *Romeo?* Why,
Romeo was as indelibly engraved on his brain as the
words on a gravestone. For the first time in his life, panic
threatened to overwhelm him. He opened his mouth in
order to give voice . . . to something. But what? He had no
idea. Then from somewhere in the deepest recesses of his
mind, the lines came back.

'. . . *for thou art*
As glorious to this night, being o'er my head
As is a winged messenger from heaven . . .'
And the audience continued to laugh.
Until finally Juliet spoke again.
'O *Romeo, Romeo! Wherefore art thou Romeo?*
Deny thy father and refuse thy name;
Or, if thou wilt not, be but sworn my love,
And I'll no longer be a Capulet.'
The audience was deadly quiet. No one laughed at Juliet.
Will directed Romeo's aside out front, as was customary.
'*Shall I hear more, or shall I speak at this?*'
There was the odd titter, but most remained quiet,
some perhaps aware of what lay ahead, others once again
waiting for Juliet to speak. She did.
'*Tis but thy name that is my enemy;*
Thou art thyself, though not a Montague.'
From that moment on, the audience remained silent.
And as Juliet's speech led into the duologue, they stopped
laughing at Romeo, who apparently no longer appeared to
them a figure of fun. The young lovers had finally become
real. The balcony scene progressed smoothly and upon its
conclusion received a respectful round of applause, but the
opening had been a humiliating farce. And Will Worthing
was incensed.
'What the blazes went wrong back there?' he hissed to
Mabel as he came offstage into the prompt side wings.
'What the hell was the matter with them?'
The curtain had closed, and behind him stagehands had
taken the blocks from the balcony and were wheeling it to
the OP side while a backcloth was being flown in for the
next act.
'Why were they laughing?' he demanded.
Mabel cued Georgie Washington and the band struck
up. Then, with the backcloth safely in place, she cued

the nearby stagehand and the curtain once again swished open. After which she cued the lights, then . . .

'You're on,' she said to Irving, who was standing by.

'Why, Mabel, why?' Will insisted as Irving Sayles bounded onstage throwing a series of backflips, delighting the audience and producing an instant round of applause; they'd fallen in love with him already from his act in the first half of the show. '*Why did they laugh?*'

'Because they thought you were funny,' Mabel said, finally free to give him her attention.

'*Why?*'

'Because of the *Pinafore* duet.' Mabel had recognised the problem from the very first titter, and was a little surprised she hadn't anticipated it. 'They didn't see you as Romeo at all. They saw you as Captain Corcoran.'

'But the *Pinafore* duet was after Gertie's opening dance,' Will expostulated with a mix of frustration and disbelief. 'It was the second turn in the first half of the bleeding show, for God's sake!'

Unusual to hear him swear, Mabel thought. 'You were very good, Will,' she said, 'very good and very, very funny. They're not going to forget a performance like that.'

The comment appeased him somewhat, as Mabel had hoped it would, but he wasn't about to let the matter rest.

'We'll change the running order then.'

'You can't hit them with the balcony scene first up,' Mabel said, 'you have to start them off with laughs, you know that.'

'So what do you suggest we do?'

'I suggest we talk about it later. In the meantime, let's hope your other number isn't affected.' Will was shortly to perform 'Never Mind the Why and Wherefore' also from *HMS Pinafore,* another frothy, comedic piece.

'Affected? In what way?' Sensing a possible affront, Will's tone was frosty.

'They might see you as Romeo and not find you funny, who can tell?' Mabel turned to the skirt dancers who'd arrived in the wings. 'Standing by, girls,' she said, although there was a full ten minutes before they were to go on. 'You have a wardrobe change, Will,' she reminded him, unnecessarily she knew, but signalling the end of the conversation. For now anyway.

Will, still smarting, stormed off to his dressing room.

They did discuss it later, back at the hotel, just the two of them, Will being loath to share his mortification with the entire company. Enough to know most would have witnessed it and those who hadn't would certainly be telling the others.

He started out on the defensive, blaming the punters.

'Ignorant peasants the whole lot of them,' he said scathingly, 'a terrible audience, no understanding of the theatre.'

'There's no such thing as a bad audience,' Mabel replied, 'only a bad show.' It was another of his favourite quotes, which he readily handed out to young actors who whinged, and she knew it would shut him up. It did.

'Now you listen to me, Will,' she went on, getting down to business. 'You and Maeve had them rolling in the aisles with "Things Are Seldom What they Seem"; the *Pinafore* duet gets us off to a great start. And in my opinion the balcony scene is the ideal way to open the second half, because by then we have the punters eating out of our hands and they're ready for a touch of the classics. The running order must stay the way it is.'

'But . . . ?' He halted, confused. What was she getting at?

'But with Max as Romeo,' she said.

'Oh.'

Mabel felt for her husband, knowing him so completely as she did. He'd wanted to show off his versatility, the great Will Worthing, master of comedy and drama, but for once his pride had proved his downfall and he'd been left humiliated. A very painful experience for any performer, especially a man like Will.

'You can't have it both ways, love,' she said gently, 'not this time.'

Will nodded. He knew Mabel was right. His ego had got the better of him and the punters had caught him out. *No such thing as a bad audience,* he thought. *Different perhaps, yes, they can vary, but one must always heed their reaction. Of course Mabel's right.*

Max proved a triumph as Romeo. The audience was quite prepared to accept the dual role of the acrobat who had so charmed them in the first half of the show and that of the star-crossed lover who won the heart of Juliet in the opening act of the second half. Mabel's genius idea that they should incorporate Max's acrobatic skills may well have helped.

When they'd met with Max and Gertie to discuss the change of casting, Rube had been only too eager to join them; this was the Shakespearean act after all. They'd asked Carlo along also as co-producer, but Carlo hadn't been interested.

'Let's have Romeo climb the balcony towards the end of the duologue,' Mabel had said. 'So romantic, the punters will love it!'

Max and Gertie had been instantly amenable to the idea, as had Rube, but Will had been aghast at the mere suggestion.

'You can't do that!' he'd exclaimed. 'Romeo never climbs the balcony.'

'Of course he does,' Mabel replied briskly, 'he climbs the thing later on in Act Three to get to her chamber.'

'But he's never *seen* to climb it,' Will insisted, 'never! The chamber scene opens and there they both are —'

'And after their duologue he climbs out of the window, doesn't he,' Mabel said. 'Which is how he got up there in the first place.'

'It's not a bad idea, Will,' Max added mildly, Gertie nodding away; she thought it was a truly marvellous idea.

'Yes, yes,' Will barked, 'he climbs out of the window, of course he climbs out of the window ... "*Farewell, farewell! One kiss and I'll descend*" ... But this is the *chamber* scene when he climbs *down*! He doesn't climb *up* in the *balcony* scene.'

'Actually, there never *was* a balcony.' The calm interjection from Rube brought them all to a halt. 'Shakespeare never wrote a balcony into the play, not in the stage directions and not in the dialogue. No mention at all. It was always a window.'

A pause. 'He's right,' Mabel said.

'Then why is it called the balcony scene?' Will demanded belligerently.

'Because at one time or another, who knows when, some bright spark director had the brilliant idea of stepping Juliet out onto a balcony instead of leaning from an upstairs window,' Mabel said. 'Very clever. Much better for audience sightlines.'

'Besides,' Gertie chimed in, 'it wouldn't sound right calling it "the window scene", would it?'

'So Max climbs up to the balcony, and that's that,' Mabel said.

Will was forced to give in. Much as he disapproved, he couldn't take on all four of them.

The balcony, which had been a rather flimsy affair, was reinforced and stabilised for the purpose of the climb, and the vines, which had served purely as dressing, were masked to hide grips and footholds. It worked a treat.

Juliet gazes down at Romeo in the garden below.

'*Good night, good night! As sweet repose and rest*
Come to thy heart as that within my breast!'
Romeo gazes up at Juliet on her balcony.
'*O, wilt thou leave me so unsatisfied?*'
She responds:
'*What satisfaction canst thou have tonight?*'
He starts to climb the vines that lead up to the balcony
railings.
'*The exchange of thy love's faithful vow for mine.*'
She watches him, thrilling to the sight.
'*I gave thee mine before thou didst request it:*
And yet I would it were to give again.'
He has arrived at the balcony, and leaps over the railings
to stand beside her.
'*Wouldst thou withdraw it? For what purpose, love?*'
Their eyes lock, their bodies meld together, her hand
resting upon his chest.
'*But to be frank, and give it thee again.*
And yet I wish but for the thing I have:
My bounty is as boundless as the sea,
My love as deep; the more I give to thee,
The more I have, for both are infinite.'
He takes her in his arms. They kiss. And the audience
goes wild! In the wings, Mabel has to wait some time before
she can interject from offstage calling out as the Nurse.

Max's athleticism undoubtedly provided an added
element to the scene, but it was he and Gertie who were
the true magic. They made a wonderful pair. Gertie really
was a young, swooningly-in-love girl, and Max really *was*
a lithe and virile, passionate youth.

Will regularly watched their performance from the
wings, dressed in the costume for his second G&S number
and each time he did his mind would go back to close on
twenty years. To the terrible cotton mill fire and the day
the two had first met, the day when they'd fallen in love.

They're actually playing themselves, aren't they, he'd think with admiration. *That's our Max and Gertie, and they're as much in love as ever they were.* But he did rather wish their voices were a little stronger and that the performance was a little more along traditional lines.

Within barely a week it became obvious to the entire company that Carlo and Maeve were having an affair. They were hardly discreet. To the contrary, they were blatant.

Will said as much to Mabel.

'They're not exactly discreet, are they,' he remarked disapprovingly. 'Dear God, they can't leave each other alone.'

'None of our business,' she replied.

'But we've only been out on the road for a week,' he protested. 'It's a bit premature, wouldn't you say?' And when she refused to comment, he protested further. 'You must admit it's not at all fair to Winifred.'

'What happens out on the road . . .' Mabel said, quoting the unwritten law that had always existed among performers on tour. 'Winifred need never know.'

Will harrumphed his disapproval at her lack of sympathy for the poor woman, then muttered something about Carlo's 'decadence' and Maeve's 'unprofessional behaviour' and stomped off.

Mabel knew exactly why he was so offended, and again it was all to do with ego. Will Worthing and Maeve Gallagher flirted outrageously in their G&S numbers, as it was intended their characters should, particularly in the bawdy duet 'Things Are Seldom What They Seem' when their performance was unashamedly suggestive. Will was now jealous that in reality it was Carlo, rather than he, to whom Maeve was sexually attracted.

Her husband's jealousy was of a strictly professional nature, Mabel was quite sure; Will so gave himself to his performances that he often *did* have a love affair onstage.

But he never strayed offstage. At least, he never had to the best of her knowledge. She recalled though the several times when she'd been heavily pregnant and unable to tour. Had he? Then she shrugged off the thought. *What happens out on the road . . .* Better she didn't know anyway.

Carlo and Maeve thrashed about in the throes of passion for the third time that morning. A Sunday that didn't involve travel to the next town was special, and they intended to indulge to their hearts' content. Carlo remained proud of his prowess as a lover and over the several weeks of their affair Maeve had proved insatiable. She reminded him of Rosie in so many ways. Strong, statuesque, well-endowed, just the way he liked a woman to be. She was not as supple and athletic as Rosie to be sure, but then she wasn't a con-tortionist – oh, the things Rosie could do with her body! But in some ways Maeve was even more rewarding. Hot-blooded, she revelled in the sexual act, whereas Rosie had always taken control, able to drive him into a frenzy while remaining somehow detached, a talent which he'd found at times exciting and at others frustrating. With Maeve he enjoyed being the one in power.

They finally collapsed in a state of mutual exhaustion, their passion spent, and within only a few minutes Maeve was asleep, lightly snoring, a sound which he rather enjoyed, bringing to mind as it did the purr of a contented cat.

He lay there, hands behind his head, looking up at nothing, but in his mind's eye seeing Rosie. He'd been thinking of Rosie quite a bit over these past several weeks. Because of Maeve. Good God, he hadn't thought of Rosie for nigh on twenty years. Which was a lie, he reminded himself; he'd thought of her for a long time after she'd left, mainly in the hope that she wouldn't return to reclaim her son. But when this had proved not to be her intent, he'd decided to forget her altogether. Although he did recall the one time he'd seen her, a whole thirteen years ago now, at the opening of Her Majesty's Theatre and Grand Opera House in 1887.

Upon Rube's insistence they'd travelled to Sydney for the occasion, Rube proclaiming it would be 'an event of tremendous historical significance', which sounded odd coming from one not given to hyperbole, and they'd taken eight-year-old Mick with them.

'Her Majesty's Theatre and Grand Opera House will be Sydney's greatest theatre,' Rube had said, 'both architecturally and in modern interior design. I think it's important Mick be witness to such an historical event. Particularly,' he'd added as if in afterthought, 'with George Rignold performing *Henry V*, which I've heard is to be a production of spectacular proportion.' More hyperbole, but no longer odd, at least not to Carlo.

Ah, so that's it, he'd thought, knowing Rube admired George Rignold, and that *Henry V* was his favourite of Shakespeare's 'military' plays. These were surely the attractions rather than the theatre itself. Personally, Carlo doubted any Sydney venue could compete with Melbourne's finest, either in architecture or modern interior design, but keen to instil a love of theatre in his son he'd been happy to go along with the idea.

Her Majesty's certainly *was* grand, he was prepared to admit, but as he'd suspected no grander than Melbourne's finest, of which there were many. And yes, George Rignold *was* a commanding Henry, he was prepared to admit that too, but he'd far rather be watching a variety show himself.

Sidelong glances at his son, however, assured him the whole exercise was most worthwhile. Mick was loving every minute of the play. But Mick's taste had always seemed to follow Rube's rather than his, a fact that far from bothering Carlo pleased him no end. After all, Rube was the smart one.

It was during the second interval he saw them, as they mingled among the crowds in the grand foyer, sipping champagne. The evening was certainly a glamorous affair, men resplendent in formal attire, women competing in all their finery, liveried waiters weaving to and fro with trays of glasses held dexterously high.

Carlo gazed around, sure there must be many a well-known face he was bound to recognise; it was a night to see and be seen after all. Most of those present were doing the same, albeit a little more surreptitiously. A wave here and there, and upon recognition the occasional connection, a kiss of a cheek, a shake of a hand, everyone eager to socialise – with the exception of Rube, who was too busy admiring the architecture, and young Mick, who was concentrating on his glass of lemonade.

Carlo saw them in an instant, Rosie and Gilda, standing barely twenty yards away, talking to a select group of people who appeared quite wealthy, but then everyone did. He nudged Rube, who dragged his eyes from the ceiling to follow the direction of his gaze, and they both stared openly at the women.

Rosie was in cobalt blue, a colour she had always favoured, an off-the-shoulder taffeta gown displaying her fine bosom and the handsome line of her back. Her body was still excellent, Carlo noted. But even in the profile view afforded him, he could tell there was a good deal of makeup on that face, on that neck too, and he doubted she would stand the test of close inspection. She had to be well over forty by now, possibly even mid-forties, although he'd never really known her actual age, had he? Gilda, in a flattering, rose-coloured silk gown, hadn't seemed to age all that much, he thought. Not as arresting as Rosie, of course, she never had been, but a pretty woman nonetheless.

Over the years since their parting, Carlo had often wondered why they hadn't bumped into each other, travelling the circuit as they did. He'd expected they would and had rather dreaded the prospect, but he hadn't even seen The Fairweather Sisters act listed on a billboard or poster and had assumed they must have left show business.

Watching her closely, he noted Rosie wasn't engaged in the group's conversation and appeared quite bored. Gilda wasn't chatting either, but at least she was feigning interest. *How typical of the two*, he thought.

Then in an open expression of disdain, Rosie turned her back on the group to survey the grand foyer, her eyes slowly raking the crowd as if seeking something, anything, that might possibly be of interest.

Carlo knew that any minute those eyes would come to rest upon him, but he did not look away. Instead, he placed his hand possessively on Mick's shoulder; he didn't know why.

Beside him, Rube did not look away either. He'd been studying the women with equal fascination, rather wishing he could say hello to Gilda, but aware it would not be wise. Now as Rosie turned and he had a clearer view of her face, he noted the finely chiselled bones were no longer delicate and the perfectly shaped lips had become thin. Perhaps being overly rouged and painted only served to emphasise the effect, but Rosie had become decidedly hard-faced. *Interesting*, he thought without rancour, *the face now reflects the true woman within.* He wondered what had made Rosie so. *A hard life no doubt*, he decided, as he too waited for her eyes to come to rest upon Carlo.

But Rosie's eyes did not come to rest upon Carlo. Oh, she would have seen him! She would most certainly have seen him, her gaze steadily sweeping the grand foyer, missing nothing, but not for one infinitesimal moment did that gaze come to rest upon him. Or, for that matter, upon the child she would have known was hers. There was no sign of recognition, no shred of interest; her eyes simply

moved on, and having completed her view of the foyer
she turned back to the group. But the way she linked her
gloved hand through the arm of the tall, obviously wealthy
man who stood by her side might have been read as a
message. If not by Carlo, then most certainly by Gilda.

Gilda turned. She looked directly at Carlo and Rube,
and also at young Mick, and her eyes took in everything.
Her eyes also *said* everything.

So that's how baby Michael turned out, they said admiringly, *what a fine young fellow*. She gave the faintest smile
and the slightest nod of approval. To both of them, not
just Carlo; Rube was included, as if they were the proud
parents, which in a way they were. *Congratulations*, her
eyes said, *well done*. Then she turned back to the group.

A whole thirteen years ago, Carlo thought, still staring
blankly at the ceiling as Maeve purred away beside him.
That was the last time he'd seen Rosie. He wondered what
she'd look like now; she'd certainly be old. But no matter,
she was of no interest to him. His 'first wife', the mother
of his grown son, had been dead for years.

By the time *The Musical Variety Extravaganza of 1900*
had completed its regional tour of Victoria and was about
to cross the border into New South Wales, every possible
kink had been well and truly ironed out, and even more
importantly the reviews from town to town had been
extremely favourable.

The usual game had been played with newspaper critics,
Will and Carlo wining, dining and generally feting the press,
both being past masters of the art, and while the reviews
had given fulsome praise to the show in general, two acts had
been regularly singled out. One was The Serpentine Dance
of The Divine Delores, which was of course no surprise, and
the other was The Wonderful Worthing, Master Illusionist,
which was particularly exciting. They now had a brand-new

act to top the bill and bring the punters running, and with Sydney looming closer, posters and leaflets were adjusted accordingly. Artie and Alfie were thrilled to discover they were now to share top billing with their Aunt Gertie.

Word was spreading, and if the grapevine continued to operate as successfully during the two-month regional tour of New South Wales, their Sydney season at the Criterion would have audiences queuing down Park Street in the hundreds, eager to welcome them with open arms.

There was a jarring moment, however, when it appeared they were about to be hit by a last-minute snag, one which in Mabel's eyes was of vast proportion.

'We goin' back home, missus.'

Young Freddy Ngala fronted up to Mabel backstage as she and the crew were busily packing out after Saturday's evening performance. The show was due to travel the following day, and they were to cross the border. Freddy's dad Jimmy was with him too, all of which was unusual. As a rule, both disappeared after the opening Serpentine Dance and their performance with the didgeridoo and clapsticks.

'You're what?' Mabel said, looking up from the large wicker skip into which she was packing props. She wasn't sure she'd heard correctly. There was much bustling going on around her, stagehands striking the set and sorting out the various rigs that travelled with them.

'Dad don' wanna go on,' fifteen-year-old Freddy said with a flick of his head at Jimmy, who stood passively rock-like beside him. A craggy man with a granite face, Jimmy didn't talk much; he was happy for Freddy to be his spokesman. 'So we goin' back home.'

'But ...' Mabel was flabbergasted. 'But ... you can't. I mean ...' She found herself stammering, which was quite unlike her. 'Well ... I mean ... you can't.'

'Sure we can.' Freddy gave his easy smile, flash of white teeth in black, black face. 'I wanna go home too. We been 'way long time now, missus. We gonna leave tomorra.'

'But . . .' Mabel looked to Jimmy as if seeking assistance, but Jimmy was simply offering a series of benign nods; the boy was doing fine, getting everything right. 'But . . . why?'

'Why what?'

'Why do you want to go home?'

'Cos it's time.'

'Time for what?'

'Time to go home.'

'Ah.' Mabel took a deep breath, and finally discovering her voice, spoke firmly. 'Now you listen to me, Freddy,' she said, 'we have a show to do. You have to perform. You too, Jimmy,' she said to the father, adding emphatically, 'that's what we *pay* you to do, you understand?'

The two shared a look. There was a further nod of agreement from Jimmy, but it was once again Freddy who replied.

'Yeh, that's good, we like that you pay us. But Dad and me, we don' wanna do the show no more, so we goin' home now.'

It was as simple as that. Mabel knew she would be unable to dissuade them. And what right did she have anyway? There was no contract, no legal arrangement, only a verbal agreement. She'd asked them and they'd said 'yes'. This was not their fault but hers; how naive she'd been.

'How will you get home?' she asked, probably for lack of something to say as her frantic mind sought a way out of this catastrophic situation. Where was she to find two more Aboriginal performers? And even more importantly, a didgeridoo?

'We walk.'

'But it's over a hundred miles to Melbourne.'

'Yeh.' A shared smile from both this time, Jimmy's showing a broad gap where two front teeth were missing. 'We like to walk,' Freddy said.

In desperation, Mabel clutched at the only solution she could come up with. 'Then I'll buy your didgeridoo, Jimmy,' she said. *Yes, that might work*, she thought. *We could blackface the trumpet player, teach him to play the thing.* 'You sell me your didgeridoo. I'll pay you really good money for it, how does that sound?'

Freddy waited for his dad to speak this time, and finally Jimmy did.

'You a woman,' he said, the statement not only incongruous but to Mabel's ears somehow accusatory.

'So?' She was justifiably mystified.

'Can't give didgeridoo to a *woman*.' His tone seemed to intimate she should have known that.

'Oh, I see. Then perhaps you could sell it to my husband,' she suggested hopefully, 'would that be possible? Could you sell it to Mr Worthing?'

But to her horror Jimmy shook his head.

'Haven't got it no more, missus. I give it away.'

'Oh dear.' Mabel was finally forced to admit defeat.

Then Jimmy made the little speech he'd come prepared to make.

'I give it to Georgie,' he said. 'I teach Georgie too. He not much good yet, but he can play. You need didgeridoo for that dance, missus.' Jimmy thumped the flat of his hand against his chest in a heartfelt gesture. 'That a dance of Country, that is,' he said, 'didgeridoo belong to that dance.'

She wanted to hug him. 'Yes, Jimmy,' she said, 'oh yes, indeed it does.' Then as father and son turned to go, she hastily added, 'But we must pay you for it. Mr Worthing, I mean, not me,' she said, in case this could be construed as some form of insult.

'No need for pay,' Jimmy replied, 'it a gift from me to Georgie.' Jimmy had become good mates with the American. They were brothers, him and Georgie.

'But the didgeridoo must be valuable . . .'

Young Freddy gave a hoot of laughter. 'Dad got two more back home, and he can make another one whenever he wanna.'

Mabel insisted upon giving them enough to cover their train fares back to Melbourne, however, and they were happy to accept that. They waited while she fetched the money from Will and Rube, who were in one of the dressing rooms counting the night's takings.

'Thanks, missus,' Jimmy said, pocketing the sum. They'd camp out tonight, as they always did, and set off first thing in the morning. They wouldn't catch the train – they'd much prefer to walk, and the money would come in handy when they got back to Melbourne.

Mabel watched as father and son set off through the backstage exit and faded into the gloom of outside. She was deeply grateful to Jimmy and thankful for his gift, her overall reaction one of immense relief. Gertie's desert dance and the didgeridoo opening of the show was, to her mind, a masterpiece.

Already she was re-envisaging the act. They would have just the one musician visible onstage, and being Georgie they wouldn't even need to blacken him up. Georgie Washington was already black, which was very convenient. He was a fine musician, but she hoped he could master the instrument; it looked difficult in its simplicity. She would operate the clapsticks herself from the wings. They must start rehearsing immediately.

Ever since that day outside the railway station in Flinders Street, Mabel had determined they must have a didgeridoo for the dance. She'd returned regularly to the station in the hope that the father and son duo would be there, but

they never were. Refusing to give up, she'd searched elsewhere in the hope of finding another didgeridoo, another
player, asking around, making enquiries particularly of
show people, but all to no avail. Apparently Aboriginal
music was not known in show business circles. It was most
frustrating. She'd tried to explain the sound to Georgie
Washington, he too never having heard a didgeridoo.
'Haunting,' she'd said, 'spiritual, mystical,' although no
specific words seemed adequate. Georgie had composed
a piece for the flute, which indeed had a mystical sound,
but it was hardly the same. *Sadly, not even similar*, Mabel
had thought.

Then, when the show was in its final stage of production
with full dress rehearsals under way and less than a week
to go, the miracle had happened. She hadn't found the
father and son duo; they had found her. Or so it seemed.

She and Rube had just stepped outside the Princess
Theatre, where they'd had a meeting with the manager
regarding their booking later in the year, and the first
thing Mabel heard was the sound of a didgeridoo. She
gazed across Spring Street to where Parliament House
stood a little further up the road, and there they were,
she could see them quite clearly. The Aboriginal man
seated on the steps with his didgeridoo, the son standing
beside him adding the rhythm of his clapsticks. Of course,
she thought, what better spot to busk than the most
majestic of Melbourne's grand buildings; tourists were
constantly drawn to the vast, colonnaded beauty of Parliament House. She noticed that, again, many passers-by
were giving the Aborigines a wide berth, although it was
also evident the same passers-by were fascinated by the
sound they were hearing.

'I'll see you back at rehearsal, Rube,' she muttered. 'Get
everything set up for Gertie's opening dance, quick as you
can.' And she was off across Spring Street, dodging the

heavy traffic of coaches and carriages, teams and pairs, single horses and drays.

Mabel on a mission, Rube thought as he watched her go. He knew exactly what she was up to; he'd heard the didgeridoo himself, and she'd spoken of it often enough. He hastily set off to do her bidding. *If anyone can make this happen, Mabel can.*

Half an hour later, she arrived at the rehearsal hall where the entire company was gathered having been working throughout the morning, and all was in readiness for Gertie's dance.

'This is Jimmy and Freddy,' Mabel announced. She'd paid them five pounds to come with her. 'There's something I want to show you,' she'd told them. 'Won't take long, it's only a block away,' and Jimmy and Freddy had been more than happy to tag along, Jimmy with his didgeridoo slung over one shoulder, Freddy tucking his clapsticks into the back of the belt that held up his baggy trousers. Why not? Five quid was five quid!

The hall that the company had hired was a regular rehearsal venue for theatre companies, being in the heart of theatre territory as it was. Also serving various community functions, dances, charity events and the like, it had ample space and an adequate stage, but the lighting was poor.

'These are rehearsal conditions only,' Mabel went on to explain, as seats were set up for Jimmy and Freddy at a perfect vantage point from the stage, 'but no matter, we have a follow spot and the projector so you'll get the general idea. We always travel with our own follow spots anyway, just to be safe.'

The two had not understood one word she'd said about 'lighting' and 'special effects', but they obligingly took their places. This appeared to be what she wanted to show them.

The other members of the company stood around
watching from the rear of the hall, wondering what was
going on and, knowing Mabel, very keen to find out;
something was obviously about to happen.

The blinds on the hall's windows were pulled down, the
place reduced to a state of semi-darkness that was satisfac-
tory, and the flautist commenced. A lingering melody that
seemed somehow otherworldly. Then, to a knowledge-
able ear, the slight whirr of a projector that would not be
audible in a proper theatre, and up on the blank screen
that was erected at the rear of the stage appeared imagery
of an arid plain, rocky outcrops, stunted mulga trees and
spinifex grasses, exactly as Mabel had envisaged in her
plans for the dance.

Jimmy Ngala and his young son stared, transfixed;
they'd never seen such a thing, how could this be possible?

These are the lands of the desert people, Jimmy thought.
How had this country of his brothers been caught in such
a way? It seemed very wrong to Jimmy, this dead image
of a land captured, motionless.

Then Gertie appeared, a billowing cloud of ochre-red,
and the imagery was reproduced on the silken expanse of
her costume. Before Jimmy's very eyes, the lifeless black
and white appeared suddenly alive and the land started
to move, pulsing with a heartbeat that was palpable. He
watched, mesmerised.

A follow spot slowly came up on Gertie, the imagery
fading now, the colour intensifying. Gertie was becoming
the land. And as he watched, Jimmy recognised the symbolism. The dancer was the land, voluminous swathes of
earth-coloured fabric floating, settling, rippling restlessly
then rising in sheer magnificence to become a mighty dust
storm, enveloping everything in its path.

Finally, the follow spot started to fade, the colour
diminished, and the imagery returned to the screen at the

rear of the stage as the dancer slowly sank to the ground, becoming simply a part of the landscape.

This was not wrong at all, Jimmy realised. This dance was a tribute to the desert country and its people.

The performance over, Gertie was given a polite round of applause by the company, the projector turned off, the blinds pulled up, and Mabel started explaining to Jimmy exactly what it was she and Gertie had in mind.

'We really want your music to be a part of the dance, Jimmy,' she said. 'You see, we feel this dance is representative of the land itself, and . . .'

She didn't need to tell him that.

Jimmy stood, nodded at Freddy, and the two walked up the side steps that led to the stage, where Jimmy sat with his didgeridoo and Freddy dug his clapsticks out from the back of his belt.

They started to play, the haunting sound of the didgeridoo filling the hall, accompanied by the rhythmic clack of the sticks.

Gertie immediately returned to the stage and between the three of them the dance became inspired. Now it was the turn of all those gathered to be transfixed. Even without back projection, even without a follow spot, the sight and the sound were a perfect marriage. Just as Mabel had anticipated they would be.

The company crossed the border, and with Jimmy and Freddy now gone, Mabel and Georgie worked hard together to try to produce the same sound. They didn't dare risk a premature attempt, so for the performances in their first several New South Wales towns they reverted to the use of the flute. But both knew nothing could ever successfully replace the didgeridoo, nor the sight of the Aboriginal man playing it.

'I'll never develop Jimmy's skill,' Georgie complained. A highly accomplished and versatile musician, the American was not accustomed to encountering difficulty mastering an instrument, but this was something altogether different. 'The circular breathing takes some getting used to,' he said, frustrated. 'Jimmy taught me how to go about it and I can manage fine for a while, but I'm having trouble maintaining it, particularly when I add the bird calls. I keep needing to take a quick pause now and then, you know? Just a matter of practice I'm sure, but it's damned annoying, I can tell you.'

'I think you're doing a wonderful job,' Mabel said encouragingly. She did too. She actually thought he was ready to perform. Who cared if he needed the odd pause now and then? The punters wouldn't even notice. But Georgie was a perfectionist, so she didn't get pushy. 'And you'll *look* wonderful too, love,' she added, determined to cheer him up. 'We won't even have to blacken you either, isn't that marvellous?'

The comment rather amused Georgie. Mabel was a highly intelligent woman, and like most show business folk there was not a shred of bigotry in her. Show business people judged, and were judged, according to talent, not colour, not race. In fact, colour and race often seemed invisible to them. *So much so*, Georgie thought, *that at times they actually fail to see any difference.* But Mabel should, he decided. This time around, Mabel really should see there was a difference.

'Jimmy is a Wurundjeri man,' he said. Very gently. He intended no insult; he liked and respected Mabel immensely. 'Jimmy told me that his people of the Kulin nation go back tens of thousands of years. To when their creator spirit Bunjil formed them and their land and all living things.'

'Oh.' She knew instantly she was being taught a lesson, and a lesson she deserved to be taught. 'I'm sorry, Georgie,' she said. It was one of those rare times in Mabel's life when she actually felt stupid. 'I'm really sorry.'

'No need to be,' he replied with a broad grin. 'I'm just explaining why I'll never be able to play the didgeridoo like Jimmy does, that's all.'

As the tour drew closer and closer to Sydney, Georgie continued his relentless rehearsal, and by the time they reached Orange, and then Bathurst, he was out onstage with Gertie, playing the didgeridoo without one single pause. Jimmy would have been proud of his pupil's progress.

They were ready for Sydney now. Ready for the Criterion Theatre and the crowds that awaited. But they were not ready for what Sydney had in store for them.

11

TERROR, TRIUMPH AND TRAGEDY ENCOUNTERED

The specific date the bubonic plague hit Sydney was quoted as 19 January 1900, this being the day it claimed the first of its victims, thirty-three-year-old Arthur Paine, a delivery man who worked at Central Wharf, where it was presumed the ship carrying the disease had docked.

The Australian colonial government had long anticipated the arrival of the plague. In fact, authorities had dreaded what they presumed must be 'only a matter of time', given the plague's fearsome ravages upon spreading south from northern China to Canton and Hong Kong during 1894. During that year alone 100,000 deaths had been recorded. Since then the disease had spread to India, and more recently, just the previous year, to Nouméa; the continent of Australia must surely be next in a pandemic that threatened to become global. While preparing for the worst, however, the government did not give advance notice to the press for fear of inciting panic among its citizens. The 'Black Death', as the bubonic plague had been termed during the pandemic of the seventeenth century, was known to be one of the deadliest diseases ever inflicted upon humans.

The bacterium was introduced by the fleas of black rats, the rats themselves having arrived on ships that had come from plague-infested ports. Once ashore, the rats quickly multiplied, the fleas transferred to human hosts, and upon being bitten a person was infected. The results were ugly. The disease moved swiftly causing acute inflammation of the lymph nodes, which then broke down spreading toxins throughout the body resulting in massive haemorrhages of the internal organs and discolouration of the skin. Hence the dreaded and aptly titled 'Black Death'.

It was therefore a sober Sydney scene that greeted the arrival of *The Musical Variety Extravaganza of 1900*. By now they were well into April, and far from keeping reportage from its citizens, the government was using the press to spread information and instruction regarding the dangers of the plague, and to issue necessary safety precautions people should employ.

Rube wondered how on earth he hadn't read about this catastrophe, he who made a rule of scouring newspapers daily. But of course they'd been reading just the country papers, and always they'd headed straight for the review section, neglecting all else. *My goodness*, he thought, *I've become a true creature of the theatre.* He would never have considered such a thing possible.

But plague or no plague, the show must go on. And it did. Just as life did in the thriving metropolis of Sydney.

On opening night they played to a packed house, and from the very first appearance of Carlo – heralded by a fanfare and captured by a follow spot as he strode out in front of the curtain, resplendent in top hat and tails – the audience was captivated.

'Ladies and gentlemen, boys and girls . . .' he announced, the pitch of his voice and the dazzle of his smile embracing one and all. 'Welcome to *The Musical Variety Extravaganza of 1900*, proudly featuring Stars of the Southern Cross. Prepare yourselves for a feast of entertainment.' The toss of his top hat into the wings (ably caught by Mabel). 'It's *SHOWTIME!*'

The plush velvet curtain swishes open to reveal a black man seated to the side of the stage, behind him a white screen, and the theatre echoes with the eerie sound of an instrument that few, if any, have heard before. An audible intake of breath from the audience as up on the screen comes an image of desert Australia, a sight few have seen, and a sight as intriguing as the photographic projection itself, which to many is also a novelty. And then on comes Gertie.

The Serpentine Dance set the standard and after that there was no looking back.

Finally the closing act: The Wonderful Worthing, Master Illusionist, and the finale reveal that brings the audience to its feet. For there, high up in a private box that overlooks the stage, is the magician himself, and in the glare of two follow spots he is revealed doing a one-armed handstand on the balcony's railing. At first there is a collective gasp of horror at the danger of such a stunt, then a moment's silence, the audience doubting this can be the magician at all, but rather someone dressed in identical costume. But very slowly and gracefully, the magician lowers his feet to the balcony, stands arms raised in triumph and acknowledges the audience, turning his gaze to every corner of the auditorium, the full focus of the spotlights verifying his identity. This is indeed The Wonderful Worthing. But he'd been onstage barely a minute ago. How had he got up there?

They watch in wonderment as the magician tosses a length of flaxen rope over the railing and, the follow spots capturing his every move, shimmies his way down to the stalls where he then bounds up onto the stage. He joins his pretty assistant, who throws open the door of the wooden box into which he had stepped only minutes previously. The box is empty.

Such a feat demands instant appreciation and Artie/Alfie takes his bows to a standing ovation, while in the narrow

confines behind the false back of the box, the other
Wonderful Worthing congratulates himself on the volume
of the applause.

They had decided, for such an impressive finale, it was
worth keeping the private boxes to the left of the stage
vacant, not just the one serving the reveal, but the others
also, for the sake of audience sightlines. And they'd been
proved right. The Worthing Brothers in partnership with
Carlo and Rube had on that night won the hearts of
audience and critics alike.

But despite the assured success of their Sydney run,
there followed the daily horrors of the plague. Everywhere
about them was evidence of the terror that threatened
Sydney and its people. The terror of the Black Death.

At the direction of the government's newly formed
Plague Department, infected areas throughout the city
were undergoing intensive cleaning operations. Houses were
disinfected with lime, carbolic water and lime chloride; all
waste, including manure and stable bedding, was removed
and burnt; a number of hotels had been closed down,
and some sections of the inner city and dock area were
demolished altogether. Rat catchers abounded, teams of
men organised by the city council to exterminate the rat
population, the government paying tuppence for every
rat delivered to the incinerator set up in Bathurst Street.

Individuals who had become infected, together with
those with whom they had been in close contact, were
taken to the quarantine station at North Head. The quarantine period had initially been ten days, but had just
recently been reduced to five.

People were living in constant fear. And none more so
than those in the business of show.

'You've been *where*, Gertie?' Will was horrified.

'Down to Circular Quay,' Gertie said. 'I had a gorgeous
walk around the Quay and The Rocks. I do so love the

harbour, you know that, Will.' Gertie couldn't understand
why he appeared upset; she always walked around the foreshore when they were in Sydney. She absolutely adored the
magnificence of Sydney Harbour.

'You cannot go near the harbour, do you hear me?
I forbid it!'

'Why?'

'Because there's a plague in this city,' he exploded, 'just
in case you hadn't noticed. And this plague has arrived on
ships! And a harbour is a place where ships dock! That's
why.'

'Oh, not at Circular Quay though,' Gertie replied airily.
'The big ships dock at the wharves in Darling Harbour;
Circular Quay's for ferries and passengers. There were lots
of people there, Will,' she assured him. 'You don't need to
worry.'

Will realised he may possibly have overreacted, but
Gertie's laissez-faire attitude simply wouldn't do; she was
too important to the show.

'Now, Gertie,' he said, quelling his impatience, 'I do
understand that ferry terminals are hardly a breeding
ground, but I still want you to stay away from the
harbour, and most particularly The Rocks. Several hotels
there have been closed, and rats are known to be attracted
to foreshore areas like The Rocks . . .' He could see she
was about to protest so he hastily went on, 'And although
you may not become infected yourself, you might well
come into contact with someone who is, which would
mean you'd have to be quarantined.' She was listening
dutifully now, so he softened his tone. 'We can't afford to
lose you from the show for a whole five days, Gertie love.
You're too valuable. Will you promise me?'

'Yes, Will, I promise.'

A mutual decision was reached among the entire
company that they would keep as much to themselves as

possible throughout the Sydney run. For the sake of the show.

But they were caught out nonetheless. By two government officials who paid them a visit on a Thursday evening.

It was just on the half-hour call and everyone was seated in their respective dressing rooms applying their makeup, when Rube, who'd been out in the foyer with the front-of-house manager, appeared backstage.

'Visitors,' he called, tapping on the door of the dressing room that was shared by Will, Max, Carlo and the twins.

It was a signal for one of the twins to disappear behind the screen in the corner, and Artie quickly did so; they were never to be seen together except by cast and crew.

'Come in,' Will called and Rube opened the door, revealing himself to be in the company of two men. But before he could say a word by way of introduction, the older of the two, a stern-faced, straight-backed man who appeared to be on a mission, barked a peremptory enquiry.

'Mr Worthing . . .' As he looked about the dressing room, it seemed more a demand than a query.

Will, Max and Alfie rose to their feet as one.

'Which of you is in charge?' The man looked accusingly from one to the other, as if the three of them were making fun of a very serious situation. 'The theatre manager and Mr Reubens here,' he said, while beside him Rube gave a slight eyeball roll, 'have told me I'm to ask for a Mr Worthing.'

Max and Alfie exchanged a glance and obediently sat, leaving Will to handle things while Carlo watched on, critical of the assumption Will Worthing was 'in charge' and prepared to take over should it prove necessary.

'Yes, gentlemen, what can I do for you?' Will's manner was dignified but distinctly authoritarian. The man deserved to be treated like an underling; his tone had been most offensive. Furthermore, Will could detect shades of a North Country accent. The man was working class; how dare he presume to be otherwise.

'Pratchett and Morley,' the man said, indicating his younger companion, a thick-set fellow, rather thug-like in appearance. 'We're from the government Plague Department.'

Pratchett and Morley, Will thought, *excellent moniker for a comedy duo. And they look the part, what's more.* 'I am the Worthing you seek,' he said with theatrical regality. 'What is your business here at this hour? We have a show to perform.'

'Not any more you don't,' Pratchett retorted with some relish; Will's tone had offended him as much as his had offended Will. 'This theatre is to be closed for cleansing and disinfecting.'

A deathly pause followed the pronouncement, and Will was about to reply, but Carlo stood, flashing the smile that won audience's hearts; Will Worthing's pomposity threatened to be their undoing.

'I'm Carlo,' he said, exuding charm, 'Master of Ceremonies and co-producer of this marvellous variety extravaganza, which we would love you and your families to attend.' His smile was flashed also at Morley. 'With our compliments, of course.'

Surprisingly enough, the tactic worked on Morley.

'I've seen it already,' the young man replied, casting an admiring glance about at the assembled performers, 'you were all wonderful . . .'

Carlo's charm, however, had fallen on barren ground when it came to the senior official, who ignored him completely.

'I have here,' Pratchett said, taking a folded piece of paper from the inside breast pocket of his jacket, 'a court order demanding this theatre be closed for two days to allow thorough cleansing and disinfecting due to possible contamination.'

It was Max's turn to intervene. He stood.

'But none of us have been in any areas prone to contagion, Mr Pratchett,' he said, addressing the man respectfully. 'We have virtually quarantined ourselves in our hotel and here at the theatre. We have been in contact with no one who —'

'Yes, you have,' Pratchett interrupted brusquely. 'One of your local workers has contracted the disease.' He briefly consulted the paper he held in his hands. 'A Mr Kelty reported to Sydney Hospital this afternoon with symptoms. He and his family have been quarantined, and both his home and his place of work are to undergo cleansing and disinfection.'

'A Mr Kelty?' Max looked a query at Rube.

'Oscar,' Rube said, with the slightest shrug that signalled *we're in trouble.*

'Ah, Oscar.' Max shared a nod with the others; they'd never known his surname, but they all knew Oscar.

Oscar was an all-round handyman and dogsbody employed by the theatre and his duties were multifarious. He would check security, ensuring all was locked up after each show; he would deliver goods and messages from front-of-house to backstage and vice versa, run errands when necessary, undertake simple repair jobs, and even oversee the cleaners in the auditorium following a performance, making sure not one apple core or piece of orange peel was overlooked. With the exception of the box office, there wasn't an area of the theatre Oscar didn't frequent on a daily basis.

'Oh my goodness, poor Oscar,' Max said in a tone that agreed with Rube's shrug: *yes, we're in trouble.* 'Why don't you come in, gentlemen,' he said to the two who were still hovering at the doorway. 'Take a seat and make yourselves comfortable while we discuss how we go about this matter.'

Pratchett and Morley stepped into the dressing room, as did Rube, but they didn't take a seat and they didn't make themselves comfortable.

'There is nothing to discuss, I'm afraid,' Pratchett said. Max's diplomatic approach had paid off and he was now prepared to be civil. 'Twelve municipal workers from the health department will be arriving first thing tomorrow to commence operations, and they'll be accompanied by two members of the constabulary whose duty will be to maintain security.' He couldn't resist delivering his next biting line directly to Will, however; he'd taken an intense dislike to this particular Worthing. 'No one will be allowed to enter the building,' he said, again relishing his power, 'and I mean *no one*!'

'But you can't do that to us,' Will protested angrily. 'Tomorrow's Friday, we always have a full house on a Friday . . .'

'I could do far more than that to you, Mr Worthing,' Pratchett said icily. 'I could have your whole company quarantined for five days.'

Rube interrupted, although gently and with care; like Carlo he was wishing Will would stop taking the high ground, it wasn't helping matters.

'But as I told you out in the foyer, Mr Pratchett, and as Mr McDonnell the front-of-house manager confirmed, none of us have been in close contact with Oscar Kelty.'

'Depends on what you mean by "close contact", doesn't it?' Pratchett said ominously: a remark, indeed a threat, that was once again intended for Will.

Max dived in before his brother could reply, Will's face a mask of fury. 'I'll just fetch the girls, shall I? They should hear this for themselves.' His look to Rube and Carlo, and even to young Alfie, said *don't let him go any further*.

'I'll only be a jiff,' he said with a brief smile to both officials, and he headed out of the door.

Behind him he heard Rube start up a conversation. 'Do you go to the theatre often, Mr Morley?' *Good old Rube*, he thought. Then he heard the younger man, whose voice was pleasant and rather out of keeping with his thug-like appearance. 'Oh yes, I do, I love the theatre.' *That might just come in handy*, Max thought.

He returned with Mabel and Gertie in only a matter of minutes and was relieved to find Will appeared to have got the message. Beneath the civil exterior, he could tell his brother was still simmering, but for the moment at least Will was under control. Particularly helpful was the fact that he had just received a compliment.

'Thank you, Mr Morley, I'm delighted you so enjoyed the duets. It is always a pleasure to meet another Gilbert and Sullivan enthusiast . . .'

'Good evening, gentlemen,' Mabel said graciously as she swanned into the room, 'I'm Mrs Worthing.' She looped her arm affectionately through Will's as if to establish which particular Mrs Worthing, but in keeping with Max's hastily delivered instruction, she was actually taking control of her husband. 'Will's in an absolute fury, Mabel, you have to keep him in check.'

'And this is the other Mrs Worthing,' Max said, introducing Gertie. 'Being a theatregoer, Mr Morley, you may know my wife as The Divine Dolores.'

'Oh yes I do, indeed I do.' Morley appeared completely overwhelmed. 'An honour to meet you. The Divine Dolores, oh my, yes, an absolute honour.'

'The honour is all mine,' Gertie replied, dropping into the deepest and demurest of curtseys, then as she rose, smiling radiantly at each of the men. 'A pleasure to meet you, gentlemen.'

'Give 'em your flirty best, love,' had been Max's instruction, 'particularly the older one, he's a hard nut.'

Even Pratchett couldn't feign indifference to the sight of Gertie. She was dressed in the sheath that she wore beneath her opening Serpentine costume, which she never donned until the last minute lest the silk be damaged. The sheath was opaque and perfectly modest, yet at the same time strangely revealing; the way it hung on her slender frame accentuating her small perfect breasts, her toned flat belly and the line of her back.

'I believe we're in trouble, is that so?' Gertie trained her attention on the older man, huge baby-blue eyes meeting his, lower lip trembling slightly. 'You want to close our theatre?' She seemed on the verge of tears.

The others thought she might be overdoing things a little, but the mix of innocence and sexuality was very beguiling to the theatrically uninitiated, and Morley looked as if he longed to cuddle her, while Pratchett too appeared taken in by the act.

'We do not *want* to close the theatre, Mrs Worthing,' he said, fighting to maintain authority while averting his eyes from the pert breasts, which he found a bit distracting. 'We *have* to close the theatre. It is our *duty* to do so.'

'Does that mean we won't be going on tonight then?' Gertie was confused; Max's instructions had been very hasty, something about closure and cleansing, but she hadn't really got the drift.

'That is correct, Mrs Worthing,' Pratchett informed her. 'There will be no performance this evening.'

'But what about our audience?' Gertie dropped her flirty act; she was horrified. 'They'll be arriving any minute. The show must go on!'

Rube described the situation, not only for Gertie but the others too.

'Mac will handle tonight's audience,' he said. Robert 'Mac' McDonnell was the front-of-house manager. 'He's already contacting those he can through telephonic communication, and he'll be standing by at the box office to reissue tickets for next week to all who turn up, and to offer refunds for those who are unable to rebook.'

'Ah, well then,' Mabel said with her customary practicality, 'that's not too disastrous, is it?' Her brain had made a quick calculation. They could live without a Thursday night – the house hadn't been a full one anyway, and most audience members could be plonked into next week. She wondered why Will had been driven into such a fury. *No doubt some wrongly perceived insult*, she thought, *he can be so unpredictable at times*. 'We'll manage,' she said, offering an obliging smile to the government officials. Then beside her, she felt Will's whole body stiffen.

'It's the next two days that are the problem,' he hissed at her through clenched teeth.

'What?' Mabel had presumed the closure and cleansing procedure was to take place overnight. Like Gertie, she had ascertained very little from Max's hasty explanation as he'd whisked them from their dressing room.

'They want to close the theatre on Friday and Saturday.' Will's hiss was now a snarl as he glowered at Pratchett.

'Oh, but you can't do that,' Mabel said pleasantly, squeezing her husband's arm in a signal for him not to overreact, but to leave things to her. 'Friday night is always a full house, you see, and we do two shows on a Saturday, the matinee and evening packed every time, always a full house for both. We couldn't possibly close the theatre on a Friday and a Saturday.'

What was wrong with these people? Pratchett wondered. Did they think plague procedures could be brought to a halt simply because they had what they called 'a full house'? Which to him had always been a poker term anyway.

'I'm very much afraid, Mrs Worthing,' he said, addressing Mabel with a tone that had again become icy, 'the theatre will be closed for two days as of tomorrow for cleansing and disinfecting purposes. This is regardless of the fact that tomorrow happens to be a Friday and that the following day happens to be a Saturday. Do I make myself understood?'

'I have a suggestion.' It was Gertie once again, no longer in flirty mode, but eager to be of assistance. 'Why don't we make it the Sunday and Monday instead?'

Pratchett looked at her blankly.

'We don't perform on a Sunday, you see,' she went on to explain, 'and Monday's audiences are usually pretty thin. Sunday and Monday would be a much better idea.'

During the brief pause that followed, Pratchett sensed the assembled company also thought this was an excellent idea. He decided they were all quite mad.

'That would work very well, wouldn't it?' Gertie said happily.

'No, it would not,' he replied.

The men left barely minutes later, but not before Morley, much to Pratchett's intense irritation, had attained autographs from Will and Max Worthing, The Divine Dolores and The Wonderful Worthing, Master Illusionist.

Only then, when the dressing room door had closed behind the two, was Artie finally allowed out from behind the screen in the corner.

The successful season at Sydney's Criterion Theatre had consolidated in the eyes of all the newfound partnership of the Worthing Brothers and Carlo and Rube. But the pressure of performing in a plague-ridden city had taken its toll, and the company was relieved when it came time to board the steamer bound for Adelaide.

The Worthings in particular were glad to get away, for they had additional cause for concern. Gertie was pregnant. She and Max had announced the news to the rest of the family on a mid-Sunday morning as they'd settled down for brunch at the café they'd adopted in Elizabeth Street.

'I've been worried for a while that I might be,' she'd said guiltily. 'I'm pretty sure now, and I'm ever so sorry. I don't know how on earth it happened,' she added in all innocence, and there'd been general hoots of laughter. 'No, no,' she said defensively, 'you know what I mean. Well, *you* do, don't you, Mabel?' She and Mabel had often discussed how one went about avoiding a pregnancy, the times of the month that were relatively safe, the precautions that could be taken – women understood such things. Smart women did anyway.

Mabel returned a smile that said *it doesn't always work, love*, but her voice was warm. 'Congratulations, Gertie, that's grand news.'

'Good thing we're getting out of Sydney in a couple of weeks though,' Max said, his arm protectively about his wife. 'You don't want to be around the plague when you're pregnant.'

'You don't want to be around the plague when you're not, either,' Artie piped up. 'The sooner we're out of here the better, I reckon.'

'I'll be starting to show by the time we open in Melbourne ...' Gertie was deeply apologetic; this was obviously her major concern.

'Oh, don't give it a second thought, love.' Mabel dismissed the notion with a wave of her hand. 'We'll work on the costumes and no one'll be any the wiser, we've done it before.'

*

The Musical Variety Extravaganza of 1900 was as eagerly embraced in Adelaide as it had been in Sydney, and without the threat of the plague, the company's season at the Theatre Royal in Hindley Street was enjoyable for all. Smaller case numbers of bubonic plague were to be reported throughout several Australian port cities over the ensuing period, Adelaide being one of them, Melbourne and Fremantle also, but none matched the pandemic's peak in Sydney, where the fear of the Black Death consumed government and citizens alike.

Lessons had been learnt, however, and in the years that followed, the Australian government's coordinated approach to plague eradication proved highly successful, the country faring far better than most due to its introduction of specialised public health departments and urban sanitary control. Australia set an example to many parts of the world with its modern, effective methods of combating a pandemic.

Following their Adelaide season, the company boarded a steamer, this time bound for Tasmania, where they would perform at another Theatre Royal. But this Theatre Royal would be in Hobart.

Hobart's Theatre Royal was situated in one of the less salubrious parts of town down near the docks, a rough, tough area known as Wapping, where brothels and pubs abounded. But the theatre itself was beautiful, none could deny that, of Georgian design, bijou, elegant, and with a history as colourful as the township of Hobart itself.

Everyone in the company had worked the Theatre Royal before, with the exception of the skirt dancers, the young troupe of six having been formed only two years previously.

'Oh, how lovely,' Lilly said breathlessly as they all stood on the stage looking out at the auditorium. 'It's everything you said it would be, Carlo, beautiful and cosy and friendly all at the same time.' She flashed him a beatific smile.

'Yes, the Royal's an excellent venue,' Carlo replied, 'very good acoustically too.' He didn't look her way, continuing to gaze out at the auditorium instead. He wished she wouldn't behave in so intimate a fashion. Just because they'd had sex twice in Adelaide, and no more than furtive couplings in a deserted dressing room, didn't give her the right to make the matter public. Everyone else knew he was sleeping with Maeve, and had been throughout the whole tour.

'You're right there, Lilly,' Irving Sayles agreed. 'The Royal always offers a welcome. She's a grand little lady with a warm, friendly heart.'

'And a warm, friendly ghost, what's more,' Gertie added.

'A ghost?' Lilly and the other skirt dancers looked alarmed.

'Yes, his name's Fred, and he's really very nice, at least *I* think so. I've seen him every single time we've played the Royal,' Gertie said with pride, and she pointed up to the rear of the dress circle. 'He's usually sitting there, right up at the very back when the audience has left, just keeping an eye on things, you know? They say he was an actor who was killed here. Don't know when, fifty years ago maybe.' She smiled fondly. 'Fred loved this theatre. He still does.'

'Most actors do,' Mabel said to Lilly and the other dancers, all of whom appeared distinctly alarmed, but then they were very young, in their early twenties. 'I wouldn't worry about Fred, girls,' she assured them, 'Gertie's quite right, he's known to be benign.' Mabel hadn't seen Fred herself, nor had anyone else in the family for that matter, Gertie being the only one so privileged. But the ghostly presence had been noted by many; not only sightings but the sound of Fred's voice, even the gentlest touch of some*one* or some*thing* passing by. No one doubted his presence. Theatre folk, always superstitious, had a healthy respect for ghosts, even hard-nosed, practical theatre folk like Mabel.

The entire company stood mute for several seconds, staring at the back of the dress circle to where Gertie had pointed, as if they were all trying to make out the figure of Fred up there in the gloom. Then . . .

'Come along now,' Mabel clapped her hands briskly, 'there's work to be done.'

The doors to the loading dock were wide open, skips and equipment had been delivered with yet more arriving, and everyone jumped to Mabel's command. The bump-in had begun.

Carlo was glad the others hadn't noticed Lilly's intimate tone. But of course, why should they? She'd only been making a comment about the theatre, and she'd said nothing he hadn't shared with everyone else; he too loved the Theatre Royal. He'd been just a bit paranoid, he told himself, but he'd have a word with her nonetheless.

One person *had* noticed, however. Maeve. And Maeve hadn't liked what she'd seen. It didn't cross her mind to suspect Carlo may have had a dalliance. Carlo was in love with her. He would never look at another woman. But it was quite obvious to Maeve that Lilly had been giving her man the eye, and Maeve wasn't going to have a bar of that. Just let the little slut try!

The company settled comfortably into their Hobart digs. Carlo, Rube and the Worthing family had hired two residences not far from the theatre, just several hundred yards up Campbell Street, befitting their status as producers. The houses, despite being in Wapping and although almost opposite the Hobart Gaol, were respectable and their location extremely convenient. The other members of the company, performers and crew alike, were accommodated in the cheaper taverns and inns of Salamanca Place at Battery Point, a good fifteen-minute walk from the theatre, overlooking the wharves and docks of Sullivans Cove.

Gertie envied the rest of the company their accommodation; she would far rather have been staying in one of the pubs by the harbour, regardless of the dim, poky rooms they offered. She said as much to Max.

'Oh lovey, you can just step outside your front door first thing in the morning and there you are.' She threw her arms wide, envisaging it all as she sat at the comfortable kitchen table in Campbell Street. 'The harbour, the docks, the piers, the ships . . . Oh Maxie, we should be in Salamanca Place.'

'No, we shouldn't, Gert.' Gertie always needed to be near water and for some unknown reason had a particular affiliation with harbours. Max preferred comfort himself. 'We're fine right where we are, love.'

So Gertie made a daily habit of walking down to the harbour. Not by way of protest – she fully accepted and understood Max's preference for comfort – but she loved to drink in the sights and the sounds of Sullivans Cove. She would set off down Campbell Street, across Collins and past the huge marketplace, where the cries of fishmongers competed and Wapping's barefoot urchins dodged among stalls nicking titbits where they could. Then after crossing Macquarie Street, she would arrive at the docks, in front of her Victoria, to her right Constitution, and there she would be confronted with the hustle and bustle that was Sullivans Cove. She'd cross over the busy Harbour Railway, which transported all the goods and cargo from the ships to the warehouses, and she'd walk to the very end of one of the piers, usually the Argyle Street Pier, where she'd gaze in wonderment upon the ships at anchor in the bay, and then beyond to the seemingly never-ending beauty of the Derwent River. Gertie never tired of the sight.

Sometimes Max would accompany her, and the sight Max never tired of was Gertie's wonderment. The docks, and even the river's beauty, failed to hold his interest, but Gertie's wonderment always did. Max loved the way his Gert found wonder in everything.

The lifestyle, too, was comfortable in Hobart, less frenetic than that experienced in bigger cities, and the company members, who had become very much a family as was often the case on tour, developed an easygoing routine.

Of the many hotels in the immediate vicinity of the theatre, two were instantly adopted as favourites. Not unsurprisingly the one right next door to the theatre itself, actually named the Theatre Royal Pub, and the one just down the road on the corner of Campbell and Collins streets, theatrically named the Shakespeare Hotel. The Theatre Royal Pub served mainly as a drinking hole where they gathered together after each night's performance, and The Shakespeare was where they downed their hearty stews or pies or lamb chops in between the matinee and evening show, such was the spirit of camaraderie that prevailed.

As the season was drawing to its close, it became evident to all that Gertie was beginning to 'show'. Although never huge in her pregnancies, her condition at close to five months was now becoming obvious, so Mabel took the requisite steps. The sheath worn beneath the silk of The Serpentine Dance was replaced by an opaque loose garment that didn't rest upon Gertie's curves, and the Juliet costume was redesigned in an 'empire' style, a fitted bodice ending just below the bustline and giving way to a flowing gathered skirt that completely disguised the rest of the body. Feminine, virginal and appropriate in every possible way.

'See?' Mabel said. 'Easy. I told you.'

With less than a week to go, everyone would have agreed that the Hobart run, where they'd played to full houses while also enjoying the easygoing lifestyle, the pretty city and the beautiful Theatre Royal, had been the most pleasurable segment of their entire tour. Until disaster struck.

It all started on the final Wednesday, the mid-week matinee day when, following the afternoon performance, the company had adjourned to The Shakespeare for their between-show meal.

'Where's Carlo?' Maeve asked as they gathered about the several huge wooden tables by the front windows, the tables they'd commandeered as their own on Wednesdays and Saturdays and which the management only too willingly kept available for them.

'He just popped over to the theatre.' Rube instantly covered, as he always did for Carlo. 'He forgot something, said he'll be back in a minute.' It was a lie, but having seen Carlo and Lilly loitering backstage, Rube had his suspicions. He knew the two had shared the occasional sexual encounter.

Everyone seated themselves around the tables, jostling for position and chattering away about the matinee or which of the several meals on offer they were going to choose, but Maeve remained standing, her eagle eye searching among the members of the company. Lilly was not there.

Only Rube noticed Maeve as she headed out of the pub; the others were too focused on their chatter.

Oh dear, he thought, *I hope they remembered to lock the door.*

They hadn't. They'd been so eager to get at each other, they'd simply dived into the dressing room the moment they were alone, slamming the door behind them, not thinking of locking it. The crowd had gone anyway, and no one ever locked a dressing room door.

When Maeve came upon them, they were in the final throes of sexual fervour. Lilly was seated on the bench-like

communal makeup table that flanked the walls and surrounding mirrors. Her skirts were hefted up to her shoulders,
her legs locked around Carlo, and Carlo, whose trousers
were down around his ankles, was pumping away between
her thighs. They didn't even hear the door open.

'You slut!' Maeve's scream was horrendous. 'You
fucking slut!'

As the couple sprang apart, Carlo diving for his trousers,
Maeve flung herself at Lilly in a state of complete hysteria.

'You whore! You fucking whore! You leave him alone!
He's mine, do you hear me, mine!'

The scene became suddenly frightening. Maeve, far bigger
and stronger than Lilly, was behaving like a madwoman,
clawing at the girl as if she might tear Lilly's eyes out.

Lilly, understandably terrified, was screaming out to
Carlo, 'Get her off me! Get her off me!'

Carlo dragged Maeve away, but she kept struggling,
deranged and bent on revenge.

'I'll kill you, you slut! I'll kill you!'

Lilly ran, still screaming, from the dressing room, not
even thinking to collect her panties that remained where
she'd dropped them on the floor.

'He's mine, slut!' Maeve screeched at the top of her
voice. 'He'll always be mine!' Then as Carlo's arms encircled her, preventing her from pursuing Lilly, the hysteria
left her and she collapsed, clinging to him, a sobbing mess.
'You're mine, Carlo,' she wept into his shoulder, 'you love
me, you're mine, you're mine.'

'Shush, shush,' he said comfortingly, holding her to him,
'shush, shush now.' He couldn't think of anything else
to say.

When she'd calmed down and appeared more or less
under control, he wiped away her tears with his kerchief.
She was about to speak, but there was nothing he wanted
to hear, nothing he cared to say himself.

'Not another word, Maeve,' he said, not unkindly but firmly. 'We'll talk about this later, after tonight's show. Now let's go and join the others.'

She allowed herself to be shepherded from the theatre and didn't even notice as he surreptitiously scooped up the panties, tucking them into his pocket.

The episode had completely unnerved Carlo. Not the fact that he'd been caught in flagrante, although that was unfortunate, but rather Maeve's deranged reaction, her possessiveness. The words she'd screamed rang frighteningly over and over in his brain. 'He's mine, he'll always be mine!' Good God, what might happen upon their return to Melbourne, he wondered. And she thought he loved her. 'You love me, Carlo, you're mine, you're mine,' she'd said. What on earth had led her to believe that? He'd presumed from the outset that Maeve had understood their affair was strictly an 'on tour' arrangement. He must put an end to it. Right now, he decided. This very night.

Maeve's performance that evening was a little low-key, but being the professional she was she covered well enough. Few would have noticed. And even if they had, everyone was allowed an 'off' night, weren't they?

Fortunately, the skirt dancers shared a separate dressing room from the leading female performers, and Lilly kept well out of Maeve's way backstage, but there appeared no threat of a further attack. And later that night, back at the house in Campbell Street, Maeve was most contrite.

'I'm sorry, Carlo,' she said, 'I know I behaved badly. It was just the shock of seeing the two of you together . . .'

Maeve had been so relieved when Carlo had asked her back to the house. She, like the rest of the company, had been booked into a room at Salamanca Place for the Hobart season, but several nights a week she slept with Carlo in Campbell Street. She'd thought that, given this afternoon's incident, he might not ask her to join him tonight. But he had.

Immediately after the curtain had come down, he'd asked her. Even before they'd had a drink with the others at the Theatre Royal Pub as they normally did.

'Come home with me,' he'd said, 'we need to talk.' She'd known what that had meant. And she couldn't wait to tell him how sorry she was.

'Not that it was your fault,' she added hastily, 'it was that little slut throwing herself at you the way she did.' *Of course it wasn't Carlo's fault*, Maeve thought, *he's a man after all. Men can't control their lust when confronted with sluts who offer themselves. And a quick fuck like that doesn't mean he loves me any the less.* But she reminded herself that she really shouldn't have lost control the way she had. Oh God, how she'd wanted to kill the bitch.

'I am truly sorry, Carlo, please forgive me. It will never happen again, I promise.' She didn't like the way he was looking at her. Why wasn't he taking her in his arms, telling her everything was all right? 'I know I shouldn't have lost control the way I did, and I know it wasn't your fault – that slut led you on – but the shock of seeing you —'

'It's over, Maeve.'

She stared back at him, almost as though she'd received a physical blow.

'But you love me . . .' Her response was a whisper of disbelief. 'You love me . . .' She whispered the words again as if anything else was beyond comprehension.

'No, I don't.' *Best to be brutal*, Carlo thought; *she must understand the rules.* 'I have never loved you, Maeve. We had a good time, no more. And that good time ends right here, this very minute. Come along now,' he said briskly, 'I'll take you back to the pub so you can walk home with the others.' The cast and crew always walked back to Salamanca Place together at night, or at least in small groups. It was not advisable, particularly for a

young woman, to be out alone in the streets of Wapping
after dark.

She followed him meekly, and they walked down
Campbell Street in silence. Carlo was relieved she hadn't
carried on with any further drama; he'd dreaded that she
might. He hadn't meant to hurt her, but she hadn't played
by the rules, and this was the way it had to end.

'Goodnight, Maeve,' he said outside the Theatre Royal
Pub, and leaving her to join the others, he turned away
and walked up Campbell Street.

But Maeve didn't join the others. She snuck into the
theatre instead, via the front-of-house, which had not yet
been locked by the night watchman, and slipping backstage she slept the night in one of the dressing rooms. Or
attempted to sleep. She was really just filling in time until
it was light. She had plans for the morning.

They found her late the following afternoon. Or rather
the Worthings did; Will, Mabel, Max and Gertie. Will
had keys to the stage door, and the four of them always
turned up to the theatre well in advance of the half-hour
call before curtain up, even before the arrival of the
backstage doorman.

She'd hanged herself from the flies. Her body was
dangling way above their heads. She'd been there since
early that morning.

12

A NEW ARRIVAL IS WELCOMED

Things were not the same after Maeve's death. The show went on, as shows always do, and as shows always must, with clinical precision. They completed the last several days of the Hobart run replacing the Gilbert and Sullivan segments with two male duets, and upon their return to Melbourne a new soprano was cast for the closing season at the Princess Theatre. But the shadow of Maeve was always there, and the company had to dig deep to resurrect a semblance of the fun and joy that had once prevailed. They succeeded, of course, as performers do, and audiences would never have suspected they worked beneath a shadow that had followed them from beyond the grave.

The task was a particularly difficult one for Carlo, and also for Will. Carlo was riddled with guilt, although he didn't understand why he should be. He had never led Maeve to believe he loved her; he had played by the rules. Theirs had been a fun affair only. But the shock of her death nonetheless haunted him. And as for Will . . . Will was consumed with anger. Carlo had told the police during questioning that he had ended his relationship with Maeve that night, revealing the reason for her suicide to be all too obvious. And to Will all too unforgiveable. That vibrant young woman would still be alive were it not for Carlo's libidinous indulgence and feckless irresponsibility.

The already fractious relationship that existed between the two men was pushed to its limits and might have caused a serious schism in their ongoing partnership, had it not been for their respective wives.

Mabel's sheer common sense came as no surprise.

'The girl was unstable, Will,' she said, 'we've all agreed upon that. If it hadn't been Carlo, it would have been someone else. Perhaps you, if she'd set her sights in your direction. And who knows, if I hadn't been on the tour, she might have done so. You might well have become the source of her infatuation.'

Will's reaction had been one of instant outrage. 'But I would never have indulged myself, Mabel, you know that.'

'Do I?' A whimsical smile and the raise of an eyebrow. 'What happens out on the road ... ?' She left the rest of the quote unsaid, and the fact that he didn't expostulate further led her to believe he understood. *Perhaps only too well*, she thought, *a bit of a giveaway?* 'Stop blaming everything on Carlo, Will. He's not solely responsible and his conscience is suffering enough as it is.'

The wisdom of little Winifred, however, came as a definite surprise. She had heard of Maeve Gallagher's death, although not of the supposed reason for the girl's suicide, apart from the fact that she'd been 'unstable'. But Carlo's introspection and uncharacteristic depression was evidence enough to Winifred. For the first time in their twelve-year marriage she confronted him about his infidelity. And very bluntly.

'She killed herself because of you, didn't she?'

'Yes.' Carlo didn't hesitate for a minute. He was eager to admit to the truth, a confession even, to get things off his chest, to clear the air, to have everything out in the open ... Keeping his secret was only compounding his guilt. 'We were sleeping together regularly, just having fun, you know how it is.'

Winifred said nothing. No, she didn't 'know how it is', but she knew how it was for Carlo, so she listened patiently.

'Maeve thought I was in love with her,' he went on, 'but I wasn't, Winnie. I was never in love with her and I never told her I was. She somehow *assumed* that I loved her, I have no idea why.' He shook his head miserably. 'I didn't lead her on. I swear I didn't. I honestly don't know why she thought I loved her.'

And that's where the problem lies, Winifred thought, *he truly has no idea of the effect he has on women.* She'd seen it so often during those years when she'd been his housekeeper and nursemaid to young Mick. The countless affairs that had been 'just having fun, you know how it is', and the hapless women who had fallen under his spell. He was irresponsible, yes, he behaved with reckless abandon, yes, but he'd never lied to those women.

'It's not your fault, Carlo,' she said firmly, 'you must stop blaming yourself. The girl was unstable, everyone says so.' *But perhaps everyone's wrong*, Winifred thought. *Carlo's been breaking women's hearts for years, and they can't all have been unstable.*

Having poured his feelings out, Carlo felt a great deal better. He was deeply grateful for his wife's understanding and support.

'I think it might be a good idea though,' Winifred added, 'if you were to temper your desire to "have fun" on tour.'

'Yes, yes,' Carlo said contritely, 'you're right, Winnie, you're quite right. I shall.'

She wondered for how long.

Since the opening of the show in Melbourne, the cast and crew rarely spoke of Maeve. They had for the last several days of the Hobart run; they'd spoken of nothing else then. But now, with a brand-new season running at the Princess, they concentrated on buoying each other's spirits.

The Melbourne run was the most important of all, taking them through to Christmas, always a busy time for the theatre. *The Musical Variety Extravaganza of 1900* would close in a blaze of triumph. Little wonder they avoided the subject of Maeve, keeping the conversation on a more general level.

Today it was theatre ghost stories, which always enthralled show business folk, and the Princess Theatre had the most famous of all.

'It happened on opening night too, would you believe,' Gertie said, 'a J. C. Williamson production. And when they finally brought him up from the basement, they pronounced him dead right here in this very greenroom.'

'Oh, how awful . . .' Nineteen-year-old Ida, the youngest of the skirt dancers, shifted uncomfortably in her chair, wide-eyed and fearful, just to think she could be sitting right on the spot where a dead man once lay. 'And they didn't even know it had happened until after the curtain call?' She was captivated nonetheless. So were the other girls; everyone loved a good ghost story, even if it scared them.

Lilly was the only one of the dancers not present in the greenroom; she stuck to the dressing room these days, wishing to avoid Carlo as much as possible, just as he wished to avoid her. Apart from Rube, no one was aware of their previous entanglement, and neither wished to be reminded of that hideous day.

It was a matinee interval and as Gertie held forth, the young dancers in particular were paying rapt attention. The others all knew of Frederick Federici's death just twelve years previously, but it didn't stop them being equally fascinated.

'That's the most amazing part,' Irving Sayles interjected. 'He had the heart attack as he was being lowered centre stage through the trapdoor into the basement, but no one knew. And when they found out afterwards, the cast all swore he was onstage with them when they took their curtain calls.'

'Isn't that marvellous?' Gertie said admiringly. 'He didn't disrupt the show for one second, not even in death. He was playing Mephistopheles, and he sang the very last note of the opera as he descended into the fires of hell bearing Faust with him, and the audience was none the wiser.'

'Yep, that's what I call a real trouper, Gert.' Max grinned. Gertie so loved a good story, and he had to agree this was a good one all right.

'And he's haunted the theatre ever since,' Pru added breathlessly, 'a ghostly figure in evening dress.' Seventeen-year-old Prudence Worthing had always adored the tragic story of Frederick Federici, and now more than ever, for she was actually performing at the Princess Theatre where it had all happened. 'He was only thirty-seven years old and terribly handsome. Isn't it romantic?'

Pru was a regular habitué of the greenroom, loving the theatre gossip that abounded there, but Artie and Alfie always remained in their dressing room, lest a front-of-house employee were to deliver a message. No one ever entered a dressing room without knocking, but the green-room was open to the occasional visit from an outsider. The necessity for the twins to remain undercover was irksome at times, particularly to Artie, who was a gregari-ous young man, but both knew it was the price they must pay, and neither ever raised a complaint.

Will Worthing, too, avoided the greenroom, under the pretext of keeping the twins company, but really in order not to find himself in the same room as Carlo. These days there seemed to be a lot of avoidance issues within the company that had once been such a family.

'The theatre used to keep a seat vacant in his honour on every opening night,' Carlo said, joining in the conversation. 'They don't seem to do it any more,' he added, 'which I think is a pity.'

'Yes,' Gertie vehemently agreed, 'they should have maintained the tradition. Every theatre respects its ghosts.'

'Have you seen him, Gertie?' Irving Sayles asked. If anyone was likely to have seen the apparition of Frederick Federici, he thought, it would have to have been Gertie.

'No, I haven't, Irving. Not yet. But I certainly intend to. I'm going to stay late now and then after the curtain's come down. That's a good time to catch a glimpse of a ghost. They like an empty theatre when there's still the feel of an audience.'

Irving was suddenly reminded. 'What about Fred at the Theatre Royal?' he queried. 'You didn't tell us whether you saw him during the Hobart run.'

Gertie paused for a moment. 'Yes. I saw him. Not during the run though. On the very last night, on the Saturday.'

All eyes were upon her. Another ghost story. Gertie was the centre of attention.

'Was he up in the back row of the dress circle, like you said he usually is?' Pru asked, wondering why Gertie hadn't mentioned it to the rest of the family.

'No. He was backstage this time.'

Another pause.

'Go on,' Ida urged. 'Oh, please go on, do tell us what happened.' Ida was hooked on ghost stories by now.

'Nothing much really.' Gertie shrugged. 'He was just a shadowy figure in the corner. I thought it was one of the crew at first, but it wasn't – everyone had gone to the pub. It was Fred. He likes a deserted theatre.'

The flicker of a glance was exchanged between Gertie and Max; she had of course told Max. And Max understood why she was now reluctant to tell her story. To do so would be to invite Maeve into the room.

Gertie smiled at Ida, who was still waiting expectantly. '*All* ghosts like a deserted theatre,' she said.

'Curtain up in ten,' Mabel announced, sticking her head through the door, and Gertie and Max left to do a quick makeup check, their balcony scene being the opening act of the second half.

The interruption had put an end to the ghost stories, for which Gertie was thankful, given the turn in conversation.

On that last night in Hobart, she *had* thought the shadowy figure in the prompt side corner was one of the backstage crew. She'd known it wasn't Mabel. Mabel and Will and Max had all said 'see you next door' as they'd left for the pub.

'You've got twenty minutes, love,' Max had warned. 'If you haven't joined us by then, I'll be coming back to get you.' He knew how much she liked to stay late in a deserted theatre now and then, particularly after the last show of a run. It was her way of saying goodbye, she said. But ill-lit theatres could be dangerous places. Obstacles abounded, and a fall into the orchestra pit was not uncommon.

Gertie watched the three of them leave via the stage door; the Worthings senior were always the last to go, just as they were always the first to arrive.

A work light had been left on; the night watchman would switch it off on his final rounds of the theatre. Cast and crew had bumped out, the packing done, skips and trunks and equipment sitting in the loading dock awaiting collection first thing in the morning. An eerie, abandoned place, in limbo until the arrival of the next show that would breathe new life into it.

Gertie walked out onto centre stage where she stood silently drinking in the atmosphere, which to her was always palpable. She could feel the past all around her, the murmur of long-ago voices, the echoes of actors and singers, of music and laughter and, above all, applause. Every theatre had a history that lived on within its walls, particularly a theatre as old as the Royal.

She looked to the back of the dress circle, wondering if Fred might be up there, but without the house lights on there was only blackness. What a pity, she'd have liked to have said goodbye.

Then to her left she heard a voice that was real, not a murmur of yesteryear, but quite distinct.

'Sad,' the voice said quietly, 'very sad.'

She turned to see a shadowy figure standing in the prompt corner, no more than a silhouette really, caught in the dim glow of the working light. The figure, which she presumed was one of the backstage crew, appeared to be gazing up into the flies, directly above her head.

Gertie looked up herself. To the very spot where they'd found Maeve dangling.

'Yes,' she said, 'yes, it's very sad.'

There was a sigh from the prompt corner and she turned back. The shadowy figure was no longer there, but she could still feel its presence. Now more strongly than ever.

'Perhaps Maeve will stay here with you, Fred,' she said. 'Perhaps you'll be joined by a friend. That would be nice for you both, don't you think?'

Gertie waited for a minute or so, but there was no reply, which didn't bother her at all. She knew he was there and that he'd heard her every word.

'Goodbye, Fred,' she said, and she left to join the others.

The New Year did not creep in gently, it exploded onto the scene. 1901 was to be a year of change for all.

On 1 January, the Commonwealth of Australia came into existence with Edmund Barton as the country's first Prime Minister. In Sydney, a great procession of thousands, led by a band of Australian shearers, marched from the Domain to Centennial Park, where the official celebration took place.

On 22 January, Queen Victoria, aged eighty-one, died peacefully in her sleep at Osborne House on the Isle of Wight. Most of her Australian subjects, like others throughout the British Empire, had known no monarch but Victoria.

The first bill to be passed by the new federal government of Australia was the *Immigration Restriction Act 1901*, which effectively banned the entry of non-Caucasians and also demanded compulsory repatriation of many of those currently resident in the country. The legislation was ostensibly in order to 'maintain Australia's British character', but the racial intentions were obvious and it quickly became known as the 'White Australia Policy'.

On 9 May, the Duke and Duchess of York opened the first Australian Parliament in the Exhibition Building, Melbourne. Later moving to Parliament House in Spring Street, the seat of government for the Commonwealth of Australia was to remain based in Melbourne until 1927.

And in the midst of all this turbulent change, on 1 February 1901, Gertie Worthing gave birth to a daughter.

That's me. Finally, here I am! At long last! Emma Jane Worthing!

As you've no doubt gathered, I wasn't planned. But oh my goodness, I was welcomed! At least, so Ma told me on any number of occasions.

'Oh Em, lovey,' she'd say with a fit of the giggles, 'you've never seen a fatter Serpentine Dancer in the whole of your life. Or a fatter Juliet, for that matter. Not that the punters were any the wiser, thanks to your Aunt Mabel who's a genius. But I can't tell you how relieved I was when you finally decided to pop your head into the world. And oh lovey, what a world you came into.'

She'd go on then about the fact it was to be another whole year before women got the vote, but she was proud that Australia had led the world. Apart from New Zealand, of course. 'They were a whole nine years ahead of us, Em,' she'd say with a sense of outrage. Then she'd add boastfully, 'But we beat the Old Country by sixteen years and America by eighteen, and that's something we can be downright proud of, that is.'

I found it funny the way Ma used the term 'we'. She was such a true suffragette that when it came to women getting the vote, she was an out-and-out Australian, but it was a different matter altogether when it came to the White Australia Policy. When that subject was brought up, oh my goodness, the shoe was on the other foot altogether!

'It's abominable, Em,' she'd say. 'It was abominable back then and it's abominable today. Australians should hang their heads in shame. Do you know what happened to all those wonderful Negro performers who came out here with the minstrel shows?'

I didn't know, and I have to tell you I was most interested, but I didn't bother answering her question, which was rhetorical anyway. When Ma was passionate about something there was no stopping her.

'A lot of the black American performers stayed here in Australia after their tours had finished.' True to form, and just as I'd expected, she went on without drawing breath. 'They didn't want to go back to their own country where they were treated so poorly. Not, might I add,' she said with acid criticism, 'that Australians treat their own black folk any better. But somehow the Negro singers and comedians who stayed on here copped things easier than they did back home. Or so they told me, and I've no reason to disbelieve them. Even when they couldn't get work as performers, they preferred to stay, taking up what employment they could. You would've seen them yourself, Em, black folk running oyster bars or pie carts around the streets of Melbourne . . .'

I had seen them too – in those early days of my youth – and when I nodded, Ma galloped on yet again.

'Retired from the theatre, all of them,' she said with an airy wave of her hand, as if she personally knew every oyster and pie seller in the whole of Melbourne, which she couldn't possibly have. 'Wonderful performers too. Jubilee singers, actors, comedians, dancers, oh so talented, and such lovely people. But minstrelsy was going out of style, you see, there wasn't the same amount of work around for them. So there they are, selling oysters and pies, some of them even cleaning the streets, but believe me, lovey, still happy and still free to live in this wonderful country they'd chosen to adopt as their own . . .'

Another all-embracing gesture and a pause for dramatic effect, then Ma's face became a mask of anger as she finally arrived at the original point she'd been intending to make.

'And then they bring in the White Australia Policy!'

She spat the words out with venom. And oh, I tell you, for a pretty woman – and Ma was certainly a pretty woman – she could show the fight when she had a mind to.

'Just like that' – a perfectly timed snap of her fingers – 'all those lovely talented men were forced to live in fear. Some worried they might be transported back to their homeland, and of course none of them dared leave the country, not even for a quick holiday or to visit a sick relative. Because if they did, the law wouldn't let them back in, see! Now what sort of freedom is that, I ask you?'

I didn't know what to say, Ma had got herself so worked up.

'At least our darling Irving wasn't threatened,' she went on, 'I was always grateful for that.' Her face softened as it did when she spoke of Irving Sayles. 'He was so talented, Irving, he rose above it all, never stopped working,' she said with an admiring shake of her head. 'And if the law had tried to send him home, Harry Rickards would have had a thing or two to say about that. So would we, for that matter. People were taking note of the

Worthing Brothers partnership after our variety extravaganza of 1900 . . .'

And I'll leave Ma right there, because she's brought me back to where the story was up to before I went off at a tangent. I'm sorry about that. But it's a habit I picked up from Ma, so we'll blame her, shall we?

The truth is, I'm very like Ma, or so they all tell me. Personally, I don't think I'm anywhere near as pretty. Certainly not as pretty as Ma was when she was young – and she was a looker, you should just see the pictures! But I'm what you call 'petite', and I'm fair-haired and blue-eyed like Ma, and most of all, like Ma, I'm deceptively strong. At the risk of sounding smug, I'll tell you something for nothing – it's very handy being perceived as 'delicate' and 'feminine' when you're really tough underneath. Tough both mentally and physically. Ma taught me that. Oh dear me, yes. 'It's your weapon, Em,' she'd say with that saucy smile of hers. 'Keep it up your sleeve for when you need it, lovey.'

So as I was saying, or rather as Ma was saying, the Worthing Brothers became quite a power after the tour of 1900. And so, of course, did Carlo and Rube. The partnership they'd set up between them was the oddest pairing of characters imaginable, which you'll no doubt have gathered by now, but somehow it worked. The clash of personalities between Uncle Will and Carlo was destined to cause problems, and of course it did. But for a good five years, with the calming influence of Aunt Mabel – and I have to say, also of Uncle Rube – it seemed they'd never look back.

I remember Uncle Rube quite clearly from those early days when I was little. He was family to us kids, always ready to lend an ear. I was the youngest by far, and all the older Worthing kids called him Rube, but to me and my brother Bertie, who was six when I was born, he was 'Uncle' Rube.

We liked Carlo too – don't get me wrong, he was great fun – but he was never 'Uncle' Carlo. Perhaps because he had his own wife and kids who were central to his life, which is just as it should be. Uncle Rube was more of a loner. I sometimes wondered whether that meant he was lonely. I do hope not.

Anyway, those early years of the brand-new twentieth century (oh dear me, doesn't that sound grand!) were good times for us. Audiences across Australia embraced the productions of the Worthing Brothers in partnership with Carlo and Rube. Particularly, or so it seemed, because their shows featured 'Stars of the Southern Cross'. At least that's what Aunt Mabel firmly maintained.

'Australians like to see their own up there onstage,' Aunt Mabel would say in that no-nonsense way of hers. 'We don't have to kowtow to overseas stars all the time, bringing them out here at great cost and then paying them a king's ransom. We can create our own stars right here in this country; there's talent enough, and it means we're providing work for local performers. Besides,' she'd add, ever practical, 'we can put the money we save into buying up theatre leases like Rube suggested.'

As always, Aunt Mabel was right. And so was Uncle Rube. New stars were created, theatre leases were bought up, some solely, some in partnership, and the money just started pouring in. Even when they didn't have a production of their own, they'd profit from their theatre rentals. And quite often they'd have two productions out on the road simultaneously, some featuring a whole programme of new performers with Carlo as the charismatic MC, others featuring highlights from their top-billing acts like The Serpentine Dance, The Heavenly Tenor and The Master Illusionist. The Worthings' old favourites – freshly revitalised, of course – were in constant demand.

In only a few years Uncle Will achieved his ultimate goal. A house in Toorak! And oh, it was posh! Well, it still is. A two-storey Italianate mansion no less, built in the late 1880s, stone colonnades, huge bay windows, an upper-floor balcony, and even a central tower. A massive circular driveway out the front, a six-horse stables out the back, and as for the interior . . . what can I say! An entrance hallway that has to be over thirty feet long, chandeliers everywhere, servants' quarters at the rear, and the rest I'll leave to your imagination.

'Will's dream palace,' Ma used to call it.

Ma and Pa bought a house too, a quarter of the size and nowhere near as grand, but still the poshest place we'd ever had. Or so I'm told; I hadn't been around to witness our previous shabby abodes. And oh, it was so pretty, with a big front verandah and a cast-iron lace balcony upstairs, and at the right time of year wisteria growing everywhere. Our house was only a few blocks from Uncle Will's and also in Toorak, mainly because Uncle Will insisted it should be.

'Toorak is a sign of achievement,' he'd say, 'and given our current success and the resulting position we hold in society, there are appearances that need to be maintained.'

Ma and Aunt Mabel always gave a bit of a harrumph when he came out with things like that, but they never openly made fun of him. Nor did Pa. This was Uncle Will's dream come true after all, and no one wants to prick another person's bubble, do they?

The other kids used to tell me how strange it seemed having separate homes all of a sudden and not living together. The Worthing offspring had always been part of one big family, more like siblings than cousins. But they quickly adapted, and being so nearby we continued to live in each other's pockets the way brothers and sisters do.

Ma told me there was quite a 'to do' between Uncle Will and Aunt Mabel when it came to the servants they'd need at the big house – which he renamed 'Worthing Manor', by the way – I forget what it had been called originally, but we kids just referred to it as the 'Big House'. Anyway, a place that size certainly needed looking after. But servants? Aunt Mabel was aghast.

'We don't have servants, Will,' she exclaimed in absolute horror, 'we *never* have *servants*!'

'Why not?' he replied, and according to Ma without a shred of pomposity; for once he was just being downright honest. 'I lack any skill as a gardener, I know nothing about horses, and you don't have time to clean a whopping great mansion. That's a full-time job, Mabel.'

He did have a point, didn't he?

They agreed to employ 'staff' – Aunt Mabel would never use the term 'servant'– and the staff came in the very handy form of the Briggs family. Mr and Mrs Briggs were a groundsman and housekeeper team, their daughters Bernice and Susan were housemaids, and son Oliver, or Ollie, was the stablehand who looked after the carriage and pair. I ask you, what could be better? The arrangement suited the Briggses perfectly. Ma and Pa Briggs, Londoners in their fifties and experienced domestics, had turned up for the interview offering their services as a couple and had successfully sold their kids into the deal. They couldn't have been happier. Mrs Briggs had one stipulation, however.

'You'll need to employ a cook, Mrs Worthing,' she said. (Aunt Mabel had instantly banned 'ma'am' as a form of address – that was reserved for the Queen.) 'I'm not trained for the kitchen.'

Aunt Mabel hadn't wanted a cook at all. 'I'm perfectly capable of cooking for the family,' she'd told Uncle Will, 'and so are the girls. I won't have my daughters being pampered; they'll end up incapable of looking after themselves.'

'But who's going to cook for the staff?' Uncle Will had countered, which brought her to a halt. She hadn't considered they'd need a further servant to serve the staff. 'And when we're away on tour, what then?' he had argued. 'You wouldn't be here to cook for everyone, would you?'

Aunt Mabel probably considered the staff capable of cooking for themselves, but in this particular instance Uncle Will was right; it was the way things were done in the running of a large house.

So Mrs Partridge joined the ranks as cook, and quickly became known as 'Party', because she was plump and jolly and so darn nice to all us kids.

The Briggs family and Party soon came to realise that the Worthings being a show business family made them somehow 'different', and that the house was always to be filled with strange people, music and song and dance.

They adjusted accordingly, but it took Aunt Mabel some time to adapt to her new position as 'mistress of the house', which we all found rather funny. Bossy Aunt Mabel, who only too readily took command of an entire show, the performers, the backstage crew and front-of-house alike, was prone to ask favours of her 'staff' – 'Bernice dear, would you mind fetching me ...' – and more often than not, she'd do chores herself, simply because it seemed easier and quicker that way. Just goes to show, doesn't it, and all due credit to her that she never lost sight of where she came from. I don't think any of us did, really, although Uncle Will made a pretty good show of it at times.

As I was growing up, I remember feeling quite thankful we didn't have servants at our house, which was so much smaller we didn't need them, because frankly I think things were simpler that way. We mucked in together like we always had, and Ma and Pa didn't want a carriage and pair, they were happy to catch the cable tram like us kids. Public transport did us fine – or shanks's pony; we all liked a good walk. Besides, the Toorak line was only a spit and a cough away; we'd be in the city before you could say Jack Robinson.

Actually – and I recall reading this only recently, can't remember where – did you know that back in those days Melbourne had one of the largest cable car systems in the whole wide world? I mean, we were right up there with San Francisco and Chicago! That's saying something, wouldn't you agree?

The tram was actually quicker than harnessing up a pair, but it wasn't the same image, so Uncle Will stuck to his carriage. When motor vehicles came into popular use some time later he made the conversion, and the stables became a two-car garage.

As things turned out, the Big House proved far more than an indulgence; the sheer size of the place was downright practical. The vast room that would once have been a ballroom was converted to a rehearsal hall, and the dimensions of various sets were marked out with different coloured tape on the highly polished wooden floor (which would have appalled the previous owners).

There was a separate music room with a baby grand, and the sizeable grounds at the rear of the house formed an excellent training area for gymnastics. Pa even rigged a highwire from one of the many upstairs bedrooms to the roof of the stables.

These practice areas were strictly for family use, of course – all production rehearsals were conducted professionally in hired venues – but it just goes to prove how very much we remained creatures of the theatre, the whole lot of us. Unlike Carlo's kids, who didn't seem to care in the least for the theatre. I can't even remember them from those early years together. Carlo and Rube I do recall (Uncle Rube in particular, as I mentioned) but Carlo's children never seemed in evidence during those hectic days of rehearsal. Mick, the eldest, had joined the army, I know that much, but the other two . . . ? They didn't appear to show any interest at all.

'What would you expect?' Uncle Will would sneer if the topic ever came up. 'The man's an amateur. How could he possibly instil a love of the theatre in his children when he has no true calling himself?'

Oh my goodness, how Uncle Will did love sticking the boot in whenever he could. Not that it bothered Carlo in the least. According to Ma, Carlo took every opportunity to thumb his nose right back, which naturally infuriated Uncle Will all the more. Things between those two were always bound to come to a head at some point, she said. And they did. In the most shocking way.

It happened in 1906, during a run at Her Majesty's in Sydney. The theatre had been rebuilt just four years previously, following a terrible fire that had gutted the place.

The fire had occurred during J. C. Williamson's 1902 production of *Ben Hur*, and there's a story for the history books, I can tell you. With a running time close to four hours *Ben Hur* was the biggest, most expensive show ever to be mounted at The Maj, boasting huge choral numbers, marches, and to top it all off a spectacular chariot race the likes of which you simply would not believe. JCW had decided that 'spectacle' was the order of the day, and he had a team of live horses pulling a chariot and galloping full tilt on a treadmill centre stage while the background scenery was rolled in the opposite direction. I mean, really, can you just imagine! Something to behold indeed, but a potential disaster, wouldn't you agree? So much could go wrong! And it certainly did. The official report said the asbestos safety curtain failed to operate, but I ask you, that's not what starts a fire, is it?

You should have heard Ma on the topic. 'All that machinery,' she'd say, 'all that metal, all those sparks!' It reminded her of the cotton mills. 'Just one spark will do it,' she'd say. 'Cotton mills and theatres, fire traps both.'

J. C. Williamson lost a fortune. Tons of special equipment and fancy machinery, not to mention the show's fourteen sets and God alone knows how many costumes. You've got to hand it to old JCW, though, he rebuilt the theatre's interior only one year later, and in a new Edwardian style that was most attractive.

And that's where the shocking event took place. In that beautiful theatre and before a full house, the Worthings were publicly humiliated. Heckled, booed and ridiculed onstage. No one knows exactly how or why it happened. No one in the family anyway. Or if they do, they've certainly never told me. But we all know, every single one of us, that Carlo was to blame.

13

A PARTING OF THE WAYS

The Worthing Brothers with Carlo and Rube presented their *Big Show Bonanza of Fabulous Favourites* in 1906, and the title was apt. The show was indeed a bonanza of acts that had proved audience favourites for years, with enticing fresh sales pitches added: 'The Divine Dolores as you've never before seen her', a new Serpentine Dance incorporating the use of film; 'Our Heavenly Tenor transports you to Italy', Will Worthing singing arias from Puccini and Verdi; and 'Introducing the talents of Baby Worthing on the highwire', the youngest member of the family, pretty little five-year-old Emma, now traversing the wire on her father's shoulders.

Carlo was Master of Ceremonies with his customary panache, and the grande finale was as always The Wonderful Worthing, Master Illusionist, but everything was given new zest and invention. The sets were more complex, as was the lighting and special effects; Georgie Washington led a sixteen-piece band; and last but not least there was the addition of film, not only as an inventive opening to The Serpentine Dance, but a comedy running a full five minutes was included as a separate act of its own. The world was by now fascinated with the novelty of moving pictures. As a result, the whole show appeared altogether bigger and grander, which was of course the intention, the budget having been increased for this very purpose.

The production was scheduled for a limited run only of major theatres in several capital cities, and minus the usual out-of-town tryout. This was evidence of the partnership's confidence in its pulling power, and advance bookings certainly attested to the fact they were right. The show would open at the Princess in Melbourne, then on to the Theatre Royal in Adelaide, then all the way to Perth where they would perform at His Majesty's, the glorious new baroque theatre that had opened only two years previously, after which the six-month season would finally close with a triumphant run at Her Majesty's in Sydney.

All went according to plan. Triumph followed triumph. From state to state, from city to city, newspaper critics wrote glowing reviews. Most evening performances were booked out in advance and matinee days, which were door sales only, saw queues lined up for blocks: down Spring Street in Melbourne; down Hindley Street in Adelaide; down Hay Street in Perth.

It was a dream run where apparently nothing could go wrong. Until the final week of the Perth season . . .

'What is the matter with the man!' Will raged to Mabel.

'He obviously has a thing for sopranos,' Mabel suggested mildly, hoping to somehow humour her husband out of an anger that appeared barely controllable.

'It's hardly *funny*, Mabel,' Will bit back scathingly, 'when you recall that Maeve suicided over the wretch!'

'Yes, I'm sorry, dear,' she admitted, 'that was tasteless of me, but I just wish you'd calm down enough to —'

'I will *not* calm down.' He paced the sitting room of their suite like a restless lion. 'I will *not* have history repeat itself in such a disgusting manner. I will *not* allow him to jeopardise the whole show to satisfy his libidinous indulgences.' He stopped pacing and stared squarely at her. 'I will have it out with him. I swear to you I'll confront him, Mabel. This must cease. Right now!'

'Very well,' she said, aware there would be no stopping him. 'But do try and control yourself first.'

History was certainly repeating itself, Mabel thought. Not just the fact that Carlo had been discovered having an affair, but that the recipient of his affections should be the soprano who accompanied Will so beautifully in the 'Mimì' duet from *La Bohème*, once again bringing her husband's ego into the equation. Why on earth couldn't Carlo have picked one of the other singers, or one of the dancers for that matter? There were any number of pretty girls in the show.

If it had been Mabel herself who had discovered the affair, she would have kept quiet about it, but unfortunately the discovery had been made by none other than Will himself.

The Worthings senior, together with Carlo and Rube, given their status as the show's producers, were staying at the opulent Palace Hotel on the corner of St Georges Terrace and William Street. The rest of the cast, including the Worthings junior, were comfortably accommodated in other very pleasant hotels nearby, even little Emma who was sharing a room with her cousin Prudence, thus proving the company's egalitarian attitude towards performers in general. But none of the hotels were as grand as the Palace, which proudly and rightfully boasted to be the finest in the entire state of Western Australia. And since the gold rush boom there were a great many fine hotels throughout WA.

So what was Adeline Stanton doing at the Palace well after midnight? Will Worthing had seen her quietly sneaking along the corridor as he'd come upstairs from the bar. He'd stayed out of sight and followed her, watching as Carlo opened the door of his room to usher her inside. And Will had fumed. How long had this been going on?

His resultant furious rave to Mabel continued until close to two in the morning and would have gone on longer had his wife not retired to bed with a brief word of advice.

'Do as you wish, Will,' she'd said, 'but whatever it is you wish to do, make sure you control your temper.'

The following day, Will confronted Carlo after the brunch he and Mabel always took in the plush downstairs dining room.

'May I have a word,' he said coldly, upon approaching the table where Carlo and Rube had also finished their brunch. The four never shared a table, for obvious reasons.

'Of course.' Carlo dabbed a damask napkin to his lips and rose leisurely, taking his time.

'Excuse us, Rube,' Will said with a polite nod to Rube, whom he liked.

Rube returned the nod amiably, but he could see behind Will's controlled facade that something was afoot. The man was angry. Had he discovered the affair between Carlo and Adeline, Rube wondered. It had been going on for a whole three months now. *Oh dear, this won't bode well*, he thought.

The two walked into the front lounge, which was relatively deserted, but they didn't sit. Will had no time for niceties.

'I know about you and Adeline,' he said, 'and your affair is to cease forthwith, as of this very moment. You are to inform her it is over, do you understand me?' Determined to take Mabel's advice and to control his temper, Will was at his pompous best.

'Oh yes?' Carlo's response was supercilious. This was the Will Worthing he really could not abide. 'And what will you do if I don't?'

'I shall tell your wife and your children of your adulterous behaviour; how does that sound?'

Carlo met Will's gaze boldly. *What happens out on the road . . . ?* His eyes made the query loud and clear; Will would never break the unspoken bond between performers on tour. It was simply not done.

Will continued however, tightly but under complete control. 'Winifred will be disappointed I'm sure, although I've no doubt she suspects you do this sort of thing all the time. But the children's knowledge of your infidelity will most certainly upset her. Mick, being grown, might view your behaviour on a "man to man" basis, but little Anne? What's she now, around fifteen, sixteen? And Marty, well he'd be coming up for seven, wouldn't he, not much older than our Em. I think they would view your tawdry affair as nothing short of betrayal.'

'You wouldn't,' Carlo said, his bravado faltering.

'Oh yes, I would. Believe me, I would!'

Will strode from the lounge into the grand main entrance, across the mosaic floor tiles and out into St Georges Terrace. He would take his mid-morning constitutional beside the Swan River.

Carlo knew he was cornered. And he despised Will Worthing. How could the man not respect the bond between performers 'out on the road'? The unspoken rule they all adhered to? But he dared not challenge Will's ultimatum; his family was far too important. He ended the affair that very day.

A fortnight later, they were in Sydney preparing for the grand opening at Her Majesty's, the final leg of a tour nothing short of victorious. And, as was to be expected, Sydney proved equally successful. Opening night resulted in glowing reviews and during the season that followed, as with the other capital cities, evening performances were invariably booked out and matinee days saw queues lined up for blocks, this time down Pitt Street. Nothing could possibly go wrong.

But it did. And again the trouble emanated from Carlo. Or so it appeared.

Nobody knew exactly how it started, nobody except Rube anyway, and even he could not believe that such an innocuous event could end up having such catastrophic repercussions.

They were barely halfway through their two-month run at The Maj when in the Cat and Fiddle Tavern late at night Carlo got shockingly drunk. He'd been drinking far too much lately and had been ever since the end of the Perth run. He was sick of Will Worthing and wanted the tour to be over.

Rube was perched on a bar stool beside him, keeping an eye on him while drinking very little himself. It being a Tuesday, he was on the verge of dragging Carlo away – they had a matinee the following day – when . . .

'You're him! You're Carlo!'

A group of revellers who appeared as drunk as Carlo himself had arrived at the Cat and Fiddle, a sleazy gathering place that stayed open until all hours and catered to all types.

'Saw your show on Saturday,' the man said, while his mates gathered at the bar, rowdily calling for drinks. 'A good night out it was, a real good night out.'

'Thank you, my friend.' Carlo gave a half-hearted salute with his glass; he wasn't in the mood to chat, but was always polite to a fan. 'Glad you enjoyed it.' He smiled glassily then returned his attention to his drink, downing its remnants. He'd switched from ale to brandy some time back, which was never a good sign.

But the man, full of drunken bonhomie, was so thrilled to meet a genuine star that he didn't get the message.

'Yep, damned fine entertainment your show,' he said jovially, 'and what about those Worthings, eh? Now there's talent for you!'

'Yeah, yeah . . .' Carlo signalled the barman who, being too busy serving the new arrivals, didn't appear to notice.

'Come on, mate,' Rube urged gently, 'time to go home, matinee tomorrow.'

'I mean, that bloke Will Worthing,' the man continued, 'what a voice, eh? No wonder they call him The Heavenly Tenor . . .'

Carlo didn't respond. He just glowered.

'And as for the young fella . . . He's his son, isn't he, The Wonderful Worthing?' An admiring shake of the head as the man accepted an ale from one of his friends who was passing glasses around. 'Now he was something really worth watching, he was . . .' A salutation, a healthy chug of ale and on he went. 'That final illusion, I mean what an act, eh? What a way to end a show! What a talent! I mean, you gotta ask yourself, how does he do it? How does he —?'

'They're twins.'

Carlo didn't yell the words out, rather he snarled them under his breath – he'd had enough of the man's ravings – but Rube froze, unable to believe what he'd just heard.

'Eh?' The man hadn't quite caught the words himself.

'They're fucking twins,' Carlo snarled again, no louder than the first time, and again the man appeared not to have heard, or if he had, he would no doubt have assumed Carlo was joking.

But Rube already had Carlo up on his feet and halfway to the door.

'Glad you enjoyed the show,' he said over-heartily, 'but duty calls. Have to put this man to bed, we've got a matinee tomorrow. Night, all.'

Then out in the street . . . 'What the hell did you just *do*!' Rube hissed, horrified.

'What? What do you mean, what did I do?' For a moment Carlo appeared to have forgotten. 'Oh, that.' He dismissed the incident with a drunken wave of his hand. 'They didn't hear, they weren't even listening and they don't even care.'

Just as well you're right, Rube thought. The men were drunk, they *hadn't* been listening, they *hadn't* heard and they *didn't* care. *Thank God for that*, he told himself as he dragged Carlo away.

But Carlo and Rube were both wrong. There was one man among the bunch who *had* heard. He didn't particularly care, it was true, but he knew someone who no doubt *would*. And that someone might pay well for the discovery of a secret that could prove ruinous.

The following day, Carlo had no recall of the event, but Rube insisted upon reminding him, and in no uncertain terms.

'Oh shit, did I really?' Carlo was dutifully appalled.

'Yep. You're safe this time – they were drunk and didn't take any notice,' Rube said, 'but you're going to have to watch your drinking, mate. You can't let things get out of hand like that.'

'I know. I know. Sorry, Rube. I'm really sorry.'

Carlo's penitence genuine, they left things there, and all appeared well enough. Until the following Saturday night's performance, which like all Saturday nights was before a packed house, fully booked in advance.

The final act . . . The grande finale . . . The Wonderful Worthing is revealed in a spotlight high above the stage. He is standing on a trapeze acknowledging the applause as it is slowly lowered. A good fifteen feet from the ground, he drops to clasp the trapeze in his hands, producing a gasp from the audience, then finally and athletically he drops five or six feet to the stage, where he stands triumphant. Beside him, The Beautiful Pandora acknowledges the feat. The door to the magician's wooden box is thrown open. The box, which only minutes earlier had housed The Wonderful Worthing, is empty.

Tumultuous applause. But along with the applause another sound can be heard. An ugly sound. And there is an ugly sight too, a disturbing sight. A dozen or so young thugs have burst into the theatre and are running down the aisles in the stalls, yelling at the tops of their voices.

The audience is distracted. The applause dies down, people look about: what is going on?

'It's a sham,' the thugs are yelling, 'they're twins!' Over and over they yell, the audience by now hearing them quite clearly. 'Fake! Fraud! It's a con! They're twins!'

Theatre employees, the doorman who had been stormed past in the foyer, several ushers, the manager himself, are attempting to round up the intruders and bundle them outside, but the damage has been done. The audience, by now thoroughly dumbfounded, is being egged on by the hecklers who have started booing. Many instinctively join in.

'Boo! Boo!' The sound swells throughout the theatre as pack mentality takes over. 'Boo! Boo!'

Up onstage Alfie, who tonight was the 'reveal', stands motionless, as does Pru. What should they do? This is normally their moment of triumph when, after numerous bows, they are joined by the rest of the company for the final curtain call, invariably to a standing ovation and invariably lasting a full twenty minutes as each act steps forward to be recognised and applauded individually. The Worthings have never been booed off stage, never once heckled and humiliated in such a way. Any minute the audience will start hurling things; they've seen it happen to others, but never, never to them.

Will, Mabel, Max, Gertie and the other performers all watch from the wings, horrified. Mabel is wondering whether she should bring down the curtain. Carlo is preparing himself to stride out onstage and attempt to take control of the situation.

However, crammed in the tiny space at the rear of the magician's box, it is Artie who makes the decision. He pulls the virtually invisible wire just above his head, releasing the spring-loaded false panel. The panel swings open and he is revealed.

He steps out in full showmanship style, accepting the boos as if they're hurrahs, bowing left, right and centre before, with a quick look to his brother and Pru, throwing a series of backflips ending in a somersault.

Alfie quickly gets the message and does the same. In an instant the identical 'Wonderful Worthings' have become an acrobatic duo.

In the orchestra pit, Georgie Washington too gets the message, and the band strikes up. As the brothers throw each other in somersaults, vault each other shoulder high, lift each other in one-armed handstands, the band under Georgie's conductorship exclaims their prowess with dramatic stabs, drowning out the boos. The hecklers are bundled outside, several audience members assisting the theatre staff.

Young Prudence is also not idle. Twirling about in time to the music as if the whole act has been orchestrated and choreographed, she emphasises each acrobatic trick with a grand flourish. By now there is no longer one boo to be heard.

Then, in the final tableau, the twins include Pru. Artie kneels on one knee, Alfie climbs to stand on his shoulders, Pru follows to stand in Alfie's cupped hand and be lifted to his shoulders and Artie slowly rises to his feet, a three-person pyramid. If the female gymnast had been Gertie, she would have performed an arm stand on Alfie's shoulders, but Pru's training isn't quite up to that standard. Not yet. As a matter of fact Pru hasn't really been trained as an acrobat at all, but every Worthing child is taught the elemental basics, just in case it might come in handy. As it does on this particular Saturday night.

The show now over, the three of them take their bows to healthy applause, cheering and cries of 'bravo', after which they are joined by the company for the final curtain call, which receives its customary standing ovation.

Through sheer theatricality the Worthings have turned defeat into victory, but they all know it is the end of The Wonderful Worthing, Master Illusionist. From this night on, the act will cease to exist.

The following morning, Will called a producers' meeting at his suite in the Australia Hotel. Once again, the six were staying in the grandest hotel the city had to offer, situated in Castlereagh Street.

They were all there, seated and solemnly silent: Will, Mabel, Max, Gertie, Carlo and Rube. The twins, who had so bravely and successfully borne the brunt of the assault, were not in attendance. They were spending the entire Sunday at the theatre rehearsing a brand-new act, The Wonderful Worthing Duo, Acrobatic Magicians Extraordinaire. As the title indicated, it would be a mixture of magic and gymnastics, but it would not be performed by identical twins, it would be performed by brothers quite discernibly different.

'Someone in the company has betrayed us,' Will gravely announced. 'God alone knows why they would do such a thing, but we must interview every single performer, every single crew member, and we must root out the perpetrator. Needless to say, whoever it is will never work in this industry again.'

Carlo and Rube exchanged a glance. They had known it would come to this and had discussed the matter in some depth the previous night.

'It was me,' Carlo said boldly, 'I'm to blame.' He was keen to get the whole thing over and done with, take whatever punishment the others saw fit, and move on.

The Worthings all turned to stare at him in open-mouthed amazement. Why would Carlo seek to ruin a production in which he was a partner?

'I'm sorry,' he said, again boldly, defiantly even, which rather detracted from the apology. 'I certainly didn't set out to "betray" the company, I can assure you. I was drunk and the words just slipped out somehow.' He shrugged, a little shamefaced. 'To be honest, I couldn't even remember I'd said it until Rube reminded me the next day.'

To Will Worthing, Carlo's boldness, followed by of all things a *shrug*, gave the appearance that the man simply didn't care.

'You destroy overnight one of the finest variety acts this country has ever seen,' he said, his voice measured, not pompous in the least but aghast to the point of disbelief. 'You jeopardise our family's entire reputation, our history as performers and producers, and you can't *remember* that you did it!'

Rube jumped to Carlo's defence. 'It's true, Will,' he said, 'I was there, I saw the whole thing. Carlo was dead drunk and he just muttered "they're twins" to a bloke who was irritating him, carrying on too much about The Wonderful Worthing and the final illusion. The bloke himself was drunk, and so were his friends; I was absolutely sure no one had heard.'

'Then you were absolutely wrong, weren't you?' Will's voice was like ice.

Rube felt the faintest sense of something resembling panic. He'd always got on well with the Worthings, all of them, including Will and most particularly Mabel. But looking around now, he could feel the alienation emanating from every single one of them.

'I understand how you must feel —' He started out addressing them all, but was interrupted by Will.

'No, you don't. You have never understood, and you never will, either of you. You don't belong in the theatre.'

But Rube was determined to be heard. 'Listen to me, Will, listen to me, *all* of you. Last night's assault was planned, a definite plot, everything organised down to the last detail. A full house on a Saturday night, hecklers paid to break into the theatre at precisely the right moment, chanting precisely the slogans they were told. There's an enemy out there bent on destroying the show, and Carlo is not that enemy.'

'Perhaps not.' Again Will was the spokesperson; no one else said a word. 'But Carlo provided the ammunition, didn't he? It was Carlo who broke the cardinal rule of the theatre.'

There was nothing Rube could say to that.

'We will complete the season here in Sydney with the twins performing their replacement act, which is bound to receive a deal of press that we can only hope will be favourable,' Will went on, addressing Rube only and ignoring Carlo. 'After which we will terminate our partnership. We will have no more dealings with your company. There will be no future Worthing Brothers, Carlo and Rube productions, you and Mabel will sort out the theatre lessee agreements, and from that moment on there will be no further contact between us.'

He darted a quick glance to Mabel, who gave a curt nod.

'For your sake, Rube, and for your sake only,' Will concluded; he couldn't even bring himself to look at Carlo, 'we'll keep this strictly between us. If word were to get out that it was Carlo who revealed the twins' identity, the two of you would never work in the theatre again. This is not a personal threat, I assure you, just a statement of the facts and the way things would play out. No one would employ you and no one would agree to be employed *by* you. Your reputations would be ruined.'

He rose from his chair. 'Meeting over,' he said, 'I'll see you at the half tomorrow.'

Carlo and Rube walked to the door, where Carlo turned back to the group.

'I really *am* sorry, you know,' he said.

Will strode off to the bedroom without a backward glance. The others remained staring at Carlo, still not saying a word. Then he and Rube left, Rube quietly closing the door behind them.

The press Will had anticipated appeared much earlier than expected, in fact the very next day. Monday's *Sydney Morning Herald* featured a lead article about the Saturday night debacle, and not just in the entertainment pages. This was obviously considered news of a broader kind and bound to grab the public's attention.

'EXPOSED!' the article's headline screamed, and below, in letters only just a little less bold, 'A Unique Performance Greets Theatregoers at Her Majesty's on Saturday Night.'

'Good God,' Will exclaimed as Mabel handed him the paper – they had the *Herald* delivered to their suite every morning – 'did we have press in the house on Saturday?'

'Not that I know of,' Mabel replied. The press was always granted complimentary seats and every newspaper in Sydney had reviewed the show a full month previously.

They sat side by side at the table and read the article together; a full account of the raid on the theatre by a gang of young thugs, the heckling that followed, and the exposure of The Wonderful Worthing as identical twins.

Another subheading followed, 'MASTER PERFORM-ERS.'

'*The Worthing twins may perhaps not qualify as a Master Illusionist,*' the journalist went on. '*Some may even refer to the pair as tricksters. To this scribe, however, they are Master Performers, and always have been. These two young men enthralled the audience with their showman-ship, turning disaster into triumph, for which they must be congratulated.*'

There followed a blow-by-blow account of the twins' talent and the sheer audacity they'd displayed in the face of such adversity, and then there was a final subheading.

A TRAITOR IN THEIR MIDST

It is a great pity that the variety industry is now destined to lose one of its most impressive acts in the form of The Wonderful Worthing. I'm sure many readers must be wondering who would take it upon themselves to break the sacred rule of the theatre, thereby shattering the illusion that has delighted so many for so long. Surely, one would assume, no member of the profession could be responsible for such treachery.

However, I have it on good authority, unbelievable though it may seem, that this is precisely the case. It has come to this writer's attention that the Worthings have been betrayed by none other than their very own partner, co-producer and fellow showman, the talented Carlo, Master of Ceremonies, who was overheard boasting of the twins' existence in a late-night tavern. That it should come down to this! That an act as simple as a drunkard boasting in a bar should cause such ruination. I must surely join all true theatre lovers in saying, 'Shame on you, Carlo.'

'Well, well,' Mabel said, 'who would have thought . . . What a bolt out of the blue.' She exhaled and leant back in her chair, amazed. 'Rube was spot on, Will, there's an enemy out there. But whoever it is, they don't just have the Worthings in their sights. Seems to me they're after Carlo.'

'And they're welcome to him,' Will said dismissively as he checked the journalist's name, an accredited critic whom he recognised. 'I wonder how Donovan got hold of the story. Or how he happened to be in the house; he reviewed the show weeks back.'

'The enemy, of course,' Mabel replied. 'Just as Rube said, this is a plot, planned and organised down to the last detail. But who on earth would go to all that trouble? It couldn't be a competitor, could it? Surely not.'

'Never,' Will stated with vigour, 'no rival entrepreneur would do such a thing. Nor would anyone else in show business, for that matter. We have only Carlo to thank for all this.'

We don't really, Mabel thought, *Carlo didn't organise the plot. He most definitely provided the ammunition, as you said, but he's not the true enemy.* But she didn't give voice to her thoughts; any further talk of Carlo would only arouse anger.

'At least Donovan's been kind to the twins,' she said. 'It augurs well for their new act.'

'Which, regardless of their prodigious talent, is destined never to achieve the heights of The Wonderful Worthing,' Will said scathingly. 'All thanks once again to our good friend Carlo.'

'Let's take a walk in the park and have some brunch out, shall we, dear,' Mabel suggested brightly, 'it's a lovely day.' That would keep them from bumping into Carlo in the dining room. *Good heavens, we can hardly continue to avoid him, though,* she thought. *There's another whole month of the show to go yet.*

Mabel wasn't really worried about any further confrontation between the two, however. Her husband would ignore Carlo, and the show would go on as if nothing had happened, the audience as always being Will Worthing's principle concern. At the end of the current tour they would return to Melbourne, sever all connections and that would be that. Mabel had to admit she would miss Rube, who was such a dear man.

As she and Will took their mid-morning constitutional in
Hyde Park, her thoughts were mainly on Artie and Alfie.
She wondered how the twins would cope with the knowl-
edge that the third person they'd created between them, The
Wonderful Worthing himself, had ceased to exist.

Had she known, even Mabel, astute as she was, would
have been surprised.

Strangely enough, Artie already felt a sense of relief.
He hadn't realised that the secrecy he and his brother
had shared, and which in the early days had so delighted
him, had in more recent times become a burden. Oh,
how they'd enjoyed fooling everyone with the hybrid
character they'd manufactured, not just the audience, but
their fellow performers, the backstage crew . . . It had
been something very special and powerful between them,
drawing them even closer together. There were times
when they'd felt they'd actually become one.

But what had been a game to start with had proved so
successful that their personal lives had slowly become lost
in a giant conspiracy. Or so it seemed to Artie. Now all of
a sudden he felt free. Bold, adventurous, audacious Artie
could finally throw caution to the wind and be himself.
Was that perhaps why he'd made the decision he had on
Saturday night? His father had congratulated him on his
quick thinking and showmanship.

'You saved the day, Artie,' Will Worthing had said. 'I'm
proud of you, son.'

But had he saved the day or had he saved himself? Artie
had known, the moment he'd stepped out of that magician's box and revealed the truth, that he was already
relishing his freedom.

Alfie, the more conventional of the two, wasn't sure
how he felt as yet. Exposed? Certainly. Vulnerable? To
some extent, yes. He'd felt supremely confident as The
Wonderful Worthing. To forego the deception and reveal

his true self had come as something of a shock. He was unprepared.

Their father had always maintained there were two types of actors and performers.

'There are those who revel in their ability to command the centre of attention,' Will Worthing was wont to proclaim, 'and there are those who revel in their ability to hide behind the mask of the character they portray. Both can be equally successful, I've found.' It was quite obvious to all which type Will himself was, and many might have thought that perhaps his brother Max fell into the other category. In any event, it appeared Will Worthing's sons epitomised their father's theory. Artie was prepared to embrace centre stage, but Alfie was not at all ready to throw aside his mask.

'Well, it's certainly true what they say, isn't it,' Gertie piped up a week later. 'There's no such thing as bad publicity.'

The Worthing family was gathered at their favourite café in Elizabeth Street overlooking Hyde Park. They invariably took over the place for brunch on a Sunday.

'For the show, yes, we've been lucky there,' Will said, 'but I'm not sure Carlo would altogether agree.' The latter comment he'd added with relish.

Since Donovan's article had appeared in Monday's *Sydney Morning Herald* the show had been inundated with press. It seemed every critic from every newspaper in Sydney wanted to write a further review of the production, or rather of The Wonderful Worthing Duo, Acrobatic Magicians Extraordinaire. Audiences too were flocking to the theatre to catch the new act, so much so that an extra matinee had been added to accommodate the numbers.

Carlo's opening appearance as Master of Ceremonies, however, would occasionally be greeted with boos, usually from the dress circle's more expensive seats or from the private boxes, most of which were the preserve of true theatre lovers. When such a thing happened, Carlo would rise above the display of antipathy with his customary aplomb and very soon the audience would be under his complete control, the brief bout of disapproval having been afforded as a matter of principle only. On matinee days there was never a boo to be heard, which was not surprising as the general audience didn't give a fig if Carlo had betrayed his fellow performers, so long as he continued to entertain.

'Everyone just loves our new duo,' Gertie said, beaming at Artie and Alfie, who were downing thick roast beef sandwiches with gusto. 'Critics and audiences alike, they all reckon you two are the best ever.' Gertie was determined to look on the bright side, and she wanted the twins to do the same. They'd lost the show's top act – so what? Artie and Alfie were fine entertainers in their own right. 'We're very proud of you boys,' she said, 'and you too, Pru,' she added. 'You look absolutely lovely up there on that stage. Your backflips are coming on a treat too, and as for that pyramid!'

Pru glowed with pride. She actually preferred being part of the new act. Her role was much more showy now, and she could top the pyramid with a handstand, what's more.

'Don't eat them all, lovey.' Gertie gave her daughter a smack on the wrist; Emma was reaching for a fourth fish paste sandwich. 'Leave some for others, there's a good girl.' Not that Gertie had any cause for concern. Little Em was the only one who had inherited her mother's love of fish paste sandwiches.

'Yes, it's a slick act all right,' Max said, agreeing with his wife and fully aware of her motives. The twins and Pru deserved the accolades they were receiving, and given the loss of The Wonderful Worthing, the twins in particular no doubt needed a reminder of their true value. 'Very slick and very professional.'

Will nodded, but said nothing. Slick, yes, professional, yes, but the duo act would never rival The Wonderful Worthing in originality, and every single one of them knew it. What was it Harry Rickards had said all those years ago? 'Identical twins – pure gold for a magic act.' As always, The Tivoli King had been right on the money.

Well, they'd lost the act now, and they'd lost it forever; there could be no going back. They would never know who had set out to sabotage them or why, but they would always know the true culprit. Will Worthing would never forgive Carlo.

14

฿ETRAYAL LEADS TO ฿HEARTBREAK

'Why did you do it, Rosie?'

Gilda had been amazed at the speed with which Rosie had carried out her plan. The trouble she'd gone to; the use of her many connections, both influential and shady; the money she'd spent, not that she didn't have any amount to spare. She'd been a woman possessed. Why?

'Why did you set out to ruin the Worthings?'

Rosie made no reply. She didn't even appear to have heard as she sipped her champagne and gazed at the beauty of Sydney Harbour.

'*Why?*' Gilda was insistent. 'What did they ever do to you? You don't even *know* them.'

'I didn't set out to ruin the Worthings, my dear.' Rosie finally deigned to turn her attention to Gilda. 'I set out to ruin Carlo. I've been wanting to pay him back ever since I left him, you know that.'

Gilda didn't actually know, or if she did, she'd forgotten. How long ago had it been since that night when Rosie had poured out the vitriol she'd apparently been harbouring for years? Close to two decades, surely; the opening of Her Majesty's Theatre, George Rignold playing *Henry V*, the night they'd seen Carlo and Rube and the boy. Had Rosie really been lying in wait all this time to seek vengeance? And if so, for what exactly? Gilda hadn't understood Rosie's reasoning on that night, and she didn't now.

'But why ruin the Worthings?' she asked. 'Why was that necessary?'

'The Worthings were opportune,' Rosie said with a weary sigh, as if Gilda really should have been able to reason this out for herself. 'They provided the means, no more than that. Besides, I haven't ruined them, I've merely inconvenienced them.'

'By destroying their top-billing act?' '*Inconvenienced*', Gilda thought, *hardly the appropriate term.* 'In exposing the Worthing twins, you've ensured they'll never be able to perform as illusionists again.'

'They'll survive,' Rosie replied with a careless shrug. 'Unfortunately, so will Carlo.' She gazed once more out at the harbour. It was late afternoon; they were seated on the balcony of her house high on the hill in Vaucluse and the view was quite splendid. 'If the truth be known, I'd rather have seen him dead,' she said calmly, 'but ruination will just have to do.'

Gilda watched as Rosie sipped her champagne, her own glass remaining untouched beside the ice bucket and bottle of Dom Pérignon that sat on the coffee table between them. There didn't seem much more to be said, did there? And her mind went back to that night . . .

'Did you see the way he flaunted the boy?' Rosie had said as the two of them sat in the downstairs drawing room of Emile Devereaux's Vaucluse mansion.

They'd returned just an hour previously, and she'd fed the Frenchman his hefty cognac while the three of them discussed the magnificent new theatre and the stirring production of *Henry V*. Then she'd stood behind her lover's armchair, gently massaging his brow, soothing away his imminent migraine. 'Poor Emile,' she'd said, 'I can always read the signs, you poor, poor dear,' and very soon the man had developed the migraine he would never have had but for her suggestion. 'You must go to bed, my poor darling,' she'd said, and he'd plodded obediently upstairs. 'I'll join you shortly, dearest,' she'd called after him, 'and I shall rock you to sleep.' She would need to do no such thing. He'd be dead to the world by the time she joined him; the brandy had been a triple measure and she invariably slipped in a sleeping draught to be sure, a regular ruse of hers. Then, alone with her very special friend, she'd settled down to voice her innermost thoughts.

Gilda was momentarily bewildered. The comment had seemed to come out of nowhere.

'Who flaunted what boy?' she asked.

Her puzzlement irritated Rosie. 'Carlo, of course,' she snapped. 'Carlo and *that* child.'

'Oh yes, of course.' *Carlo and* that *child who just happens to be Rosie's own son*, Gilda thought, *and* that *child who just happens to be called Michael, or has Rosie forgotten?* 'Rube was there too,' she said with a smile. 'I must say, he's not ageing as well as Carlo.' Gilda was determined to play the moment lightly; Rosie was in one of her moods. God only knew what was going on in her mind.

'He had his hand on the boy's shoulder,' Rosie said, 'and he stared me down. Or he tried to. A brazen confrontation, daring me to react. And the boy was so beautiful.'

'Yes, he was, wasn't he?' Gilda agreed, still lightly, but recognising the signs of danger. 'A very handsome lad indeed.'

'I despise them both.'

The comment was made with such quiet loathing that Gilda felt a frisson of shock. She offered no reply, but her eyes asked the question.

'I never wanted a child,' Rosie said, 'he knew that. But I suffered the whole ghastly business of pregnancy and birth, and then he expected me to embrace motherhood. Me! The hide of the man! Carlo took the best years of my life, Gilda, and one day I intend he shall pay. I don't care how long I have to wait, but I can promise you he will pay, and dearly. I'll see him ruined. Or better still,' she added, 'I'll see him dead.'

Rosie hadn't once raised her voice, which made the vitriol of her words and the threat they carried somehow more menacing. Gilda had believed her that night. There was a madness in Rosie.

She'd wondered briefly whether perhaps she should get in touch with Rube and warn him, but the following morning all seemed forgotten. And in the days and weeks and then months that ensued, Carlo's name was not once again mentioned. Rosie had married Emile the following year and two years later the Frenchman was dead. He'd died peacefully of a heart attack, asleep in his bed; an enviable way to go, many agreed.

With his passing Rosie had become a very wealthy woman, and she and Gilda now lived in the Vaucluse mansion, regularly escaping the city to the beautiful home Emile Devereaux had built at Wentworth Falls in the Blue Mountains. A comfortable lifestyle for two middle-aged, but still fashionable, women who mingled in the upper echelons of society.

Now, all these years later, Gilda could only presume Rosie's determination to ruin Carlo had been freshly aroused by the fact they'd attended the opening night of his variety show, once again at Her Majesty's Theatre, a coincidence that may perhaps have helped fuel the flames. At the time, she'd been astonished Rosie would even suggest such an outing.

'But you can't stand the man,' she'd said. 'Why would you want to go to the theatre and see a show featuring Carlo of all people?'

'Why not?' Rosie had replied with apparent indifference. 'I've heard the production is very good. Besides, the opening night will be one of the events of the season. Everyone who's anyone is bound to be there.'

So they'd attended. And the night, as promised, had proved a social highlight. So much so that Gilda had half expected a further outpouring of venom from Rosie upon their return to Vaucluse, for Carlo had featured in much conversation among the set with whom they'd mingled, particularly the women.

'He's ageless, isn't he?' 'Utterly magnetic . . .' 'I saw him twenty years ago, and he hasn't changed a bit.'

While the men's discussion had evolved principally around The Divine Dolores, The Wonderful Worthing and The Heavenly Tenor, the society matrons' focus had seemed particularly trained upon Carlo.

Gilda had awaited the outburst. But none had been forthcoming.

'An excellent production,' Rosie had said as they'd prepared for bed. 'In fact, an excellent night all round.' Not one mention of Carlo.

Now, watching Rosie gaze serenely out at the harbour and hearing her chilling words, delivered so calmly – 'If the truth be known, I'd rather have seen him dead, but ruination will just have to do' – Gilda realised Rosie must have been planning her attack ever since that opening night barely a month ago. Sending out word among the many shady connections she'd always maintained. Letting it be known there was money to be had for any news that might bring down the showman known as Carlo. And, of course, Carlo himself had presented the perfect opportunity. A drunken comment in a bar, that's all it had taken. And in only a matter of days Rosie had set everything in motion.

Gilda picked up her own glass of champagne. She took a sip. It had lost a little of its chill having been sitting there for some time, but the bead was still fine.

'You were lucky Carlo made things so easy for you,' she said, wondering if perhaps she was treading on dangerous ground, but still curious, still with questions circling.

But there was no danger. Rosie actually laughed.

'Yes, I suppose I was,' she agreed. 'Mind you, there was another tack I could have taken; my sources came up with some very interesting information. Did you know several years ago a girl he was fucking on tour committed suicide over him? They managed to keep it out of the newspapers, naturally, but I don't think his wife and children would be happy to hear of it, or his fans for that matter. My contacts in the press could have come up with an excellent feature article; the theatre-going public just adores salacious stories.'

She gave another laugh, obviously pleased with herself. 'But you're quite right: Carlo handed me his own destruction on a platter, and I couldn't be more grateful.'

'Why?' Gilda asked. It seemed she was always asking 'why' of Rosie, whose actions she so often could not fathom. 'You said all those years ago that he'd ruined your life, but look at everything you have, Rosie.' She gestured at the luxury that surrounded them. 'You could not possibly want for more; you have everything you need.'

For the first time, Rosie ignored the prettily fading light over the harbour waters and turned her full focus upon Gilda.

'And look at everything I've had to do to get it,' she said meaningfully.

Gilda knew the reference was to Emile. She knew also that Rosie was implying she herself had been an accomplice who had benefitted from his timely death. Which in a way was true. She'd been unaware of Rosie's actions at the time, but she'd said nothing to the authorities when, following his death, she'd discovered the bottle of arsenic at the back of the kitchen cupboard. She'd known there and then that Rosie had murdered her husband, but she'd said not a word. No matter what Rosie did, Gilda would never betray her.

'Why Carlo?' she now demanded unflinchingly. Emile was a long time ago and she refused to be distracted. 'Carlo didn't ruin your life and you know it. So *why*, Rosie?'

Rosie smiled. Not the captivating smile of her youth and middle years, which had served her so well, but the triumphant smile of an old woman who'd won, hard and bitter.

'Because I can,' she said.

No, Gilda thought, her mind sifting through the facts, *no, there's something more*. Why had Rosie wanted to go to that opening night given she so detested her former lover? Had she wished to see the changes time had wrought upon him? If so, she'd been destined for disappointment. The man's magnetism, his agelessness . . . Could Rosie's malice perhaps be a mere product of envy? She was sixty-three years old and could no longer disguise her age. *Oh, the vestige of beauty is still there, yes*, Gilda thought, *true beauty never altogether dies, but there's no denying she's old. Can it really be this simple? Does she wish to destroy him because she's outlived her beauty and he still possesses his?*

Then another thought struck Gilda, and with blinding clarity or so it seemed. *She loved him!* Surely only love could breed such hate. Wasn't that what all the melodramas were about? Why else would Rosie have remained obsessed with Carlo all these years?

'Did you love him?'

'Who?' The harbour view had once again claimed Rosie's attention.

'Carlo. Did you actually love him? Is that why you've gone to such lengths to destroy him?'

Rosie's laugh was mirthless. 'Good heavens above, what a fanciful notion,' she scorned, 'and what an active imagination you do have, my dear.'

Rosie drained her glass and stood. 'It's starting to get dark. Let's go inside.'

Gilda rose to her feet.

'Leave that,' Rosie said as she was about to pick up her barely touched glass. 'The maid will bring things in. We'll have another champagne before dinner, shall we?'

Then two steps and Rosie was by Gilda's side . . . turning Gilda towards her . . . taking Gilda's face in her hands . . .

'How could you possibly suggest I might have loved Carlo,' she whispered, 'when you know there has never been anyone but you.' And very gently she kissed Gilda. A true lover's kiss.

❧

Uncle Will's prediction proved spot on. Following the exposure of Carlo's treachery, he became show business poison – no one would work for him, and no one would employ him. At least, this is what Ma told me years later. I was only five or six at the time, so of course I had no idea back then. But I do recall, all of a sudden, Uncle Rube and Carlo were no longer a part of our lives. They just seemed to vanish. Apparently they left Melbourne altogether and settled in Sydney, which pleased Uncle Will no end. 'The less we see or hear of the man the better,' he said, and he refused to talk of Carlo ever again, or even to have his name mentioned. 'That man has ceased to exist for as long as I live,' he announced to the family.

You won't be surprised to hear, I'm sure, that the parting of the ways between the Worthings and the man who must not be named brought about big changes for the family.

Although now a solo production company no longer working in partnership, the Worthings continued to produce two shows simultaneously, which was no mean feat I can promise you, but with the younger generation taking on much of the load, they were exciting times for us all.

Uncle Will was finally living his long-envisioned dream, having moved into the world of legitimate theatre, principally Shakespeare. One of the company's two productions presented 'the classics', you see, although the term 'classics' was open to interpretation. Shakespeare certainly qualified, but I'm not so sure about Gilbert and Sullivan, or Oscar Wilde for that matter. But such productions were so popular worldwide they were no doubt destined to be the classics of the future, and this was 'legit theatre', so who cared? Certainly not Uncle Will, who was in his element. My big brother Ted too, he was over the moon – oh dear me, such a lovely actor! And as for cousin Prudence . . . Well, I can't begin to tell you! The acrobatic magical act that had replaced The Wonderful Worthing was now a well-rehearsed and highly polished duo by the twins, and no longer required the distraction of a tantalisingly costumed pretty assistant, which meant Pru was at long last able to give voice to the actress she truly was and had always wanted to be. Pru was more than over the moon, Pru was in seventh heaven!

The other production, performed yearly under the banner of 'THE WORTHING BROTHERS' VARIETY EXTRAVAGANZA OF . . .' continued along much the same lines as previously, and yet this was variety with a difference, as more and more the use of film was incorporated. Aunt Mabel, who'd had an interest in film for quite some time, had acquired a very valuable contact in London, an agent called Leonard, who regularly sent her short films that ran about five or six minutes. There were any number of companies churning out these things apparently – selling them for around fourpence a foot (plus Leonard's commission, of course) and very good value it was, according to Aunt Mabel. They came in all varieties too, some dramatic (*A Father's Revenge*), some comic (*The Milkman's Wedding*) and some simply piquing general interest, like a motor vehicle race (motor cars were quite the thing by then). Aunt Mabel tended to favour the comic, and every Worthing Brothers variety production featured two short films, one in each half of the show, proving very popular, I must say.

Funny when you think about it, isn't it? Back in those days it didn't occur to us we were introducing the public to the very medium that would one day threaten the downfall of live theatre. But you must understand that back then producers couldn't really envisage folk wanting to see images up on a screen rather than the real thing. Ma certainly couldn't.

'A few minutes of novelty's one thing,' Ma would say, 'but just imagine a packed theatre full of real, live people sitting for two whole hours watching a flat screen with moving pictures.'

Aunt Mabel didn't altogether agree. Or perhaps Aunt Mabel was more prescient.

'I wouldn't be too sure about that, Gertie,' she'd say.

'Oh, tosh,' Ma would reply with that impatient flick of her head, 'people aren't so silly.'

The two different productions did split the family up quite a bit, some working variety, some working classical, but nobody minded, and the Worthings were so versatile there'd be regular crossovers anyway. The Serpentine Dance would be given a breather and Ma would take on Desdemona to Uncle Will's Othello, or perhaps something light and frothy like Gwendolen in *The Importance of Being Earnest*, her own niece Pru as her protagonist Cecily (Ma was still playing juvenile roles, or 'juves' as we called them, well into her forties – oh, Gertie was a marvel, really she was). And then there was our Sarah and Izzie, whose musical skills were invaluable wherever and however they were cast. Pa, funnily enough, was more involved with the classical productions these days, having handed the acrobatic reins over to Artie and Alfie following his fiftieth birthday. He could still highwire with the best of them, but firmly maintained it was time he called it a day.

'Acrobatics is a young man's game,' he'd say.

But oh my goodness, you should have seen his athleticism in the fight scenes! And as for his swordsmanship! There are heaps of duels in Shakespeare, and even if there weren't we'd invariably stick one in just for spectacle. Pa would choreograph the sword fights and we'd milk them for all they were worth. Max Worthing quite took your breath away, I swear he did.

Cousin Alice was the only one of all the Worthings who didn't pursue a career onstage. Isn't that strange? For some unknown reason, Alice had always wanted to get married, settle down and have babies, which we others found most odd. And that's exactly what she did. At the age of twenty-three, she married Raymond Sparks, an accountant, and went to live in Adelaide.

In 1910 when my brother Bertie turned fifteen, he was finally able to leave school and join the theatre full time instead of just during the holidays, which thrilled him to bits. He'd never been able to understand how I'd been allowed to escape the rule writ in stone for all Worthing offspring. But being the youngest by far and so unexpected, I was spoilt right from the beginning. All of my schooling was done at home during rehearsals, or out on the road, or while playing the major theatres of capital cities. And I simply cannot begin to tell you how many teachers I had! 'Little Em' was never found wanting for attention, I can promise you. Spoilt? Oh gracious me, yes, spoilt rotten I was, and I loved every minute of it.

Artie and Alfie still proved our top-billing variety act, even above The Serpentine Dance, mainly because their routine was so original, quite unlike anything else that was going around. Not that Ma didn't regularly freshen up her act, goodness me, yes! Gertie and Mabel were continuously inventive – new themes, new choreography, new costumes – and people still queued to see The Divine Dolores. But The Serpentine Dance had become something of an institution, if you know what I mean, a sort of variety show 'ritual' – like the way everyone who goes to Paris has to see the Eiffel Tower.

I must say, we all found it marvellous that despite the loss of The Wonderful Worthing, Artie and Alfie's individual talents placed them right up there at the top. Which sort of goes to prove, doesn't it, that the man who must not be named didn't altogether wreak the havoc of which he was accused? But one would never dare say that to Uncle Will, not in a million years!

The twins symbolised the new generation of Worthings, and I mean that quite literally. Their acrobatic magical act was even billed these days as 'The Amazing Brothers Worthing', proof they truly were chips off the old block. They never worked as twins, mind – always brothers – each expressing himself as the individual he was in real life, and the act reflected their differences.

Artie was the consummate showman, strutting his stuff with pride, and he was vocal, always vocal. Every acrobatic trick was followed with a 'hoopla' or an 'olé', every magical sleight of hand with a 'voilà'. He was cheeky and bold as brass, and he'd front his sea of admirers demanding an instant round of applause – and getting it, what's more, regular as clockwork.

Alfie was far more subtle, and never ever vocal. Alfie loved mime. He always had. And like all true mime artists he communicated with such delicacy, such finesse. His timing was impeccable and his relationship with his audience intimate. When conveying a triumph, instead of hoopla-ing or olé-ing he'd gaze about the house as if lost in wonderment. You could swear he was saying, 'Can you believe that?' and all those folk out there in the darkness would feel the contact, as if he was playing directly to them. He had that personal touch, same way Pa had, a wonderful talent, and oh dear me, how they'd laugh. There was a touch of the clown in Alfie. He was funny and charming and eminently loveable.

As you can no doubt imagine, the pairing of the two was a real treat. They worked off each other beautifully, the showman and the mime, sharing their talents in a way that delighted audiences. Ma always said they were Will and Max Worthing all over again.

'You should have seen the twins back then, Em,' she'd say. 'Oh, those boys were a marvel. Well, they weren't boys at all, were they, goodness no, they'd just turned thirty, but they were always boys to me. And there I'd be, standing backstage watching your Uncle Will and your pa, seeing them as young men.' She'd wipe away a tear, quite openly, never bothering to hide the fact. 'Oh Em, you should have seen the twins back then!'

I had seen them, of course; Ma tended to forget that, probably because I was only ten when it happened. But the memory of a ten-year-old is crystal clear. If you don't believe me, just ask a really old person and they'll tell you I'm right. They probably can't remember what they did yesterday or what they had for lunch even, but they remember when they were ten years old. I certainly remember the twins back then.

❧

The publicity stunt was Artie's idea, typically bold, typically brazen, but Alfie was eager to carry it out. Artie always had the best ideas, and Alfie was only too keen to follow wherever they led.

'We'll have to do the climb in the dead of night, Art,' he said as they sat on the grass by the stables eating their lunchtime sandwiches – ham, cheese and pickled onion scrunched between two huge slabs of Mrs Partridge's home-baked bread, which was sometimes still hot from the oven. They always sat on the grass during their lunch break and the sandwiches were always ham, cheese and pickled onion, their joint favourite, lovingly prepared by Party, who absolutely adored the twins.

The stables of the Big House had been converted to garages and the rear grounds grassed and landscaped, but in the centre a hard surface space the size of a large stage in one of the grand theatres had been retained for rehearsal purposes.

'We'll be stopped if someone sees us,' Alfie went on.

'Only if that someone's a copper,' Artie interrupted through a mouthful of sandwich, 'or a railway employee. Anyone passing by will just stand there and gawk.'

'Yep,' Alfie agreed without a further second's thought, 'you're right. Human nature; they'll want to find out what we're up to.'

'But we'll make the climb before dawn anyway,' Artie said. 'Dunno what time those railway blokes arrive for work, and we want to be fully set up before they do.'

The idea was to climb the facade of the magnificent, newly completed Flinders Street Railway Station, which had opened just the previous year. They would rig a huge banner that would hang above the grand arch of the main entrance reading 'THE WORTHING BROTHERS' VARIETY EXTRAVAGANZA OF 1911', and beneath, in letters only slightly smaller: 'Featuring The Amazing Brothers Worthing at their Most Spectacular'. They would hire a photographer to picture them from the street far below, posing way up there on either side of the banner as the hustle and bustle of early morning materialised and crowds gathered to, as Artie put it, 'gawk at the sight'.

'The most famous building in Melbourne,' he'd said as he'd excitedly pitched his idea. 'One of the biggest and grandest railway stations in the whole, wide world, Alfie! We'll give the picture to the press; it's bound to make the front pages. Come to think of it, we probably wouldn't even need to hire a photographer – the newspapers would send their own as soon as they heard we were up there. Maybe we should tip them off in advance just to be sure . . .'

Alfie had commented at this point that their actions would no doubt be against the law and they'd probably be arrested, which hadn't in the least bothered Artie.

'More publicity,' he'd said, 'all the better. Ma and Pa would bail us out.'

Alfie was all for it. And he had his own ideas, as usual along very practical lines.

'We'll need a lightweight banner,' he said, 'canvas will be too heavy for the climb. We'll get Ma to make one up out of cotton.'

It was understood from the outset that the family would be in on the idea, for this was the perfect derring-do form of promotion that made headlines.

'Why, Harry Rickards did it just last year,' Mabel said, 'around this same time in February, when he brought Houdini out for a season at his Opera House. Do you know, the newspapers said there were *twenty thousand* people gathered around the Queens Bridge to see that man dive manacled into the Yarra. *Twenty thousand*, possibly *more*,' she emphasised. 'Can you *believe* that!'

'Yes, perhaps so, Ma,' Alfie said cautiously, once again favouring the pragmatic approach, 'but the Houdini stunt was advertised. Furthermore it was legal; Harry obviously had permission. We don't, and if we tried we wouldn't get it.'

'No matter' – Mabel waved the fact aside as the triviality she considered it to be – 'if there's any trouble, we'll bail you out,' and the twins exchanged a smile.

A lot of preparation went into the stunt. For several days, and nights also, Artie and Alfie studied the site; the footholds, the handholds, the lighting, the best time to scale the walls pre-dawn before the workers arrived. Melbourne's electric street lighting was switched off at midnight, so it would be dark, but that presented no problem. They often did stunts blindfolded anyway, in order to give the audiences an extra thrill. Blindfold was easy, they both maintained. 'You just picture the layout you've rehearsed over and over and you're right there,' they'd say. 'No need to see, your brain does it for you.' To Artie and Alfie, the mind of an acrobat had its own special vision.

'Look at that, will you, just look at that,' Artie now said, 'as easy as climbing a ladder.'

They gazed up at the splendid facade towering above them. Built in French Renaissance style over an area of two city blocks and topped by a mighty central dome, Flinders Street Station was truly impressive. But the twins were taking in neither its splendour nor its beauty.

'Yep,' Alfie agreed, 'a drunken amateur could make it up to that ledge. Rendered brickwork with hand and footholds all the way – you're right, Art, just like climbing a ladder. Fifty feet or so would put us up there, wouldn't you say?'

'I would, maybe a bit more. And the ledge'd be about forty feet or so across . . .'

'And a ten-foot drop for the banner would see it hanging just above the top of the central arch . . .'

As they made their calculations, the brothers squinted up at the third floor, where five stone columns flanked each of the four windows that looked out over the ledge. Behind these windows, which were always firmly closed, they presumed were the station's administration offices or the like, but the windows themselves presented no interest as a possible source of access to the ledge. The theatrics and heroics of the climb was of paramount importance to the stunt and its publicity value.

They'd even discussed whether they shouldn't perhaps climb higher, well above the windows and the ledge, to the apex of the building's facade, beneath which sat the huge central clock.

'We wouldn't have to climb to the top of the apex,'
Artie had said, 'just stand either side, it'd look pretty
spectacular.'

'Yep, we could do that,' Alfie had agreed. 'Much harder
climb, though, and it'd take us away from the banner.
Might be best to keep things simple, both of us on the
ledge, the banner directly below. What do you think?'

'Yeah, that makes sense. We'll stick with the ledge.'

Alfie usually did make sense; it was always Artie who
wanted to go that one step further.

'Pity those columns aren't free-standing,' Alfie now said
thoughtfully, his full focus upon the ledge. 'Would have
been easy to sling a rope around the ones at each end.'

'Yeah, they're just decorative, built into the stone,
shame about that. We'll have to lock clamps onto the ledge
instead.'

The plan was to hang the banner from the ledge, let it
drop for all to see, and pose either side for the photographs
that were bound to make the front pages of newspapers all
over the country, possibly even the world. According to
Artie anyway.

'The greatest billboard Australia's ever seen,' he boasted,
'displayed on one of the greatest railway stations in the
world. You don't get bigger than that, Alfie.'

And Alfie wholeheartedly agreed.

So did their mother who, as was to be expected, took
over the directing and staging of the event. To Mabel the
logistics were no more complicated than the rigging of
the countless cycloramas and backdrops and scrims she'd
designed, erected and used to great effect over the past
thirty years.

'I'll use a thick-weave cotton and sew evenly distributed
weights into the hem in order to keep it in place,' Mabel
said, having agreed that the forty-by-ten-foot banner would
be easier to handle in cotton rather than canvas. 'You can't

have the thing flapping about everywhere. But you won't need to be concerned with weight,' she added. 'We'll have the banner carefully folded concertina-style on the top of the main entrance steps to one side where it'll be virtually out of sight, and well out of people's way, and you'll make the climb with twine, Artie. Then once you reach the ledge you won't haul up the rope, you'll wait for Alfie to climb up from his side. The only weight you'll have to contend with will be the clamp, but you'll carry that in a shoulder satchel, so it shouldn't present a problem.'

She turned to her other son. 'Same goes for you, Alfie, you'll carry a satchel and climb with twine – I've estimated the length as closely as possible before attaching the rope – but you'll have to move fast because as you climb, the banner will unfold across the top of the steps, attracting attention and possibly getting in the way of any night office cleaners who might be around. Once you're both on either side of the ledge, you can haul up the banner and it'll be out of everyone's way.'

Mabel had not only studied the building herself, she'd accompanied the twins on their pre-dawn vigils, and they'd discussed the occasional coming and going of cleaners. She was of the same opinion as Artie and Alfie.

'Oh, they won't be any problem,' she'd said dismissively. 'No cleaner's going to call the police or report something that's none of their business. Like anyone else who happens to be passing, they'll just stand and gawk.' Mabel, too, was of the firm opinion 'gawking' was what everyone did when they saw something unusual. 'You only need to put on a show and look as if you know what you're doing,' she'd said, 'and they'll keep gawking until they find out what it is.'

The fact that night cleaning took place, they had decided, was really to their advantage, the spillage of light from the station's interior making visibility no problem.

'Pity, I'd quite looked forward to the test of working blindfolded,' Artie had quipped, and his brother and mother hadn't quite known whether or not he was joking.

The whole family was in on the act, and come the chosen night, a mild-weathered, cloudless, mid-February pre-dawn, most were actively taking part, playing the roles allotted them by Mabel.

Mabel and Gertie were standing either side of the arch at the top of the station's main entrance steps to ensure the banner first unfolded across the landing and then unfurled upon its ascent as smoothly as was intended. Ted, his sisters Sarah and Izzie, and his younger brother Bertie, were positioned in pairs as lookouts up and down Flinders and Swanston streets. Ted and Bertie both had whistles, and if any police were seen on patrol they'd sound the alarm: one short toot for 'freeze' if there appeared no immediate threat of discovery, and two loud bursts signalling the need for a distraction. Should the latter be necessary, Pru and her young man, Tom, were standing by in a side street. Pru was to start screaming with all the considerable power she had at her command, and when the police came to her rescue, her fiancé Tom Buxton – a lovely performer with a most promising baritone – would be comforting her, saying she'd been accosted by a young thug who'd tried to steal her purse before running off in the opposite direction. The police, it was presumed, would give chase, and if by any chance they didn't, Bertie was to spring into action as the young thug, appearing from nowhere and on the run, presumably having accosted someone else.

Apart from little Em, the Worthing brothers senior were the only family members not playing a role, this again upon Mabel's directive.

'We'll keep you two out of it,' she'd said. 'The blame can rest with the younger ones. If we get into trouble, the whole thing can be put down to the impetuosity of youth.'

But of course there was no way Will and Max could be kept from witnessing the event. The Worthing brothers senior together with ten-year-old Em set themselves up outside St Paul's Cathedral on the corner of Swanston and Flinders, diagonally opposite the station. They were to be the audience.

There would be a further audience arriving shortly in the form of Ritchie, the stills photographer they'd employed, although for press purposes he was hardly necessary. Mabel had tipped off the press, telling them there was to be something afoot at Flinders Street Station early the following morning. 'Something highly newsworthy,' she'd promised.

'They'll be there all right,' she'd assured the others, 'even if they don't turn up at first light. But I've hired Ritchie anyway; nice to have our own set of publicity shots.'

The twins commenced the climb in the early hours, well before the first glimmers of dawn. They were costumed in full acrobatic regalia, navy and sky-blue leotards with Mabel's handstitched sequins that so successfully caught the lights, but they'd opted to work barefoot rather than in the thin, flexible slippers they favoured onstage.

Artie went first, climbing the left-hand side of the facade as viewed from the street, and it took him only minutes to reach the narrow ledge. Once there, he stood twine in hand leaning against the pillar at the far end, and giving a tug on the twine he alerted Mabel below that he was in position. It was now Alfie's turn.

Alfie climbed the right-hand side with equal dexterity and even greater speed, behind him the immaculately concertinaed banner starting to unfold and snake its way across the platform. Both women followed its progression with care, ready to lend assistance, but not for one second was there any sign it might foul. Then . . .

'He's there,' Gertie called across to Mabel. Feeling a tug on the twine, she knew he'd arrived.

Up on the ledge, the twins could see each other vaguely silhouetted at either end. They exchanged a wave and set about attaching their clamps, a delicate balancing exercise given the narrowness of the ledge, but they worked fast and in unison.

All was going smoothly. No sign of a policeman, no sound of a whistle.

As anticipated, however, there was an encounter with cleaners, two women going home from their night shift.

Bessie and Martha were surprised to find as they walked out of the station that their way was impeded by what appeared to be a rolled-up length of cloth stretched across the breadth of the platform at the top of the steps.

They hesitated simultaneously.

Then, to their right, a figure appeared from out of the shadows, a rather matronly woman judging by her shape, and her voice was very pleasant as she reassured them.

'It's all right, ladies,' she said, 'we'll have this out of your way in just a jiffy. If you wouldn't mind stepping over it?'

Another woman appeared from the shadows on the left, a petite woman, slim, much younger.

'Sorry, loveys, we won't be a tick.'

Bessie and Martha obediently stepped over the cloth.

'What's going on?' Bessie whispered as they walked down the steps to the street.

'Dunno,' Martha replied, 'no idea whatsoever.'

But they were certainly going to find out, and when they reached street level they turned back to watch.

Fifty feet above, Artie and Alfie had attached their clamps to the far ends of the ledge.

'I'm right,' Artie called, 'you on?'

'Yep, I'm on. Let's go.'

Together, they steadily counted out loud as hand over hand they hauled up the twine, which then became rope, and the banner slowly rose.

'Oh my, look at that,' Bessie whispered. 'Can you see what it says?'

'Nope.' All Martha could see in the dim, dim light was a massive, great banner. But she wasn't going anywhere until she found out what it said and how on earth it was rising up out of nowhere the way that it was.

The banner unfurled perfectly, without fouling of either cloth or rope; Mabel's preparation had been impeccable.

After detaching the twine, which they placed in their shoulder satchels, the twins fed the ends of their respective ropes through the C-shaped frame of their clamps. They took their time, carefully ensuring the banner was hanging straight and at the exact height they wished, with the top just below the ledge, before tying it off. Then, the balancing act over, they rose to their feet and settled themselves, leaning back against the windowsills directly behind them to await the dawn.

They didn't need to wait long, for barely twenty minutes later the first glimmer of light edged across a clear sky promising a beautiful day. They leant out and looked at each other, exchanging grins and a 'thumbs up' sign. And they looked down at the streets below too, where they already had an audience.

Bessie and Martha, having patiently watched on for a full half-hour, had been joined by any number of early morning passers-by, either those heading home from night work or those on their way to a dawn start, probably at the markets. Whenever anyone stood looking up at something, others were bound to stop and look up too. Human nature.

There was another audience also. Across the street, outside St Paul's Cathedral, the twins could see quite clearly the whole family gathered. They gave them the thumbs up sign too. And they noted that Ritchie, the photographer, was with them, camera in hand and tripod over his shoulder. It would shortly be time to put on a show. But they would wait just a little longer. Every performance needed good lighting.

Then, all of a sudden and as if on cue, there it was. Dawn. Flooding the sky. A brand-new day. Showtime!

The twins stood, breathing deeply and steadily, expanding and contracting their lungs in anticipation. Rising up onto their toes, fingers interlocked, they stretched their arms above their heads, tightening their abdomens and buttocks, preparing their muscles for action, easing out any possible cramps that might have resulted from their inactivity.

Even their preparation was graceful, and below in the street there were 'oohs' and 'ahs' as people, perfect strangers, nudged each other and pointed. The performers had been barely visible, tucked away motionless up above. Now, as the pair surfaced and the first rays of sunlight caught the spangles of their costumes, the crowd, for it had already become a crowd, knew it was in for a treat. The banner after all said everything. These were The Amazing Brothers Worthing.

Ritchie crossed the road and set up his tripod. He'd get in some early shots before the newspaper boys arrived with their press cameras.

Artie and Alfie went into their routine leisurely, no need to rush.

Resting his right hand against the pillar, Artie lifted his left knee, and taking hold of his heel very slowly raised his leg higher and higher until he was in full splits position. Then, rising onto his toes, he released his hold on the pillar and gave a loud 'hoopla' as he made the grand gesture with his right arm.

It was a bravura performance high up on the narrow ledge, and made all the more impressive by Alfie, who gazed down at the audience, gobsmacked, gesturing wildly and miming *look at that, oh what bravery*, inviting an instant round of applause.

Then, as he got carried away with the crowd's enthusiasm, Alfie jumped up and down on the ledge and in his excitement stumbled. Turning to clutch at the pillar, legs dangling, toes of right foot seeking a hold in the grooves of the brickwork, it was touch and go; he was about to fall to his death. Or so it appeared. Alfie, of course, knew exactly what he was doing. He managed to save himself, 'just in time'.

It was now Artie's turn to mime. He fanned his face, mopped his brow – *phew* – and initiated the thankful round of applause.

They continued their performance thus, working together as a team, adding to each other's act, never drawing focus until it was their turn. And the audience grew larger and larger, loving every minute and swelling ever more as early morning commuters arrived.

By now the press had turned up, journalists and photographers vying for position, and the twins rested between performances to pose for still shots. But the press heralded the arrival of the police who, having been informed of the 'goings on' at Flinders Street Station, were determined to break up the proceedings.

'Get down!' the commanding officer called up to the twins. 'Get down from there immediately!'

But the twins had no intention of leaving, at least not until they'd experienced the full rush hour they knew Flinders Street Railway Station had to offer. It was their intention that hundreds and hundreds of travellers and commuters should relay the news of their daredevil escapade. 'The Amazing Brothers Worthing' were to be not only the headline story in every newspaper, but the wondrous experience encountered by many and passed on to yet more. 'Word of mouth' was the true catchphrase of all entrepreneurs. 'Word of mouth?' they would say. 'Nothing better.'

So Artie and Alfie reacted accordingly and in character. Artie pretended he couldn't hear the officer's command. Cupping his ear with his left hand, he leant out at a most precarious angle, to the consternation of the crowd who drew audible gasps. 'What was that?' he yelled, fingers of his right hand firmly finding a hold on the grooves in the stone pillar beside him, prehensile-like toes gripping the side of the ledge maintaining his balance.

Alfie in turn feigned obedience to the order, appearing about to make his way down. His back to the crowd, he edged inch by inch along the ledge, one tentative arm and leg going out to the side, reaching for the brickwork, only to return. Then, facing the front, he looked down at the crowd, fearfully gnawing his fingernails, gazing at the fifty-foot drop, his mime saying *oh dear, I can't do this.* A turn away, another try, a turn back, another despairing *I give up.*

The audience's attention went from one performer to the other, a gasp at the bravura, a laugh at the mime; this was true entertainment.

The police had now been joined by railway officials, all of whom were bent on resolving this unseemly incident before the onslaught of the peak business rush hour.

They conferred, and barely ten minutes later the twins' performance was rudely interrupted.

Up on the ledge, Artie and Alfie heard the sound of keys turning in locks, and all of a sudden the two central windows opened out onto the ledge. This presented no direct danger to them, but they were taken by surprise. Why had it never occurred to them that the police and the authorities might approach them this way? For some strange reason the windows had never once entered the equation; they had made no plans for such a contingency. The windows simply hadn't mattered. They mattered now, however. Now they mattered a great deal.

A man stood at each window, one a police officer, the other a railway official.

'Get off that ledge and come inside immediately,' the policeman commanded, the same officer who had issued orders from the street.

Artie and Alfie exchanged a look that said everything; no words were necessary. *This won't do*, their eyes said, *the crowd might think we climbed out through the windows. This won't do at all.*

'Did you hear me,' the officer barked, 'I said get in here. Right now, this minute!'

'I'm sorry, but we can't oblige, sir,' Alfie said, respectfully but firmly. 'We climbed up here from the street and that's the way we intend to climb down.'

'I will not allow that.'

'With all due respect, sir, I'm afraid you can't stop us.'

The officer was left in a quandary. He certainly couldn't climb out on the ledge himself, and any attempt to open the other two windows and wrestle the young men inside would no doubt lead to disaster.

He disappeared from view, issuing orders to his men, and several minutes later the main entrance to the station was cordoned off and the platform and stairs cleared, policemen preventing anyone from entering or leaving.

'Come down immediately!' the police officer commanded from the street below.

Another look was shared between Artie and Alfie. Alfie gave the slightest of shrugs, signalling a query. *Do we go straight down? Do we give them a show on the way? What do we do, Art?*

Artie's decision was instant. *Not yet,* the shake of his head said, and then he pointed: *I'm going up. You stay here.*

Alfie nodded: *Right you are.* Artie was going to put on a final show, and he was to mime accordingly, Alfie realised. This was a good plan. And as Artie commenced his climb up the left-hand side of the facade, he mimed shock and horror for the benefit of the hundreds who now stood watching, no doubt thrilling to the sense of fear and trepidation he was communicating. *Yes, good showmanship,* he thought, *good teamwork all round.*

Within only minutes Artie had disappeared from his line of vision, but Alfie knew the audience below wouldn't realise that, so he kept up his performance.

The crowd had spilled out into the streets now to get a better overall view. Trams and vehicles, both horse-drawn and motorised, had come to a halt; people were even getting out to watch.

Alfie continued his mime, looking down at the audience, fingers to mouth, aghast, terrified, then up to where Artie had disappeared, hands indicating his thumping heart, then held as if in prayer, all the while awaiting the signal that would tell him his brother had arrived at the apex of the station's grand facade beneath which sat the central clock.

Then he heard it. The loud cry of '*Olé!*' The signal that Artie was striking a pose upon the ledge above, and that his reaction was to follow suit.

Alfie raised his fisted hands high and pumped the air in a gesture of triumph. And then he heard the screams.

Artie's '*Olé!*' had aroused the pigeon pair nesting in the nook where the apex met the ledge. Startled, they wittered out noisily at his feet, distracting him for just that one vital moment.

Alfie didn't see his brother fall. He didn't hear him either. He heard nothing but the screams of the crowd. And when he looked down, there was Artie, sprawled out far below, the thick pool of blood that circled his head already starting to wind its way down the stone steps.

15

LIFE MOVES IN MYSTERIOUS WAYS

It goes without saying (as I'm sure you can imagine) that Artie's death had a profound effect upon the whole family. None of us will ever forget that dreadful morning. It's forever etched in our collective memory and still openly talked about all these years later. Which, come to think of it, is probably healthy, wouldn't you agree? You can't keep things bottled up; you have to move on from a tragedy like that or it'll eat you alive. But, unfortunately, there was one of us who couldn't move on.

The person most deeply affected (as I'm sure you can also imagine) was Alfie. Alfie never got over Artie's death. They shared the bond of twins, you see. Different though they were as personalities, their bond was so strong that when Artie died a part of Alfie died too. He stopped speaking after Artie's death, choosing instead to live a wordless existence, communicating only through mime. At least, this is so to the best of my knowledge. There may have been an occasion when he spoke, I really wouldn't know, but if he did no one has ever told me. I've not heard my cousin Alfie utter a single word, not since the year I was ten, the year Artie died.

From that awful day on, Alfie adopted his stage persona in real life. His whole world became mime. Oh, he continued to work as a performer. It was obvious to everyone that Alfie simply *had* to perform, that he *lived* to perform. He developed a truly wonderful solo act, a mixture of magic and mime with an acrobatic trick thrown in now and then to surprise the audience. But the character performing the act was no longer funny, no longer the clown. Instead, the character was somehow touching . . . a soulful creature . . . poignant . . . Ma always said that watching Alfie was like watching a ballet. 'So graceful,' she'd say. 'All great mime artists are wonderful dancers, but Alfie's something else. Alfie's a true work of art.'

I'm sure any psychiatrist would say that the character Alfie created was his escape from reality, but we in show business would say it was also his entrapment. He couldn't leave that character up there on the stage the way performers normally do. Instead, he lived his whole life behind the mask he'd fashioned for himself. I think that's so terribly sad.

Uncle Will held Carlo responsible for all of this. For Artie's death . . . For Alfie's retreat into his world of silence . . . Uncle Will firmly maintained none of this would have happened if the twins had still been performing as The Wonderful Worthing, Master Illusionist.

'That man's to blame for everything,' he'd say – he still refused to mention Carlo by name. 'Whatever hardship he may be suffering following his fall from grace cannot possibly be punishment enough for the crimes he has perpetrated upon this family! May he rot in hell!' My goodness, how Uncle Will hated Carlo.

'Terrible business,' Rube said, as he and Carlo studied the front pages of their respective newspapers. Rube always read the *Sydney Morning Herald* and Carlo the *Daily Telegraph*, and on this particular morning the headlines all over the country were screaming the death of Arthur Worthing, one of the two 'Amazing Brothers Worthing'.

'It most certainly is,' Carlo agreed, 'a real tragedy. Poor Artie, such a nice young bloke.'

'Poor Alfie, too. I wonder how he's taking it. Those boys were always so close.'

The two were seated in the breakfast room of their brand-new house, Winifred having left with the chauffeur to drive twelve-year-old Marty to school, after which she would go shopping. The house, which Carlo and Rube had purchased through their company, Carlovsky & Reubens Real Estate, was in Wolseley Road, Point Piper, considered by many the wealthiest area, and indeed the wealthiest road in the whole of Sydney, if not Australia. Point Piper certainly vied with Melbourne's Toorak for status ranking, a fact Carlo brought up on any number of occasions.

'Will Worthing always loved crowing about his Toorak mansion,' Carlo would gloat, 'but we've shown him, haven't we, Rube?'

Rube always found it wisest not to comment.

The house, built of solid brick in the modern 'Federation' style, was not as grand as Will Worthing's Italianate mansion in Toorak, but it was most attractive and commodious with ample room, allowing separate quarters for Rube and a spacious office, which the two men shared. Gable-roofed with a decoratively tiled front porch and pretty lead-light windows, it boasted splendid harbour views, and the sizeable block of land upon which it sat was, furthermore, destined to skyrocket in value. As Rube well knew.

In fact, Rube knew a great deal about real estate; he'd made it his business to do so.

'Property, Carlo,' he'd said upon their arrival in Sydney. 'We'll go into the property market, that's where the money is.'

And so they had, forming a new company and investing the considerable funds which were at their disposal, following the termination of their partnership with the Worthing Brothers, into real estate. Now, five years later, with a most impressive portfolio, their plans were taking an even grander turn.

'We'll build our own theatre,' Rube had announced just the previous year. This had followed an evening when Carlo, a little the worse for drink, had bemoaned the fact that he missed the world of show business.

'I have a natural talent, mate,' he'd said. 'I like to strut out there onstage and win over an audience, it's what I was born to do. I miss the theatre.'

Rube hadn't replied with the obvious: that Carlo was exercising his natural talent on a regular basis. That in the endless buying and selling of property he was constantly strutting out there and winning an audience, the only thing missing being the stage itself. But he hadn't reminded Carlo of that fact. And after mulling things over during the night, he'd awoken the next morning with a plan that he thought made a great deal of sense.

'Sydney is challenging Melbourne as the country's centre of entertainment these days,' he'd gone on to explain. 'Entrepreneurs are crying out for new venues, the bigger the better, and I can see no greater property value to be had than a brand-new theatre. We build it, we own it and we lease it out for a fortune, they're bound to come running. Then, once the theatre's established and people are flocking to it, we'll produce shows of our own.'

Rube gave his boyish grin. For a podgy, balding man who looked all of his fifty-seven years, he remained amazingly baby-faced.

'With a company called Carlovsky & Reubens, theatre folk won't even know it's us,' he said. 'No one ever took note of our surnames, did they? And even if they were to twig who we are, no one would dare blacklist us. We'll be more than just producers, Carlo, we'll be theatre owners. What entrepreneur doesn't need to lease a theatre, eh? And when we're back in the business and producing our very own shows in our very own venue, who will refuse to work with us, eh? Performers can't afford to knock back jobs offered to them on a platter, not in a career as risky as the theatre.'

Carlo shook his head admiringly. 'God but you're clever, Rube.'

So they'd set about planning their new venture, scouring the inner city for prime locations, properties they could buy, buildings they could demolish, and now, a year later, they'd decided upon the perfect position with the perfect frontage.

'Castlereagh Street,' Rube triumphantly declared. 'We'll make Castlereagh Street the grand boulevard of theatres, like Bourke Street in Melbourne . . .'

'Like Shaftesbury Avenue in the West End . . .' Carlo chorused with equal enthusiasm. 'Like Broadway in New York . . .'

'Exactly,' Rube agreed. 'George Marlow and Ben Fuller have just opened the Adelphi in Castlereagh Street; J. C. Williamson holds the lease on the Theatre Royal down the road; and in a couple of years we'll launch our brand-new venue called . . .' He paused briefly before continuing, 'Well, whatever we call it . . . And in doing so, we'll turn Castlereagh Street into the West End of Australia!'

Carlo paused for a second. Then: 'We could call our theatre the Carlosseum,' he suggested.

Rube looked at him askance. Was he serious? Given Carlo's ego it was often quite hard to tell.

Carlo threw back his handsome head and laughed. 'Just joking, Rube,' he said, but the way he added, 'honest I am,' left room for doubt.

'Good gag, Carlo.' Rube decided to give him the benefit. 'But you might actually have something. The Colosseum's not a bad idea at all; it certainly has the ring of grandeur we're after.'

So the Colosseum it was. And as the year dawdled to an end with 1912 looming ever closer, the demolition of sites in Castlereagh Street was well underway and plans were being drawn up for the construction of the most modern, state-of-the-arts theatre in the Southern Hemisphere. Carlo and Rube were destined to be back in business.

Will Worthing would have detested the mere thought of Carlo's resurrection, but as yet Will Worthing had no idea of what lay in store.

Apart from missing a career in the theatre, Carlo had actually never been happier. Despite now being in his early sixties, his libido did not appear to have greatly diminished; he was still drawn to attractive women, just as they were still drawn to him. But without the freedom of being out on the road or performing interstate, the temptation no longer presented itself, and he was content for things to remain that way. Carlo had become a true family man. He loved Winifred, in his own way, which was a mixture of fondness and gratitude, for she was the perfect mother to young Marty, upon whom both he and Rube doted. He loved his daughter, Anne, too. Anne had recently married her beau, a doctor called Christopher with a practice in Orange, 150 or so miles west of Sydney, and a grandchild would surely be forthcoming in a year or so, a prospect that thrilled Carlo immeasurably. But his greatest pride was without doubt his firstborn son, Michael.

Mick Carlovsky had followed his heart's desire and joined the army as planned. But he hadn't joined the army in the exact *way* that he'd planned. Again he'd followed the advice of his Uncle Rube who, as usual, had made all the pertinent enquiries.

'If it's a lifetime military career you're after, Mick,' Rube had said, aware that this was exactly what the lad was after, 'the best way to go about it is to graduate from university. That way, when you enlist you'll be sent directly to Officer Candidate School. I suggest a law degree myself,' he'd stated emphatically. It wasn't really his personal suggestion at all, but rather that of his source of enquiry. 'What do you think, Carlo?'

'Oh, undoubtedly.' Carlo had played the game with equal emphasis, as if he too knew what he was talking about. 'Law would be ideal.' *A son of mine at university!* His chest had swelled with pride at the mere thought.

Mick had followed Rube's advice, attending the University of Melbourne where, having always been an excellent student, he'd gained a law degree with ease, and in 1904 he'd joined the Australian Army.

As expected, he'd been sent to Officer Candidate School at Victoria Barracks on St Kilda Road where he'd undergone a year's training, focusing primarily on military skills and leadership, and in 1905 he'd graduated as Lieutenant Carlovsky.

They'd toasted his success over the dinner table, the whole family, even six-year-old Marty allowed a thimbleful of champagne.

'To Lieutenant Carlovsky,' Rube had said, and Carlo, Winifred, Anne and little Marty had repeated the words, clinking their raised glasses.

My son, an officer in the Australian Army! Carlo had thought at any moment he might burst with pride.

As far as Mick was concerned, there was just one problem with everything going so seemingly to plan. Thanks to his law degree, he'd been installed at the Legal Offices of the Department of Defence in Victoria Barracks. Where was the action? He was willing to bide his time for now, but he longed to serve a more active purpose.

Following the move to Sydney, Carlo didn't see as much of his eldest son as he would have wished, but there were brief trips interstate, the two had regular telephonic communication – a form of contact that had changed the lives of so many – and Mick continued to be his father's greatest pride and joy.

Now, with the prospect of a new theatre taking shape, Carlo's life appeared charmed in every possible way. How Will Worthing would have loathed the fact. But there was someone else besides Will Worthing who wished Carlo the direst of ill-fortune. And that someone else was much closer to home.

Little had Carlo and Rube known when they'd bought their Point Piper house that in Vaucluse – another choice suburb on the southern side of the harbour – lived the women from their past, Rosie and Gilda. Not that the women were in permanent residence at Vaucluse, for they spent much of their time these days escaping the chaos of Sydney traffic to holiday at Rosie Devereaux's spacious country home in the Blue Mountains. But the four friends of yesteryear were nonetheless 'neighbours' in the wealthiest of Sydney's 'eastern suburbs'.

The two respective houses were not visible to one another across the broad expanse of water that separated them, but Rosie knew exactly where Carlo lived. She'd made a point of finding out all she could after she'd caught sight of him at an organ recital she and Gilda had attended in the Sydney Town Hall just the previous year.

'That's Carlo,' she'd hissed with a bony nudge of her elbow.

'So it is,' Gilda had replied in a whisper, careful not to disturb those seated beside them. *Here we go again*, she'd thought, having registered the acid tone. 'And he still hasn't aged, how does the man do it?' She'd played the moment casually, as she always did when sensing Rosie's irritation; best not to arouse the snake for fear of becoming the object of its venomous attack. 'Rube hasn't changed either. He's really rather gnome-like, wouldn't you agree?'

Rosie, distracted, had not deigned to reply. 'That'll be his wife with them, I suppose,' she'd said, leaning forward for a better view. 'What a plain creature. I take it they must be living here in Sydney.'

'Yes, perhaps they are.' Gilda had been intrigued by the way Rosie was making such a study of Carlo, who was seated to the side and several rows in front of them. Surely she wasn't still obsessed with the man. 'I'll say hello to Rube after the recital and find out if you like,' she'd offered.

'Don't be so *stupid*, Gilda, you'll do no such thing.' Rosie's muttered reply had dripped with contempt. 'I have my own ways of finding out.'

And she had, sifting enquiries through her grapevine of contacts.

'Carlovsky & Reubens Real Estate agents,' she'd announced, 'that's what they're up to these days. Quite a step down from the standing ovations of the past, but I've heard the company's rather successful. Hardly surprising, I suppose,' she added scathingly, 'Carlo would excel as a *real estate salesman*.' Rosie managed to make the phrase sound not only unsavoury but verging on the disgusting.

Gilda said nothing, hoping this latest development would blow over.

But it didn't.

'He's bought a property in Point Piper,' Rosie exclaimed only several months later, 'how dare he!'

The remark had come out of the blue, but Gilda hadn't needed to ask who 'he' was. And why wouldn't Carlo buy a property in Point Piper, she'd wondered. The man dealt in real estate, after all, and Point Piper was one of the choicest real estate areas in the whole of Sydney.

'So we're more or less neighbours then,' she'd said flip-pantly, hoping once again to avoid the venom. A wrong choice.

'This is not something I take lightly, Gilda' – Rosie's look of contempt had been withering – 'and I certainly do not appreciate the fact you appear to find the situation amusing.'

Gilda had wisely remained silent, but she'd wondered whether they might see Carlo around the place from time to time. It was quite likely; the eastern suburbs social set had their favoured haunts and she and Rosie, although now in their late sixties, still regularly mingled.

Gilda proved right. They saw Carlo quite often, much to Rosie's chagrin. But to Rosie's far greater chagrin was the fact that Carlo never saw them. Or rather the fact that Carlo never saw *her*. She could understand why he failed to notice Gilda, who'd grown old and fat, but even as his eyes scanned the restaurant or café or theatre foyer, seeking those he might know, they flitted right by her without a shred of recognition. She was deeply insulted. Why was he not confronting her as he had all those years ago, when he'd defied her not to acknowledge him and the child she'd borne him? Then she realised, with an immense sense of shock, that he didn't even *see* her.

It was true. Carlo never saw old women.

But Rube did. Rube recognised them both instantly. Gilda had grown plump, but she appeared to him the same, viewed from a distance anyway; the same animation, the same unpretentiousness that he'd always found so attractive. Rosie was something altogether different. Her body had remained slim enough – she'd gained no weight – but the once proud and impressive breasts had dropped considerably, rendering the uplifted décolletage crêpey, matching the texture of her weathered neck. Her hands were claw-like and her face, hard at the best of times, had now firmly set into the lines of one dissatisfied with life. Rosie had grown decidedly old.

Gilda and Rube had caught one another's eyes from the outset and a secret exchange had taken place, each reading the other's thoughts to perfection. Rube's querying look (*shall we say hello?*); Gilda's response (*under no circumstances*) a clear directive. So from that moment on they'd taken care to avoid all contact. And Rosie continued to fume.

'The man's everywhere,' she said, 'it's utterly insufferable.'

By now Gilda was wondering whether they shouldn't move semi-permanently to the property at Wentworth Falls. Rosie was once again becoming obsessed, which was not at all healthy.

Then, in early 1912, things took an even more worrying turn as word began to circulate among their theatre-going social set.

'Have you heard about the Colosseum?' Violet asked.

Violet, known fondly as Vi to her friends, was a doyenne of eastern suburbs society. With a great love of the theatre, she could always be relied upon to gather together a group of like-minded theatregoers, and tonight her party of eight was to attend a production of *The Mikado* at the Theatre Royal in Castlereagh Street. As was customary, they had met for pre-show drinks at the ultra-fashionable Australia Hotel, which also fronted proudly onto Castlereagh, the two magnificent edifices separated only by the narrow laneway of Rowe Street. Now, having left the hotel, Vi and her party were about to cross Rowe.

'Colosseum?' As they arrived at the corner, Vi's lawyer Angus halted, sharing a puzzled glance with his wife, Vi's very good friend Mary. The others halted alongside him, equally bemused. 'What, you mean the Colosseum in Rome?' he queried. 'Good heavens, of course we've heard about it.'

'No, the Colosseum here in Sydney,' Vi said a little smugly, pleased to be the bearer of fresh news. 'In fact, right here in Castlereagh Street.'

'What, a new theatre?' Angus looked most pleased.

'That's right. You've probably noticed the demolitions, and they've started on the first stages of construction already.'

'Oh I say, how grand. Who's building the thing?'

'A company called Carlovsky & Reubens,' Vi said.

'Never heard of them.' Angus gazed around at the other members of the party, who also appeared mystified. With the exception of Rosie and Gilda.

'They're real estate agents,' Rosie said bluntly, her tone dismissive, 'property developers, no more than that.'

'Oh no, my dear, I beg to differ, they're *much* more than that,' Vi replied. 'I have it on good authority that Carlovsky is none other than that wonderful performer who hosted those marvellous variety shows some years back – Carlo, don't you remember him?'

'Vaguely.' Rosie's response was tight-lipped.

'Oh, *I* do,' Angus's wife Mary chimed in eagerly, 'and you're quite right, Vi, he was absolutely *splendid*. High time he was lured back to the stage, such a talent. Don't know why he disappeared the way he did.'

'I believe he was blacklisted,' Angus said, taking Mary's arm and leading the troops as they stepped from the kerb. 'No idea what for, but I'm sure people will have forgotten by now. He's such a brilliant showman they're bound to welcome him back.'

Gilda gathered up her skirts and crossed Rowe Street, eyes front, not daring to cast a glance at Rosie, whose face she knew was thunderous.

'We'll certainly find out in a year or so,' Vi said as they arrived at the Theatre Royal's main entrance. 'I shall be organising a party for the grand opening of the Colosseum, whenever that may be, and you're all invited to join me.'

She beamed magnanimously as she swept into the foyer.

Rosie barely saw or heard *The Mikado* that night, her mind reeling with the possibility that Carlo might be destined to rise phoenix-like from the ashes of his destruction.

'How could they possibly welcome him back?' she raged when she and Gilda had returned to the house in Vaucluse. 'Don't they realise he committed the unforgivable sin? Don't they know that no one is accepted back into the theatre after an act of disloyalty such as his?'

'Obviously not,' Gilda said, pouring them both a sherry from the decanter on the sideboard in the hope that a nightcap might calm Rosie down but, in the knowledge that it probably wouldn't, rather needing one herself. 'But you see they're not theatre folk, are they, they're audiences – they don't know the rules.'

'Then they should be told,' Rosie said, accepting the glass without a word of thanks. 'They should be told of his past and they should boycott his theatre.'

'I think ultimately they don't really care about his past or his misdemeanour so long as he keeps them entertained,' Gilda said reasonably. 'That's all that really matters to an audience.' She could see in an instant that her comment was not helping matters, but she was tired and couldn't be bothered with any further discussion. Not now anyway; it was late and she wanted to go to bed. Best to placate Rosie though.

'I wouldn't give the matter too much thought,' she said. 'They've only just started building the theatre – it won't open for at least another year, possibly two, according to Vi. And when it does, it may well turn out to be just a Carlovsky & Reubens property development as you suggested.' She downed her sherry in one healthy hit; bed beckoned. 'This may be no more than a storm in a teacup. Shall we go to bed, my dear?'

It proved, however, far more than 'a storm in a teacup'. Vi having set the wheels in motion, by March her theatregoing set could talk of little else than the possible return of the charismatic performer known as Carlo.

Gilda pretended to lose all interest in the theatre, hoping to avoid the gossip that abounded, or rather hoping to keep the gossip from Rosie's ears. But Rosie would have no bar of it. She went to the theatre, she listened to the gossip, noting every word that was said, and she seethed.

'This must not be allowed to happen,' she threatened. 'Something must be done about Carlo.'

Gilda was concerned. What was the 'something' that Rosie might do? What was there that Rosie possibly *could* do? Nothing, surely.

Then one morning in early April, the chilling exchange that Gilda found so frightening.

'Do you remember when you asked me why I did it?' Rosie queried.

'Why you did what?'

The maid had just delivered their breakfast grapefruit and the question had come out of nowhere; Gilda was understandably puzzled.

'Why I set out to ruin Carlo.'

'Oh. Yes.' *That*, Gilda thought.

'And you remember I said at the time that I would rather have seen him dead, but ruination would just have to do.'

Rosie's voice was distant, a monotone, as if coming from some other world altogether, and Gilda looked down at her grapefruit, which suddenly lacked appeal.

'Yes, I remember,' she said. Of course she remembered, just as she remembered that Rosie's words that evening had been delivered in this same alarmingly detached manner.

'I should have killed him,' Rosie said, 'ruination didn't work. Much better if he were dead.' She set about tackling her grapefruit, calmly, methodically, but she appeared distracted, her mind elsewhere. 'Something must be done about Carlo,' she said thoughtfully. 'I shall have to look into it.'

Gilda worried throughout the day and the whole of that night, convinced that once again Rosie was in the grip of madness. What did she intend to do? Was she going to kill Carlo herself? She had the means. The .45 calibre Derringer pistol that she kept in the top drawer by her bed. 'In the event of intruders,' she'd said when Gilda had questioned her, 'very effective at close range.'

Gilda could see her right now. Walking brazenly up to Carlo in full public view, putting the pistol to his chest and firing. Rosie was ruthless. She was perfectly capable of murder. She'd killed her husband, hadn't she? Or she might perhaps prefer to have someone else do the deed; she might hire a professional. Her links with the underworld no doubt gave her the means to avail herself of that choice also.

As Gilda's mind raged through the options, she became firmly convinced it was only a matter of time before Rosie's madness would demand action. *I must get her away from the city*, she decided, *away from the city and away from herself. I must save Rosie.*

By the following morning she had decided upon a plan.

'Why don't we go to the country,' she suggested, once again over the grapefruit the maid had delivered. 'Just for a week or so. Wentworth Falls is beautiful in April with all those glorious autumnal colours; you always say it's your favourite time of the year.'

'Yes I do, don't I?' Rosie agreed.

'And you'd relish a break from the jangle of traffic surely, all those dreadful vehicles that threaten life and limb.' Gilda was doing her best to sound casual, hoping Rosie wouldn't sense her desperation.

But Rosie didn't. In fact, Rosie appeared very normal this morning.

'Yes, they are truly ghastly, aren't they,' she said. 'Very convenient for one's own use, of course' – Rosie had a chauffeur herself – 'but there are so many lunatics out there who really should not be allowed behind the wheel of a motor.'

They'd had this conversation any number of times before, and Gilda was thankful Rosie didn't seem to find the fact suspicious.

'It might do us both good to have a rest from the noise and the chaos of the city,' she suggested. 'What do you think?'

'Yes, just for a week or so as you say, perhaps a fortnight – it might indeed do us the world of good.' Rosie's smile was affectionate. 'Will you make the arrangements, Gilda dear?'

'Of course.'

They left the next day. Gilda's plan of action was drastic she well knew, but it was also essential. She could think of no other way.

Their bodies were discovered a week later, in the late afternoon of 16 April. Their distraught housekeeper returned from her day off to find her mistress laid out on the bed like a queen, and her mistress's companion slumped in an armchair nearby, chest drenched in blood, a pistol in her lap.

Gilda hadn't wanted Rosie's death to be messy.

She'd felt sorrow as she'd dressed Rosie's body in the beautiful ivory lace gown that had been her favourite, and she'd felt regret, too, that it had had to end this way. But there had been no torment in her decision. She'd done exactly as she'd set out to do; she'd saved Rosie from herself.

She'd sat in the armchair for several minutes admiring her love. The serenity of death had restored Rosie's beauty. *How glorious she looks*, Gilda had thought, before raising the pistol to her chest.

The police finding was a double suicide, although the reason for the women's deaths remained a mystery; no one had an answer. No one had even an inkling why such a terrible and unexpected event should have occurred. But it was reported, a very small article in the *Sydney Morning Herald*.

'DOUBLE SUICIDE MYSTERY', the article was headed, although the letters were not large and the report was at the bottom of page three.

> *Two elderly ladies, Mrs Rosie Devereaux and her companion, Miss Gilda Grant, well-known in social circles, were discovered dead at their holiday home in the Blue Mountains. Mrs Devereaux died of supposed poisoning and Miss Grant of a self-inflicted gunshot wound to the heart. No motive is known, but police are ruling the case a double suicide.*

The report was granted no more space than that. But the newspaper had no further space to offer. During the early hours of 15 April the RMS *Titanic* had sunk in the North Atlantic, taking more than 1,500 passengers and crew to their watery graves. Who cared about the deaths of two old women in the Blue Mountains?

It was some time before the news filtered around among the eastern suburbs set, for few even noticed the article, the whole world reeling as it was over the sinking of the *Titanic*. But Rube, who scoured every inch of every newspaper, the first always being the *Sydney Morning Herald*, read the report, tucked away where it was at the bottom of page three. And he was saddened.

Poor dear Gilda, he thought, *poor, poor dear Gilda. And Rosie too, much as I didn't really care for her. What a tragedy. Why on earth would they wish to kill themselves?*

He didn't say anything to Carlo. There would be no point; Carlo wouldn't be interested. Besides, Carlo was too excited about the prospect of the new theatre, which was beginning to take shape, and also the snippets of rumour that apparently abounded – in the eastern suburbs anyway.

'Word's got out that it's us, Rube,' he'd said eagerly upon returning home only several days previously and bursting into the office they shared. 'Word's got out and people are saying they want to see Carlo back onstage.'

He'd seemed puzzled that Rube wasn't instantly jumping up and down.

'Don't you realise what this means? We won't have to hide away any longer. When we open the theatre, we can open it with our very own show and with me as Master of Ceremonies. Carlo and Rube, mate! We'll be back in business!'

Rube had never seen Carlo in such a state of elation. He was a little more circumspect himself, however. The rumours of a relatively small social set of local theatre-goers hardly guaranteed a welcome return to the industry that had blacklisted them.

'We've a long way to go yet, Carlo,' he'd warned, not wishing to be a dampener, but feeling under the circumstances reason should prevail. 'I doubt we'll be opening the theatre any time soon. The architect predicts at least another two years . . .'

'No matter, no matter.' Carlo had flashed his easy, breezy grin. 'Whenever it happens we'll be ready, and we'll *show* 'em, Rube. It'll be showtime all right, it'll be showtime like they've never seen before!'

And now, even the dreadful news of the *Titanic* failed to deter Carlo. The ship's disastrous foundering continued to be the topic on everyone's lips, but it failed to provide an ongoing distraction to Carlo, whose conversation invariably reverted to the Colosseum.

During the weeks and then even the months that followed, the subject of the *Titanic* consumed the entire nation, shocking reports appearing about a shortage of lifeboats, mismanagement of the ship's evacuation, appalling treatment of those passengers travelling in the lower classes. People were outraged the world over, even this far away in Australia.

Finally, after months and months of newspaper coverage that seemed to relate to nothing but the *Titanic*, another topic altogether offered itself up by way of diversion. Particularly to those in Melbourne. The construction of Luna Park was nearing completion. Australians were about to experience a contemporary entertainment phenomenon of vast proportion, akin to the original Luna Park on New York's Coney Island. Or so the advance publicity boasted. And when towards the end of the year the date of the park's impending gala opening was announced, people could talk of little else. 13 December 1912 was a day firmly marked on many a calendar, and not only those of Melburnians, but others who intended to travel from far and wide to experience the marvel of Australia's very own Luna Park.

'It's a novelty, that's all' – Will Worthing was most dismissive – 'just a novelty, it won't pose any threat to us.'

'Of course it won't,' Mabel crisply agreed. 'It's an *amusement park*, for goodness' sake.'

'People like to be amused,' Gertie remarked as she picked up another sandwich, 'particularly on a Saturday afternoon when the weather's fine.'

The four Worthings senior were gathered on the back verandah of the Big House for a light Sunday lunch, and with Luna Park due to open the following week the topic had inevitably come up.

'You might have a good point there, Gert love,' Max said, and before his brother could pooh-pooh him, as he knew Will was about to, he continued. 'We are after all in the middle of summer, and our Saturday matinees could well suffer.' The company was currently performing a season at the Theatre Royal, and the prospect that Saturday matinees, which invariably played to packed houses, might come under threat was something none wished to contemplate.

Gertie took a bite of her sandwich, gave a complacent nod that said 'exactly' and chewed on, savouring every mouthful. The others had long finished eating, but Gertie always chose to linger over the plate of fish paste sandwiches Party made especially for her.

'Well, we'll see, won't we, we'll see. All in good time.' Will's tone was benevolent; he refused to argue with his brother, but as he didn't believe for one minute he could possibly be wrong, he also managed to sound patronising.

Will Worthing still didn't believe he was wrong well over a month later when not only were Saturday matinees suffering, but also Friday and Saturday's evening performances. He admitted Luna Park may possibly be a contributing factor but refused to acknowledge any ongoing threat.

'It's just a fad,' he insisted, 'just a passing fad. People will tire of Luna Park eventually, you wait and see.'

'I think nonetheless, dear, we should pop along and check the place out for ourselves,' Mabel suggested mildly.

And so they did. On a Sunday. The entire family, with the exception of Pru, who was at home looking after her newborn, David. Pru had married her young man, Tom, just one year previously, although in typical fashion she'd refused to change her surname. She would remain Prudence Worthing, she'd insisted, but Tom, being himself a creature of the theatre, had totally understood. Worthing was a name to be proudly borne in the business of show, a name that carried a great deal more weight than Buxton.

They travelled to the St Kilda foreshore by tram, much to Will's annoyance. He would far rather have driven his Model T Ford, but Mabel was insistent.

'We're going as a family and we'll go by tram, Will,' she said. 'Everyone travels by tram these days.'

Will's expression clearly said *not if they can afford to do otherwise*, but he was wrong, including in the case of his own family. Max and Gertie and their tribe always travelled by tram despite the fact that Max too owned a 'Tin Lizzie', which these days were not exclusive to the realms of the well-to-do anyway, but were rapidly becoming available to the common man in the street.

'Oh my, just look at that,' Gertie said, after they'd piled out of the tram at the special Luna Park stop on The Esplanade. 'Bit scary, isn't it?' She gazed up at the mammoth mouth of the entrance, which appeared about to engulf them. 'Like being chewed up and swallowed alive. If it's got to have teeth it could be a bit more smiley, don't you think?'

'Yes, it is rather ferocious,' Mabel agreed, 'and it's certainly bigger than it looked in the newspaper pictures.'

Will said nothing. He wasn't prepared to admit that he found the thing rather impressive.

They walked through the giant mouth to join the crowds that mingled in the magical world of fantasy towers and rides and stalls and myriad attractions the park had to offer. Here the 'Palais de Folies', 'River Caves of the World' and the 'Palace of Illusions' stood side by side with the 'American Bowl Slide', the Whitney Bros 'While-U-Wait Photo Booth', and a very busy Penny Arcade, not to mention a colourful carousel and other children's delights; there was certainly something for everyone. But reigning supreme was, without doubt, the Scenic Railway, a massive wooden roller coaster ride that encircled the whole park, offering intermittently between its dipping and diving spectacular views out over Port Phillip Bay on the one side and the city of Melbourne on the other.

'Well, you can't say it doesn't have atmosphere,' Max remarked wryly to Will.

But Will appeared not to hear. He was too busy studying the man on the highwire that was rigged across a section of the park.

'I didn't know they had live performances,' he said.

'They do in there too.' Mabel pointed to the sign above the entrance to the Palace of Illusions, but again Will appeared not to hear, or perhaps he chose not to listen, still intently focused as he was upon the highwire act.

'He's nowhere near as good as you,' he said, then turned as Alfie tapped him on the shoulder. 'Or you, Alfie.'

Max and Alfie exchanged a meaningful look.

'Of course he's not,' Max said. 'Alfie and I are the best in the business, aren't we, Alf?' to which Alfie nodded. 'And don't forget after all,' he added, including Mabel as he quoted her, 'this is just an *amusement park*.'

Alfie nodded once again and with a childlike grin squatted, holding an imaginary set of reins at chest height, and bounced gently up and down miming a six-year-old riding on a carousel. He was very funny.

Mabel smiled. 'All right, all right,' she agreed, 'I know I said that.'

Despite the fact that Alfie's onstage persona was no longer that of a clown, his offstage mime was often performed with the intent to amuse. And invariably to amuse one person in particular, his mother.

The Worthings senior, together with Alfie and Ted, decided to check out the performers in the Palace of Illusions, while the younger members of the family opted for personal preferences.

Sarah and Izzie, now well into their twenties, had arrived with their respective beaux and all four were keen to experience the River Caves of the World. Or rather, the girls were. The beaux, however, appeared quite happy to go along with the idea. They were coincidentally both Henrys, although upon the Worthing sisters' suggestion they'd agreed to adopt the nicknames Harry and Hal – lifted from Shakespeare's *Henry V*, of course. Being good-natured young men they'd accepted the arrangement, although their ignorance of the theatre very often landed them in trouble.

'What did you do that for?' Izzie's Hal had exclaimed when he'd visited her backstage on opening night with a pretty bouquet of flowers, which she'd promptly thrown out of the window.

'Lily of the Valley, can't have them in the dressing room.'

'Why on earth not?'

'Lilies are funeral flowers; they mean death to the show.'

Hal had been quite peeved – how was he to know that? And Harry had fared no better.

'Shush,' Sarah had said when, upon escorting her from her dressing room after the show, he'd started to whistle 'A Bicycle Built for Two'.

Harry had been in a jaunty mood off to supper with his girl and he was taken aback; she'd sounded very sharp, which was not like Sarah.

'Sorry, love,' she'd said, 'no whistling backstage.'

'Why?' Rather than taking offence, he'd been most interested.

'Goes back to the old days. Stagehands signalled with whistles when they were dropping scenery and weights from the flies; you could have copped something on the head.'

'Right' – that made sense, he'd thought – 'but they don't use whistles any more, do they?'

'Nope. Still bad luck to whistle backstage though, you just don't do it.'

'I see,' he said, although he didn't actually. 'I'm sorry.'

'That's all right, love.' She'd given his arm a squeeze; he was such a dear.

Both Harry and Hal had a lot to learn about the theatre, but they considered Sarah and Izzie worth the trouble, just as they now considered the River Caves of the World no hardship.

Seventeen-year-old Bertie and Emma, who would shortly turn twelve, both had an altogether different idea. They intended to try every ride the park had to offer.

'Except for the carousel' – Bertie flashed a warning glance at his little sister – 'that's just for kids.' But he had no cause for concern; it was a sentiment echoed by Em.

'Yep, no carousel,' she agreed, 'and we start with the roller coaster.'

Despite their six-year age difference, Bertie and Emma were very good mates, with only the occasional clash for both were feisty. Bertie looked so young for his age that people would at times assume there were only two or three years between them, which tended to annoy him.

'She's my kid sister,' he'd snarl contemptuously, 'she's only a *baby*,' which would arouse an equally contemptuous rejoinder from Em.

'Race you!' Em said, and she took off for the roller coaster before he had a moment to prepare himself.

But Bertie was happy to give her a good head start; he usually let her win, anyway.

The others watched them sprint off.

'I'd like to have a ride on the carousel,' Gertie said, eyeing the colourful horses longingly.

'After we've checked out the performers,' Will ordered. 'What if they have a Serpentine Dance?'

'Oh.' Gertie hadn't thought of that. 'They better not.'

They didn't. And the general consensus of the group upon emerging from the Palace of Illusions was that Luna Park's live performances presented no threat to the acts offered up in a Worthing Brothers production.

They gathered at two of the benches in the picnic area and sat to discuss their findings.

'I liked the marionette show,' Gertie said.

'Yes,' Mabel agreed, 'the marionettes were rather good. Perhaps we should incorporate a puppetry act – what do you think, Will?'

But both Will and Max appeared dubious; puppetry obviously wasn't their thing.

'Look.' It was Ted who drew everyone's attention to Alfie.

Seated at the end of one of the benches, Alfie had raised his right arm, resting his fist on the top of his head, and was now slowly raising his hand, hauling himself up by an invisible thread. Alfie was becoming a puppet.

They all watched, entranced as they always were when Alfie put on one of his shows.

When he'd finally reached full height, the 'thread' was released, the arm dropped, and Alfie hung there as if in thin air, head and limbs dangling lifelessly. Then limb by limb, joint by joint, he became a marionette, operated by an invisible puppeteer. First his head jerked up, a look of surprise on his face as he was brought to life. Then one arm, one hand. Then the other arm, the other hand. Then one knee lifted and a foot reached forward to take a tentative step. Then the other knee, and the other foot. All the while, Alfie closely and carefully studied each individual movement, communicating to his audience a sense of delight and wonderment as one by one everything worked. *Look*, his face was saying, *my, my, just look at that!* Then finally, his marionette body fully operational, he skipped about revelling in his freedom, sharing his joy with those watching, but most particularly with his mother. He came to a halt before Mabel and performed his marionette bow, just for her.

Mabel laughed her lovely laugh and applauded. Only then did Alfie come out of character and bow to the others, who were also applauding. And not just the family, but any number of passers-by, all of whom had gathered to watch.

Alfie acknowledged the applause, then sat quietly back on his bench.

'We don't need a puppet act, love,' Will said to his wife, 'we already have the best there is.'

'Yes,' she agreed, 'we do.'

Will Worthing was grateful to his son. There had been a time when he'd thought he would never again hear Mabel laugh.

Gertie studied the love shared between Alfie and his mother, the love that had preserved them and continued to do so. She found their bond intensely moving. It was two years now since Artie had died, and for some time after his death his brother and his mother had both suffered guilt. Why they should, Gertie had no idea, but she would never forget the night Mabel had unburdened herself.

'Alfie thinks it's his fault,' Mabel had said. 'He blames himself, which of course is wrong.'

'Of course it is,' Gertie had agreed.

But Mabel hadn't been listening. 'I'm to blame, you see,' she'd gone on, 'it's all my fault. I encouraged the boys to do that climb. I helped them plan it, every step of the way. What sort of mother sends her son to his death? What sort of mother does that make me?'

Gertie hadn't even answered, knowing Mabel was searching for a reason why her son was dead. But there wasn't one. People just died, didn't they? Particularly people whose profession was as dangerous as that of The Amazing Brothers Worthing. Show business abounded with accidents like Artie's. She didn't say this though. She just held Mabel close instead. It was the one and only time Gertie had ever seen Mabel cry.

'I'm going for a ride on the carousel,' Gertie announced.

Alfie jumped to his feet, intent upon joining her. His impromptu performance had unwittingly called attention

to their group and a number of people were seeking autographs, having recognised these were none other than 'The
Worthings'.

Very gently and politely, they excused themselves from
the burgeoning number of fans and, as one, headed for the
carousel. All except Will, that is. Will stayed on signing
autographs. One never left an admirer wanting, it was
simply not done.

They enjoyed Luna Park.

After the carousel ride, Will joined them and they
bought ices from the special Sennitt's Ice Cream stall
bearing its proud M.I.M. sign ... *Guaranteed Pure
and Wholesome. Latest American Process. Manufactured
only by the Melbourne Ice (Cream) Manufactory, Sennitt's
Ice Works.*

Then they joined up with the rest of the family and took
a ride on the Scenic Railway (third time around for Bertie
and Emma) agreeing it was truly spectacular, the highlight
of their day.

Finally, on the trip back to Toorak, having commandeered virtually the whole of the tram, they agreed also that
Melbourne was lucky to have Luna Park. Even Will was
prepared to admit to the fact, albeit a little condescendingly.

'Something of which Melburnians have every right to
be proud,' he declared, 'although it'll never replace the
theatre. Luna Park, grand though it is, belongs to the past.'

'But it's the most modern, sophisticated amusement park
this country has ever known,' one of the Henrys argued.

'Yes, and that's exactly what it is, young man.' Will
could never remember which Henry was Harry and
which Hal, so he avoided using names, succeeding only in
making himself sound more pompous. 'It's an *amusement
park*. The world of entertainment has moved on from the
cheap thrills of mechanised rides, and the simple offerings
of sideshows and fairgrounds ...'

'I love sideshows,' Gertie said. 'I love fairgrounds too. And rides. Especially carousels.'

Will glared at her. She was supposed to be on his side; these young Henrys knew nothing of show business and it was time they were informed.

'The uninitiated naturally experience personal excitement from amusement parks, Gertie,' he said icily, 'but as you well know, theatregoers are more discerning. They require talent, substance.'

He readdressed his attention to the Henrys. 'Audiences want to see artistes of true calibre, they want to experience content of true worth, comedy, drama, opera . . . Shakespeare, of course,' he added, 'stories that capture them.' Will was becoming ever more declamatory as he warmed to his theme. 'They want to see real, live people up there on that stage offering them an escape from their mundane existence.'

'They happily accept people who aren't live too, Will,' Mabel drily reminded him. 'Film is becoming very popular these days.'

Mabel did not intend to belittle her husband – she never deliberately punctured Will's ego – but it was time to put a halt to his rant; he did tend to carry on at times.

'Yes, yes,' he admitted with a touch of impatience, annoyed at being interrupted midstream, even by Mabel. 'But it's hardly the same thing, is it?'

'No, it's not, I agree entirely, but it *is* a step in a new direction, and a step we need to take note of if we're to move with the times.'

Mabel, always innovative, had kept herself well abreast of the latest changes. The Worthing Brothers no longer imported film footage via their agent in London. The short films incorporated in their variety shows were purchased from local producers instead, producers right here in Melbourne.

It had all started with *The Story of the Kelly Gang*, directed by one of the five Tait brothers just six years previously. Shot around the city of Melbourne, Charles Tait's film had premiered at the Athenaeum Hall on Boxing Day 1906, and with a running time of more than one hour, was the longest narrative yet seen in the world. Furthermore, *The Story of the Kelly Gang* had been both a commercial and critical success, creating a 'boom' period for Australian cinema and putting Melbourne at the very forefront of production.

'Film is definitely something we need to acknowledge,' Mabel said.

'But what about the punters?' Gertie suddenly jumped in, keen to offer her two-penneth. 'The punters will always want to see the *real thing*, surely. I mean, people have been making bio pics of The Serpentine Dance for years now, but it's hardly like watching the *real thing*.'

'Oh, I don't see film ever replacing us, Gertie,' Mabel agreed. 'Live theatre will never die. But I can't help wondering what lies ahead. Show business is evolving in so many new ways.'

Time to lighten the mood, she thought, and she smiled at Bertie and Emma, the youngest members of the group, who were leaning over the respective backs of their tram seats paying avid attention.

'Who knows what's going to happen next?' she said. 'It may well be over to you two to find out.'

ACT III

16

KING AND COUNTRY CALL

Rube's warning to Carlo about the architect's prediction proved correct. It was well over two years before the Colosseum was finally approaching completion. Given the complexity of its design and the grandeur of its interior this was hardly surprising. With an auditorium licenced to seat an audience of approximately 2,500, its tiers and galleries constructed on the modern cantilever principle, iron columns supporting the front of each tier, it was a pioneering structural wonder.

The décor of the interior too was breathtakingly stylish. Gone was the customary discomfort of 'the gods', to be replaced now by the grand circle whose seats and carpets matched those of the stalls and dress circle. The colour scheme was of rose, silver and blue, and the effect was further softened by the filtered light that emanated from strategically placed chandeliers. The overall mix of modernity and elegance was nothing short of magnificent.

There was still much work to be done, fittings and furnishings for the foyer and the bars, completion of the dressing rooms backstage. It would be a full six months or more before they would be in a position to advertise their presence to the public. But it was surely now time to start planning their opening show. What would it be? Who would they hire? Did they dare mount a Carlo and Rube production openly publicising Carlo as the star attraction?

Rube thought it was far too dangerous himself. But he had no cause to worry that Carlo might insist, for Carlo had lost all interest, and Rube knew only too well why. Carlo didn't care what show they decided upon for their grand opening, or even whether or not he was included. Carlo had far more on his mind these days than the rebirth of his career as a performer.

'You decide, mate,' he said. 'I leave all decisions to you, I'll go along with whatever you say.'

It was 1914. War had broken out in Europe. Britain had summoned her dominions to take up arms and Australia was answering her call.

All Carlo could think about was his son. Lieutenant Michael Carlovsky had been promoted to Captain and transferred to the 1st Division of the Australian Imperial Force, his deployment to France imminent. Carlo was worried. What the hell was going to happen to his son?

The average Australian was a little confused by the finer details, and also the speed of events that led to the war in Europe. Few had even heard of an Austrian Archduke called Franz Ferdinand, but his assassination on 28 June 1914 in a place called Sarajevo, another name unfamiliar to most, led to a series of consequences so dire that the whole of Europe was thrown into chaos. Countries were being invaded, neighbours were declaring war on one another, and to the average Australian it all appeared something very messy and very far away. Until 4 August when, only six weeks after the assassination of an obscure aristocrat in an obscure European city, England declared war on Germany and the world became involved. The average Australian was now forced to take notice. King and Country were calling. They must answer.

And answer they did. In droves. Young men flocked to recruitment centres all over the country. In major cities, in regional centres, in tiny backwater towns, they signed up by the thousands, determined to get to Europe before the war was over. What an adventure!

Thirty-five-year-old Captain Michael Carlovsky, too, was eager to see action. At last his years of military training and experience were to serve a purpose other than deskwork and court appearances. Deployed to France, he would fight at the front in defence of the mother country.

He made a final telephone call to his family in early November.

'We leave in a week or so, Dad,' he said. 'We'll be training at a military camp before our arrival in Europe, but we're not allowed to say where, not yet anyway.' Mick himself knew the camp was in Egypt, but the location was at this stage a military secret. The lads who'd signed up would have no idea where they were heading. Most would presume they were going directly to France, or possibly England.

'You take care, Mick,' Carlo said, 'you take care, son.'

Carlo was aware his words were inadequate, but what else did you say to your boy when he was going off to war?

'Sure I will. I'll write as soon as we get to camp. Let you know where we are and how we're going.'

Mick's voice, brisk, business-like, held the edge of authority that reflected the professional soldier he was, and Carlo, although concerned, couldn't help but feel a stab of pride.

'I'll put your mother on.'

Carlo handed the earpiece to Winifred, who was standing nearby. By her side fifteen-year-old Marty waited impatiently for his turn.

Winifred, too, felt inadequate as she offered her well wishes, but always a strong little woman she kept her exchange brief and to the point.

'God speed, Mick,' she said as she signed off, 'here's Marty.' And she handed the earpiece to her young son, who all but grabbed it from her.

'G'day, Mick!' he yelled. Marty always yelled when he was speaking on the telephone; like most he didn't realise that it actually wasn't necessary. 'You're taking off to see the world, eh? You lucky bastard.'

'Language,' Winifred said automatically.

'Wish I was taking off with you.' Marty didn't even hear his mother. 'I'm going to sign up as soon as I can.'

Mick could feel Marty's passion vibrating down the line, such an earnest kid, and his own voice bore a smile as he replied.

'No you won't, mate,' he said fondly. 'The war'll be well and truly over before you're old enough. Besides, you're not the right type. This isn't just one big romp, you know —'

'Course it is,' Marty broke in eagerly, 'you'll get to see the world, Mick. Crikey, you're going to France! You'll get to see the Eiffel Tower ... the Arc de Triomphe ... you'll get to eat snails and frogs' legs ...'

Mick laughed. 'I'm not going on a holiday, Marty, I'm going to fight a war, and military rations aren't likely to include snails and frogs' legs.'

How typical of Marty to romanticise things, Mick thought. *He's a dreamer. He'd never make a soldier, not in a million years.*

Mick and Marty Carlovsky were as close as two siblings could be. The fact they were half-brothers had never entered the equation, although given their twenty-year age gap Mick's attitude towards Marty had a distinctly paternal quality. But the two were also as different as could be, Marty a product of his father's theatre world and his Uncle Rube's love of books and plays, a world that Mick had so forcefully rejected in favour of the army. Mick was a soldier and Marty a romantic, it was as simple as that, and it seemed from the very outset they'd been born that way.

'You stay put, mate,' Mick instructed. 'You stay put and I promise I'll send you a report on France when I get there.'

'A description of everything, you promise? The Champs-Élysées, the Louvre . . .'

'If I get to Paris, yes.'

'And you'll try and eat frogs' legs and snails?'

'For you, Marty, yep. Just for you, I'll try.'

But as things turned out, there was a change of plan. After several months' training at Mena Camp in Cairo, the Australian 1st Division was not sent to France, or to England for that matter. Instead they were sent directly from Egypt to Turkey as part of the hurriedly formed Australian and New Zealand Army Corps. The ANZACs, as the troops were instantly termed, were to support the British in their newly launched campaign against the Turks at a peninsular called Gallipoli.

The Gallipoli landing on 25 April 1915 proved disastrous, but back home in Australia, the general populace was kept in total ignorance of the fact. The British Army refused to admit to the ineptitude of its military planning, which led to the devastating loss of life suffered by the ANZACs, and the Australian government, having promised to provide a quota of troops to the British, dared not risk affecting its recruitment drive by frightening off volunteers with news of the slaughter that had occurred on the stony beach of 'Anzac Cove', as the site became known.

But the truth could not remain hidden for long. Families needed to be notified. Brutal telegrams arrived informing parents and wives and siblings that their men had been killed or lost or wounded in action. The first five days from 25 to 30 April saw a toll of 643 killed in action. These statistics were not published. But the telegrams kept coming.

And the following month of May was worse – 1,805 KIA. The official military reports remained heavily censored, but back in Australia, word was spreading. The names of the dead were now published in newspapers; lists were posted on the walls and windows of town halls and post offices in country towns throughout the land. This relentless death had not been anticipated; this slaughter of a generation of young men was not right.

Australia was already becoming a nation divided, and the further horrors that ensued during the first week in August turned the tide of public opinion decidedly against the government's support of the war. The Battle of Lone Pine and the Charge at the Nek resulted in the deaths of thousands who fought bravely – seven Australians were awarded the Victoria Cross – but to what end? And at what price!

In total, the Gallipoli Campaign, which proved a resounding military defeat for the British, cost Australia in excess of 8,000 dead and over 19,000 wounded. The only successful element to the entire operation was the ingeniously managed evacuation of 36,000 troops smuggled out over five nights in December; troops who would thereby live to fight another day in another bloody battle in another part of a rapidly becoming war-torn world.

Captain Michael Carlovsky was one such man, a survivor of Gallipoli, but he wasn't among those evacuated between 15 and 20 December. He'd left Anzac Cove much earlier than that.

Serving in the 3rd Brigade under the command of Lieut. Col. Ewan Sinclair-Maclagan, Mick had been one of those first ashore on 25 April. He'd been wounded twice, once in the arm during the landing and several weeks later in the leg while leading troops into battle. Twice, too, he'd been mentioned in dispatches for showing exceptional command and control under fire, but Mick's days in

Gallipoli were to be numbered. When his leg wound became infected and his condition diagnosed as serious, he'd been medically evacuated to Alexandria in Egypt, where his recuperation had taken some time.

Finally, when he was well enough to be returned to camp, he'd written to his highly relieved family who had been scouring the newspapers daily, dreading the sight of his name among the latest published lists of the fallen. He'd addressed the letter to his father, apologising for the dearth of mail over the past several months but admitting to having 'copped a blast that put me out of action for a while'.

I'll be left with a bit of a limp, he wrote, *but at least I won't lose the leg, which is a blessing – it was touch and go for a while, so they tell me. All hunky-dory now though. I'll 'get to fight another day', as they say. That's a favourite saying among the medics here, by the way – 'you'll get to fight another day, lad,' they assure our boys. And their assurances are all hale and hearty as if that's just what the poor young buggers need to hear, when all most of them want to do is come home. It's a joke, Dad, honest it is. So many of them are kids. Just kids. And that brings me to what I really need to tell you, or rather to ask of you. In fact, without sounding overly dramatic – because let's face it that's your area – to beg of you.*

Unlike the missives Mick had sent from Cairo during the earlier training days, when he'd always kept his news light and entertaining for Marty's amusement, this letter had a much more serious tone.

Don't, whatever you do, let Marty lie about his age and join up, he went on. *He'll try to, because like most of the lads he thinks it's all one big adventure and a way to see the world – you know what a romantic he is. But he's not soldier material, Dad. God, who is at his age? But they think they are, and that's the problem. Off to*

fight for King and Country, some even have their parents'
permission – Mum and Dad are proud of them, they
say. Others sneak away and sign up on their own – Jeez,
I see so many boys over here who've done just that. And
the army accepts them! Some are still sporting bumfluff,
they've barely started shaving! They're kids. Babies. This
is no place for them.

Mick appeared then to experience a sense of guilt, as
if he'd been disloyal to the young troops with whom he
served, but he'd meant no disparagement, and he continued in all honesty.

Don't get me wrong, Dad, our boys are brave soldiers,
they're fighting to the death, even the youngest among
them, they're not going to let down their mates. But
seeing so many of them dead, so many of them shock-
ingly wounded, young as they are, lives ended or changed
forever . . . I don't want Marty to be one of them.

He signed off rather abruptly, having said what he'd
intended to say.

Well, I'll leave it at that. Goes without saying this letter's
just for you. And for Rube too, of course, be good if Rube
keeps an eye on the boy as well. I'll enclose another letter
here for Mum and Marty and I'll make it on a jollier
note. Although in all honesty there's not much to be
jolly about over here. This whole campaign is proving a
disaster. A bloody shambles, if the truth be known.

Cheerio for now,

Mick.

Mick didn't hand the letter to a runner to be delivered
to HQ for postage as was the normal procedure. Instead
he paid a visit to HQ himself and delivered the letter
directly to the mail room, which was perfectly permis-
sible for an officer of his rank. In doing so he would
bypass the censorship of general troop correspondence. It

was a precautionary measure on his part, just in case the military might choose to cut a phrase of his here and there, although he didn't see why they should.

Following the evacuation from Gallipoli, the ANZAC troops were returned to the military camp at Cairo for a period of long-overdue recuperation. It was Christmas. They were to rest up and see in the New Year. Then, as their numbers grew ever larger with fresh recruits from Australia, they were to retrain and await further orders.

And the new recruits arrived in their thousands, wave upon wave of them, swelling the ranks of the Australian Imperial Force. They were to be rigorously trained in Egypt before setting off for France and the Western Front. Their orders had come through and the newcomers were excited. Most had never been overseas before; the prospect of Europe was thrilling.

Captain Michael Carlovsky was assigned to the 5th Division of the AIF, which was chiefly composed of raw volunteers, specifically because of the battle experience he'd gained in Gallipoli. These as yet untested troops would need hardened, seasoned leadership.

Here we go again, Mick thought, wondering how many of these boys he would have to watch die.

Under the command of Major General James Whiteside McCay, the 5th was the last of the Australian divisions to leave Egypt bound for France, where it was to be placed as part of the British XI Corps commanded by Lieutenant General Richard Haking.

The troops arrived in Marseille in late June and travelled across France by train in open carriages. Their reception was enthusiastic wherever they went. Peasants waved at them from the fields and a welcome awaited them at every quaint little village they passed, people lining up along the track, children running beside the carriages, girls blowing kisses, old men saluting. The French were amazed that men should travel from the ends of the earth to help France in her greatest hour of need.

The young troops relished every minute of the attention afforded them, waving to the children, returning the girls' kisses and the old men's salutes. They drank in with relish too the beauty of the countryside, the fields and forests, the old stone farmhouses and barns, and above all a land-scape so fresh and green.

'It's a different sort of green from home, isn't it?' Jonno of the 57th Battalion remarked thoughtfully. 'A much greener green somehow.' Jonno always noticed such things.

Pete didn't; not when there were girls around, anyway. 'I reckon that one back there had her eye on me.' Pete was still craning his neck for a last glimpse of the girls who'd been blowing kisses. 'The one with the check dress and fair hair.'

They arrived in Armentières in northern France near the Belgian border, and on 8 July were transported to the camp and trenches near a village called Fromelles. The Australian 5th Division was now part of the British XI Corps, and they would shortly be ordered into battle.

It was a week after their arrival, early in the evening, and Mick was wandering through the camp near the British sector, his mind distracted by thoughts of the young men he would shortly be leading into battle. Orders had just come through to the commanding officers, although not as yet the troops. They were to make their attack on the morning of the 19th. Just four days now. The British military intended the attack as a tactical manoeuvre to divert German attention from the Battle of the Somme, and Mick couldn't help but wonder what was about to happen. *My boys are so young*, he thought, *so bloody young, and so bloody inexperienced. Dear God, what's going to happen to them?*

Then he saw a kerfuffle up ahead and he heard a Pommie voice.

'You thieving little git,' the voice bellowed, 'I'll have your guts for garters! You Aussies think you can get away with whatever you want, don't you? Well, not this time, laddie.'

A British provost sergeant, a burly man who must have been close to forty, was laying into a young Australian soldier. Mick marched up to them briskly.

'What appears to be the problem, Sergeant?' he demanded.

'Sir.' The sergeant stood to attention, snapped a salute and then referred disdainfully to the Australian private who, despite his extreme youth, didn't appear particularly fazed by his predicament; indeed he seemed quite prepared to tough it out. 'This lad here, Captain, I caught him stealing British equipment. Won't do, sir, won't do at all.' The sergeant glared at the young private. 'We'll throw the book at you, laddie,' he growled. But the 'laddie' squarely met the sergeant's eyes, and Mick couldn't help liking him for it. He could tell the sergeant enjoyed bullying.

'What did you nick, Private?' he asked.

'Haversack, sir.' He gestured to the bag the sergeant was holding. 'Shaving kit, tooth powder, personal stuff like that.'

'Don't you have your own kit, soldier?'

'Yes, sir. But our kits aren't anywhere near as good as the Poms'.'

Mick wanted to laugh; it was true after all. 'You know you've got yourself into a whole lot of trouble, don't you?'

'Yes, sir.'

'Right. Come along with me then.'

They were about to set off, but the sergeant interjected. 'Excuse me, Captain —'

'It's quite all right, Sergeant,' Mick assured him, 'I'm taking the lad into Australian custody . . .'

'But, sir . . .'

'We'll deal with this ourselves; he'll be duly punished, I can assure you.'

Mick's tone was dismissive, and the sergeant could do nothing but snap to attention with another smart salute.

'Yes, sir,' he said.

The young private followed Mick at a brisk march back towards the camp's Australian sector, but they stopped well short of HQ.

'Right you are, son,' Mick said, coming to a halt. 'I'm going to let you off this time, but you do know you did a bloody stupid thing, don't you?'

'Yes, sir.' The boy grinned, not cheekily, but rather a grin of unadulterated relief. He'd thought he was going to have the book well and truly thrown at him, and he'd been covering his nerves with a show of bravado. The way he always did, the way he always had, even as a child. 'Thank you very much, sir.'

'How old are you?' Mick asked, thinking the boy looked no more than eighteen, if that, perhaps even seventeen. *Another one with bumfluff*, he thought.

'Twenty-one, sir,' the boy said. He wasn't lying; he'd always looked young for his age. 'Just,' he admitted.

'Which battalion are you with?'

'The 57th.'

'Ah, right.' Mick nodded. The 57th was to be held in reserve. *If the kid's lucky he might miss out on the battle altogether*, he thought. 'And what's your name?'

'Worthing, sir, Albert Worthing.'

A pause followed, then: 'My, my, my' – it was Mick's turn to grin – 'little Bertie Worthing, eh?'

'Yes, sir.' Bertie was puzzled. How did the captain know that?

'I'd say you were around five years old when I first met you,' Mick said. 'Possibly even younger,' he added, recalling that day at the Worthings' house in Cremorne when the little boy had thrown himself into the Yarra to prove he could swim when he really couldn't. His big brother had had to fish him out. *Such a bold little bugger*, Mick thought.

Bertie continued to look blankly at the captain. What on earth was the man talking about?

'*The Musical Variety Extravaganza of 1900*,' Mick said. 'Ring any bells?'

'Crikey, yeah.' Bertie nodded vigorously. 'My dad and my uncle produced that show.'

'They did, "in partnership with Carlo and Rube,"' Mick quoted the slogan. 'I'm Mick Carlovsky, Carlo's son.'

He offered his hand. He knew that being an officer it wasn't the done thing. But then letting a soldier off after he'd been caught stealing wasn't the 'done thing' either, was it? And when troops were about to go into battle, a lot of 'done things' didn't seem all that important.

'Golly.' Bertie shook the hand on offer, feeling more than a little overwhelmed. 'Carlo and Rube, eh, that's going back a while.'

He could remember Carlo and Rube, particularly Rube. Uncle Rube, all the kids had called him. He'd been eleven years old when the partnership had split up, and he didn't know exactly what had happened, but something pretty awful. Nobody talked about it even to this day.

'I saw you a couple of other times when the families got together,' Mick went on, 'but mostly I was away studying and you were at school, so we weren't really part of the show business side of things.'

'You didn't want to be,' Bertie blurted out as an image of Uncle Will flashed through his mind, ranting as he so often did. *That boy has matinee idol written all over him, damn good-looking, presence and charisma to boot, and he wants to go into the* army! *Why Carlo's letting him is utterly beyond me!*

'You wanted to go into the army,' Bertie announced with an air of triumph that said, *there you are, I remember.*

Mick nodded. 'And as you can see, that's exactly what I did.'

'Uncle Will could never understand why,' Bertie said. Looking at the captain now, he could see what Uncle Will had meant. The bloke was handsome all right, in a battle-worn sort of way. Tall, fair-haired, blue-eyed, everything that set theatre-going hearts aflutter. But he wasn't a matinee idol, not at all. This bloke was tough, Bertie could tell.

'I'll see you later, Bertie,' Mick said. 'You keep yourself out of trouble now.'

'Yes, sir.' Bertie saluted, then watched as Mick walked away. *Mick Carlovsky*, he thought, *well I never!*

Bertie Worthing had volunteered for service in the latter part of 1915. He'd signed up with a number of his Melbourne mates, boys he'd known from school, boys who lived down the street, each egging the other on, keen to experience the thrill of it all before the war was over. None appeared overly deterred by the reports that had filtered back from the Gallipoli Campaign, but young men of twenty considered themselves invincible.

The Battle of Fromelles was the first occasion the AIF saw action on the Western Front, and proved a disaster. Over 2,000 Australian soldiers were slaughtered on one solitary day and night, and even greater numbers were to die from their wounds. Little wonder it was later described as 'the worst twenty-four hours in Australia's history'.

The troops of the Australian 5th had been introduced to the Western Front in a veritable bloodbath.

Mick had no idea how he'd cheated death at Fromelles. A bullet had clipped the rim of his helmet, leaving a jagged groove in the metal as proof. Another had gone straight through the material of his trouser leg. But he'd remained miraculously unscathed as thousands around him were killed and wounded. Boys, so many of them ... To Mick anyway ... Just boys ... Relentlessly mown down by German machine gun bullets.

Young Bertie Worthing had escaped the carnage. The reserve troops had not been called in. What would have been the point? The attack had served no purpose whatsoever. The entire battle was, to quote Australian Brigadier General H. E. 'Pompey' Elliott, 'a tactical abortion' and should never have happened.

But Bertie had nonetheless been introduced to the horrors of war. He and his mates of the 57th Battalion had seen the aftermath. From that day on they knew what to expect, and they knew, furthermore, that they must prepare themselves for the worst.

Barely a day or so later, Bertie and his brothers-in-arms found themselves encamped near the township of Albert in northern France, two miles south of a village called Pozières, with the expectation of going into battle sooner rather than later, although as was customary they had been told very little.

In the meantime, during the several days while they waited, the troops enjoyed the picturesque township of Albert with its impressive centrepiece, the Basilica of Notre-Dame de Brebières, which invariably invited comment.

'There she is, our Fanny,' Pete said, gazing up at the towering spire atop of which was the statue of the Virgin Mary that, having been hit by a German shell early in 1915, remained slumped to a near-horizontal position. 'She's a beauty all right, isn't she? Bound to win a gold medal,' he said, and Jonno, Bertie and the others laughed heartily.

The incomprehensible fact that eighteen months after its shelling the statue still had not fallen had earnt it legendary status. The British maintained that whoever caused 'The Leaning Virgin', as she had become reverently known, to fall would lose the war, while the Germans maintained the opposite. The Australians, upon their arrival, however, had viewed the statue in an altogether different light.

'Looks just like she's diving, doesn't it,' one had remarked.

'Yeah,' another had agreed, 'she's a high diver at the Olympics, that's what she is.'

So the statue had been christened 'Fanny' after Fanny Durack, Australia's gold medal swimmer at the 1912 Stockholm Olympics. The Australians' irreverence, as always, had not endeared them to the British.

Bertie and his mates had made a point of visiting the church as soon as they'd arrived at Albert; 'Fanny' was famous.

'It's a pity the place is so damaged,' Jonno said, looking around at the quaint streets and stone houses that surrounded them, many displaying the ravages of war. 'This is a pretty town. It's old too,' he added, 'it's really old, you can tell.' Jonno noticed things like that.

But his mates had already started wandering off. Pete and several others had their eyes on some girls who were walking up the hill, and Bertie was heading over the road to the colourful little marketplace where vendors were selling fresh produce from stalls, although being late on a Saturday afternoon most appeared to be packing away their wares. Jonno shrugged and set off up the hill; Bertie would join them all in good time.

'*Madame*,' Bertie said to the woman behind the wooden counter of one of the stalls, a dark-haired, worn-looking woman of forty or so. '*Vendez-vous des pommes?*' he painstakingly enquired, determined to practise his French and hoping he was getting it right.

The woman, who was stacking wooden crates of various sizes, stopped what she was doing and looked at him with a puzzled expression. Then, as if having worked out what it was that he'd said, she shook head.

'*Légumes?*' He was sure this was the word for 'vegetables' but she was studying him so quizzically he was starting to feel unsure. '*Vendez-vous . . . ah . . . légumes?*'

The Frenchwoman continued to study him for a further several seconds. Then: 'I do, but I have sold them all,' she replied in attractively accented, excellent English.

'Oh good,' he said with a touch of relief. 'That's good, you speak English.'

'It will be necessary. Your French is truly appalling.'

'Ha,' Bertie snorted, 'you should hear my German.' He grinned broadly. 'I've been practising that too and it's even worse.'

The woman smiled, a heartfelt genuine smile that erased the weariness from her face, transforming her completely. 'We are all hoping you young Australians will have little cause to speak German.'

Bertie was transfixed by her smile. He'd miscalculated her age, he realised. She was nowhere near forty; she was far closer to thirty, and furthermore she was beautiful. Or rather handsome, strong-boned and arresting. He stood openly gaping, at a loss for words, which was very unlike Bertie.

'What is your name?' she asked.

'Oh. Bertie,' he said, 'Bertie Worthing.'

'Ah.' She appeared most interested. 'Bertie, as in *Albert*, yes?'

'No, not Albair,' he corrected her. 'It's pronounced Albert.'

'*Non, non, non,*' she said with an impatiently dismissive wave of her hand. 'This is a French name. The English use it, yes, but they do not pronounce it correctly. It is *Albert*, the name of this town, you know?' She held her arms out wide, a dramatic and expansive gesture embracing the whole of the township. 'You are standing right here in the centre of *Albert*.'

'Really?' He was surprised. 'I thought it was Albert.' He gave another grin. 'Actually, I've been telling all my mates it was named after me.'

This time she laughed, and he thought he'd never seen a more beautiful woman. Which was strange, because he'd seen a great many beautiful women over the years. He'd grown up in the world of show business and show business was the home of beautiful women. But her beauty was different, he thought. It was something to do with her smile and her eyes, not the perfection of her features but rather her expression. Even now as he watched, mesmerised, her face once again transformed, the smile fading as she turned her head from him and gazed out to the west.

'The war will be here again soon, no?' she asked, but it wasn't really a question.

'I reckon you're right,' he replied.

'Out there,' she said, 'along the river through the Somme Valley, there have been many recent battles.' She turned to face him once again, and he could see the sorrow mirrored in the dark depths of her eyes. 'You can hear the cannons fire at night. So many dead.'

'Yep.' He nodded. 'We'll be fighting soon, at least that's what my mates are saying. Could be as soon as a day or so.'

The sorrow in her eyes was instantly replaced by concern, and as her face again transformed, Bertie realised this was where her beauty lay, in her expressiveness. Hers was a beauty that came from deep within.

'What's your name?' he asked.

'Elise,' she said, 'Elise Fouchard.' Elise was chastising herself for the words that had accidentally sprung out. How could she have said that? *So many dead.* How thoughtless, how insensitive. He was little more than a boy and he was about to go into battle. How *could* she! But she'd thankfully seen no flicker of a reaction in him; in fact he'd appeared hardly to have heard her.

'How old are you?' she asked.

'Twenty-one,' he said, noting her instant surprise and once again entranced by the fact that she was so readable. 'I know,' he added with a smile, 'everybody tells me I look eighteen.'

'I am thinking you are seventeen,' she said, displaying the one hiccup in her so far faultless English. She returned his smile, but the concern remained in her eyes. *Still too young to die,* she was thinking. 'Ah' – then she looked beyond him to the street that led out of town – 'here is Pierre come to collect me.'

Bertie turned to see a horse and dray plodding towards them.

'Pierre is your husband, is he?'

'No, no,' she smiled, 'Pierre is my farmhand.' She leant in towards him and lowered her voice, even though the dray was still well out of earshot. 'Actually, Pierre is just a little simple,' she explained, 'so much so that they will not have him in the army.' Then she slapped her hands together loudly, startling Bertie. 'Now, enough talk,' she said briskly, 'I must pack my things.'

'Let me help,' he offered, and before she could reply he'd already set about stacking wooden crates and cardboard boxes.

'The scraps we put there,' she said, gesturing to a large cardboard box into which she was tossing the discarded outer leaves and stems of various vegetables. 'Nothing must go to waste,' she said. Then, with the humorous raise of an eyebrow, she added, '*Des légumes*, they are for the chickens.'

'*Les poulets*,' he said triumphantly.

'*Oui, très bien*,' she congratulated him, although his pronunciation had been atrocious.

'We call them chooks back home.'

Elise chose to make no enquiry but returned to her work, and by the time Pierre pulled up the horse and dray, everything was stacked and sitting by the side of the road ready for transport, the colourful tablecloth that had covered the counter tucked under her arm and the stall now a bare wooden construction awaiting the next market day.

She introduced Bertie to the farmhand, a gawky young man in his mid-twenties wearing baggy trousers, a grubby check shirt and braces. Even upon first meeting, Pierre did appear a little on the simple side, wordlessly tapping his cloth cap by way of salute, but as Elise explained, he was shy and didn't speak a word of English.

When the dray was loaded, she made Bertie an offer.

'Would you like to visit my farm?' she asked. 'It is no more than a kilometre from town. I will give you a bag of apples you may share with your friends.'

He beamed, his face radiant with pleasure; he'd been so loath to say goodbye.

'I would *love* to visit your farm,' he said.

'Come along then.' She climbed up onto the dray, placed the tablecloth on her lap and wriggled alongside Pierre. 'There is room enough for three,' she said, patting the bench in a maternal way, as if she were issuing orders to a child.

They chatted amicably as the horse plodded along and during the fifteen-minute journey Bertie, always inquisitive, learnt a lot about Elise. He didn't hesitate in delivering his questions, and she didn't hesitate in answering them. He relished her honesty, just as he relished the feel of her thigh against his, although he knew he shouldn't. He knew she looked upon him as no more than a boy.

He discovered that her grandmother was English, which was why she spoke the language so well, and that her grandmother lived on a farm nearby.

'Mamie lives with my mother and father,' Elise explained. 'We are a farming family of three generations on my grandfather's side. When my husband and I married, André bought the property close to the farm of my parents. He too came from this region, and he too was of farming stock.'

Bertie didn't pick up on the past tense. 'Do you and André have children?' he asked.

'Yes, two little ones. I leave them in the care of Mamie when it is market day and I come into town.'

'Ah.' He still didn't get the inference. 'Handy to have a babysitter living next door,' he said.

'Yes, very handy. For I need to work. My husband is dead.' She realised he hadn't registered her situation and she didn't mean to sound brutal but was just stating a fact. 'He was killed in the war eighteen months ago.'

'Oh.' Bertie was brought jarringly to a halt. 'I'm sorry.'

'Yes. So am I.'

They travelled in silence for a while. But it was not an uncomfortable silence, the honesty of her response having saved him from that.

They could see the farmhouse up ahead now, an attractive stone cottage, surrounded by groves of trees and vegetable plots. A barn and stables, several small wooden outhouses. A modest property, but pretty.

'We French never asked for this war,' Elise said, gazing out at the countryside. 'We wanted no part of it. But when Germany invaded us, what else could we do?'

She hadn't addressed the comment to him, and Bertie rightly assumed her query was rhetorical so he didn't reply.

But he noticed, for the first time, her cynicism. She was bitter, he realised, and she had every right to be.

They drove up to the stables where they alighted, leaving Pierre to look after the horse and dray and the cartons and boxes.

'Let me help,' Bertie insisted.

'No, no,' she said, 'it is his job.' She nodded to the Frenchman, '*Merci*, Pierre,' and the young man returned the nod, once again touched his cloth cap by way of salute, and went about the routine of his business.

'Come up to the house and I will get you those apples.' The tablecloth once again tucked under her arm, Elise marched on ahead and he followed.

The cottage was as attractive on the inside as it was on the outside.

'It's pretty,' he said, gazing around at the cosy little sitting room.

She didn't acknowledge the remark, paying him no heed as she walked through to the kitchen. He followed.

'Very pretty,' he said. It was. Another small room, but bright and sunny with pots and pans hanging from hooks on the walls, bowls of fruit and vegetables sitting on the bench by the windows and on the central wooden table. '*Très jolie*,' he said. 'That's right, isn't it?'

He was clearly so eager for approval that Elise didn't laugh and tell him 'jolly' was an English word for 'happy', but she did correct him nonetheless. 'Yes, that is right,' she said, 'but it is pronounced *jolie*.'

'Ah, good,' he nodded, filing the word away for later, 'good, thanks.' He had a small English-to-French phrase book and dictionary, but he found a lot of the spelling strange. He intended to practise though; he'd get it right in the end.

She took a cloth bag from one of the several hanging on a hook by the pantry door and tipped a whole bowl of apples into it.

'For you and your friends,' she said. *He is so young*, she thought.

'That's very generous of you, Elise, thank you.'

'You are welcome.' She handed him the bag.

'Oh.' He took it from her but was a little confused; it was a nice bag, sturdy, made of linen. 'But what about . . . ?'

'You may keep the bag,' she said, 'I have many. Mamie makes them; they are very useful.'

'Ah, well in that case,' he grinned, '*merci* very much.'

'*Merci beaucoup*,' she said automatically. *So very young*, she thought.

'*Merci beaucoup*.' Bertie filed that one away too. He'd actually seen it in the phrase book, but hadn't been sure how it was pronounced. Good to know.

'I have some wine,' she said. 'Will you share a glass with me?'

His face lit up. 'I'd love to,' he said. '*Merci beaucoup*.'

'Do please sit down.' She gestured to the table with its four wooden chairs.

He sat while she fetched a bottle of red wine and two glasses, and when she'd opened the wine she joined him at the table.

She poured the wine and raised her glass. '*À votre santé*,' she said.

That sounded a little difficult to Bertie. 'Cheers,' he said, raising his own glass.

As they made the toast their eyes met, and for a moment that seemed very long to both they remained motionless.

Elise Fouchard's heart ached for this boy who was no doubt destined to die in a foreign land. An Australian boy ten thousand miles from home and family. He could not even speak the language of France and yet he would probably die on its already blood-stained soil. She wanted to hold him in her arms, to stroke his hair, to tell him everything would be all right and that she would care for him.

Bertie wasn't sure what he was thinking, or perhaps even hoping. He just knew he was looking at this glorious woman and that her eyes were telling him something.

Elise broke the moment and made the decision for them both. She put down her glass and stood.

'Come,' she said, offering her hand.

He put down his own glass, stood and took her hand, now knowing what was about to happen.

She led him into her bedroom.

17

AWAKENINGS

At 12.30 am on 23 July 1916, Bertie Worthing was one of the many who went over the sandbags in the frontline as the Battle of Pozières erupted.

He and his mates, so many new to the shocking reality of war, were being thrust headlong into battle, and like the troops at Fromelles their initiation was brutal.

Bertie didn't see those falling beside him as he charged across no man's land. He knew men were copping it right, left and centre, but he didn't know who, he didn't know one of the first was Pete; you didn't stop to find out, did you? You had to kill or be killed, that was the object of the exercise. And, like many, Bertie screamed as he ran. Then, when they reached the German lines, he screamed as he shot and he screamed as he stabbed. Yelling murder to the enemy, screaming out vengeance seemed to help somehow, if only in numbing the brain to the mindlessness of it all. You didn't dare think, did you?

But he did think later on. When the onslaught was finally over and he lay in a shell hole surrounded by the detritus of war, gazing up at a sky where the first streaks of dawn might have signalled normality had it not been for the smoke and the stench that remained and the cries of wounded men nearby. He couldn't *stop* thinking then. How many men had he killed? He couldn't possibly remember. And *had* he killed them, or did they, too, lie wounded, crying out for help? He could only remember the world exploding all around him, and when they'd reached their objective, a frenzy of shooting and stabbing. He'd been stabbed himself. A bayonet had pierced his arm, even as his own had found its mark in the young soldier's stomach. He could still see the wretched look in the man's eyes, a man no older than himself with the sure knowledge that he was dying. Yes, he'd killed that bloke, all right.

In a matter of only hours Bertie Worthing had aged twenty years, and he knew he would never be the same again. *Which one among us can ever be the same again?* he wondered.

Then, perhaps in an act of self-preservation, an image came to his mind, blocking out the surrounding carnage and the young soldier's eyes. Blocking out the smoke and the stench and the cries of pain. It was the image of Elise, tousled hair splayed on her pillow, eyes beseeching him, lips gently parted as she whispered her goodbye. *Be safe, Albert. Be safe, my young soldier from Australia.*

Bertie knew at that moment that Elise would stay with him, that the memory of her would help him through the horrors he was destined to endure, perhaps even through his own death, should it come to that. Elise would be with him. In the tenderness of their lovemaking, a tenderness he'd never before experienced, this had been her intention. He knew that now.

The Australian 1st Division suffered 5,285 casualties on its first tour of duty at Pozières, one observer remarking that when the survivors were relieved on 27 July, 'They looked like men who had been in Hell ... drawn and haggard and so dazed that they appeared to be walking in a dream ...'

The battle, which finally culminated on 3 September, proved a victory for the British, but at tremendous cost to the Australians. Charles Bean, the Australian official historian, wrote that Pozières Ridge was 'more densely sown with Australian sacrifice than any other place on earth'.

As was customary, statistics were not broadcast to the Australian public, but word had its own way of getting around back home. Word even received directly from the battlefront.

Our boys are doing it really hard over here, Dad, Mick wrote, *the Somme is proving a bloodbath for our young troops. Just between you and me (and Rube, of course, I presume he'll be reading this – in fact, I'm hoping he will), the number of losses are already far greater than Gallipoli. They're fine boys and they're putting up a brave fight, of course, but it's a baptism by fire, and like I told you before, so many of them are just kids! Tough to see them go down in such numbers. All the more reason you and Rube need to keep your eyes on Marty. No bloody romancing about seeing the Eiffel Tower and eating frogs' legs. Tell him there's nothing over here but mud. Endless bloody mud . . .*

Bertie's letter to his parents recounted no statistics, no comparison to Gallipoli, but then Bertie didn't know any statistics. And had he, his letter would have been censored. But, if anything, Bertie's letter conveyed even more of the horror, given the harshness of its tone.

My two closest mates copped it, he wrote, *and on the very first night, which doesn't seem fair to me. Jonno'll come home, but probably without a leg, at least that's what I heard. Pete won't be coming home at all.*

Bertie wasn't pulling any punches; it felt better that way, to just say things out loud, or rather write them out loud. It helped somehow. But he knew in doing so he would worry his family, so he backed off a little, although at first he wasn't sure how to help put them at their ease.

I don't want you to worry about me, he went on. *I know you will, of course, but I've got a funny sort of feeling that I'm going to come out of this all right.*

Then the idea hit him. He wanted to write honestly, so why not tell them the truth? Not all of it, naturally, but he could tell them the way he felt.

I reckon I've got this sort of guardian angel, you see. I know that sounds a bit queer, particularly given I'm not a religious bloke, but something happened just before we went into battle. And now I have this kind of angel looking after me . . .

'He fell in love, that's what happened,' Gertie said. 'He met a woman and he fell in love, I bet that's it.' She and Max were seated side by side on the bed reading the letter out loud in the privacy of their upstairs bedroom. Or rather Max was, as Gertie hung breathlessly onto his every word; they'd pass it around among the family later. Max didn't look up, but read on.

Sounds really stupid, doesn't it, but I tell you it's true. I don't feel scared when she's around . . .

'I told you.' Gertie bounced up and down on the edge of the bed. 'It's a woman. He's in love . . .'

'Be still, Gert,' Max said, eyes still focused on the letter, 'I can't read.'

'Sorry.' Gertie obediently stopped bouncing.

So there you are, see? You mustn't worry. Just know that, weird as it seems, I'm being looked after. And hell, let's face it – the tone of the letter changed as Bertie continued in a practical vein – *there's no point in worrying anyway, is there? I mean, no amount of worry's going to change things, is it?*

Right, that's enough about me. What's happening at home? You must be heading off to Sydney with 'The Shrew' sometime soon. You said in your last letter you were about to start rehearsals. That'll keep Uncle Will happy, Petruchio's always been one of his favourites. Are you playing Kate, Ma? And what about the rest of the casting? Which theatre are you playing and when do you open? I want all the news. The boys over here can't get enough gossip about the theatre. I'm a real hero just being a Worthing, so send me whatever bits and pieces you can.

Give my love to the girls and tell Ted not to feel bad about being too old to join up – there's not much 'fun' he's missing out on, I can promise you.

Keep the letters coming, we read stuff out to each other when mail arrives from home. Helps boost morale and all that.

Cheers for now,

Your loving son, Bertie.

'Oh dearie me . . .' Gertie took the letter from Max and, after gazing at her son's signature for a moment, she kissed it, then clutched the pages to her chest. 'Oh dearie, dearie me . . .'

'Come on, Gert love,' Max said, 'no point in tearing up, that's not what Bertie's after.' But he put his arm around her anyway.

'I know.' Gertie forced back the tears and stood. 'I know just what he's after and it sure as heck isn't blubbing. He wants news about the theatre, doesn't he, that's what he said. Well, that's just what he'll get.' She handed the letter back. 'You share that around, love, I'm going to write to him.'

'Good girl,' Max said, as he watched her march resolutely from the bedroom and set off downstairs.

In the front drawing room that served as an office, Gertie sat at the desk, took up the brand-new Waterman fountain pen Max had bought her and started to write.

Hello lovey, it's me. We got your latest letter, and I'm very glad to hear about your guardian angel. Honest, Bertie, I really, really am. You tell her from me I expect her to look after you good and proper.

She wouldn't ask him any private questions, she decided, nor would she voice her presumption this 'angel' was a woman. That wouldn't be right. She'd tell him all about *The Taming of the Shrew* instead, just like he'd asked her to, and she'd give him bits and pieces about the theatre that might amuse his mates. That's what Bertie wanted.

Yes, we're just finishing rehearsals and we'll be taking 'The Shrew' to Sydney at the start of next month. We're playing the Criterion, which is one of your Uncle Will's favourite venues for Shakespeare – he says The Cri's got that more 'intimate' feel. And no, I'm not playing Kate, I'm playing Bianca. Will reckons my voice isn't strong enough for Kate, and I'm sure he's quite right. He's cast a lovely young actress in the lead, a girl called Millie. Millie Hampton. Fairly new on the scene. She doesn't really look like a Millie, though, you know the way people look like their names? She's not pretty and feminine the way I see a Millie, she's more what you'd call 'arresting'. And she's tough too, even a bit fearsome, at least I find her so. All of which makes her a splendid Kate. But you know the funny thing, Bertie? At least I find it funny. Actually, I find it downright hilarious. Kate is the older sister and Bianca the younger, as you know. Well, Millie's twenty-five years old, which is about the age Kate should be, but oh my lordie, I'm coming up for fifty! Isn't that a hoot! Of course, Will's a good thirty years older than Petruchio should be too, but nobody ever cares about men's ages, do they? None of the others seem to find any of this funny, by the way – they all say I look half my age – but truly, Bertie, our little Em'd be a better Bianca than me.

Which brings me to the rest of the casting – you asked about that too. Em's coming with us to Sydney, just playing bits and pieces, there are so many of them in 'The Shrew', but here's the other really funny part – oh, your mates can have a laugh about this one all right. Ted's playing Lucentio, who's in love with Bianca, and your dad's playing Baptista, the father of Kate who Petruchio's courting. Now how's that for a good old mix-up? Your dad's younger than your Uncle Will and he's playing his father-in-law, and I'm being wooed by my own son! Oh, Bertie love, only in the theatre, eh?

We've two productions under way as you know. Sarah and Izzie have been performing their musical segment in 'The Variety Extravaganza of 1916' tour, and they're about to set off on the final leg, a two-month run up to Christmas at His Maj in Perth, one of my most favourite theatres ever! Alfie, of course, has been topping the bill, and that's probably why the tour's been all but booked out. Which really is proof of his drawing power because, I have to tell you, Bertie, theatres aren't doing too good at the moment. Numbers are down because of the war, see? But your Uncle Will is quite sure they'll pick up. Oh my heavens, he does carry on.

'In times of adversity, the public needs escape ... !' 'Never forget the noble purpose we serve ... !' I bet you can just hear him saying all that, can't you.

No doubt he'll be proved right – he usually is, and it's certainly why we're sticking to comedy at the moment. I mean, when the whole world's falling apart you'd rather see 'The Shrew' than 'Hamlet', wouldn't you? A few more laughs to be had. Let's face it, we all need a bit of cheering up these days.

Well, I've rabbited on long enough. The others will write soon, I know they will because we talk about you all the time. I just wanted to be the first.

I'm sending you all my love, Bertie. And you tell that guardian angel from me to keep doing her job. That's an order now.

Bye, lovey,

Ma.

Gertie shed a tear or two as she signed off. Why not? *You can't put on a brave face the whole bleeding time, can you*, she thought. Of course she worried about her son, just like so many mothers all over the country. What terrible times. She hoped her letter might give Bertie's mates a few smiles way over there in France.

A fortnight later *The Shrew* was in Sydney, preparing for the season at the Criterion Theatre on the corner of Pitt and Park streets. There would be a week set aside for the bump-in, technical and dress rehearsals, two preview performances, and then it would be opening night.

Fifteen-year-old Emma stood in the stalls and gazed about the auditorium. Uncle Will was quite right, she thought. Despite the three tiers of levels there was an intimate feel about the place. Even empty as it was now, you could tell it offered a personal contact between audience and players; no wonder they all loved The Cri.

There would be no rehearsal today as they were setting up, the backstage crew and principal performers working alongside one another; the Worthings always took an active part in the bump-ins and bump-outs. Their presence wasn't altogether necessary, but old habits die hard and memories from early touring days, when everyone mucked in, were still fresh in the minds of most.

Em looked up at the stage, which appeared a clamorous mess of activity, but which, with Mabel as always at the helm, was actually progressing with military precision.

'What can I do, Aunt Mabel?' she called above the din.

'Are you all set up in the girls' dressing room?' Mabel called back. 'Checked your costumes, set up your possie and makeup?'

'Yep, done all that. What else can I do?'

'Nothing thanks, love. Too many cooks as it is.' Mabel was wishing a number of the others would bugger off, Will in particular, who was fussing about the props when they weren't unpacked, and she hadn't even set up the props tables yet. 'Go for a walk, Em,' she called, 'or buy yourself a cup of tea somewhere nice, we're doing fine here.'

'Rightio.' She'd do both, Em decided. She'd go for a walk down to Circular Quay, where she'd buy a cup of tea and watch the ferries coming and going.

Emma had inherited her mother's love of Sydney Harbour. Like Gertie, she enjoyed nothing more than a wander along the forefront, particularly the Quay where the waterway was so busy and there was so much to see.

She chose to walk down Castlereagh Street instead of Pitt, in order to check out the theatres, and discover what was on at each.

It was a fine morning in late October, but there was still a bite of spring in the air and she drew her wrap around her as she walked. Not that she minded a mild chill; if she was in Melbourne she'd probably be wrapped up in an overcoat and scarf, wouldn't she?

The Theatre Royal was playing *The Importance of Being Earnest*, which was hardly surprising; everyone was doing comedies these days. *And you can't go wrong with 'Earnest'*, Em thought.

She wandered on a little further and came to the Colosseum. This was the brand-new theatre that had opened less than a year ago, she realised, the one about which Uncle Will had been most scathing.

'No, no, we won't be booking into the Colosseum,' he'd said dismissively when she'd suggested it as a possible option for *The Shrew*. 'The Worthings will never be booking into the Colosseum.'

'Why not, Uncle Will?' She'd been puzzled; the full-page article she'd just read in *The Age*, complete with picture, was quite splendid, which was why she'd brought up the subject in the first place. She'd referred to the newspaper. 'It says here that the theatre is "a pioneering structural wonder",' she quoted, 'a "state-of-the-art" design, they say, and just look at the picture.' She held the paper out to him, but he ignored it altogether.

'The Colosseum is banned,' he said.

'Why?'

'Ask no questions and you'll be told no lies,' Will had tersely replied. 'It just *is*, that's all.'

'Oh.' Emma's interest had naturally been piqued, but even her mother had been unforthcoming.

'Best give it a rest, lovey,' Gertie had said upon being questioned, 'just a bit of personal history, that's all,' which had only served to further pique her daughter's interest.

Em looked up at the impressive facade of the theatre, where the title of the current production was emblazoned above its main entrance: *The Merry Widow*. Another good choice, she thought; operettas and musicals were also popular these days. Or rather, like comedies, they were a safer bet than dramas.

She couldn't resist sneaking a look inside. That is, if the theatre was open; it was a Monday morning after all.

She pushed one of the two main doors, and to her surprise it opened. Then she stepped into quite possibly the most magnificent foyer she'd ever seen, and in her relatively short existence young Em had seen many.

A floor of ornate mosaic tiles, a vaulted, cathedral-like ceiling with a huge central crystal chandelier, heavy oak doors leading to the stalls either side of a broad marble stairway up to the dress circle. Even the programme seller's little wooden booth beside the stairs was a work of art, decoratively carved and highly polished.

She wandered about the foyer looking at the posters and pictures of *The Merry Widow*, which was evidently in the final month of its run, as there were other posters declaring the show that would be opening in early December.

'GRAND GALA VARIETY SPECTACULAR,' the posters screamed. 'A CHRISTMAS BONANZA FOR ALL.'

And in smaller letters below she read, 'A Carlovsky & Reubens production'. She hadn't heard of either Carlovsky or Reubens. They must be new producers in the business, she thought.

'Can I help you?' a voice asked.

She spun about, startled. She'd been so distracted she hadn't noticed the young man who'd come out from the box office and was standing right behind her.

'Oh, I'm sorry,' she said, 'I probably shouldn't be here, should I? I mean, you're not actually open, are you?'

'No, we're not,' he replied bluntly, but he didn't appear upset by her presence.

'I just wanted to look around.' Em noted that he wasn't really a young man at all but more a youth, possibly not much older than herself, although he seemed very mature and self-assured. 'It's a beautiful theatre,' she said.

'Yes, it is, isn't it,' he agreed. 'Very innovative too. "State-of-the-art" as they say.'

'Yes, I read that direct quote in a newspaper,' she said, 'that's why I snuck in to have a look.'

'I'd be happy to show you inside the auditorium,' he said, 'but I'm afraid I can't at the moment. We're in rehearsal, you see, for the Christmas revue.'

'Are you in the show?' She was a little surprised. He didn't look like a variety performer or an actor, she wasn't sure why; perhaps because he appeared so serious. There wasn't anything 'theatrical' about him.

'Oh, gosh no,' he replied, 'I don't belong onstage. I'm in the management side of things.'

'Really?' she queried disbelievingly. *But you're so young,* she thought.

Her reaction was clearly readable, but he wasn't in the least offended. He smiled instead.

'I work for my dad,' he said, indicating the poster. 'I'm Marty Carlovsky.'

Em liked his smile, genuine and unassuming. She thrust her hand out boldly, as was her custom; Em was anything but timid.

'Hello, Marty,' she said, returning his smile. 'I'm Em. Emma Worthing.'

He was relishing the firmness of her handshake when the name suddenly registered.

'What?' His reaction bordered on comical in its disbelief. 'You're *who*?'

'Emma Worthing,' she said, 'my family's in the business too.'

'I know.' Of course he knew. Everyone knew the Worthings. 'Is Will Worthing your father?'

'No, he's my uncle.'

'Oh hell.' Marty looked around warily. His dad might appear at any moment; Carlo and Rube were both in the auditorium. 'You'd better not tell your uncle you were here – he hates my dad with a vengeance.'

'Why?'

'I don't know, to be honest. But it goes both ways, there's no love lost on either side.'

'Really?'

'Yep, from what I can gather anyway. My dad's always very scathing about Will Worthing and he makes it obvious the feeling's mutual, but when I ask why he just clams up.'

'How interesting.' Emma was most intrigued. 'My Uncle Will told me the Colosseum was banned, but he wouldn't say why. He just said that the Worthings will never perform at this theatre.'

'I doubt they'll be asked,' Marty commented wryly, and Em was treated to another very likeable smile.

'I suppose I'd better get out of here then, before your dad discovers there's a Worthing on the premises.'

'Probably best.' He accompanied her to the door. 'Where are you off to?'

'A walk to Circular Quay and a cup of tea,' she said.

'I know a really good café near the Quay that serves the very best chocolate cake. Generous portions too. Do you want some company?'

'That'd be nice.'

'Good. I'll just nip out to the back office and let the front-of-house manager know I'm leaving; he might want to lock the main doors.'

'And so he should,' she said curtly, 'you never know what sort of stray might wander in off the street. I'll wait outside.'

Marty grinned. He liked Emma Worthing. Not because she was fair-haired, blue-eyed and pretty as a picture, none of which particularly attracted him; there were numerous pretty girls in show business. But because Emma Worthing was gutsy. And what's more, she was funny.

He joined her in less than two minutes and they set off down Castlereagh Street, talking nineteen to the dozen.

'You're just about to open *The Shrew* at The Cri, aren't you?' Marty queried.

'Yep, in a week.'

'The pre-publicity's been excellent. How are your bookings?'

'Should I be telling the competition?'

'Not if you don't want to.'

His response to her arched comment was so simple and direct that Emma dropped the act.

'According to Aunt Mabel the advances are excellent, particularly given the current climate.'

'That's good to hear. Theatre's certainly doing it tough at the moment.'

'Uncle Will thinks the slump is only temporary. He says that as the war continues people are bound to seek the escape theatre offers.'

'Let's hope Uncle Will's right,' Marty said with a smile. Then all of a sudden he became deadly serious. 'I agree with your Uncle Will. I think there are very tough times ahead, and I think people *will* need to escape. My brother's serving in France and he says things are getting grimmer by the minute over there.'

'My brother's serving in France too,' Emma said.

'I think just about everybody's brother is,' he replied drily.

'I wonder if they know each other.'

'I doubt it somehow, it's a pretty big army.'

They were walking past another theatre, but Em didn't even notice. They'd stopped talking shop now and she'd forgotten her intention to check out the competition.

'You never know, though, do you,' she said. 'Bertie signed up last year so he's been gone for quite a long time. They might have bumped into each other.'

'It's possible, I suppose.' Marty didn't think it was himself, but she seemed to like the idea so he went along with it. 'My brother Mick didn't sign up – he's much older than me and he's an officer, been in the army for years. That's why we get a bit more detail in the letters he writes; he's not censored the way the general troops are. There's a lot the military keeps from the general public, you know.'

'Is there?' Em hadn't really known that. 'Like what?' she asked.

'Oh, statistics for starters, the numbers of casualties, and the success or failure of military campaigns. Mick doesn't give us specific information, of course, but he makes regular comments about some battle being "a farce" or a "bloodbath" or "a useless waste of men", stuff like that. You can tell he's pretty bitter about the way the British are running things.'

'Yes,' Em was thoughtful, 'Bertie's bitter too. He said in his last letter that his two best mates copped it on their very first night. He reckoned it wasn't fair.'

'He's right, it wasn't. There's nothing fair about war.'

They walked on in silence for a while, each lost in their own thoughts but comfortable with the other's company, and upon arriving at Circular Quay they sat at Marty's favoured café, where they ordered a pot of tea and two slices of chocolate cake.

'When Mick took off for the war,' he said, picking up the conversation from where they'd left it, 'I envied him like mad. I thought going to war was the most exciting thing a bloke could do. Heck, you get to travel to France and see Paris, the Eiffel Tower and all that.' He laughed. 'Do you know, I actually told him he had to eat snails and frogs' legs so he could tell me what they were like – how naive is that!'

Em thought it sounded quite reasonable herself. 'If I was going to France I'd want to try snails and frogs' legs,' she said.

He laughed again, but he was laughing at himself, not her. 'You wouldn't when you're fighting a war, believe me.'

The sparkling waters of Sydney Harbour and the busy to-ing and fro-ing of ferries presented as colourful a picture as ever, but Em wasn't paying the surrounds her customary attention. She was too busy studying Marty, who she decided was not overly serious at all. He had a distinct sense of humour, it was just that he didn't show off the way she did.

The tray with the pot of tea arrived and she played mother while Marty continued.

'That was nearly two years ago,' he went on, 'and Mick still thinks I'm naive. He calls me a romantic and worries constantly that I'm going to lie about my age and sign up. He's forever nagging Dad and Uncle Rube not to let me.'

It was Em's turn for a name from the past to register, and it did, with astounding impact.

'Uncle Rube,' she said, and everything suddenly fell into place. *Carlovsky & Reubens*, she thought, *of course!*

She'd never known their surnames. Had anybody? 'Your dad and your uncle are Carlo and Rube!' she exclaimed.

'That's right.' He had no idea why she appeared so excited. 'They used to trade under that name years ago.'

'And they formed a partnership with the Worthing Brothers.'

'Did they? I never went on any of their tours as a kid – I always stayed home with Mum – but I think you may be right.'

'I *know* I'm right,' Em declared emphatically, plonking down the teapot. '*The Big Show Bonanza of Fabulous Favourites.* It was 1906, I was five years old and I was *in* that show.' She painted a billboard in the air. '*Introducing the Talents of Baby Worthing on the Highwire,*' she announced. 'Actually I just stood on Dad's shoulders,' she admitted, 'but you know how audiences adore little kids – do a handstand and they'll think you're a star. Milk?' she asked, jug instantly poised.

'Yes. Thanks.'

'I remember your Uncle Rube,' she said, passing him his cup of tea and pushing the sugar his way. 'I used to call him Uncle Rube too, he was a lovely man.'

'Still is.'

'And I remember your dad. He was Master of Ceremonies in the *Fabulous Favourites* and gosh, he was a wonderful showman.'

'Yes, he doesn't perform any more these days, doesn't seem interested. I think he's too worried about Mick and the war, to be honest.'

Their chocolate cake arrived, two overly large slices on delicate plates that appeared far too small.

'Told you they're generous portions,' he said, picking up his cake fork.

As they dug into their cake, Emma agreeing it was delicious, they discussed the situation. Or rather Emma did.

'Your dad and your uncle don't trade under the name Carlo and Rube any more,' she said, a statement as much as a question.

'Nope.'

'Do you know why?'

'Nope.'

She toyed thoughtfully with her cake, pushing the slice around on its pretty little plate. 'It was straight after the *Fabulous Favourites* that the partnership split up, you know.'

His mouth full of chocolate cake, he just looked a query.

'Something happened in that production,' she said. 'There was some terrible disagreement that caused a rift between Carlo and Rube and the Worthings. Or at least between my uncle and your dad,' she added, 'because it does seem to have become a personal vendetta, doesn't it?'

'Mm hmm.' Having taken a further mouthful, he mumbled agreement.

'I wonder what it was to have become so bitter,' she mused, 'so all-consuming that it's virtually an obsession. To Uncle Will, anyway. And you said it's more or less that way with your dad too, didn't you?'

He nodded, chewed further and swallowed.

'I wonder what it could be, Marty.'

'Are you going to eat that, or are you just going to play with it?'

'Oh.' She looked down at the cake. 'Oh, I'm sorry.'

'No need to be sorry, but if you don't want it, I'll have it.'

'No, you won't. It's delicious, you're not getting one mouthful.' And she attacked the cake with relish.

They finished their cake and their pot of tea, and before they left it was Marty who had the final word on the subject.

'I don't think it matters what happened between our families, Emma,' he said.

'You're a Worthing and I'm a Carlovsky, and according to them the two don't mix. But we're not them, are we?'

'No, we're not.'

'We must do this again some time, what do you say?'

'I say yes,' she returned his smile, 'and sometime soon.'

As they walked back up the hill, they made plans for their next meeting. He would put aside a seat for her at this Wednesday's matinee, he said.

'It's a good *Widow*, I think you'll like it.'

'And when we open next week,' she said, 'I'll have a seat put aside for you at *The Shrew*. We can compare notes.'

'Excellent,' he agreed, 'and we'll meet up afterwards for tea and cake and endless discussion.'

'What names will we use?'

He looked blank.

'To book the seats,' she said. 'We can hardly put them aside for a Worthing and a Carlovsky, can we?'

'Ah. Yes. Just first names then. Emma and Marty?'

'I'm not sure. Even that could be risky. I'll be Charlotte.'

He raised a querying eyebrow.

'Charlotte Brontë, she's my favourite author.'

Marty grinned happily; what a lot they had to talk about. 'I'll be Anthony,' he said. 'Anthony Trollope's mine.'

Over the weeks that followed, Charlotte and Anthony became regular pseudonyms, sometimes shared jokingly, but on occasions they even left messages for one another at their respective theatres.

Until one day, right out of the blue . . .

'Who is this Anthony?' Gertie asked. 'When are you going to introduce him to us?'

'Oh, he's no one important, Ma, just a boy I met in a café. We sometimes get together for a cup of tea, that's all.'

But Emma's attempt to shrug things off didn't work; Gertie was eyeing her shrewdly.

'You're not getting involved with someone you shouldn't, are you, my girl?' she asked. 'You're only fifteen, and that's far too young for any sort of hanky-panky.'

Emma felt herself flush. 'Don't be silly, Ma, it's nothing like that at all.'

'Then bring him around to the hotel some time so we can say hello, lovey, that's all I ask.'

Em and Marty stopped leaving messages for each other after that, arranging instead to meet on Sundays, a different time and place each week.

But Gertie remained suspicious. Where did her daughter go every Sunday? She voiced her concerns to her husband.

'I don't mind her having a young fella, Max,' she said, 'but why won't she introduce us to this Anthony boy, eh?'

'I dunno, love.'

'I'll tell you why. Because he's not a young fella at all, that's why. He's some dirty old geezer who's after a pretty young thing like our Em.'

'Really? You reckon?' Max was horrified.

'Yes, I do,' Gertie said firmly, having persuaded herself this must be the case. 'She meets up with him on Sundays, God knows where. I only hope they're not doing it already, she's miles too young for that sort of thing.' Gertie tended to forget she herself had married at seventeen.

'Right.' Max took instant action. 'You just leave this to me, love. I'll follow her on Sunday, and if this bloke's up to no good I'll knock his block off.'

When he came home the following Sunday and confronted his wife, he could barely stop laughing.

'Well, the bloke's sure as hell no dirty old geezer, love, and they're sure as hell not doing it.'

'Yeah? Go on.'

'Anthony's a really nice-looking boy, just a kid, can't be more than a year or so older than Em, two at the most.'

'You didn't *meet* him, did you?'

'No, no, I just followed them like I said I would. Didn't want to intrude – it wouldn't have felt right, her knowing I'd been spying on her like that.'

'And?'

'They met in the park and they walked, and they sat on a bench and they talked. Then they went to a café and had a pot of tea and talked some more. They didn't *stop* talking, that's all they did.'

'I wonder why she doesn't want us to meet him then.' Gertie was mystified.

'No idea, but it's her private business,' Max said firmly. 'Not up to us to interfere, Gert love.'

Early the following year, when the three-month Sydney run of *The Taming of the Shrew* came to a close, the company was to return to Melbourne for a further season at the Princess Theatre.

Coincidentally, only one month after that, in March 1917, *Carlovsky & Reubens' Grand Gala Variety Spectacular* was to open the first leg of its national tour at Her Majesty's Theatre in Melbourne.

'So I'll see you in a month then, Charlotte,' Marty said jokingly. He was trying to sound casual, but not quite succeeding so decided to give up. 'Just four short weeks, Em,' he admitted. 'Frankly I can't wait.'

'Me neither.' Em too was prepared to be honest. 'I'm glad your dad's given you the tour manager job.'

'Yep. He was over the moon when I asked him.'

Carlo had been delighted when his seventeen-year-old son had professed interest in managing the interstate tour.

'I'm not too young, Dad,' Marty had said, hopefully quelling the one argument his father might present. 'I've had a lot of experience and I know all the ropes now.'

''Course you do, son, 'course you do.' Carlo had been thrilled his youngest son was now devoted to the family business; he hadn't realised Marty had become so passionate about the theatre. And besides, the tour would distract the boy from any desire to go to war; it was an excellent idea all round. 'You're not too young at all.'

'I'll miss you, Emma.'

They were seated on a bench in Hyde Park, the bench they had often favoured over the past several months.

'I'll miss you too, Marty,' she said.

And they kissed, for the very first time.

18

OF LOVE AND WAR

The battlefields of France had rapidly become a blur to
Bertie. Place names rang indistinctly in his mind and the
battles themselves all merged into one blood-red image.
But he was a hardened soldier now. Focused upon the job
at hand, he barely even heard the din that surrounded him,
and he no longer screamed as he ran. His mind remained
empty to all but the mantra 'kill or be killed'.

It was only after the mayhem that the sounds returned,
the relentless rat-tat-tat of machine guns, the explosions
of heavy artillery, the cries of the wounded and dying.
And the sights too, the mutilated bodies and the blood. So
much blood . . .

That was when Elise came to him. He would feel the
touch of her skin, he would see the look in her eyes, and
he would hear her parting words: *Be safe, Albert. Be safe,
my young soldier from Australia.* And he *was* safe, wasn't
he? He wasn't one of those bloodied corpses strewn about
so obscenely in the mud, so carelessly, so indecently,
like rotting garbage awaiting collection. She'd saved him
once again. And she was saving him right now, from the
thoughts that drove men mad.

In his letters home he continued to mention his guardian
angel, knowing that it made his mother happy. And it did.
Gertie had come to believe quite firmly that her son had
some form of angel protecting him.

Hey Ma, you'll be happy to know I'm still being looked after, he wrote. *My guardian angel's doing her job, just the way you ordered. Came out of the last scrape with flying colours. In fact, I'm no longer an ordinary private, but an NCO (that's non-commissioned officer, for the edification of you ignorant lot back home). Only a corporal but it's a step up the ladder. I got promoted in the field at Bullecourt. At least, I think it was Bullecourt – I get the names of a lot of these places mixed up, I think quite a few of us do. But a promotion, not bad, eh?*

He wouldn't tell them that being promoted 'in the field' meant they were running out of officers during battle. Nor would he tell them that NCOs tended to cop it more than the general troops.

Good news about Sarah and Harry's baby, and fancy them calling him Max. That'll please you no end, won't it, Dad? Glad to hear Izzie and Ambrose have set a date too. A mid-July wedding in Melbourne sounds a bit on the cold side to me, but I'm supposing it's a choice that fits in with production schedules.

Knowing that his letter would do the rounds, Bertie invariably addressed individual members of the family.

I must say, Izz, I'm rather glad you didn't end up with Hal. Nice bloke, don't get me wrong, but he never really fitted in, did he? We probably scared him off right from the start insisting he be a Hal when he'd always been a Henry. We're a bossy bunch, we Worthings, and probably difficult to take for those not in show business. Of course Ambrose is quite safe; being a musician he's one of us. But you, Harry old mate, presuming you read this letter as I'm sure you will, in my opinion you have the patience of a saint.

As usual, he finished off with the same request.

So what's next now The Shrew's about to close? I want you to give me every bit of theatre news you can lay your hands on. And that includes you, Em, you've been a bit slack with your letters of late. The boys over here just eat up the gossip – they say it's better than anything you could get in a magazine or the papers because it's the real thing. I reckon I must be the most popular bloke in the whole battalion.

Cheers for now and love to you all,
Bertie

Em replied immediately. Her brother's reprimand, mild though it had been, made her feel guilty. She had been distracted of late certainly, but that was no excuse for not writing to Bertie.

Yes, I've been most remiss, Bertie, she wrote, *and I do apologise, but I'll make up for my slackness with as much theatre news as possible so you can share it with your mates.*

I'm happy to report the business has picked up hugely over this past year, just like Uncle Will swore it would. Actually, there was an article in the newspaper the other day that said, and I quote, 'people are turning to the theatre as a means of escaping the harsh realities of the war'. Uncle Will read it out loud to us all in that 'told-you-so' way of his. You could have sworn he'd written the article himself. Who knows? Maybe he did.

By the way, I agree with you about Harry having the patience of a saint. I mean, without Hal around he could have gone back to being a Henry, couldn't he? But he accepts the fact he was made a Harry by us Worthings and is content to stay that way. And although he has no real interest in show business himself, he's quite happy for Sarah to continue her career when baby Maxie's a bit older, which is further proof of his sainthood. I think he's an exceptionally nice brother-in-law, and I agree with Ma that it's very handy to have a lawyer in the family.

Now, on with the theatre news. Unbelievable though it may sound, we've just started rehearsals for 'King Lear'.

Yes, yes, I can hear you say it, 'but I thought you were sticking to comedies,' and yes, yes, we were. But you see, this is the change that's come about of late – it seems comedy has done the rounds for long enough and audiences are now prepared to embrace drama. According to Uncle Will, anyway.

'People no longer need to be fed frippery,' he says, 'they crave escape to another world altogether, and "Lear" is a big canvas, the biggest of them all ... Shakespeare's masterpiece ...'

And then he goes on and on as you can well imagine. Personally, I think it's because he's been longing to play Lear for years and now believes he's the right age. This is not altogether a bad thing, I must say, because that means he's leaving the Romeos and Hamlets to our Ted, as I believe he should. Petruchio and the other comedy leads he can get away with, indeed he's magnificent, but Romeo and the Dane belong to a younger actor. At least, that's my opinion and I'm sticking to it.

Now, Ma says you'll want to know the rest of the casting, so here's the other bit she reckons will give you a laugh. She said to tell your mates (just in case they don't know, which between you and me I think is quite likely) that Goneril, Regan and Cordelia are King Lear's daughters. Well, Ma's been cast as Goneril, and Millie Hampton as Regan, which means she's once again playing sister to an actress half her age while at the same time playing daughter to her own brother-in-law. Ma finds all this hilarious, of course, as Ma always does, but to the rest of us it seems absolutely fine, because up onstage where you can't see any wrinkles she still looks twenty-five.

And just guess who's playing youngest daughter Cordelia? Yep, yours truly. And can you guess why? Yep, I bet you got that part too, but it'll be something to share with your mates. Because I'm the lightest, that's why – I weigh even less than Ma and she's still tiny. I bet your mates don't know that just about every Lear tests the weight of his Cordelia. This is for when he has to carry her on in his arms, stone cold dead, at the very end of the play. I'd actually be willing to bet most Lears would prefer a skinny bad actress to a fat brilliant one. Which is sort of understandable, isn't it? I mean, it's an exhausting role to start with – the poor bloke shouldn't have to lug around a barrel of lard after all that hard slog, should he?

The 'Lear' production's pretty much a family affair, like 'The Shrew'. Pa's playing Gloucester and Ted's playing Edgar, so that's a nice piece of real-life father and son casting, the sort of thing the average punter just loves to read about, so we make it very clear in the programme.

We open here in June – a three-month season at the Theatre Royal and then off on a tour of the major capital cities. It'll take us well into next year, so let's hope Uncle Will's right and that audiences are now happy to embrace drama as well as comedy. I don't fancy the idea of spending the first half of 1918 playing to empty houses all over the country – I ask you, what could possibly be worse?

That's just me trying to be funny, as I'm sure you realise, Bertie. I can't imagine what you must be going through over there. I'm aware you spare us detail so as not to worry us, but I know things are terrible for our young men at war, and I do feel for you, really I do.

I'm sorry I haven't written more often lately, it's unforgivable of me, and it won't happen again. But I can promise any lapse on my part doesn't mean you've been out of my thoughts. Far from it. I talk of you and think of you more than you could possibly imagine, and like Ma I pray your guardian angel will send you home safely to us.

My love to you always, dearest Bertie,
Em

Emma *did* think and talk of her brother a great deal. And she *did* know that things were terrible for the young Australian soldiers in France. She probably knew far more than the average girl her age, for she and Marty constantly spoke about the war, and also about the letters they received from their respective brothers.

Marty had arrived in Melbourne with the *Gala Variety Spectacular* in mid-March, just a month and a half after Em's sixteenth birthday. The company had booked him into the Grand Hotel in Spring Street, aptly named for it was one of the grandest hotels in the whole of Australia. 'Only the best for our new tour director,' Carlo had boasted, although it had been Rube who had made all the tour arrangements, as Rube always did.

'The Grand is commensurate with your rank, Marty,' Rube had said when Marty had queried the choice. 'Out on the road you're the boss, and the company needs to be aware of that.'

'But Wallace isn't booked into the Grand,' Marty had argued, 'won't he be offended?' Wallace was to be his assistant, an older and highly experienced man who would prove invaluable on tour.

'Not in the least,' Rube replied smoothly. 'Wal prefers more modest accommodation, always has.'

'To be honest, Uncle Rube, I think I might too.'

Rube could understand the boy's reasoning; Marty wasn't anything like his father, who always demanded the finest, but due to his youth it was necessary to create a sense of hierarchy. To start with anyway.

'You're the new Carlovsky at the helm, Marty,' he went on to explain. 'Once the cast and crew have adjusted to your leadership you can stay wherever you like, but for now I suggest we stick to the Grand. Is that all right with you, mate?'

'Sure.' Marty rightly sensed this was part of the test that had been set for him. He needed to prove himself capable. He even sensed that Wal was being sent along as backup in case he didn't, all of which he considered quite fair. 'Sure, Uncle Rube,' he said, 'of course it's all right.'

The day after his arrival Marty had left a note for Em at the Theatre Royal box office, signing it Anthony, but this time in a sealed envelope to avoid any awkward questions.

They'd met that first Sunday at his suggestion on the steps of Parliament House, which was just up from the Grand on the opposite side of the street. *Because that way I can't get lost*, he'd said in his note. Marty wasn't familiar with the layout of Melbourne.

'I've missed you,' he said.

'I've missed you too.'

They didn't embrace. The steps of Parliament House being such a public place, they walked up to Fitzroy Gardens instead. And there among the trees and the leafy laneways that meandered through the park, they kissed. For the second time.

Then they wandered hand in hand along the paths, talking animatedly, not noticing the beauty of their surrounds, eyes only for one another. To passers-by they presented a pretty picture, two young lovers clearly besotted.

But they weren't lovers. Not yet.

During the weeks and then months that followed they would meet on Sundays as they had in Sydney, and they would walk through Melbourne's parks or, hunched over pots of tea in obscure cafés well away from the popular haunts of theatre folk, they would talk. They would talk about everything; their respective childhoods, their brothers, the war, the world in general and everything in between. The books they'd read, their views on life, and of course they talked about the theatre.

'No wonder the critics hail him as "the great Will Worthing",' Marty said on this particular Wednesday late afternoon. 'His Lear's nothing short of spectacular. I cried at the end of the play, Em, I actually *cried*. I *never* cry in the theatre.' Marty was genuinely overwhelmed. 'By golly, he deserved that standing ovation.'

'Yes, he gets a standing ovation after every single show, even a mid-week matinee like today. You should just see them on a Saturday night – they go wild.'

'I can understand why.'

'It's a bravura performance all right,' Emma agreed. 'Uncle Will's always been impressive, but he's really made Lear his own. He's been wanting to play the role for years, only he said he was too young . . .' She went on to proclaim in her best Will Worthing impersonation, '"To play Lear, it is essential one has a wealth of life experience! One must be at least fifty years old, preferably sixty . . ."' Then she dropped the act. 'He's just about to turn fifty-nine, so he obviously qualifies.'

The two of them were huddled together over a pot of green tea and a plate of dumplings at their favourite eatery in the old area of Chinatown, which had been established during the early gold rush days. Nestled downstairs in a laneway that led off Little Bourke Street, the restaurant was tiny and seemed to cater exclusively to its local community of Chinese, which very much suited Marty and Emma. As Caucasians, they'd received the occasional look of surprise initially, but the locals now accepted their presence and paid them no attention at all.

'You're not a bad Cordelia either, Em,' he said admiringly. 'In fact, you're very, very good.'

'I'm a convenient Cordelia,' she replied.

'Convenient, how so?'

'To quote Ma, "I don't weigh no more than a feather, lovey",' she said with the accent Gertie lapsed into when she forgot her Ps and Qs, or more importantly when she intended to make a point.

Marty smiled as Em went on to explain the all-important factor of Cordelia's weight. He loved the way she performed at the drop of a hat, and he loved the way she talked about the theatre and her family and, most particularly, about her mother. He loved everything about Emma.

'Better a skinny, appalling Cordelia than a fat, oh-so-brilliant one,' she declared with theatrical flair, and he laughed out loud.

The production of *King Lear* had opened just the previous week and Em had left a ticket for him at the box office for the first mid-week matinee.

'I'll have it put aside in the name of Rochester,' she'd told him on Sunday. 'I've decided Anthony's surname must be Rochester.'

'Don't tell me,' he'd said, instantly meeting the challenge, '*Jane Eyre*, am I right?'

'Of course,' she'd replied, 'my absolute favourite of Charlotte's.'

They ordered another pot of green tea and another plate of prawn dumplings as they continued to discuss the production, Marty praising the staging and the lighting and above all the brilliant storm effects.

'So real,' he said, 'frighteningly effective.'

'All due to Aunt Mabel,' Em replied with a nod. 'Aunt Mabel's a genius, the best in the business.'

They were very much enjoying this mid-week treat, their meetings normally being reserved for Sundays, theatre's one day off. Marty devoted the rest of his days to his duties as tour manager; keeping the books, looking after the show's takings, checking on advance bookings and publicity, travel and accommodation arrangements: the list was endless. He was determined to prove himself capable in the position. And he was succeeding. The *Gala Variety*

Spectacular was running like clockwork, the reviews had been excellent, and the Melbourne bookings far exceeded those of the Sydney season. The *type* of audiences seemed different too, or they did to Marty.

'What is it, Wal?' he'd queried. 'Melburnians seem so eager to embrace the theatre – they don't sit back in judgement the way Sydneysiders do, waiting for the performers to prove themselves before they show any appreciation.'

'Melbourne's always been a theatre town, Marty,' had been Wal's laconic reply. 'Always has been, always will be.'

Wallace Stanley was a likeable, laid-back fellow in his early forties and the two got on immensely well. If there was any piece of advice Wal thought the youngster might need, he offered it in a helpful 'matey' way, and he appreciated the manner in which it was accepted. He'd been only too pleased to discover the kid wasn't the bratty son of the boss he'd feared he might be, but a nice young bloke, bloody intelligent and eager to learn.

As a result, Wal had been happy to oblige when Marty had asked him to take over for the mid-week matinee while he checked out the opposition.

'Sure, boss,' Wal had said. 'Which particular opposition do you intend to check out?'

'I'm booked into a matinee at the Theatre Royal.' Marty saw no reason to lie. 'The Worthing Brothers production of *King Lear*.'

'Ah,' a droll raise of eyebrows, 'the Worthing Brothers. Better not tell your dad that, eh?'

'I reckon you're right.' Wal's reaction intrigued Marty. 'There's no love lost between Dad and Will Worthing, is there?'

'That's putting it mildly.'

'Do you know why exactly?'

Wal was now intrigued by Marty's reaction. *So the kid doesn't know? His father hasn't told him? Although hardly surprising*, he supposed. *You wouldn't want your kid to know you'd betrayed your partners and broken the cardinal rule of the theatre, would you?*

It had been over ten years ago now, but Wal clearly remembered the article in the *Sydney Morning Herald* exposing Carlo as the traitor who'd revealed the Worthing illusionist was twins. Unforgivable, of course. Killing a prize act like that. But if Michael Carlovsky wasn't prepared to share this information with his son then it was hardly his place to do so, was it? Besides, he liked Carlo.

'Don't know the specifics, Marty,' he said evasively, 'but it caused a right royal bust-up of the partnership your father had with the Worthings. So much so that your dad was blacklisted for years afterwards. No one would work with Carlo and Rube. That's why they changed the name of their production company. I suppose your dad blames Will Worthing for that.'

Blacklisted, Marty thought. That would certainly be reason enough for his father to detest Will Worthing. But why would Will Worthing set out to destroy his father? Marty remained at a loss. And when he told Emma of his latest findings, so did she.

'No idea,' she said. 'Whenever I ask, the whole family clams up on me. But you know what, Marty? I don't care any more. I really don't.'

Marty decided he didn't, either.

'I find it amazing,' he now said as they dived into the fresh plate of dumplings, 'that even in these dark times audiences are prepared to embrace a tragedy like *Lear*. Dad and Rube have been carefully sticking to comedies and musicals, given the war and all that.'

'So did we, but Uncle Will predicted the punters would want something meatier after a while,' Emma said. 'I didn't believe him at the time; I thought it was wishful thinking on his part because he so wanted to play the role. But he was right. Here in Melbourne anyway. It'll be interesting to see how keen they are in the other states.'

'Yes,' Marty agreed, 'Melbourne audiences certainly seem more receptive than most. I've discovered that recently.'

'Aunt Mabel says the bookings in Adelaide and Perth are well above her expectations though,' Em went on as she poured them both another cup, 'so word's obviously got out.'

'With the reviews you've had so far, I'm not surprised. It's wonderful advance publicity, Em, they'll be queuing up for blocks by the time you get there.'

Even as he said the words, Marty realised how much he was speaking her language. And also how much he cared. Not only for Emma, but also for her world. He'd come to love show business. He hadn't been sure before – working for his father's company had seemed just a 'job' – but being with Emma had changed his life. Her world had become his, he realised. As Em herself was wont to say, he'd become 'a creature of the theatre'.

They hadn't noticed the passing of time in the dim little downstairs eatery, but when they realised it was approaching seven o'clock, they hastily settled the account – Em insisting on paying her half as she always did – and left. They must return to their respective theatres for the evening performance.

Emerging into the narrow laneway above, they were hit by the wintry night. A chill wind whistled through the gloomy backstreets of Chinatown, but they barely noticed as they held each other close. Every single parting ended in a kiss, and every single kiss became more fervent.

'I love you, Emma,' he said.

'And I love you, Marty,' she replied.

These days every parting ended with the same whispered vow, and every parting was fraught with a passion they both recognised.

Pulling their heavy winter coats and scarves tightly about them, they headed off in their separate directions.

It was early spring and the *Gala Variety Spectacular* was nearing the end of its Melbourne run. Only three weeks to go. Emma was feeling desperate.

'It's time we made love,' she said. As always, Em was direct.

They were in Alexandra Gardens, another favourite Sunday walk of theirs, setting out from the city, over the Princes Bridge and along the banks of the Yarra.

'Are you sure?'

Her words had shocked him, and he drew away from their embrace to study her closely. Much as they recognised the passionate nature of their kisses, he'd taken care to avoid any overtly sexual move. He needed to be certain.

'Are you *really* sure?'

'Of course I am,' she said brusquely. 'And you know I'm right, so stop trying to protect me.'

'Why would I *not* protect you, Emma,' he said, 'I love you . . .'

'And I love you,' she said, the desperation in her voice now obvious. 'We know we love each other, Marty, and we're running out of time – you leave in three weeks.'

She kissed him fiercely and he responded with the same urgency. She was right, they both knew it was time.

'How do we go about this then?' he said several minutes later, as they sat on a bench looking out over the Yarra. 'How do we smuggle you into the Grand?'

Now that the decision had been made, Emma was far more relaxed. She was even prepared to enjoy the test that lay ahead.

'We could disguise me as a youth,' she said, 'so wonderfully Shakespearean. I could be an old college friend visiting from interstate who's popped into the Grand to say hello.'

He looked at her quizzically. Pretty little Em with her blonde hair and blue eyes? A youth?

'We whack a moustache on me, hair up in some sort of hat,' she replied. 'It always worked for the Bard.'

'Very funny,' he replied, wondering whether perhaps she might actually be serious; it was sometimes difficult to tell with Em.

'Or I could pose as the daughter of a hugely important politician,' she suggested, 'that would impress them at reception.'

His look this time was one of bemusement.

'Parliament House over the road,' she explained, 'the federal government meets there regularly. Bigwig politicians arrive from all over the country and they invariably stay at the Grand. I could be the daughter or the niece of a member of parliament.'

'And where would that get us?' He remained puzzled.

'I'd just tell the receptionist I wanted to pop upstairs and see Uncle What's-his-name,' she said airily.

'In which case we'd have to have a name for Uncle What's-his-name, he'd have to be real and he'd have to be booked in at the Grand.'

'Oh.' Emma realised she hadn't thought the scenario through properly. 'Yes, I suppose you're right.'

'Why don't we keep things simple?' he suggested. 'Why don't you pose as my sister?'

'We don't look at all alike,' she said, studying him critically.

'Many siblings don't.'

'All right,' she agreed with reluctance, disappointed they hadn't decided upon something more exciting, particularly the 'youth'; she'd have enjoyed that role. 'I suppose it's better to be practical.'

'Yes. I think it is. So when do we enact this charade?'

'Now,' she said, 'we enact it right now.' And she stood.

He rose to his feet, and as they kissed he didn't ask her once again if she was sure. The game playing was over; they were now in earnest.

As they walked back to the Grand, they discussed their plan of action. Or rather Emma did. They would not enter together, she said; that would look suspect, and anyway, if they did, how would people know they were brother and sister? He was to collect his key at the front desk, tell the hotel manager he was expecting his sister Charlotte and that he wished to be informed of her arrival, after which he was to go up to his room. She would arrive a good half an hour or more later, and he would be summoned to the lobby, where she would be waiting.

'What happens then?' he asked.

'Then the performance begins,' she said, as if the whole process was extremely simple, which to Em it was. 'Don't worry, Marty,' she added, aware of his uncertainty, 'take your lead from me. We just have to be bold, that's all.'

They were walking up Collins Street now, and a block or so before they reached Spring Street she halted outside a small café.

'I'm going to have a pot of tea,' she said. 'I'll see you within the hour.' And she disappeared inside, leaving him standing in the street.

He walked on alone, visited now by a sense of uneasiness. She appeared so sure of herself, but did she really know what she was doing? Did she really want to surrender her virginity to him, or was she surrendering herself to some romantic illusion? Emma was very theatrical after all. But then she was also very practical.

Marty was confused. He was not a virgin himself, having experienced a torrid exchange the previous year with a chorus girl nearly twice his age in a dressing room at the Colosseum. It had been a coupling about which his father had been most congratulatory.

'You're a man now, son,' Carlo had said with pride, 'well done.' Then he'd added unashamedly in true giveaway fashion, 'At seventeen it's high time a fellow lost his virginity.'

Marty had suspected, and rightly so, that his father had paid the woman to seduce him; she'd certainly been experienced and had tutored a raw beginner well.

Now as he entered the main lobby of the Grand, he was starting to feel insecure. He loved Em with all his heart and the mere thought she might later regret her actions worried him.

He crossed to the reception desk and collected his key.

'I'm expecting my sister Charlotte within the hour,' he said to the hotel manager. 'Will you inform me when she arrives, please.'

'Of course, Mr Carlovsky.'

And he went upstairs to nurse his doubts.

Inside the little café, Em was feeling no insecurity, no doubt whatsoever. She knew exactly what she was doing.

She had a cup of tea, left the remainder in the pot and departed the café half an hour later.

When she arrived at the Grand she paid a brief visit to the ladies' room in the lobby, after which she strode confidently up to the reception desk.

'I'm Charlotte Carlovsky,' she said, 'I believe my brother is expecting me.'

'He is indeed, Miss Carlovsky, do please take a seat.'

The hotel manager, a dapper man of around fifty, tapped the bell on his desk with the flat of his hand, and in only seconds a bellboy appeared from nowhere.

'Inform Mr Carlovsky, room 207, that his sister has arrived,' he said briskly.

Setting her handbag on her lap, Emma positioned herself primly on one of the plush sofas in clear view of the magnificent main staircase down which Marty would descend, and she watched as the be-capped bellboy trotted up those same stairs.

Barely three minutes later, Marty appeared.

He saw her instantly from the top of the stairs.

Oh my God, he thought, *how are we going to play this?* and he started down towards her.

She rose to meet him, her arms outstretched, her smile exuding a wealth of joy and affection.

'Dearest brother,' she called, crossing to the stairs, and as he reached the bottom she embraced him. 'Oh Marty,' she said, 'it's wonderful to see you.' She kissed him cheek to cheek, either side, three times, European style. 'I've missed you so.'

'It's lovely to see you too, Charlotte,' he said with surprising ease. *What now?* he wondered.

She linked her arm through his, guiding him effortlessly about the lobby.

'Isn't this the most *marvellous* hotel,' she enthused, running her fingers lightly over the magnificent pieces of furniture, gesturing expansively all about them at the abundant floral decorations and plants in their fine vases and pots ... up at the ornate ceiling ... down at the floor ... and all the time not once drawing breath. 'The design,' she went on, 'the architecture, the furnishings, the art works, and oh Marty, the facade!' She stopped, gripping his arm in breathless wonder. 'The view from the street! Those twin towers, sheer magnificence! I'd heard the hotel was wonderful, but I was quite overwhelmed by the sight. We don't have anything nearly as grand as the Grand in Sydney, you have to admit.'

Marty wanted to burst out laughing. Surely she was going too far. But in his peripheral vision he could see the manager paying attention while pretending not to, and he could tell the man was personally delighting in the compliments, particularly as others in the lobby were looking around appreciatively admiring the hotel's beauty.

'Yes,' he agreed, 'it's a very beautiful hotel.'

'How sweet of Father to book you in here for the whole Melbourne season,' she went on. 'Poor me, I've been relegated to Aunt Sybil and the cousins in Toorak for my three-week visit. It's all quite frightful. Why couldn't he book me in here with you?'

'I'm sure he's just being protective, Charlotte, you know how he is.'

'What's your room like? Is it divine? I'm madly jealous. You must show me, this very minute.'

He allowed himself to be gently steered towards the main staircase.

'Of course, come on up.'

'Aunt Sybil sends her love by the way, and so do all the little cousins,' she continued, as they sailed arm in arm up the stairs. 'Oh my goodness, those children are absolute monsters.'

'Are they really? Still? I thought they might have mellowed by now.'

'Not in the least. Spoilt, you see. You and I were never like that. Aunt Sybil should have taken a leaf out of Father's book.'

She prattled on all the way up the stairs to the landing, and up the next flight of stairs also, despite the fact they were by then well out of sight of the lobby.

Marty had no problem fielding the questions she fired at him as they went. Yes, the show was going wonderfully, he said, and yes, Father would indeed be proud of him in his new position as tour director, and yes, he'd be happy to arrange seats for her to Saturday's matinee, although surely she'd be bored having seen the production so many times in Sydney . . .

The hotel manager, whose name was Francis, watched them disappear from sight, and as their voices faded into the distance he wondered whether they really were brother and sister. He rather doubted it himself, and personally he didn't care. Young Mr Carlovsky was an impressive fellow, a successful entrepreneur no less, and the girl was obviously a young woman of breeding.

As long as decorum was maintained, Francis never intruded upon a guest's privacy; it would be such poor form to do so. But the pair fascinated him nonetheless. If they weren't brother and sister, then it was a fine performance.

'You were very good, Marty,' she said as he closed the door behind them, 'you could have been an actor.'

He laughed, surprised to discover that he'd actually enjoyed the performance. 'You made it pretty easy for me, Em.'

'Oh, just look at this room. Isn't it glorious? I meant every word I said down there by the way, this really is a magnificent hotel.' She tossed her handbag on a chair and crossed to the window, which looked out over Spring Street. 'And what a wonderful view.'

Marty's doubts returned in an instant. She was still making small talk, he realised, and at such a rapid pace. Was it a sign she was nervous or having second thoughts?

She sat on the bed, testing it with a girlish bounce. 'A nice, comfy bed too,' she said teasingly.

Yes, he thought, *she's nervous*. He sat beside her, taking her hand in his.

'Emma,' he said gently, 'we don't have to do this. If it doesn't feel right . . .'

'Of course it feels right,' she insisted, still playfully. 'You're not getting out of it you know, I simply won't let you.'

'But you're nervous, I can tell, and —'

She interrupted him. 'I'm not nervous, Marty,' she said, 'I'm excited.'

'But are you sure, Em? Are you *really* sure?'

'Of course I'm sure!' She sounded exasperated now. 'I've been sure for months! Do you know, I've been sitting in that wretched café for the past half-hour thinking, "Gallop apace, you fiery-footed steeds, towards Phoebus' lodging . . ." I can't *wait*, Marty, that's how sure I am.'

This isn't helping, Marty thought. In fact, she was just confirming his suspicions.

'But do you think that perhaps you might be romanticising things a bit? You know, the way you do?'

'What way is that?'

'Well, quoting Juliet for a start.'

'Why not? I feel just as strong a longing as Juliet did. And you're just as romantic as Romeo was.'

She rose and crossed to the washstand, where she gathered up the towel that sat beside the large bowl and water jug.

'We must be practical though,' she said, dropping the towel on the bed. Then she walked to the windows, drew the curtains closed and turned back to him. 'I'm sure, Marty,' she said, 'I'm absolutely sure.' She kicked off her shoes and, unfastening the buttons of her blouse, slipped it from her shoulders and let it fall to the floor. She wore no undergarment. She'd taken her camisole off in the ladies' room and stuffed it into her handbag. She'd had a feeling it may come to this, that his principles might perhaps get the better of him and that she may have to play the seductress.

She walked slowly towards him, undoing the waistband of her skirt and stepping out of it as it, too, dropped to the floor. She was naked now but for her panties. She'd considered removing those also, but had thought this might be a little too confronting for him. Marty was no doubt unaccustomed to the flagrant immodesty born of backstage quick changes and shared dressing rooms.

He stood, unable to drag his eyes from her she was so beautiful, and as she walked into his arms all doubt and insecurity faded to nothingness. Everything was as it should be. They were born to be lovers.

They kissed with a tenderness that quickly became erotic, and as they did she dropped her panties to the floor, then started undoing the buttons of his shirt. For a virgin, Emma was not lacking in confidence and Marty found himself instantly aroused.

But after they'd made love, he was horrified by the sight of the blood on the towel she'd laid out for them.

'Did I hurt you?' he asked. 'Was it painful?'

'Yes, a bit,' she admitted. 'I'd expected it would be though. Ma told me the first time usually is.'

'I'm sorry.' He was overwhelmed with guilt. He'd tried to be as gentle as he could and to go as slowly as he could, remembering his time in the dressing room and the dancer's advice. 'Slowly, sweetie,' the woman had said to him over and over, 'go slow . . . slow down now, there's a good boy . . . better for the girl that way . . . better for you too . . .' He'd tried his very best to adhere to the advice, but he was inexperienced, and he'd been so excited. He felt thoroughly wretched now. 'I'm so sorry, Em. I really am so sorry.'

But she laughed. Sitting up, she leant back against the bedstead and laughed out loud. 'Oh Marty, stop worrying, you didn't do anything wrong.' Her laughter subsided and she gazed at him fondly. 'You're a true innocent, aren't you,' she said.

'How do you mean?' He sat up too and they propped side by side.

'A girl's loss of virginity isn't meant to be comfortable. It's meant to hurt a bit and there's always blood.'

'Oh.' He hadn't known that. His sexual education had been sadly lacking, his father having simply thrust upon him a woman of experience. 'I was hoping it'd be a magical experience for you,' he said.

'The second time will be,' she replied, and there was a distinct promise in her eyes. 'The second time will be a magical experience for both of us. And the third time and every time after that too.'

She kissed him with infinite caring, and Marty thought it was impossible for anyone to be more in love than he was at that moment.

'I love you, Emma,' he whispered.

'I know,' she whispered back to him, 'isn't it wonderful?'

She nestled into him, naked skin on skin, and as she ran her fingers gently over his chest, he could already feel the fresh stirrings of arousal.

'Of the two of us, you're the true romantic, Marty, not me,' she said. 'You do realise that, don't you? I'm theatrical, yes, but I'm not really romantic. Romance is your domain.'

'And yet you think of us as Romeo and Juliet?' he queried with a touch of whimsy; the fact did seem a little contradictory.

'Of course I do,' she replied. Then she drew back and looked him squarely in the eyes. 'Because we are, aren't we? Young, forbidden lovers from two families at war?'

Was she serious? he wondered; once again it was hard to tell. And did it matter anyway? She was either unable to differentiate between fact and fiction, or else she simply didn't care. It appeared that to Em the real world and the theatre world had become enmeshed, and Marty decided that he liked things that way.

'Let's hope we don't come to the same sticky end,' he said.

'Oh no, we only choose the bits that suit us,' she replied, 'no tragic end for us.'

She snuggled back against him, and even as he delighted in the feel of her he couldn't help thinking how mercurial she was, such a tantalising mix of the romantic and the practical.

'Besides,' she added, 'there are the odd discrepancies. For a start I'm two years older than Juliet; she was only fourteen.'

He wondered how old Romeo was supposed to be. 'I'll be eighteen next week,' he said.

She knew he was aroused. As was she. They were ready now for the second time.

'Happy birthday,' she said, and rolling on her side, she parted her legs and guided him into her.

When they returned downstairs, they continued the sibling act for the benefit of anyone who might be watching, most specifically the hotel manager.

'Do you have time for a spot of lunch before returning to Aunt Sybil's?' Marty asked her.

'Absolutely,' she replied, taking his arm, 'I was hoping you'd suggest we dine. I'm starving.'

From the reception desk Francis watched the charade with amusement. *A long time to show your sister your room*, he thought. But even without the time element, their performances, although creditable, could not disguise the fact they were lovers. They were *so obviously* lovers, he wondered whether perhaps he should discreetly look away. But he didn't. Francis was not without his own talents as an actor and his nonchalance never deserted him.

'Thank you, Mr Carlovsky,' he said as Marty handed him the room key, 'have a pleasant afternoon,' and he nodded politely to Emma. 'Miss Carlovsky.'

'He knows,' Emma muttered as they walked out of the main doors and into Spring Street.

'Does he?' Marty asked. 'Oh hell, what will we do?'

'Nothing at all,' she boldly replied. 'He's happy to play the game, and so am I. So long as he doesn't find out who I am.'

The following Wednesday, they returned to the hotel in the late afternoon during the break between matinee and evening show. And they returned once again the next Sunday, when they spent a whole blissful two hours together. On both occasions the exchange between Emma and the hotel manager was conducted with the utmost courtesy.

He greeted her with a 'Good afternoon, Miss Carlovsky' on the Wednesday, and a 'Good morning, Miss Carlovsky' on the Sunday, and each time she smiled charmingly back at him. 'Good afternoon,' and 'good morning,' she replied. But they both acknowledged the understanding that passed between them.

Unbeknownst to Emma, however, the hotel manager *had* found out who she was. Not deliberately. Francis went to the theatre a great deal and he was particularly fond of the classics. Upon attending the Tuesday night performance of *King Lear*, he'd recognised Cordelia immediately. *Miss Carlovsky*, he'd thought. And then upon consulting the programme, he'd discovered her to be none other than Emma Worthing, the youngest daughter of the Worthing family.

That certainly explained how her sibling performance had been so accomplished, he'd thought; she was a marvellous Cordelia.

Francis, who was an admirer of talent, had no intention of exposing the girl's identity or admitting to his knowledge of it. Why should he? Young Mr Carlovsky and Emma Worthing both had a profile in the theatre. They were deeply in love and no doubt conducting their affair in clandestine fashion to avoid the attention of the press. Their secret was quite safe with him.

'Oh Marty, I'll miss you so.' She clung to him on this, their last Sunday.

The *Gala Variety Spectacular* had just one week to run. The company would be leaving for Tasmania the following Sunday, and the young lovers couldn't bear the thought of parting.

But Marty had a plan. He wouldn't tell her yet, not until he'd spoken to his father. He would make the telephone call first thing Monday morning. Mondays were always busy in the office of Carlovsky & Reubens, and Carlo and Rube would both be there. If his father didn't agree to his proposition then he would appeal to Uncle Rube, who would surely see it as an excellent business plan.

'I'll miss you too, Em,' he whispered and he kissed her. Then among the rumpled sheets they made love again, tenderly, achingly, as if for the very last time.

But on the late Wednesday afternoon, their final meeting at the Grand, he had good news for her, and he burst out with it the moment he'd closed the door behind them. Before they'd kissed even.

'I'm not going away with the tour,' he announced. 'I'm staying right here in Melbourne.'

She made no reply but stared back at him, dumbfounded. How was this possible?

Enveloping her in his arms, he kissed her deeply then led her to the bed, where they both sat while he explained briefly and succinctly what had happened, trying all the while to keep his jubilation in check.

'I spoke to my father on the telephone Monday morning and we came to an arrangement,' he said. 'Wal, my assistant, is taking over management of the tour, and I'm to set up a Carlovsky & Reubens office here in Melbourne.'

'Good heavens.' Her smile was a mix of joy and incredulity. 'I don't believe it – that was your *father's* idea?'

'No, it was mine actually, and he took a little convincing, but Uncle Rube backed me up.'

'Oh Marty, that's wonderful.'

'Yes, it is, isn't it. But you know something else, Em?' He couldn't help his excitement showing now. 'It really does make sense. Melbourne's the theatrical capital of Australia. The show's done great business here, better than in Sydney, and we really do need to set up a Melbourne base. I wasn't lying to Dad. Although,' he admitted with a smile, 'I wouldn't have come up with the idea at all if it hadn't been for us.'

'But how amazing your father agreed,' she said. 'I mean, allowing your assistant to take over the tour management.'

'Oh, that was the easy part,' he scoffed with a laugh. 'Wal's far more experienced than I am. He was really sent along to keep an eye on me and make sure I didn't mess things up. When I told Dad I'd known that right from the start, he was left without a leg to stand on.'

He gathered her to him. 'So now, my love,' he said, 'now, my very own love, we have another whole two months until you're out on the road with *Lear*.'

They kissed, already undressing each other as they sank back onto the bed.

He wouldn't tell her his father's parting words after the lengthy discussion where Rube had taken his side, finally convincing Carlo of the idea's merits.

'Now you listen, son,' Carlo had barked down the line, 'and you listen carefully. Melbourne is the Worthings' home base. You steer clear of doing any business with them, do you hear me, Marty? No matter how enticing a prospect appears financially or artistically, no matter how remote the link, be it even a member of their tribe as crew or performer, I'll have no connection whatsoever with the Worthings. Do I make myself understood?'

No. He wouldn't tell her that.

19

THE BEST LAID PLANS
OF MICE AND MEN

It was late April 1918 when Bertie found himself once more promoted in the field; he was a sergeant now. He still wore the insignia of a corporal as his stripes hadn't come through yet, but the men with whom he served happily accepted his command. They liked Bertie Worthing, he was one of them, and most important of all they respected him. Which was just as well, given what lay ahead.

A strategic battle of the utmost importance was about to be launched, a battle that might well prove a crucial turning point of the war.

At dawn on 24 April, the Germans had captured the tactically important town of Villers-Bretonneux just south of the River Somme, thereby opening the way to their main objective, Amiens. The British commanders planned an immediate counterattack with two Australian brigades and three British battalions.

The surprise attack was to take place that very night. The Australian brigades were to approach the town from opposing directions in a pincer movement, which would trap the German forces. A dangerous manoeuvre, conducted in the dead of night with no prior reconnaissance, there were many even among the hierarchy who had their doubts about the efficacy of such a plan. But surprisingly enough the Australians themselves were in no such doubt.

As night fell and the troops waited in the gathering darkness for their orders to move, word passed among the Australians, steadily building and giving them purpose, lending them strength for the battle ahead. Then, as midnight ticked over to the 25th of April, the words were whispered louder and with ever more vigour . . . *'It's Anzac Day!'* To a man, they were exhilarated by this knowledge. They would fight to commemorate their brothers who had fallen at Gallipoli. They were fellow Anzacs.

It was well past midnight when they were ordered to move, and by now they were imbued with a fervour bordering on euphoric. This was to be a battle that would go down in history.

The night was cold and clouds had gathered, blackening the sky from any light that might have been cast by the moon, a blessing given the attack's all-important need for surprise. But as the hundreds of troops neared Villers-Bretonneux, they became eerily lit by the distant burning houses and the flash of exploding artillery fire that evidenced the Germans' capture of the township. Every man could see quite clearly the play of light and shadow on those who filed ahead, and every man knew the element of surprise was quickly running out.

Then suddenly it happened. All need for stealth was gone and they were in the thick of battle. Fired up by the knowledge it was Anzac Day and with single-minded purpose, they rushed fearlessly forward and into the German machine gun posts. As some later wrote, 'the Australians charged like a pack of wolves'. And once there they killed with devastating efficiency, bayonets slicing mercilessly into grey-clad bodies.

The area around Villers-Bretonneux became a charnel house that night. Slaughter and mayhem ruled as hundreds upon hundreds of German troops were killed. The orders had been clear. No prisoners were to be taken.

Bertie and five of his men charged full-on at a German machine gun post. Their commanding officer had fallen and Bertie was now leading this small band that had separated from the others, as so many had in the chaos. But upon landing in the dug-out, prepared once again to kill without mercy, they discovered all six of the machine gun crew were already dead.

To their surprise, an Australian officer was standing there. Pistol in hand, he pointed it vaguely at them, not in a threatening manner, just issuing an order.

'Nothing to see here, lads,' he said, indicating with the pistol a change of direction, 'move on to the next one.'

In the flashes of light that illuminated the battle scene, Bertie had seen the officer quite clearly; he knew who this was.

'Strewth,' he said, 'Captain Carlovsky, as I live and breathe.'

'And who might you be, Corporal?' the captain queried, lowering his pistol.

'Albert Worthing, sir.'

Mick peered at the soldier. 'Well, well, little Bertie Worthing, and all grown up into a corporal.'

'Actually, I'm a sergeant now. Got promoted in the field three days ago. My stripes haven't arrived yet.'

'Congratulations.'

'Hey, Captain,' one of Bertie's men interrupted, 'did you climb in here on your own?' Young Joe had been looking around at the bodies of the Germans, six in all. Surely the captain hadn't killed the whole lot of them single-handed.

'Yes,' Mick said, thinking that the private, like so many, looked no more than a baby. 'I ran out of men some distance back, don't know where they got to in this blackness.'

'And you killed all this lot on your own?' Young Joe was awestruck.

'Not really,' Mick replied briskly. 'One was already dead, two were wounded.'

Bertie sensed Mick Carlovsky was impatient to move on. 'So you have no men,' he said, 'and we have no officer. Shall we join up, Captain?'

'We shall.' Mick nodded to the young privates, who all seemed like kids to him. 'Let's go,' he said. And the seven of them climbed from the dug-out to re-join the fray.

By dawn of 25 April, three years to the day from the initial landing at Gallipoli, the Australians had successfully broken through the German entrenchment at Villers-Bretonneux. It would take the Allies just the rest of that day and into the next to secure the township and create a new frontline to the east. The battle had indeed proved a crucial turning point of the war. But it had cost the Australians dearly; over 2,400 of their men had died that night.

As first light streaked the sky, Mick Carlovsky, Bertie Worthing and the two remaining members of their small band walked across the field towards the house where they could see Australian soldiers were gathered. They'd lost three of their seven, including young Joe, but the fighting in this particular area was over. They'd won their battle.

What followed seemed quite bizarre to Bertie. After the horrors of all the killing, things had become suddenly and strangely dreamlike, as if somehow this couldn't really be happening.

The house was grand in a rustic sort of way, no doubt the farmhouse of a well-to-do landowner, and it was relatively unscathed. Soldiers were lounging around outside, leaning against its stone walls and seated on its two wooden benches, sharing a smoke and a drink and a chat, and inside music was playing.

The four crossed the verandah and stepped through the front door. A middle-aged man was sitting at a piano playing ragtime and a woman was handing around drinks on a tray. Soldiers were gathered about the piano, tapping their boots in time to the music, chatting and smoking as if it was any old Saturday night.

Mick, Bertie and the boys did the same. They accepted a drink from the tray, they each took a cigarette from the pack Mick offered around, even Bertie who didn't even smoke, and they all tapped their boots to the music.

Bertie couldn't remember exactly what it was they chatted about, although it didn't seem to have been the killing, he surely would have remembered that.

They stayed for a good half-hour or so before going their separate ways to re-join their battalions. Or what remained of their battalions. Despite the success of the attack, they were yet to discover the extent of their losses.

Mick offered Bertie his hand as they parted.

'See you back home, Bertie,' he said.

'Yep' – Bertie accepted the hand and they shook warmly – 'see you back home, Mick.'

He watched Michael Carlovsky walk away, straight-backed, positive, despite a barely discernible favouring of his left leg, the gait of a true military man. And he wondered if Mick too had felt how strange this farmhouse gathering had been. Probably not.

God, he's tough, Bertie thought. *Fancy him taking out a whole machine gun post on his own! That deserves recognition, that does.* There and then Bertie decided he'd put Mick up for a medal. *Me and the boys are witnesses*, he thought, *we'll get together and send in a report through our CO. Mick Carlovsky's a fair dinkum hero.*

Little did Bertie know, Mick was a haunted man . . .

'You killed all this lot on your own?' the young soldier had clumsily queried, and he'd answered truthfully enough; one had been already dead, two wounded, he'd said. But he hadn't told the boy that the other three Germans had their hands held high above their heads. He'd killed three men who were in the act of surrendering. He'd killed the two wounded men also, although they may possibly have survived, who could tell? The orders had been 'take no prisoners', and Mick always obeyed orders. But he was haunted nonetheless, knowing that the image would stay with him for as long as he lived.

I do believe the end is in sight, Marty, he wrote a week later to his brother. *In securing Villers-Bretonneux the Allies have effectively put paid to the German offensive on the Somme, and we may even be home for Christmas. At least that's what we're hoping. And I must say, mate, now that you're old enough to join up, I'm bloody glad it'll all be over and you'll be too late.*

Mick was deeply thankful his baby brother was not destined to go the way of so many young men who had lost their lives in this war that now appeared to have been so futile. It seemed a whole generation of young men from all parts of the globe had died for no real purpose. Mick Carlovsky had become decidedly cynical.

Although I have to admit, he went on, *it's obvious from your letters you've grown up a bit by now and don't see war in the romantic light you once did, which is a damn good thing.*

Fancy you setting up a family office in Melbourne! I'm most impressed. And planning a co-production with the Fullers no less! Doubly impressed. As I'm sure you're aware, I know bugger all about the theatre, but even I've heard of the Fuller family's entrepreneurial skills.

Which brings me to a connection you may find of interest. Guess who I bumped into just a week or so back? And in the middle of a bloody great battle, what's more! None other than young Bertie Worthing. You wouldn't remember him personally, you were just a kid when the families' partnership split up, but of course you'd know of the Worthings – they're as famous a theatrical mob as the

*Fullers, probably even more so. And I'm sure you've heard
Dad carry on about Will Worthing – by golly, he'd have
the man's guts for garters if he could, although God only
knows why. Anyway, Bertie Worthing's a really nice bloke –
a young fella, only a few years older than you, and a damn
fine soldier to boot. Makes this whole family palaver so
stupid, doesn't it? So downright petty! Whatever took
place between them – who gives a damn! I certainly don't,
and I know Bertie wouldn't either. If we manage to come
through these final stages of the war, I'm going to make a
point of catching up with young Bertie Worthing. You'll
like him, Marty, you really will . . .*

Upon receiving Mick's letter, Marty couldn't wait to
show Emma. By now she was out on the road with the
Lear production, so he posted it to her in Perth where they
were playing at His Majesty's. The lovers corresponded at
least twice a week.

See, Em, he wrote in the most jubilant fashion, *we'll
have our brothers on side when we tell our families. Everything's going to be fine, my love. Everything's going to be
just fine!*

Em wasn't so sure herself. Marty didn't know her Uncle
Will.

Emma and Marty's affair had continued to prosper in
the living quarters above the Carlovsky & Reubens office
that Marty had hired. A small converted terrace house
in Carlton's Lygon Street, it was within easy walking
distance from the city.

Their love now consumed them, but inevitably the time
came when *King Lear* was to leave on its interstate tour and
they were forced to make their farewells. No matter though;
by then they had their future plans firmly in place.

'We'll confront them as soon as you get back, Em,'
Marty said, running his fingers through her hair as they
lay, naked bodies entwined on the little upstairs bed,

'and we'll tell them we're getting married. No seeking permission, we'll just make the big announcement. "Hey, everybody," we'll say, "we're getting married!" How's about that, what do you think?'

She laughed, loving the touch and the smell of him, already feeling the ache of parting, knowing this was their last Sunday.

'I think Uncle Will is likely to explode,' she said.

'Yes, so is Dad,' Marty agreed, 'but we shall pick up the pieces and carry on regardless.'

For once it was Emma who, rather uncharacteristically, addressed the problem in all its potential seriousness.

'What if they forbid the marriage, Marty?' she said, rolling onto her side and gazing at him. 'They could, couldn't they? I'm only seventeen.'

'Then we'll run away and marry in secret,' he replied. 'Juliet was only fourteen, remember?'

She laughed once again, she couldn't help herself. 'Since when did you become so theatrical?'

'It rubs off, my love, you're solely to blame.'

Em's mood quickly sobered. 'But what about the co-production you're discussing with Ben Fuller,' she said, 'wouldn't that be jeopardised if we ran away?'

'We'd only run around the corner,' he said, 'and when we come back people wouldn't even know we were married. Isn't that the way Shakespeare planned it?'

Marty drew her close. 'Let's not spoil our last day together, Em, we'll worry about all this when the time comes.' He kissed her gently. 'But I promise you, nothing and no one will ever part us. Just let them try! We'll go to war if need be.' He kissed her again, more deeply this time, and any further argument that might have been about to formulate in Emma's brain ceased to exist. There was only this moment.

It's me again, Em. I have to interrupt here. I'm terribly sorry, but I simply must. And it's been a long time since I did, so do please forgive me.

You see, I'm becoming aware that Marty and I might sound like a couple of lovesick fools – heavens above, let's face it, we were – but oh my goodness, as Marty said, we really were prepared to go to war if need be. Nothing was ever going to stand in our way.

So as you can imagine, when Marty sent me the letter he'd received from his brother, Mick, I was as elated as he was. The thought of confronting Uncle Will remained as daunting as ever, but we would have allies in Mick and Bertie. Allies from both families. If it turned out we really *did* have to go to war then we would have soldiers on our side ready and willing to join us in battle – *real* soldiers, what's more. Oh dear me, we were excited.

The newspapers reported the victory at Villers-Bretonneux as a turning point and even hinted the end of the war was in sight, just like Mick had said in his letter to Marty. It may well be over by the end of the year, they said. A cause for rejoicing indeed! But oh, I simply must digress for a moment and tell you a little of the sadness, and also the injustice, we civilians had been witnessing back home. And for some time now.

During the early days when all the lads had signed up for their overseas adventure, the war had seemed somehow remote to us civilians. It was something we just read about in the newspapers for the most part. Then, of course, came the realisation of the terrible numbers of casualties, so many families with sons killed in action; the lists were endless, names after names. Then finally the wounded started arriving home from the various hospitals and rehabilitation centres where they'd been recovering from their frightful injuries. At long last we civilians were witness to what they must have been through, fighting in those far-off places that to us were just foreign-sounding names in a newspaper. You'd walk down the street and you'd see a man without an arm, another with a leg missing; it was frightening to behold. There was any number of these poor, limbless souls searching for work, and there was ample work to be had – with all the young men off to war there were plenty of jobs around. But do you want to know the truly awful, horrible, shocking part? Just about everywhere you looked there were signs saying 'no ex-servicemen required' or 'returned soldiers need not apply'. Isn't that absolutely appalling!

I'm pleased to report no such attitude existed in the theatre. In fact, the theatre openly welcomed returned soldiers. A one-armed man could liaise between front-of-house and backstage, we always needed a runner, and a one-legged man could sit on a stool and operate a follow spot. There was always work in the theatre for our boys who'd come home, at least there was in a Worthing Brothers production. And I reckon I'd be safe in saying it was the same throughout show business. Theatre folk are like that.

Strangely enough, the most heartbreaking returned soldiers were not necessarily those who bore their wounds for all the world to see. There were some poor creatures who lived in torment, emotional wrecks, their minds crazed by war. Yet to look at them you'd never know it.

We encountered one such in Perth on the *Lear* tour, a young man who called himself 'Fish' – I think his surname was Fishbourne, I can't really remember. Anyway, Aunt Mabel and Ma bumped into Fish standing on the corner of St Georges Terrace and William Street with a sign around his neck that said 'returned soldier in need of work'. They immediately dragged him along to His Majesty's, of course; we'd only just arrived and were setting up, so the timing was perfect.

Fish was a strong, able-bodied young man with a big build and powerful shoulders, just the sort you need for hauling up back-drops and scrims, and I must say while we were bumping in and rigging the set he worked like a navvy.

He didn't talk much, mind, seemed pleasant enough, but kept pretty well to himself. Ma was the only person who made any direct contact with him. It was as if she recognised there was something broken inside. But that was Ma – she had a sort of 'sixth sense', as they say. And of course, being Ma, the contact was made in her own saucy way.

'My, my, you're doing a grand job there, Fish,' she'd say. 'If this was a variety show, I'd bill you as The Strongman.'

She'd give him a flirty smile and Fish would smile back. You could tell he was pleased by the compliment and that he really liked Ma.

Things were fine during the two days of bumping in and setting up, and then the technical cut-to-cue runs where you just checked everything was working. But after that came the big dress rehearsal when it was all fitted together. This was what the audience would see in only a few hours' time when they poured into the theatre for opening night.

Well, everything was running like clockwork. I mean, you'd expect it to, wouldn't you? After a full season in Melbourne and then Adelaide we were a pretty slick production.

Fish was working away as diligently as he had for the past two days. Together with the other stagehands he was hauling up scrims, flying in backdrops, moving furniture for scene changes and pushing hefty great trucks onstage during blackouts. Backstage crew do real hard yakka, I can tell you, although from out front you'd never know it, everything working smooth as silk the way it does. That's theatre for you.

Anyway, then came the storm scenes in Act Three. We hadn't run the storm effects in the technical rehearsal, just checked the lighting cues, no need for all the rest.

'Blow, winds, and crack your cheeks! Rage! Blow!'

By the time we reached the peak of the storm when Lear rages at the elements, the thunder sheet and the wind machine were going full bore, all technical effects working as smoothly as they should, but Aunt Mabel had cause for worry.

From her position in the prompt corner she'd noticed something was wrong with Fish. At least that's what she told us later. He'd taken her cue at the opening of Scene One and hauled on the rope that flew in the backdrop of 'the heath', but as the storm's sound effects had slowly grown she could see he was becoming agitated.

Our two regular stagehands who travelled with the show were extremely adept at handling the thunder machine. Wearing gloves to protect themselves from the giant metal sheet – which is extremely thin by the way, because the thinner the sheet the more impressive the noise – they'd 'warm it up' between them, producing a sort of distant rumble of thunder. Then gradually they'd shake it with more and more vigour, building the sound to a crescendo. So come the opening of Scene Two, when the storm reaches its zenith, with demon winds whirling and lightning tearing the sky asunder, the cracks from the thunder sheet were truly fearsome. It's always the test of a great actor's vocal power to rise above the storm. And it goes without saying Uncle Will had more than enough power, which was why he demanded a particularly ferocious storm.

'*You sulphurous and thought-executing fires,*
Vaunt-couriers to oak-cleaving thunderbolts,
Singe my white head! And thou, all-shaking thunder,
Smite flat the thick rotundity o' the world!'

Oh my goodness, you should have seen Uncle Will's *King Lear*, really you should have, a tour de force if there ever was one; no wonder the critics raved. And he didn't hold back in a final dress rehearsal, I can promise you. He was testing everyone's mettle, you see, we all had to rise to the occasion, particularly the backstage crew. If anyone was found slacking they'd cop it from Uncle Will.

But on this occasion, one of the backstage crew simply couldn't handle it. With the storm now at its zenith, our new stagehand had become a complete mess.

I wasn't witness to the onset because I was in the dressing room at the time, but Aunt Mabel said Fish was shaking uncontrollably. Then all of a sudden he put his hands over his ears, dropped to his knees and let out a mighty great howl.

It stopped the show in its tracks. We all heard him, not just those onstage and in the wings, but we lot in the dressing rooms too. He was louder than the storm. Louder than Uncle Will, even. I've never heard a sound like it. It wasn't a scream, and it wasn't a shriek or a yell or anything like that. It was a wail of anguish from the depths of a man's soul, at least that's what it sounded like to me. And it didn't stop, it went on and on and on.

Aunt Mabel called an instant halt to the rehearsal and the rest of us rushed up onstage to see what was happening.

Oh, it was awful. Fish was on his knees, rocking backwards and forwards, and he seemed in agony. His face was distorted, and he was clawing at his head as if trying to haul out whatever it was he could see in there. I've never in my life witnessed anyone so tortured, and I never wish to again.

Pa and our Ted tried to help him to his feet, but the moment he felt the touch of their hands on him he shrank away terrified, arms flailing, warding them off.

No one knew what to do, we just stood around helpless. But, as one, we turned to Aunt Mabel for leadership, which wasn't strange really; we always had, even Uncle Will although he'd never admit to the fact.

'The storm triggered it,' she explained, 'it was the noise that set him off.' Then she looked directly at Ma. 'Over to you, Gertie,' she said.

Everyone watched in silence as Ma crossed to where Fish knelt, still rocking back and forth, still clawing at his head, but by now the wailing had subsided, becoming more of a moan, a sort of keening sound, still agonising, still painful to hear.

Ma knelt beside him.

'The storm's over, Fish,' she said quietly, so quietly that I wondered if he'd be able to hear her above his moans.

'No more storm,' she said. 'No more noise. It's all gone now. There's only me here.'

He heard her. And he also heard the silence. He kept rocking back and forth, but he stopped clawing his head and he stopped moaning. Instead he went limp; that big strong body slumped forward and went limp as a rag doll. Then – oh so heartbreaking to watch – he started to cry.

'Make it go away,' he whimpered over and over through tears that just poured down his face. 'Make it go away, make it go away.'

Ma put her arms around him, joining in perfect time with his rocking, stroking him gently all the while. A diminutive mother comforting a giant baby.

'There, there, lovey,' she said, 'it's going away now, it's all going away. No more noise, lovey, no more noise.'

We had to let Fish go after that. I often wonder what happened to the poor man, whether he remained haunted for the rest of his life. And I often wonder how many others there might be just like him. The memory's never left me, you know, even now after all these years. Oh, war is a terrible thing.

When the *Lear* tour finally came to an end in late June and we returned to Melbourne, I told Marty all about the episode with Fish.

'It could have been your Mick or our Bertie,' I remember saying. 'Oh Marty, what those poor men have been through!'

I was really shaken as I recounted the story, and of course Marty comforted me the way only Marty could, but it led to a serious and productive discussion between us. We'd always talked about our brothers and the fact that, miraculously, they both appeared to have escaped the war unharmed. But what if they hadn't? What if they were injured the way Fish was – the way so many might be? We'd never thought about that before. Probably because we'd been so preoccupied with each other.

Anyway, we decided not to immediately enlist the help of our siblings upon their return, but to assess their condition first. It didn't seem right to drag them into another battle when they'd just returned from the theatre of war. If that sounds a little indulgent on our part, or even pretentious, believe me I mean it to. As if our predicament could be in any way meaningful given all they'd been through! But young lovers are so selfish, aren't they? When you're young and in love there's no world other than your own. We meant well though, truly we did. The war would soon be over and our boys would be coming home, if not for Christmas then certainly sometime in the New Year. Marty and I determined to curb our impatience and put any thought of family confrontation aside until then. Our marriage could wait until we knew all was well. In the meantime, we must continue to guard our secret.

However, I have to tell you, only a short time later we were nearly caught out. Oh my goodness yes, a very close call. It actually appears quite funny in retrospect, but at the time it was most alarming.

The *Lear* season having now closed, we were not governed by evening performances, and Marty and I became a little careless. We never spent the whole night together, of course – that would invite far too many questions – but more often than not we'd meet up after Marty had closed the Carlovsky & Reubens office for the day. We'd make wild, abandoned love in the upstairs bedroom (oh, the divine passion of youth!) and every now and then we'd walk into Chinatown, where we'd have an early meal at our favourite downstairs haunt. We never worried about being caught out there as the clientele were all Chinese, but I realise now it was nothing short of reckless for us to wander so openly about the theatre area of Melbourne.

One night, unbelievable though it may sound, you'll never guess who we bumped into in the middle of Bourke Street! Ma and Pa no less! Actually, it's not in the least unbelievable when you think about it. In fact, the only unbelievable aspect was my own foolishness! Whenever the family was in between productions they'd invariably catch up on the other shows about town – Marty and I were only too lucky we hadn't encountered the whole Worthing tribe.

Ma and Pa were on their way to the Theatre Royal, and right there amidst the glaring lights of Bourke Street, as if caught centre stage in a follow spot, we all but barged into them. We weren't looking where we were going, wandering along arm in arm with eyes only for one another.

'Em?'

Ma came to an abrupt halt and I could tell in an instant she was demanding an introduction. But funnily enough (and here's the really weird part), Pa got in first.

'Anthony?' he queried.

Ma threw a brief glance at Pa, which seemed to signal something, then she looked back to Marty. She and Pa both seemed in a state of complete surprise. And they weren't the only ones, I can tell you. I was flabbergasted, to be honest. How on earth could Pa know this was the 'Anthony' we'd invented in Sydney, the 'Anthony' who'd left messages for me at the Criterion? Mind you, I was grateful he'd made the assumption. Mysterious though it was, he'd given us a springboard.

'Yes, this is Anthony, Pa,' I replied. 'He's visiting from Sydney. Anthony, this is my mother and father.'

Oh, you should have seen our performance, smooth as silk we were.

'Anthony Rochester,' Marty said. 'How do you do, sir.' And with a nod to Ma, 'How do you, Mrs Worthing.'

There were warm handshakes all round; Ma was always one to offer her hand.

'Lovely to meet you, Anthony,' she said. No one uttered a word about how or why they'd assumed this was 'Anthony'. Funny that, don't you think?

'How long are you staying in Melbourne, dear?' Ma asked. 'You must come around for dinner one night, the family would love to meet you.'

She gave me one of those 'all-knowing' looks of hers, which quite clearly said, 'Ah ha, so this is the one, is it?' She seemed quite pleased to discover my 'amour' had turned out to be 'Anthony'.

Ma, as I'm sure you'll have gathered by now, was frightfully canny. She'd known I was no longer a virgin for some time, in fact well before we'd left on the *Lear* tour. She'd confronted me quite openly.

'It shows, lovey,' she'd said, 'you can always tell.' She'd passed no judgement, mind. 'You're of an age now, Em, where passion can take over your life' (she'd know all about that, wouldn't she; she'd been passionately in love with Pa at the age of sixteen) 'but you mustn't allow it to ruin your life, lovey, that's where the danger lies. You are taking care of yourself now, aren't you?'

She'd said it in that 'deeply meaningful' way that left no room for doubt, but I pretended not to understand one single word she was talking about. A typically youthful reaction, to close off from one's parents – we all do that, don't we, every single generation? But the truth is, my reaction wasn't one of youthful rebellion at all. I didn't want to close off from Ma; I adored her and dearly wanted to tell her the truth. But how could I? Marty was Carlo's son. He and I both knew that when we confessed to our love for each other it would be essential we confront the whole family. The feud was too strongly embedded, it had gone on far too long.

Ma had continued to be pushy, albeit in a gentle way. 'Why don't you bring him home, lovey,' she'd say, and I'd remain non-communicative. 'And if it's a girl, then that's all right too.' I'd felt myself blush when she said that – oh, Ma could be so embarrassing. But she'd persisted, obviously thinking this might be the cause for my reluctance. 'Plenty of that goes on, you know, lovey, and I don't see anything wrong in it. People sow their oats in different ways, not up to us to judge.'

I'm aware such a comment will no doubt seem very odd to you, but believe me Ma wasn't alone in her views. Theatre folk have always been liberal-minded. No one really cares what goes on behind closed doors, so long as it's not hurtful to others.

She still hadn't been able to get anything out of me, though, and finally she'd given up trying, so I think meeting 'Anthony' on that early evening in June pleased her immensely.

Marty replied to the dinner invitation as cool as a cucumber; he really had become the most accomplished actor – swearing it was all due to my influence, of course.

'How kind of you, Mrs Worthing, I'd love to accept,' he said, 'but I'm afraid my stay in Melbourne is very brief. I'm shortly to return to Sydney.'

'But you do come to Melbourne quite often, do you not?'

Ma was looking at him eagle-eyed, and I could tell she was thinking if this was the boy with whom I was having an affair then he must surely be a regular visitor to town.

I was about to flash a look to Marty but there was no need; he'd realised the same thing and was quick on the uptake.

'Oh yes, indeed I do, ma'am.'

(Ma'am! Really! I thought that might be going a bit too far myself, but Ma seemed to approve; I could read her like a book. *What a nice young man*, she was thinking.)

'Then you must come to dinner when you're next in the city,' she said.

'Indeed I shall, Mrs Worthing, indeed I shall.'

Pa interrupted at that point. 'We'd better get a move on, Gert love,' he said, 'or we'll be late for the curtain.'

'Oh dear me, yes,' Ma replied, 'that wouldn't do at all.'

And they hurried off.

I knew I was going to cop it from then on. 'When is that nice young Anthony coming back?' I could hear her ask. Which of course she did, any number of times. Until I invented a long overseas trip.

'His father's in the import-export business,' I said. 'He's been sent off to America.'

'Oh, what a pity. Well, when he returns home . . .'

After that Marty and I became a great deal more cautious, aware we were playing a dangerous game. The little terrace house in Carlton was perfectly safe; no Worthing was likely to visit the office of Carlovsky & Reubens. But I daren't be suspiciously absent for too long, and of course we daren't be seen together around town.

Oh, how we longed for the time when Mick and Bertie would be home and we could put an end to the whole charade. However disastrous our confrontation might prove, even if our parents chose to disown us, at least we would no longer be forced to skulk about in the shadows.

20

AN END TO CONFLICT?

Captain Michael Carlovsky stood on what, until only several hours previously, had been a picturesque green sloping pasture. It was now a decimated wreck of shell holes, beyond which he could see the blackened burnt-out remnants of a once-pretty village. Le Hamel had been aptly named. With a population of less than a thousand, mostly farmers, shopkeepers and their families, it could only be described as a hamlet. Now barely a single house remained untouched, destroyed by the Australian artillery barrage which, closely followed by the Allied troops' infantry insurgence, had evicted the Germans in an attack lasting all of ninety-three minutes.

By God, you've got to admire Monash, Mick thought. *Why they didn't give him higher command earlier in the war is beyond me. We sure as hell wouldn't have suffered the losses we did if Monash had been running the show.*

Australian Lieutenant General John Monash had proved himself a military genius, in Mick's opinion anyway, and in the opinion of many. Having finally been given charge of his own troops and several brigades of Americans, Monash's plan of attack at Le Hamel had been carried out with flawless precision. Employing aircraft, artillery and armour in effective combination with infantry, the attack had commenced at 3.10 am, and as Mick now surveyed the scene at 6 am, the conflict had been over for an hour or more. A lesson in military coordination and efficiency.

How many of our boys might still be alive, Mick thought with contempt, *if the British generals had followed Monash's tactics instead of shoving the troops headlong into the fray like so much fodder.*

He walked down the ravaged slope towards the town, picking his way between bomb craters, abandoned trenches, weapons and dead bodies, and as he went he pondered his luck at having survived the war. From Gallipoli through the campaigns of the Western Front, the endless Battles of the Somme – and he was still in the Somme Valley, wasn't he, only a mile or two from Albert where he'd fought two years previously. *Christ, was it that long ago?* Amiens, Pozières, God alone knew how many other hideous battles, all the way back to Fromelles, and more recently Villers-Bretonneux. But his mind halted at that point. He didn't want to go there; that place held the worst of his nightmares. He'd recently learnt he was to be awarded the Military Cross, which in itself was a brutal reminder. *The Military Cross? For what? For murdering men in the act of surrendering?* No, no, he wouldn't think about that. He'd think about home instead, home and family.

And home was already beckoning. Having been placed into Monash's Headquarters Unit as an observer, he'd heard from several senior officers that Le Hamel would see the end of the Australians' action on the frontline. The troops were to be sent to the rear and hopefully would be on their way home in a couple of months. One general had even said the Australian troops would no longer be needed, that the Germans were beaten, that an armistice would be called and that surrender was imminent.

He'd reached the bottom of the slope now, and he stopped at a shell-torn hedgerow where the town's shattered houses stood on the other side. He lit up a cigarette, feeling all of a sudden extremely weary. This had been such a very long war.

'Mornin', Carlo.' A brash voice cut through the stream of his thoughts. He found the American accent jarring, this particular American's anyway. He'd fought alongside English accents, Irish, Scottish and Welsh accents, even Indian and South African accents, but the Texas growl of young Lieutenant Nathanial 'Buck' Buckston, whom he'd met only the day before, he found particularly abrasive.

'You can call me Buck and I'll call you Carlo,' the Texan had said upon introduction. 'That OK by you, amigo?'

'Suits me, Buck,' he'd replied. He hadn't told the American that as 'Carlo' was the lifelong diminutive of his father's name, he'd far rather be 'Mick'. He simply couldn't be bothered.

'Goddamn but that was some fight, wasn't it,' Buck now said as he swaggered up to join his newfound amigo. 'We went through 'em like a knife through butter, I'll be damned if we didn't.'

'Yes, I suppose we did.'

The bravado in both the swagger and the voice was evident, but the eyes told a different tale. Mick could see fear there. This was Buck's first taste of battle and it showed. In fact, the battle they'd just fought was the first time in the war that American troops had acted as part of an offensive. No doubt many of Buck's young comrades in arms were feeling the very same way, Mick thought with a touch of sympathy; getting blooded was never easy.

'That goddamn boy of yours, that Monash,' Buck went on, still playing the bravado for all it was worth, 'I recall him saying at the briefing it'd all be over in ninety minutes. Well, hellfire and damnation, you could've knocked me down with a feather when they called a ceasefire and I looked at my watch. He was right on the money!'

'He's a very good general,' Mick said.

'For a Jew, yeah, he darn sure is.' Buck dragged a packet of cigarettes from his shirt pocket. But I guess even a Jew boy can surprise, ain't that so, Carlo?'

Mick wanted to take umbrage at the Texan's comment, but sheer fatigue told him not to bother, so he just stood silently as Buck lit up.

'I'll be damned.' The American took a hefty drag. 'I just realised,' he declared, exhaling a plume of smoke into the morning air. 'Do you know what today is?'

'Another day to stay alive?' Mick suggested drily, wishing Buck would move on.

'Today is the goddamn Fourth of July, that's what it is. Today is Independence Day!'

'Congratulations.'

'Hey, Carlo, let's us go find some buddies and some good ol' boys sippin' whiskey.' Buck gave him a hearty smack on the back. 'We gotta lot to celebrate, what do you say?'

Thank God he's going, Mick thought, dropping his own cigarette and grinding it into the ravaged earth with his boot. 'Not right now thanks, Buck. You go on along, I'll join up with you later.'

'Right you are, buddy,' a hearty punch to the shoulder this time, 'we'll raise hell, all right.' He swaggered off. 'Independence Day, can you believe that?' he said as he went, whether to Mick or himself it was unclear.

Mick didn't watch the man go but, relieved by the semblance of silence, remained staring at the ruins of the once-pretty township just the other side of the hedgerow. He wasn't really seeing the township and he wasn't really hearing the distant, vague sounds of voices and vehicles as he gave himself up to his weariness and the all-enveloping blur. Even his thoughts had deserted him.

Then, shattering the blur, came a sound he knew all too well. The crack of a rifle. *Sniper*, he thought as the bullet hit him in the chest.

The force flung him backwards into a crater and he lay there looking up at the sky. Other sounds came to him then, a Texan voice nearby screaming, 'Jesus Christ!' Other voices from further away, the sound of chaos and gunfire. But they all meant nothing as, with the sure knowledge he was dying, thoughts once again came flooding back. Pictures more than thoughts really. He now saw the whole war in a series of images. So many different wars it seemed.

High, impossible cliffs reaching up from a pebbled beach. Heat, flies, trenches, the stench of rotting flesh . . .

Horse teams of sixteen dragging guns, light railways for supplies, petrol engines so the Germans wouldn't see the steam . . .

A vast sea of mud, a boy no more than sixteen struggling in the slime, others looking on helpless as he succumbed to the mire dragging him under . . .

Then the image above all else, the Germans in the act of surrender . . .

But this image was no longer detached, opening the gates as it did to a flood of recrimination that he knew he would never be able to justify. The bloodlust had been running so strong that night, 'Anzac Day' screaming in everyone's mind, some yelling the words as they ran. Like all the others he'd been in a frenzy. Upon storming the trench, he hadn't even noticed the Germans had their hands in the air. He hadn't even known he was alone, that his men were either dead or far behind him, he'd just killed as he'd been ordered. 'Kill every German in sight, take no prisoners,' they'd been told, and he'd passed on those very same orders to his men. He'd killed two of the three before he'd realised they were surrendering, but that hadn't stopped him killing the third. *Unconscionable*, his mind now said in judgement, *unconscionable, whatever the orders*. He'd killed the two wounded as well. One was in agony with a gut shot; surely an act of mercy? But his mind would allow no escape. *A decision that was not yours to make*, it said. The other wounded was semiconscious. Would he have survived? *Quite possibly, yes. Who would ever know?* And all of them young. Just like the Aussie boys. So terribly young. Far too young to die.

As oblivion slowly engulfed him, Mick was thankful to escape the guilt that would have plagued him for the rest of his life. And when all was said and done, he was one of the lucky ones, wasn't he? He had actually lived a life. A life far longer and fuller than any of those boys.

Michael Carlovsky died on 4 July 1918. He would have turned forty the following year.

Later that month, when the family was informed of Mick's death, their reaction was one of utter shock.

'But he was due home any minute,' Carlo said desperately, as if sheer disbelief might render the report incorrect. 'He wrote and told me so. The war was virtually over, he said. The papers have been saying the same damn thing too. The Germans are on the verge of surrender, our boys will soon be coming home, they've been saying. How the hell could the government allow this to happen! How the *hell* could they let this bloody well *happen*!'

Carlo had lived in fear for over three long years, expecting at any time to be informed of his son's death. Now, having been lulled into a sense of security for the past month or so, his grief was mingled with rage.

As he paced the living room, ranting about the government and railing against the injustice being served, Winifred sat quietly on the sofa, Rube beside her, holding her hand in both of his, although she barely seemed to notice.

Winifred never cried in the presence of others, not even her husband; in fact, particularly not in the presence of her husband. Winnie always cried alone.

'The war's over, for God's sake! The war's bloody well *over*, everyone knows that!'

As Carlo continued to rage, Rube didn't dare say what was uppermost in his mind. *There may well be further deaths. War isn't over until an armistice is signed and peace is declared. How many more are yet to die?*

In his own silent way, not unlike the woman whose hand he presently held, Rube was mourning the death of one who had felt like a son to him. Mick and Marty had always been the sons he knew he would never have. Now one was gone.

'And I'm supposed to be *grateful* for his Military bloody Cross, am I?' Carlo demanded. 'They inform me of my son's death and at the same time tell me I'm to be presented with his award at Government House! That's my pay-off, is it? They murder my son, but I get a bravery medal to show off so that makes everything all right.'

Carlo didn't even notice as Winifred stood.

'I'm going to have a lie down,' she said quietly. 'Stay with him, Rube, he'll need you.'

Rube nodded. They both knew that Carlo's grief and rage was wearing him out, that very soon he would sit down and weep. *Which will do him good*, Rube thought as he watched Winnie disappear upstairs where she, too, would no doubt give in to her tears.

In the meantime, Rube himself set about making plans. He must inform Anne and her family who were in Orange and Marty who was in Melbourne of their brother's death. Or rather, Carlo must do so as soon as he had calmed down. And he must arrange a family get-together in Sydney, he decided; sharing their grief as a family would lessen the burden. It might perhaps be a good idea to tie up the family visit with the presentation at Government House, he thought. Yes, if that could be arranged it would be an excellent idea, a most fitting memorial for Michael Carlovsky.

Rube's way of dealing with grief was to keep his mind as busy as possible.

In Melbourne, Marty's reaction, although less dramatically expressed than his father's, was one of equal disbelief.

'But he told me he'd be coming home soon, Em,' he said. 'Mick wrote that the war was all but over . . .'

'I know, I know,' she replied, gently stroking his hand as they sat side by side on the bed.

He made no attempt to stem the tears that unashamedly poured down his face, but just stared instead at the hand stroking his, which was somehow comforting. He had no one but Emma with whom to share his grief, and it was now a good hour or so since he'd received the phone call from his father. He'd been sitting numbed by the news, longing for her arrival.

'It's just such a shock,' he said, 'we'd all thought he was safe.'

'I know, I know,' she repeated, still stroking his hand, feeling dreadfully disloyal that her thoughts had strayed to her own brother. If Mick Carlovsky had been killed, was Bertie still in danger, she was wondering. Emma too had been lulled into a sense of security, mainly through Mick's news from the front, which Marty always shared with her.

'He's to be posthumously awarded the Military Cross,' Marty said, the tears gradually subsiding; it had been an immense relief to share his anguish so openly. He released his hold on her hand, took his handkerchief from his pocket and blew his nose. 'Uncle Rube's organising a family memorial in Sydney,' he went on, trying to sound business-like. 'He wants to tie it up with the presentation at Government House if he can, but doesn't know when that'll be yet. I'll put things on hold here and go up to Sydney next week, though, the whole family's getting together. Anne's bringing her tribe in from the country.

She and Chris have three kids now, so Dad can play proud
grandpa, that'll help.'

Tears once again threatened and he took her in his arms.

'Oh Em,' he said, 'war's such a bloody awful thing,
isn't it?'

'Yes, it is,' she said as they clung to each other. *Oh
Bertie*, she thought, *please, please be safe!*

Marty was gone for over two months, during which
time he and Em missed each other more than ever, this
separation having a greater impact somehow than her
simply being 'out on the road'. At first Emma had even
wondered whether they dared write to one another.

'I've painted us into a bit of a corner, haven't I?' she said
just before he left.

'In what way?'

'I've sent "Anthony" off to America. If letters keep
arriving from Sydney, Ma's bound to ask questions.'

But Marty was quick to solve the dilemma. 'I'll post
mine here to the office,' he said, giving her the key. 'You
can pop in regularly and collect them. There won't be a
problem my end,' he added, 'any letters you send could
just be business.'

As was the case during their previous separation, they
wrote continuously, at least twice a week, and their letters
became their lifeline.

Darling Em, Marty wrote after the first several weeks,
*I'm sorry to be the bearer of bad tidings, but the bravery
awards presentation at Government House isn't going to
be held until the end of September. I've promised Dad
I'll stay on in Sydney until then – he really is so broken
by Mick's death, and having the family around him is
doing wonders. Anne and the children are staying on too,
although her husband, Chris, has to return to Orange.
He's a doctor with a practice there, so business calls.*

Actually, in a lighter vein, hopefully to give you a bit of a smile, I tried to claim business necessitated a return to Melbourne for me too. Even just for a few days! Oh God, I miss you so! I approached Dad in my most impressive 'theatre producer' style – you know, the full-on performance the way I've learnt from you.

'I really must go back to Melbourne and see Ben Fuller, Dad,' I said with all the positivity I could muster. 'There's so much to discuss about next year's co-production.'

Well, you won't believe this, but Dad actually telephoned Ben Fuller himself! Once he'd found out where he was anyway. And he's not even in Melbourne. In fact, he's not even in Australia. He's in New Zealand – the Fullers own just about every theatre there is in New Zealand, and they're always making trips over there.

Naturally I had to pretend ignorance. 'Golly, I hadn't realised he'd left yet,' I said, although apparently he's been in New Zealand for weeks. Dad didn't fire questions at me to start with, he just went on about what a good bloke Ben Fuller is. Evidently Ben (who is always 'Mr Fuller' to me, by the way) told Dad he'd heard about Mick – it appears everyone in show business has, there was a mention in the variety pages. Anyway, he sent his deepest sympathy to us all, and said I was to take as long as I like, that he wouldn't need any further discussion with me until the end of the year.

How's that for getting caught out, eh? But here's the really funny part, Em. After Dad had raved on about 'good old Ben Fuller', I waited for the awkward questions that were bound to follow. Instead I copped something else right out of the blue.

'Who's this George bloke Ben's bringing from overseas for the farce we're co-producing, Marty?' he asked me. 'Ben reckons he's a comic genius.'

'George?' I asked. I didn't have a clue what he was talking about.

'Yeah. George Faydow, or something like that,' he said, 'never heard of him.'

I had to tell him that Georges Feydeau isn't coming out here, that he's not an actor, he's a French playwright, and that he wrote the play we're producing.

Which then led on to a whole discussion about Feydeau. Dad was aware we were doing a farce called 'The Lady from Maxim's' and that it was a saucy, vaudevillian style of play, the likes of which are hugely popular in France, and now also London and New York. That's what attracted him to the project in the first place, that and working with the Fullers, of course. But he didn't know anything more than that, he'd left it all in my hands. So he was fascinated when I told him our co-production with Ben Fuller would see the first Australian production of a Feydeau farce. He greatly approved.

'Well done, son, I'm proud of you,' he said. 'Really proud. Always good to be in the history books.'

So there you are, Em. After a very close call, my bacon was saved by none other than M'sieur Feydeau himself. I bet that'll give you a bit of a laugh, or at least put a smile on your face. I hope so anyway . . .

Emma did smile as she read his letter. Marty's love so delighted her that perhaps deep inside she even laughed for she knew exactly what he was doing. He was trying his utmost to distract her from her worry about Bertie. While mourning his own brother's death! That's how much he loved her.

Marty had been aware from the outset, even as she'd comforted him in the height of his grief, that Mick's death must have aroused her fears. How could it not do so? He never enquired about news of Bertie in his letters, whether or not her brother had written, whether or not the family had heard something. As soon as she received word, she would let him know. In the meantime, they would play the waiting game together.

Then finally . . .

He's alive! He's alive! The words screamed out at Marty from the page; he heard her voice and rejoiced for her. *A letter to the whole family arrived just today and I couldn't wait to write and tell you. He's not wounded or anything, the same cheeky Bertie as always, and everyone's wondering why I'm carrying on the way I am. 'The mail always takes an age,' they keep saying, 'it hasn't been any longer than normal between letters . . .' But I can't help myself, I'm delirious with joy after all this worry, and oh I love you so much for sharing the burden with me . . .*

Marty smiled as he read on, Emma recounting every bit of Bertie's letter, most of which had been written in his customary light-hearted vein. Em's voice, and also that of her brother, rang out so loud and clear.

I refuse to feel even the tiniest bit of guilt at how shamelessly selfish I'm being, she wrote in closing. *I'm simply too happy to care! But I can promise you, my darling, I will be thinking of you next week. The award presentation at Government House will be a sombre affair I'm sure, bitter-sweet, but a wonderful and fitting tribute to Mick.*

And then . . . Oh Marty, I can't wait to have you back home!

See? Selfish to the very end.

My love to you forever and ever and ever. Amen.

Your Em.

The award ceremony was every bit as Emma had predicted: sombre, bitter-sweet, but also wonderful. For all Carlo's earlier protestations, the Military Cross awarded posthumously to his son proved a source of great pride. As he listened to the citation recounting the bravery of Captain Michael Carlovsky in single-handedly overpowering an enemy machine gun emplacement at Villers-Bretonneux, he found comfort in the knowledge that Mick had fought so heroically. Marty, too, was comforted by the fact that the brother he idolised had not died in vain, that the part Mick had played in the war had served so great a purpose.

Rube and Winifred had arranged a post-ceremony party back at the house, where the family gathered to make speeches about Mick, and the men proceeded to get very drunk. All in all, a most successful wake and celebration of Mick's life.

Then, barely a week later, Marty was back in Melbourne.

The young lovers' reunion in the little upstairs bedroom of the terrace house in Carlton was as joyous, as passionate and as all-consuming as ever. This time, however, there was one notable difference in their lovemaking.

They had always taken care to protect themselves in the past. This time, upon Emma's insistence, they did not.

'No, no,' she urged when, at the height of their passion, he was about to withdraw, 'no, Marty, don't leave me.' And with all her strength she held him inside her.

They remained locked together well after he was spent, kissing and murmuring their love for one another. And when finally they fell apart, breathless from their exertion, they both, inexplicably, laughed.

'Do you think that was wise?' Marty asked as they lay side by side, gazing up at nothing.

'Most definitely,' she said. 'If I'm pregnant they'll *have* to let us marry, won't they?'

'Or else disown us altogether,' he replied. 'Either way, I don't care, do you?'

'No.'

They knew, both of them, that they *did* care really. But not at this moment. At this moment they would happily abandon their families, the lives they had led, and everything else that might stand in their way.

He rolled on his side to face her. 'You conniving woman.' He smiled as he ran his fingers lightly over her breast. 'Was that really your plan? To get pregnant?'

'Not at all,' she said, turning to him in all seriousness, 'I just didn't want you to leave me.'

'I'll never leave you, Em. Never.'

They then set about making their plans afresh. There was no longer any point in waiting for their brothers to come home. Mick was never coming home, and as the war dragged on who knew when Bertie would be back? So they chose a date, a very pertinent date. They would inform their parents of their intention to marry on the 2nd of February the following year. The day after Emma turned eighteen.

The Great War came to an end on 11 November 1918, and the world rejoiced. A cause for celebration throughout the Commonwealth, not least of all Australia.

'Our boys are coming home!' was the refrain that rang out across a nation deprived of a generation of its young men. But there was a conundrum facing the Australian Imperial Force, one that had not been considered when the government had so eagerly sent its sons off to fight for the motherland. No thought had been given as to how these same sons, or rather those of them who had survived, were to be brought back home.

Following the declaration of peace, 100,000 soldiers of the AIF were billeted throughout Northern France, living in barns and farm buildings and any other places of shelter that could be found. After jubilantly embracing the armistice and the fact that the conflict was over, they were now informed it could be as long as two years, even more, before they would see their homeland and families. The Australian government had no contingency set in place for their return. The men could not stay where they were; Australia was not even officially a part of the Allied Occupation Force. What was to happen to them?

Proving once again his military acumen, it was Australian General John Monash who came to the rescue. Within one month of the armistice, Monash planned the demobilisation and immediately began executing the repatriation of all AIF personnel. He was ultimately to achieve his aim in little less than a year, a feat nothing short of extraordinary.

Within the first few weeks and months, drafts of men sailed for England, where they were accommodated in barracks awaiting transportation to their homeland. Those destined for the speediest repatriation to Australia were, as was to be expected, the wounded, who would be immediately followed by the 'originals', those who had graduated to the Western Front having first served in Gallipoli.

Many of the troops found themselves at the Australian military camps on Salisbury Plain in the county of Wiltshire, and among them was Bertie Worthing, whose battalion was one of the first repatriated to England in early December. He and his mates counted themselves lucky, but they were now resigned to wait for what would possibly be a very long time.

Luck, however, seemed to follow Bertie Worthing.

'Sergeant Worthing!'

A week after their arrival in England, Bertie and several of his mates took off on a day's leave to visit Portsmouth, around forty miles south of the camp on the English Channel coast.

It was here on the docks that Bertie could have sworn he'd heard his name called.

'Sergeant Worthing!' Again, louder this time.

He turned to see Lieutenant Colonel Timothy Gray making his way towards him. He and Gray had shared a trench on the Western Front on more than one occasion, and despite their vast difference in rank had formed an excellent friendship, principally due to Gray's passion for all forms of theatre. It turned out Timothy Gray particularly adored any show that bore the Worthing Brothers name, and he'd constantly pestered Bertie for news from the world of entertainment.

'Hello, sir,' Bertie said as the lieutenant colonel, a fit-looking man in his mid-thirties, joined the group, 'good to see you.'

'Well, you certainly didn't waste any time getting out of France, did you, man,' Gray snorted good-humouredly. 'In those battalions that arrived last week, eh?'

'Yes, sir. Struck it lucky, we did.'

'Camped up at Salisbury Plain, are you?'

'That's right, sir.' Bertie gave a careless shrug. 'God only knows for how long.'

Bertie's battalion mates were shifting uneasily beside him. They were not comfortable with the easy relationship shared between their sergeant and such a very senior officer.

'Excuse us, sir,' one of the men said deferentially to Gray before turning to Bertie. 'Us lot are off to find a pub, Sarge,' he muttered. 'We'll leave you to chat on and catch up with you later. Otherwise we'll see you on the five o'clock train back to camp.'

'Oh, rightio.' Caught off guard and a little disconcerted, Bertie could only look on as his mate saluted the lieutenant colonel.

Gray returned the salute, and he and Bertie watched as the men scurried away.

'Always disappointing when people are desperate to get out of one's company,' Gray said. 'If we were back home in civvy street, they probably would have asked me to join them for a beer.' There was a touch of regret in his smile to Bertie. 'Something I've never quite adjusted to, I'm afraid, try as I might. It's one of the less pleasant aspects of being an officer.'

'A *good* officer, though, sir.' Bertie grinned reassuringly. 'There's a distinct difference between an officer and a *good* officer. And believe me, you're one of the good ones, sir, one of the *really* good ones.'

The comment obviously pleased Gray. 'That's very nice of you to say, Sergeant.'

'Bertie. The war's over, sir. Bertie'll do.'

Gray smiled and extended his hand. 'Timothy,' he said, 'or better still, Tim.'

They shook.

'So, Tim, why don't we find a pub and have a beer?'

'Why not?' Gray laughed. 'I have an hour to spare, more than enough time for you to tell me the latest news from the Aussie world of show business. What are the Worthing Brothers getting up to these days?'

They set off along the docks.

'Shakespeare's all the go in the world of the Worthings,' Bertie replied. '*King Lear* in particular. Uncle Will decided it was finally time he took on Lear; he swears it's the greatest role of them all. And he's had a huge triumph with it evidently, rave reviews, shows sold out all over the country. I'll never hear the end of it when I get home. That is if I ever *do* get home,' he added wryly.

'Marvellous,' Gray enthused, 'I can't wait to see it. I'll be home around March myself, will it still be running then?'

Bertie shook his head. 'The tour finished months ago.'

'What a shame.' Timothy Gray appeared crestfallen, his disappointment genuine. 'What a damn shame, I'd so love to have seen it.'

'Oh, I've no doubt you will,' Bertie said. 'With a success like that, they're bound to do a return season. I'd put money on it myself, Uncle Will won't be able to resist.'

'Marvellous, simply marvellous.'

They made for the pub they could see directly ahead.

'Will Worthing's Lear,' Gray said with an admiring shake of his head, 'now that really would be something.'

They entered the bar and bought their beers, Gray insisting it was his shout, but the conversation soon turned from show business to something quite different.

'You're keen to get home as soon as possible, I take it, Bertie?'

'Who isn't?'

'I might just have a job for you. I'm after a sergeant orderly, you see. We leave right here from Portsmouth docks aboard the HMT *Lutana* in late December. That'd get you home by early March. What do you say?'

Bertie was gobsmacked. 'I say it's my round,' he replied when he finally found his voice.

He wrote to his family that very same day, making no attempt to disguise his jubilation.

Bumped into an old mate this arvo, he started out casually enough, *a high-ranking officer in fact. Not quite the done thing for an NCO to be pally with the likes of a lieutenant colonel, but Tim's a great fan of the Worthings, so ... Like I told you, I'm a hero to every soldier who loves the theatre.*

Anyway, it turns out Tim (Lieutenant Colonel Timothy Gray to you) has been appointed OCT (Officer Commanding Troops) on board His Majesty's Transport 'Lutana', which is one of the first vessels to be used as a hospital ship for the repatriation of wounded soldiers to Australia.

And here's the best bit! I've been assigned to the ship as a sergeant orderly and we leave Portsmouth at the end of this month.

Do you realise what this means? he continued ecstatically. *I might even be home before you receive this letter! It's possible, isn't it – knowing how slow the military are with their mail!*

Tell Uncle Will he has to reprise his Lear – my mate Lieutenant Colonel Tim can't wait to see it.

I'm not writing any more now. Have to get this to the mail room so it'll go out with the first batch tomorrow.

Love to everyone.

See you in March!

Bertie.

Luck followed Bertie Worthing wherever he went, a fact he always put down to Elise, his beautiful French guardian angel who continued to watch over him.

21

A PLAGUE ON BOTH YOUR HOUSES

There was no lengthy delay at all in the arrival of Bertie's letter. To the contrary, not having been sent from a battle zone, it reached Melbourne far more swiftly than military mail previously had. Max and Gertie received news of their son's imminent arrival towards the end of January, and jubilance reigned throughout the various Worthing households as the letter was circulated from one family member to another.

Emma and Marty immediately decided to postpone their confrontation plans until after Bertie's homecoming.

'It's been so long now,' Em said, 'what's one more month, and we could certainly do with an ally.'

Marty agreed. Furthermore, he told her, the timing was perfect. By March they would have cast their production of *The Lady from Maxim's*.

'I'll suggest to Dad that he come to Melbourne and be introduced to the company,' he said. 'I'll tell him I've set up a meeting with Ben Fuller and the cast. It's perfectly normal procedure for a co-production, the director and cast getting to meet the money men at the top.'

'Oh dear,' Emma grimaced, 'and instead he gets confronted with his arch-enemy Will Worthing – that won't go down at all well, will it?'

'Nope, it certainly won't, but at least it'll get them in the same room.' Another thought occurred to Marty.

'I'll suggest Uncle Rube comes along too. He's always an excellent buffer when Dad's ire is up.'

'And Bertie will be our buffer against Uncle Will's ire.' Emma held up both hands in the classic gesture. 'Fingers crossed, lovey, as Ma would say.'

Bertie arrived home to a hero's welcome, the whole Worthing clan gathering at the Big House, even cousin Alice and her family, who'd taken the train from Adelaide. A grand Worthing reunion was not something to be missed, and there was always ample room for extra guests at Will's mansion in Toorak.

The celebrations were endless. Bertie had been gone for almost three years, and there was any number of newborn Worthings who had to be introduced to the family hero. And Bertie was most certainly a hero! Why, he'd been mentioned in dispatches twice! He'd received the Military Medal!

'Just doing my job,' he insisted self-effacingly.

But the others would have none of it, particularly Gertie.

'You're a bleedin' hero, lovey,' she insisted, reverting to her origins as she did when excited. 'Gawd, it's a Military Medal we're talking about!'

'Plenty of those going around, Ma,' he replied with a shrug. 'Other blokes have got them too, you know.'

But again he was howled down by all, so he put on a show and played up to the accolades.

'All right, all right,' he replied, arms held high in surrender, 'I acknowledge the truth. You're right, every single one of you, I'm a hero. Just like Ma said, I'm a bleedin' hero.' And he bowed theatrically as if to the stalls and the dress circle and the back seats of the gods, acknowledging their applause.

Same old Bertie, everyone thought, cheeky as ever, hasn't changed one bit.

It was big brother Ted's comment in private that meant the most to Bertie though. Big brother Ted, who'd always been his childhood hero.

'I'm proud you're my brother, Bertie,' Ted said. And Bertie glowed.

A further private meeting a week later, however, had an even greater impact upon Bertie Worthing.

'There's someone I want you to meet,' his sister Emma had said.

Bertie had presumed she wanted to show off her 'hero brother' to a girlfriend, and he'd good-naturedly accompanied her on a tram to the city from where they'd walked to a small terrace house in nearby Carlton. No harm in humouring her; Em was a bossy little thing when she set her mind to it, and he admired her for that.

The sign on the door he found intriguing: 'Carlovsky & Reubens, Theatrical Producers'.

Carlo and Rube, he thought, his mind immediately going to Mick Carlovsky and the first time they'd bumped into each other in France. 'I'm Mick Carlovsky, Carlo's son,' he remembered Mick saying. *What's going on?* he now wondered as he followed Em inside to the small front office.

A young man was standing by the desk, a very young man, no more than twenty at the most.

Emma closed the door behind them.

'This is Martin Carlovsky,' she said. 'Marty, this is my brother, Bertie.'

The young man stepped forward, offering his hand.

'Pleased to meet you, Bertie,' he said.

As they shook, the realisation suddenly hit Bertie. This was Mick Carlovsky's kid brother. The two didn't look at all alike and there was at least a twenty-year age difference, but this was Mick's brother, all right.

An image flashed through Bertie's brain. Villers-Bretonneux, the farmhouse, the bizarre way they'd stood around chatting over a beer, or was it a cider, he couldn't recall, and having a smoke when only moments previously they'd been slaughtering men. He heard Mick's words: 'I've got a kid brother a bit younger than you.' He hadn't been able to remember what they'd talked about that morning. He did now. They'd talked about home and family.

'Hello, Marty.' He grabbed the young man's hand in both of his and pumped away enthusiastically. 'It's great to meet you. I know your big brother, we met up a couple of times in France. He's a beaut bloke, I really admire him.'

Marty's eyes flickered to Emma; Bertie clearly hadn't heard the news. But then why would he have?

'Mick's dead, I'm afraid.'

'Oh.' Bertie froze, their hands still linked, then he broke from the handshake. 'Where,' he asked briskly, 'when?'

'July,' Marty said, 'Le Hamel.'

Bertie nodded. He'd heard about the victory at Le Hamel, the huge success of Monash's battle tactics, which had presumably led to the last of the Australian troops' action on the frontline. *What rotten luck*, he thought. *What rotten luck to cop it right at the end like that.* A wave of bitterness swept over him. *What rotten, fucking luck!*

A little nonplussed by the lack of reaction, Marty felt a need to fill in the silence. 'They awarded him the Military Cross,' he said, 'but that was for action he saw at Villers-Bretonneux, not Le Hamel.'

Another nod from Bertie, although still no comment as his mind ticked over. *So the report we put through our CO paid off*, he thought with a vague sense of satisfaction, *the military came good.* Then the bitterness once again enveloped him. *So what! So fucking what! Small fucking solace!*

Emma too was feeling awkward. Her brother's reaction, or rather the lack of it, was unexpected and somehow out of character, his expression so hard, so seemingly unmoved.

'Mick wrote in a letter to Marty that the two of you had met,' she said, feeling, as Marty had, a need to fill in the silence. 'He really liked you, Bertie, said he wanted to meet up with you again if you both got through the war.'

Bertie finally realised something was expected of him.

'Yes, I'd have liked that too,' he said a little stiffly, the anger still burning inside. 'I'm sorry to hear about your brother, Marty.'

'Thanks.'

'So' – Bertie suddenly clapped his hands together loudly, breaking the awkward moment – 'this is a turn-up for the books, isn't it,' he said, looking brightly from one to the other. 'A Worthing and a Carlovsky in the same room. How has this come about?'

In that instant, Emma realised her brother was not at all the same cheeky Bertie they'd all assumed him to be. He'd changed. Of course he'd changed. She hoped this act he was now putting on, this bold front he insisted upon presenting to the world, didn't hide a man who was broken.

'We love each other and we're going to get married, and we need your help.' She got straight to the point.

'Oh shit,' Bertie said. Then after a pause he added, 'You know you're asking for trouble, don't you?' But the light in his eyes signalled he was only too ready to do battle. Em was right. Bertie had changed. He was a different man. But he was not a broken man.

When Carlo was informed the meeting with Ben Fuller and the entire company of *The Lady from Maxim's* was to be held at a grand house in Toorak, he was not in the least surprised.

'The poky little office in Carlton's far too small, Dad,' his son had informed him over the telephone, 'and we want to impress everyone, don't we?'

'Of course, of course.' Carlo naturally presumed the meeting was being held at Ben Fuller's house. Or one of them. Ben Fuller and the Fuller family in general were bound to have houses all over the place, including New Zealand, and any Melbourne property would naturally be in Toorak.

'Marty's most insistent you come too, Rube,' he said, after hanging up the telephone handpiece and recounting the conversation he'd had with his son.

'Why?'

'Haven't a clue.' Carlo shrugged. 'But you know how much he values your opinion. Good God, he listens to you far more than me most of the time.'

Rube was happy to accompany Carlo to Melbourne – the current show was running smoothly and their two assistants could ably handle the office in their absence – but he had his suspicions nonetheless. It would seem Marty wanted his backup. Why? Had the boy made some casting decisions his father might disapprove of? *Ah well,* Rube thought, *we'll find out soon enough.*

Emma and Bertie had brought their parents over to the Big House.

'There's someone we want you to meet,' Em had told Max and Gertie. 'He's a friend of ours, isn't he, Bertie?'

'Yep.' Bertie's response had been monosyllabic, but Em had expected nothing more. He'd assured them he'd be there to lend support but would only enter the fray should it prove necessary; the battle was ultimately theirs.

'We want Uncle Will and Aunt Mabel to meet our friend too,' Emma had added, looking to Bertie who gave an affirmative nod.

Max and Gertie had been puzzled. A friend of Bertie and Emma's – how was this possible? Bertie had been away for so long, and now home for only two weeks; how could they have discovered a mutual friend in such a short time?

Will and Mabel's reaction had been along similar lines, but all four were most definitely intrigued.

They now sat, the Worthing brothers senior and their wives, in the less formal front drawing room of the Big House reserved specially for family gatherings. A large, spacious room with sofas, chaises longues, armchairs and hardbacks scattered around to comfortably accommodate the full Worthing clan. Here they awaited the arrival of Emma and Bertie's friend, while standing by in the kitchen was ever-loyal Party, her fresh scones warm in the oven, ready for the delivery of morning tea.

'Is it all right if we wait until our friend gets here, Aunt Mabel?' Em had suggested, when upon the family's arrival Mabel had offered tea.

'Of course it's all right, dear,' Mabel had said, thinking that Em looked just a little nervy.

Em and Bertie were now seated on the sofa by the bay windows with a clear view of the landscaped front gardens, the circular driveway and the tiled porch with its magnificent stone colonnades.

Gertie, too, was thinking her daughter appeared a bit jumpy, the way she kept turning to peer through the bay windows.

'So this friend of yours and Emma's, Bertie,' Will queried, lounging back in his comfy armchair, wondering why on earth they needed to stand on ceremony and couldn't start their morning tea before the arrival of this presumably young guest. 'What's the connection? How do you know him?'

'I served with his brother in the war, Uncle Will.' Unlike Emma, Bertie was quite at ease, not casting so much as a glance out of the window. *What will be will be*, he was thinking; after all, he was only here to lend moral support.

'Ah' – Will nodded sagely as if this remark explained everything, which it didn't – 'and this chap's brother arrived home early like you, did he?'

'Nope. This chap's brother's dead.'

'Oh.' Another nod as Will gathered no connection at all had been made. 'Sad, very sad.' He was about to question Emma regarding *her* connection with the mutual friend, but Em jumped in first.

'They should be here any minute now, shouldn't they, Bertie?' she said, glancing anxiously over at the giant grandfather clock that read a quarter to ten.

'Yep, the overnight train gets in at half past nine.' Bertie too glanced at the clock. 'A cab from Flinders Street, and yep, any tick now I'd say.'

Everyone had registered the plural.

'They?' Gertie queried.

'Overnight?' Mabel asked. 'They're coming from Sydney then, are they?'

'That's right,' Emma said.

More intriguing by the minute.

'Well, well,' Max said benignly, 'whoever *they* are, we can't wait to meet them.' He flashed a warning glance at his brother, knowing that Will was irritable about the delay in the delivery of morning tea.

Em, on full alert, was the first to hear the sound of motor vehicle tyres on gravel, and she turned to look through the bay windows at the cab pulling up in the circular driveway.

'They're here,' she said.

Outside, Carlo stepped from the front seat of the cab, dapper in his grey felt fedora and his well-cut suit with its slimline jacket. He'd naturally dressed for the occasion.

As they'd turned into the driveway, he'd admired the house, surely one of the grandest mansions in Toorak – who could possibly fail to be impressed? Just the sort of house Ben Fuller would have, he'd thought. He really must show off his own property in Point Piper when Ben was next in Sydney.

Marty had met his father and Rube at the station, and he now sprang from the cab's back seat, diving in front of Carlo to lead the way, as Em had instructed, up the steps to the smaller side door that opened directly into the family's informal front drawing room, thereby avoiding the main entrance and reception hall. Behind them, Rube stayed back briefly to pay the driver.

Inside, Emma had jumped to her feet and was first to the door.

'We do have a maid, you know,' Will muttered.

'We're expecting a *friend*,' Mabel hissed from her hard-back chair beside him; Mabel always preferred a hardback. 'We don't need a maid to open the door to a *friend*.'

She rose graciously, prepared to be introduced to the friend, a signal for the others to do likewise, which they did, Will obeying begrudgingly.

Emma opened the door to reveal Marty.

'Hello, Marty,' she said over-brightly, 'come on in and meet the family.'

Marty stepped inside.

Good heavens above, Max thought, *it's young Anthony from Sydney*. He looked to Gertie, who was equally amazed and already one step ahead in her reasoning.

How on earth could our Bertie know Em's friend, Anthony? Gertie was thinking.

Then behind Marty, Carlo appeared, and bringing up the rear was Rube. The three of them stood side by side taking in the sight of the Worthing family, all of whom appeared equally gobsmacked to see them.

Oh dear God, Rube thought, *that's why Marty wanted me here. He's been doing business with the Worthings.*

There was a moment's breathless silence, confusion clashing with disbelief, everyone's mind reeling, then Carlo and Will Worthing burst out in unison.

'What the hell's going on?' Carlo demanded.

'What are you doing in my house!' Will roared.

Chaos ensued. The grandfather clock started to chime the hour; other voices clamoured to be heard, Max telling his brother to calm down while they got to the bottom of this, Gertie demanding an explanation of her daughter; Mabel stage directing right, left and centre in a bid to keep order; and finally Bertie's voice rising above them all, even above that of the great Will Worthing.

'Can everyone shut up while we make the introduction!' he bellowed. The tone of command belonged to a sergeant on a military parade ground and the effect was instantaneous.

During the brief hiatus that followed, the clock continued to chime and Bertie nodded to his sister.

'Go on, Em,' he said, stepping back to lean casually against the mantel over the fireplace, reverting once again to his role of observer.

The clock's final chime sounded. Emma and Marty took each other's hand and crossed to the centre of the room where Em addressed her family one by one.

'Ma, Pa, Uncle Will, Aunt Mabel,' she said, nodding deferentially to each, 'this is Martin Carlovsky.' She took a deep breath, finding strength in the feel of Marty's hand so firmly clasping hers. 'We love each other and we intend to get married.'

Will Worthing looked only briefly at the young man, who was of no interest to him, before his eyes turned to Carlo.

'Over my dead body,' he snarled, his contempt directed solely at the man he detested above all others.

'That can be arranged,' Carlo snarled with equal loathing. 'I'd happily do the job myself.'

The mutual hatred between the two arch-enemies was palpable, and as Marty embarked upon his speech he realised its probable uselessness, but he stuck to the script regardless.

'Emma and I love each other very much, and we would like to receive the blessing of you all,' he said respectfully. 'But if we don't gain your permission, I must tell you that we'll marry, anyway. We have the right to do so; Emma is eighteen.'

'There'll be no link between our families, boy,' Will growled, but he wasn't looking at Marty, his eyes remaining fixed upon Carlo. 'Your father killed my son.'

The statement hung there unchecked for a moment or so, met by disbelief from most, but not all.

Emma and Marty shared an incredulous glance. How was this possible? It couldn't be, surely.

Emma looked to her parents, but Gertie and Max said nothing. They knew exactly why Will believed this to be true. In their grief at the time they'd even believed it themselves, and they would both admit that deep down they still tended to blame Carlo for Artie's death.

Bertie too, despite his determination to remain detached, was taken aback. But Artie's death had been an accident. He remembered vividly that awful morning. He'd been sixteen years old when he'd seen his cousin plummet from the top of Flinders Street Station. How could Carlo be held responsible for such a catastrophe?

But the greatest disbelief of all sprang from Carlo himself.

'What the hell are you talking about?' he demanded. 'I had nothing whatsoever to do with your son's death.'

'You killed him as surely as if you'd put a gun to his head. I have a dead son!' Will screamed out his rage. 'I have a *dead son*! And all because of you!'

'You're not the only one who has a dead son!' Carlo's abuse was hurled from the well of grief he bore daily; how dare Will Worthing claim the sole right to anguish! 'You're not alone in suffering the death of a son! I've lost my boy too, damn you!'

'But I didn't *kill* your boy, did I!' With that Will launched himself at Carlo and they both came crashing to the floor. 'You killed my son!' he kept screaming over and over as they grappled together. 'You killed my son!'

Carlo was approaching seventy, a good eight years older than Will, but it was evident in only seconds Will Worthing was no match for him. As his old boxing skills came quickly to the fore, Carlo could have pulverised the younger man had he wished. But he didn't. Instead, he successfully fended off Will's clumsy blows, overpowering him with ease.

Max and Marty separated the two, Max seating his now breathless brother in the armchair, Carlo shrugging away his son's helping hand, picking up his fedora and brushing it off. He did so hate to appear ruffled.

Bertie merely watched on from his position by the mantel-piece. He'd come to the rescue if necessary, but at the moment they seemed to be sorting things out for themselves.

'You crazy bastard,' Carlo said. He was calm now, his tone a strange mix of contempt and pity as he studied the great Will Worthing, defeated and gasping for air. 'What in God's name gives you reason to think I killed your son? How could you entertain such a demented notion?'

'Because it's the truth.' All fight had left Will, but his hatred remained. 'My son is dead directly because of you,' he said. 'You might just as well have killed him with your own hand.'

Carlo said nothing but stared back uncomprehendingly.

'You really have no idea, do you?' Will appeared equally uncomprehending of the fact Carlo could be so ignorant.

'You honestly don't know what you did when you exposed the twins to the world.'

'Oh yes, yes, The Wonderful Worthing, Master Illusionist . . .' Carlo replied contemptuously. 'I broke the cardinal rule of the theatre, yes, yes, I'll never work again, I'll be blacklisted . . . You certainly made sure of that, didn't you?'

'No, you did that to yourself.'

'So what?' Carlo felt the familiar surge of irritation at the return of the pompous Will Worthing he so despised. 'I'm a producer now, I'm as successful as I've ever been. My breaking your precious cardinal rule didn't end up breaking *me*, did it?'

'No. It ended up killing my son.' Will rose to his feet; he felt stronger now. 'Let me spell out the truth for you, Carlo, as in your ignorance you're clearly unable to grasp it. If you had not revealed the twins' identity, my boys would still be performing as an illusionist. They would be performing as *one*, do you get my drift? They would never have been promoting a duo act. They would never have climbed that wretched building together. Artie would never have fallen to his death . . . They would have remained *one*! Can you understand that? *One* solo act, *one* sole identity they shared with the world. There can be no denying your betrayal *killed my son*!'

In the brief pause that followed, Emma glanced at her mother and father, expecting some form of rebuttal, but none was forthcoming. Gertie and Max stood gazing at Carlo as if they too condemned him.

It was Mabel who broke the silence.

'That's not true, Will,' she said.

Will stared in amazement at his wife. How could she refute him? How could she deny the facts?

'Artie and Alfie would never have continued to perform as one,' Mabel went on. 'Artie had tired of the illusionist act long before Carlo exposed the twins. He didn't like the subterfuge. He wanted to perform out in the open, to be the star that he was.'

'Oh, is that so?' Will sneered. 'And he told you all that himself, did he? Before he died, Artie actually told you that he'd been wanting to break up an act as brilliant as The Wonderful Worthing!'

'No, Artie didn't tell me. Alfie did. And he told me *all that*, as you say, *after* Artie died. He said Artie was relieved to be free of The Wonderful Worthing, that he was actually grateful they'd been revealed as twins. That's what Alfie told me.'

Will not only refused to believe his wife, but he saw Mabel's declaration as the height of disloyalty.

'How could Alfie have told you that?' he snarled accusingly. 'Alfie can't even fucking talk!' Once again he turned his wrath upon Carlo. 'That's something else you don't know, you murderous bastard,' he hissed. 'Ever since Artie's death his twin brother has been mute. I blame you for that too. It's because of you Alfie can't bloody well speak.'

'Yes, he can, Will.' Mabel again, defiant. 'He can speak. To me. He speaks to me always.'

The whole family was now amazed. Every pair of Worthing eyes was trained upon Mabel.

'We'll ask him in, shall we? He can tell you the truth himself.' Without waiting for an answer, Mabel turned to Bertie. 'Bertie dear,' she said, 'would you mind fetching Alfie, he's rehearsing out the back.'

Bertie obligingly disappeared and Mabel, once again in full stage management mode, took over the proceedings.

'Do please sit down, everyone,' she said calmly. 'So silly to let things get out of hand the way they did.'

Surprisingly enough they all obeyed her, as people tended to when Mabel issued orders, although Carlo made sure Will Worthing had resumed his armchair before, with a nudge from Rube, he perched himself on a hardback by the table.

Gertie flashed an encouraging smile to her daughter who, together with Marty, had returned to the sofa by the bay windows where they sat holding hands. 'Goodness me, lovey,' she said, 'you have sprung it on us, haven't you?' Her gaze included Marty as she added, 'I can certainly see why the need for "Anthony".'

'Thanks, Ma,' Em replied gratefully, squeezing Marty's hand to say, *at least we have support from one quarter.*

Will's baleful glare left Gertie undaunted. *Sins of the Father* ... her eyes boldly replied, and she sat back, joining the others in stony silence.

The door opened and Mabel rose to her feet as Bertie arrived with Alfie in tow.

'Alfie darling,' she said, and crossing to her son she took his hand, leading him into the centre of the room. 'I have a favour to ask of you.'

Alfie stood listening very carefully to his mother's instructions, his eyes not once leaving hers. Now in his late thirties, he was an inconspicuous man to look at, no particular feature demanding of attention, no body language sending an immediate message. But Alfie's face and body provided the blank canvas upon which he drew his characters. When Alfie performed, he became whatever or whoever he wished others to see.

'You remember when you told me about Artie wanting to be free of The Wonderful Worthing?' Mabel asked. 'You remember how you told me he'd felt trapped by the illusionist act for years? You said that for Artie the character you created between you was no longer the game you'd both loved playing as boys.'

Alfie slowly nodded, his focus still intense but unfathomable, as if querying his mother's intention.

'I want you to tell everyone else here that, Alfie,' Mabel said. 'I want you to tell them just what you told me.'

Alfie's eyes finally left his mother's to gaze around the room, taking in one by one all of those watching. Then he turned back to his mother, and something passed between them. Was it a query from Alfie? Was it an agreement from Mabel?

'Yes,' Mabel said, 'you tell them in your own way, love. Tell them just what you told me.' She released her son's hand and stepped aside.

Alfie once again gazed around the room, and everyone watched in breathless anticipation. Alfie Worthing was about to speak. For the first time in eight years his voice was about to be heard.

But Alfie did not speak. Instead, he transformed himself, the blank canvas becoming another person altogether.

Using the central floor space like a stage, he performed 'in the round', engaging individually with each of his spectators as he circled among them, his movement unbelievably graceful – 'like watching a ballet', as Gertie always said. The person he presented was outwardly flamboyant, a confident young man, joyfully embracing the world, but the true essence of the character within was readable to all who had known him. A boldness lay beneath; an unconquerable spirit of adventure and a daring that could belong to only one. This was unmistakably Artie Worthing.

'G'day, Art,' Bertie wanted to say as he was flashed a wink in passing.

A special smile for Emma, which she immediately recognised. 'It's Artie,' she whispered with a squeeze of Marty's hand; he was the only person present who hadn't known Artie Worthing.

Will and Mabel would have shared a glance, but neither dared risk losing a second of this magical rebirth, as their eyes met those they could have sworn were the eyes of their dead son.

Having made his connection with all, Alfie returned to the centre of the room, where he reverted to his blank canvas, before once again transforming.

To the amazement of those watching, he appeared imperceptibly to shrink, in both the physical and mental sense. He became a withdrawn, conservative young man, the antithesis of the character he'd just presented. Again circling gracefully among them, he now avoided their direct gaze, as if preferring to hide from the world, perhaps even to seek some furtive form of escape. This was the young Alfie Worthing of yesteryear.

Oh lovey, Gertie thought. She'd always wanted to cuddle young Alfie, who'd lived his whole life in the shadow of the brother he so adored. *Oh Alfie, lovey.*

Although avoiding direct contact, Alfie's eyes briefly met those of his mother, and Mabel gave the slightest nod. He was telling the story beautifully.

Having clearly defined the two characters, Alfie now returned to the centre of the room where he created a third. Standing momentarily as the blank canvas, he held his arms wide then slowly drew his hands together, merging the brothers to become The Wonderful Worthing, Master Illusionist.

Now as he paraded among them, he was pure showmanship, and showmanship at its finest, presenting wizardry to the world with the wave of a hand. The balance of bravado and delicacy was superb. A sweeping grand gesture, a gentle uncurling of the fingers to reveal what? A flock of white doves? An image of incredible beauty? He even *became* the doves and the image, one moment appearing to be in flight, the next enveloping them in a sea of colour and movement that might have been anything. It was all in the mind of the audience. Anything was possible, and every-thing believable, or so it seemed.

Watching on, Will and Carlo's reaction was exactly the same. *He was the greatest performer of them all*, both were thinking, neither realising in that moment that The Wonderful Worthing had never really existed.

Alfie had finished his mime, and returning to the centre of the room there was a spontaneous round of applause, but with a raise of a hand and a shake of his head he called an immediate halt. The purpose of his performance had not been to entertain. He intended now to inform them of the consequences that had attended the creation of The Wonderful Worthing.

This time he no longer paraded among them, remaining instead in the centre of the room, but with each transfor-mation, which was performed in slow motion, he circled on the spot, making eye contact with everyone, ensuring they all read his intention.

First he was The Wonderful Worthing, but as he rotated he became Artie, then a further rotation and, holding up his hands, fingers splayed, slowly drawing them down over his face, Artie himself was transformed. Gone was the joy. The face was now mournful, unhappy, lost in a character that was not of his own making.

Then still rotating and still in slow motion, back came The Wonderful Worthing who gradually transformed into Alfie, but hands again held up, fingers splayed as before, the younger Alfie too was transformed. No longer insecure, but freed of his inhibitions, happy, confident to have discovered a new self.

Each metamorphosis was hypnotic, and the audience gazed on in spellbound wonder.

Having made his point, Alfie concluded his mime with a statement. Unmasking the dual faces with his hands revealing first mournful Artie, then happy Alfie, he became the classic theatrical images of tragedy and comedy. The creation of The Wonderful Worthing had come with a price, he was saying, and his brother had paid that price for too long. He called a halt, shaking his head and drawing a rift in the air with his hands. It had been right for The Wonderful Worthing to come to an end.

Then finally, mime over, he returned to the blank canvas he presented in real life. He had told his story.

'Thank you, Alfie,' Mabel said. 'Satisfied?' Her question was directed to Will.

'You told me he spoke,' Will replied, sullen, but obviously very much affected by what he'd witnessed.

'He does. He just did, didn't he?'

'You said he spoke to you personally.' A touch of accusation, but everyone including Will himself knew he had lost the argument.

'And he does speak to me,' Mabel quietly insisted. 'He speaks to me often. Would you like to know what else he told me?'

Without waiting for a response from her husband, she looked to Alfie who nodded.

'He told me the only reason Artie remained locked into The Wonderful Worthing character was because of you, Will. Not because he feared you – Artie was fearless as we all know. But because he loved you. And because he knew it would break your heart to lose the act of which you were so proud. Isn't that right, Alfie?'

She looked to her son, who once again nodded.

Then surprising them all, including his mother, Alfie decided to have the last word. Crossing to stand before his father, he held out his hands, which was an unusual gesture; Alfie never sought physical contact, preferring always to distance himself.

Will rose, taking his son's hands in both of his, and they stood looking into one another's eyes.

This time Alfie was neither a blank canvas, nor was he playing any character other than Will Worthing's son. But as he placed his father's hands against his heart, he was speaking for both sons. In the intensity of his gaze, Artie was there too.

This is the truth, both sons were saying. *What we have just told you is the truth, we both swear.*

There was the suspicion of a tear in Will's eyes as he met Alfie's. He'd never truly shared Artie's death with his other son; he'd been too busy hating Carlo. He was moved, and made as if to embrace his son.

But Alfie withdrew his hands and stepped back, reclaiming the space he needed. Having broken the moment, he looked from his father to Carlo, and raising both arms in the broadest of gestures that could not be misread, he wiped the air clean. It was over.

He glanced at his mother and again something passed between them. Then he turned and walked from the room.

His departure raised questions in people's minds and silence remained as everyone wondered what would happen next. Alfie's performance had expressed more eloquently than words the fact that the twins were destined to part as performers, that The Wonderful Worthing would not have survived as a single identity, that Carlo could not be held responsible for Artie's death. But did that mean all was forgiven between Will Worthing and Carlo?

Em and Marty's hands were locked tightly together as they looked from one family patriarch to the other. Who was about to make the first move?

But no move was made, the hatred between the two being so long ingrained neither man was prepared to give way. They simply glowered at each other from across the room.

Carlo, still seated like everyone else, even rose to his feet in order to be on the same eye level as Will Worthing.

Was he waiting for an acknowledgement, perhaps even an apology from his arch-enemy? If so, none was forthcoming. Finally . . .

'Come on, Marty,' he said, 'we're leaving.'

'Good riddance,' Will snarled.

Marty remained where he was, putting his arm around Emma, signalling he was going nowhere and that if Will were to throw him out Em was coming with him.

Em's eyes boldly signalled the same message, but neither Will nor Carlo seemed aware of anything but their own personal hatred as they continued to stare each other down.

Bertie decided it was time he lent a hand. He was here, after all, to do battle, wasn't he?

'I think we're forgetting the main purpose of this get-together,' he said, rising languidly from his chair with a nod to Emma and Marty to do the same, which they did. 'We have here before us a young couple seeking the blessings of their respective families,' he went on, very calmly but with a dangerous hint of something approaching mockery. 'Perhaps it's time we turned our minds from the petty events of the past to address the future of two young people who wish to marry.'

Will and Carlo both took instant offence. *Petty? Petty* events of the past? The boy was ridiculing them.

But Bertie continued, unruffled by their obvious animosity. 'Let's wish Em and Marty well, shall we?' He addressed his own parents first. 'Ma, Dad, what do you say? Do they have your blessing?'

Gertie instantly dived in. ''Course they do, from the bottom of my heart.'

'Yep, I'm happy for you, Em,' Max said to his daughter. Then to Marty, 'And you too, mate.' He had to stop himself from saying 'Anthony'.

'And you, Aunt Mabel, do they have your blessing?'

'Of course.'

Bertie could see Rube across the room nodding benignly to Marty; it was clear the couple had his blessing too. Which left only this monstrous pair with their monstrous egos, he thought. *Here goes.*

'So,' he said, taking up his position 'centre stage' and addressing the both of them, 'that just leaves you two, doesn't it?' The element of mockery had now become derision.

'Surely the blending of families as noble as the Worthings and Carlovskys would be a fine thing,' he went on, deliberately goading them. 'Just think of the new blood born of such a union. The offspring of kings! A fresh dynasty to rule the world of show business!' Bertie gave it his all, revelling in his performance and relishing their outrage. 'How could you resist such an alliance —'

Carlo and Will both burst out in unison.

'How dare you belittle me, boy!' Carlo had his fists up as if about to attack.

'You insolent young bastard!' Will yelled.

But Will's voice was no match for his nephew's.

'Just look at you!' Bertie yelled back, unleashing the anger that had been simmering. He was not only ready to do battle, he was aching for it. 'Just look at the two of you! You're petty! You're shallow! You're beneath contempt! This fucking war between our families has been brought about by your egos and means nothing. Nothing, do you hear me!'

He rounded on Carlo first.

'I've fought in a *real* war,' he went on. 'I've fought alongside your son. I've seen men die. I've killed men. Mick and I killed men together, standing side by side, protecting each other's backs. *That's* war!'

He then turned on Will. 'This feud you've invented between you, this stupid, bloody vendetta, is meaningless.'

His anger was already on the wane, dying down as quickly as it had erupted.

'You've both lost sons,' he said, addressing the two of them, 'one in an accident and one in the war . . .' After which he addressed the whole room. 'There's hardly a family in the country not mourning the loss of a son. But the war's over now. And so is this one. This war ends right here.'

He stopped abruptly, having said his piece. And he shep-herded Em and Marty forward to receive their blessings from the two patriarchs, who were forced to accept a *fait accompli*.

Will embraced his niece and Carlo his son, but rather conspicuously neither man offered the other his hand. Bertie decided against such a suggestion. That would perhaps have been asking too much.

The room then erupted in noisy relief, congratulations openly expressed to the young couple, Mabel ringing the bell to signal the maid it was time for morning tea, despite the fact it was really getting closer to lunchtime.

Then over the top of it all, Bertie simply couldn't resist. Turning to confront the two family patriarchs, he yelled at the top of his voice, '*A plague on both your houses!*'

And he roared with laughter as Will Worthing and Carlo turned to glare, first at him and then at one another.

Oh, what world do these people live in, Bertie thought, *what bloody world do they live in?* Then he smiled to himself. *The world of the theatre, of course, what else?*

CURTAIN CALL

A FINAL WORD,
YEAR UNKNOWN

So there you have it. With the approval of our families we got married and, unlike Romeo and Juliet, lived happily ever after. Don't you just love an ending like that?

A few bits and pieces I'd like to fill you in on.

Following 'The Great Showdown', as Bertie chose to call it (oh, the impertinence), the main question on everyone's lips was 'Did Alfie really talk to Aunt Mabel?'

Truly, we were all dying to know whether Alfie ever spoke to his mum when they were alone together. I actually asked Ma because if anyone would know it'd have to be her; she and Aunt Mabel told each other everything.

But Ma didn't know, and she had no intention of asking.

'Something that big has to stay personal, lovey,' she said to me. 'It's just between her and him. But I'll tell you something for nothing, Em. Your Aunt Mabel says Alfie's grown to love his world of silence. He's happy there, he tells her. As happy as he can be without Artie, anyway.'

It's still sad, though, don't you think?

The rift between families was healed to the point where the revival of our *King Lear* production ('returned by popular demand!' naturally) had a gala opening at the Colosseum in Sydney. This was mainly due to the influence of Aunt Mabel and Rube, who'd instantly reforged their friendship. Uncle Will and Carlo were never destined to become friends. Well, they hadn't been from the very start, had they? Egos like that are bound to clash, but somewhere deep down they respected each other's talent, or recognised it at least.

A sad note to add here. Rube died later that same year, 1919. The Spanish Flu. Oh my, what terrible times. The deadliest pandemic in human history! Killed millions all over the world, including our own dear Rube. As you can imagine, Carlo and Marty were hit hard by his death, but so were we Worthings, particularly Aunt Mabel. She and Rube were birds of a feather, clever people who saw things in their own artistic way and spoke the same language.

By the time the pandemic was over in 1920, theatre had undergone quite a change. With silent films proving so immensely popular some venues had converted to cinemas, and as the twenties progressed many others were tending to go the same way. Understandable, I suppose, but for those of the old school, like us Worthings, it was a shame to see some of our really glorious theatres converted to 'picture palaces'.

Then out of the blue came the rumours of 'talkies'. The American studios were experimenting with talking pictures, Aunt Mabel said, and then she floored us all with her announcement. I remember the moment as clearly as if it was yesterday.

'We must go into the film business,' she proclaimed.

I thought Uncle Will would die of apoplexy.

'It's only a matter of time before the Americans pull it off,' she went on, as cool as a cucumber. 'If we already have our own Worthing Brothers Film Company established, we can lead the way in the production of Australian talkies. Makes sense, don't you think?'

Well, dear me, that got everyone going.

Ma said she'd love to be in the pictures, and Bertie said, 'Just imagine the range one would have as a director.' Bertie had become the most marvellous director, by the way – a true visionary, he left his own stamp on any production he undertook, which is the sure sign of a born director.

I thought the idea quite splendid myself and was about to say so, before Uncle Will could take over and veto the whole thing. But my Marty got in first and it was he who really sealed the deal.

'Of course, we'd need actors with *voices*,' he said, giving me a meaningful nudge in the ribs with his elbow.

Pa instantly got the message and took up the baton. 'You're spot on there, mate; talkies would need *real* actors, wouldn't they?'

The stage was set.

Uncle Will's ego didn't allow him to believe he'd been sent a message. This was now his idea, and his alone.

'Any talking picture would require actors with a background in the theatre,' he declared, the proposition having suddenly become something of interest. 'Proper actors with proper voices trained to take command. Voices skilled in reaching the back seats of the gods, captivating the audience . . .'

He was off and running.

The Worthings never left the theatre, which remained their true love, but they did buy up a studio and they did go into movies. And when the talkies came along, they were at the forefront of Australian film production. It was yet another beginning in the Worthing family saga.

But that's another story.

AUTHOR'S NOTE

Showtime! was inspired by, and is a tribute to, the early entrepreneurial giants of Australian show business. A number of these are mentioned throughout the book, including James Cassius Williamson (JCW), Harry Rickards (The Tivoli King), Ben Fuller of the Fuller theatrical family dynasty, and Charles Tait of the famous Tait brothers (five in all).

Several real people feature in *Showtime!*, including Harry Rickards himself together with two of the variety stars of the time, Ada Delroy and Irving Sayles. All other characters are fictional.

The theatres mentioned throughout the book were actual theatres of the time with the exception of the Colosseum. In design, however, the Colosseum is very much based upon the St James Theatre, which was built by Ben and John Fuller and opened in Sydney in 1926.

The two ghosts who feature in *Showtime!* are historically documented, so can be considered real – if you believe in ghosts, that is. A number of actors profess to having seen 'Fred' at the Theatre Royal, Hobart, including my good friend Jacki Weaver. Sadly, despite having played the Royal twice myself I have not been so privileged, but I thoroughly believe in his presence.

The death of Frederick Federici at the Princess Theatre, Melbourne, on 3 March 1888 during the opening night of

J. C. Williamson's production of *Faust* is particularly well documented, as is the wide-held belief that he remains the resident ghost at the Princess to this very day, with claims of theatre staff having regularly sighted his figure in evening dress.

ACKNOWLEDGEMENTS

As always, love and thanks to my husband, Bruce Venables, who has once again been with me every step of the way, his input on all levels invaluable.

My thanks also to the usual suspects – my agent James Laurie and other loyal friends who offer encouragement, together with practical assistance in their various areas of expertise: Sue Greaves, Michael Roberts, Colin Julin, Susan Mackie-Hookway and Ross Hitt.

Many thanks to my publisher Beverley Cousins, my editors Brandon VanOver and Claire Gatzen, my publicist Karen Reid, and the wonderful hard-working team at Penguin Random House Australia.

Given the travel restrictions imposed during this last year due to COVID-19, I've been unable to conduct the field trips I would normally have undertaken, and as a result have relied more than ever upon literature for research rather than the usual 'one on one' contact with people and places.

I've been immensely lucky to have had several books up my sleeve right from the start that have been far more than a source of research; in fact, they've been nothing short of inspirational.

First and foremost among these, I wish to recognise *Ada* by Kaz Cooke (Viking, 2017). I read this delightful novel about Ada Delroy long before embarking upon *Showtime!*, but when I finally chose the theme for my next book, *Ada* was the first reference material I turned to. Many thanks, Kaz.

A second treasure I already had up my sleeve was *Actors Blood* by my very dear friend the late great actor and director Alastair Duncan ('Fabric of a Nation' series, Lexington Avenue Press, 2004). This book, too, proved inspirational.

And a third, also written by an old theatre mate: *Tivoli King: Life of Harry Rickards, Vaudeville Showman* (Allambie, 2009) by Gae Anderson.

Other books I wish to recognise include:
Stars of Australian Stage and Screen, Hal Porter (Rigby Limited, 1965)
On Stage, Monroe H. Fabian (Mayflower Books, 1980)
Theatrical Anecdotes, Peter Hay (Oxford University Press, 1987)
Clothes in Australia, Cedric Flower (Kangaroo Press Ltd, 1984)
Gallipoli, Les Carlyon (Pan Macmillan Australia, 2001)
The Great War, Les Carlyon (Pan Macmillan Australia, 2006)